MW01624832

The Initiation of
Lady de Winter

~~~~~A Novel~~~~~

Crystal McKinnis Allen
&
Carole McKinnis
~~~~~

The Initiation of Lady de Winter

ISBN: 978-1-7374484-1-9

Editing: H.G. Mac, Lorraine Reguly

Cover design by Crystal McKinnis Allen

Cover art by Abdul Momin Ariu

www.crystal allen author.com

facebook.com/crystal mckinnis allen

Reference Guide

A list of hierarchies of the royal peerage and Catholic religion can be found at the end of the book starting on page 368.

A Cast of Characters designating which characters are fictitious and which are historical follows on page 374.

This information clarifies the social relationships and historicity of the era, which can help readers better understand this work of historical fiction.

Table of Contents

In 1623, Prince Charles of England embarked on a journey to Madrid, seeking the hand of Infanta Maria Anna of Spain. English commoners were alarmed at the thought of a Roman Catholic queen on the English throne, as it conjured the specter of their most recent Catholic regent, Queen Mary I, also known as Bloody Mary. Spurred on by the Duke of Buckingham, the prince and his traveling party disguised themselves as merchants and crossed into France, and then Spain, on horseback. Undetected, they entered the city gates of Madrid. The affair became known as "The Spanish Match."

1

The Keeper of the Kingdom

February 1623
Southampton, England

Lady Anne looked up, amazed the day had flown. The diamond-paned windows glimmered with the colors of the setting sun. She lifted a burning candle from the candelabra and lit three more wicks before re-fastening it to its base.

Quentin, her four-year-old, looked thoughtful as he knelt on the chair next to hers. Lady Anne selected a slender paintbrush from the tray and dipped it into the watery, brown ink.

"Here is what a bunny looks like," she said, as a chubby rabbit flowed from the brush's tip.

"Can I make a bunny?" Quentin asked, reaching for her brush. Just as his little fingers closed over it, an outside movement caught her eye. She glanced through the window and her blood ran cold.

In the mid-distance, a thick man in a black cloak and a black, flat-brimmed hat strode up the walkway.

How did he get past the guard at the gate?

Anne rose, darted to the side of the bay window and peered outside. Flames from the fireplace reflected in the windowpanes, partially obscuring him. She touched a hand to the prim bun at the back of her head, knowing the blonde curls at the side of her face, along with her well-formed figure, could invite the wrong kind of attention from the dark stranger. Her position afforded a clear view of the château across the broad lawn. She had convinced her husband to move into the cozy parson's house for the winter, finding the three-story manor far too drafty and eerie after dark—unsuitable for a child.

She waited for the man to approach the château. No doubt, he would assume the lord and lady of the house resided there. Instead, the stranger turned toward her window, as if he knew where to find her. Her heart sped as she stared into his cruel eyes, shadowed by thick eyebrows. His chin drooped into his fat neck, but his gait made him seem as solid as a boulder.

"Harald! Come down!" she shouted, hoping he could hear from his upstairs study. She breathed more easily at the sound of her husband's massive feet pounding the wooden steps. Harald stormed down the curved stairway into the parlor.

"There's a man coming up the walkway. Please, hurry! Meet him on the landing. I do not want him in our house."

Harald swung open the door, allowing in a rush of winter air. Anne noticed he wore nothing but a chemise over his trousers. The icy breeze lifted his auburn hair from his shoulders. He motioned for Anne to step out first, then followed, shutting the door behind them.

"Greetings!" he called, his baritone voice booming into the evening air.

The stranger peered at them with tiny, reptilian eyes as he closed the space between them.

Harald stepped in front of Anne and asked, "May I ask who I have the honor of meeting on our doorstep at the end of day?" His voice dripped with sarcasm.

The stranger's expression was as cold as a crypt.

"I am an envoy from the Vatican."

Anne stifled a gasp. The man's attire was devoid of Roman Catholic insignias. Yet, it made sense. In Protestant England, an obvious papist would be mobbed on sight, even burned alive.

"And you are?" Harald prompted.

"But a humble Keeper of the Kingdom." His accent was unmistakably Italian.

Harald pulled his head back. "What do you want from us?"

"I have come to do *you* a favor. But first, a revelation. All of Britain is returning to the fold of the True Church." He paused to let the words sink in. "A match has been made between England's Prince Charles and the Spanish infanta. This is a proud blessing upon the House of Stuart. By the grace of God, this match shall allow the prince to retain his father's throne."

The threat was veiled, but Anne caught it at once. If the king declined the match, the Roman Church would prevent Prince Charles's succession to the throne, somehow. She looked into Harald's stormy eyes and their communication was instant: play along and discuss the matter later.

"If it is the king's will for his son to marry the infanta," Anne said, her tone obsequious, "of course, we will support the match and do all in our power to carry out his wishes."

"You will make it the king's will, Lady Audley. I understand you possess the powers of persuasion."

Anne froze as she met the stranger's glass-green eyes. He spoke of the espionage training she had received; she could sense it in her bones. *How does he know?*

The stranger shifted his cold gaze to Harald. "If you assist the Church in converting the prince and vouchsafing this union, the Vatican will reinstate the House of Audley to our good graces. We know the enemies of God in this land. They will be stripped of their fortunes. As it is written, 'To those who have much, more will be added unto them.'"

Anne hoped Harald would hide his disgust. He lifted one eyebrow in a pantomime of greed, but asked, in a more conciliatory tone, "Pray tell, how can we be of service to the Keepers of the Kingdom?"

The stranger smirked, fooled by Harald's counterfeit deference. "Your mission is simple. Go to King James. Tell him there are whisperings from the Duke of Buckingham's quarters that a match between the Spanish infanta and Prince Charles is under consideration, but say nothing of our meeting. You must convince the king it is the only way to pass his throne on to his son. Remind him, in the most courteous fashion, that he is old and his son is naïve. Prince Charles can be easily replaced by his cousin, Ann Stanley,

Countess of Castlehaven. She is devoted to the Church, and her claim to the English throne is far stronger than James Stuart's, let alone that of Prince Charles. Our original plan was to replace Charles with her, upon his father's death, but the Lord is kind. He has chosen to give King James an opportunity to return Britain to the True Church and escape damnation.

"You, Lady Audley," he continued, his predatory eyes back on Anne, "will play Cupid to this royal couple. Explain to Prince Charles how delightful a Roman Catholic wife could be, with a never-ending appetite for producing heirs. Although your task is woman's work, it is vital.

"That is all. Fini," he said with a twirl of his thumb and forefinger. "Go now, to the king. Both of you."

He spun on his heel and glided into the shadows, leaving nothing but the sound of boots on gravel echoing in the evening air.

2

Kitty

Kitty awoke to the sound of feet pounding on the stairs. A volume of Romeo and Juliet fell from her lap as she bolted up. The parlor door opened and slammed shut, shaking the rafters above.

She rushed into the parlor, surprised to find the room empty, save for Quentin, who stared at her with large, blue eyes from behind the desk.

"Mummy and Daddy went outside to see a man," he said, as if disappointed he had not been invited.

She peered out the window of the parlor, but it was difficult to see the portico from there. Noticing her reflection, she finger-combed the tight, bronze curls that crowded her ears. If Anne and Harald had a visitor, she didn't want to look like a rag doll when they came in. A turn of her head revealed her bun was still presentable. Her tawny complexion made her self-conscious, but Anne and Harald had remarked on her golden glow often enough to put her at ease.

She went to the desk and gave Quentin a cuddle as she sat beside him to examine the painted creatures. Anne had hired her to be her lady's maid, but Kitty spent more time with Quentin, which suited her. The flaxen-haired boy was the most adorable tot she had ever known.

"What is this?" she asked playfully. "Are we making foxes and bunnies?" She picked up a thin brush and tried her hand at painting, glancing repeatedly at the diamond-paned window as she did so. Their candlelit faces reflected against the encroaching dusk.

"I don't like your bunnies," Quentin complained. "Mummy's are better."

Kitty looked down at the blotting paper. Indeed, her bunnies looked like hedgehogs with clumsy spatulas rising from their heads.

"You are right, Little Master. My bunnies look silly, next to your Mum's. How about I tell you a story about a bunny, instead?"

"I want to hear a story about a bunny named George," Quentin said as he studiously painted another one.

"Very well." Kitty put down the brush and rested her hands in her lap. "There once was a little bunny named George Villiers," she began, referring to the avaricious Duke of Buckingham, whom she loved to mock. "He flattered the king endlessly, held his hand, and blew him kisses, thereby becoming the king's favorite bunny. George didn't give two figs that no one else liked him."

The story entwined the boy in its spell. Quentin stared at her with unblinking eyes.

"One day," Kitty continued, "George the bunny told the king, 'I want to be a duke.'

"The king said, 'That is a splendid idea, but I have no ducal titles to give.'

"'Yes, you do,' said George the bunny. 'Yonder lies an old man, almost dead, who has a ducal title. Very soon, he will need it no longer.'

"'But what about the duke's heirs?' cried the king.

"'But what about precious me?'" cried George the bunny.

"'But, of course,' said the king. 'I nearly forgot. You are the key to my happiness. I hereby pronounce you Third Duke of Pickpocket, by royal decree.'

"'But I very much wanted to be the First Duke of Pickpocket,' said George the Bunny.

"'First Duke you are, then,' said the king.

"'Now, I want a big house,' said George the bunny, 'even bigger than yours.'

'The king hesitated. Such a house could cost him his entire treasure, but George the bunny batted his eyes, clasped his hands over his heart, and swayed his hips to-and-fro until the king could stand it no longer—'"

Kitty jumped at the sound of the front door opening. Anne looked anxious. Harald looked grim as he stomped up the stairs.

Anne rushed over to gather Quentin into her arms, hugging him tighter than usual. His short, blond curls melded with her long ones as he struggled to break free.

"Look, Mummy. Look at the critters I made!" Quentin exclaimed. He resumed his perch on the chair.

Anne ummed and aahed at Quentin's painted creatures as she carried on a conversation with Kitty over his head.

"Who was at the door?" Kitty asked in a low voice.

"A beastly man. He wouldn't say his name, but the Vatican sent him. Have you ever heard of the Keepers of the Kingdom?"

Kitty put her hand to her mouth.

"But, of course, you have," said Anne. "You overhear everything."

"Some time ago, an old traveler was passing through town. He was full of tales. I chatted with him at the market. He told me The Keepers of the Kingdom are a nest of Vatican spies appointed by the pope to function as overlords to the Inquisition. I thought he was spinning a yarn."

"I wish he had been," said Anne.

"What did the man say?"

"I can't discuss it here. But we must pack—" Anne mouthed the rest of the words, "For a long trip."

At midnight, their coach pulled up to the two-story guest house, where Harald's brother, Cedric, and his wife, Aelfreda, lived on the far side of the château.

Anne looked down at Quentin, perched next to her. His wide eyes signaled he was still awake.

"We're at Uncle Cedric and Auntie Aelfie's house," she said. "Would you like Daddy to carry you, or would you like to walk?"

"I want Daddy to lift me from the coach. I can walk to the house myself," he said.

Kitty lifted Quentin onto her lap to bring him closer to the coach door.

Cedric came out onto the portico holding a lamp. "I received your message," he said. "Janie and Tommie would be most honored to host their distinguished Cousin Quentin. We have many adventures to conduct, and I fear we may not succeed in our endeavors without your help, my lad."

Once Harald set Quentin on the flagstones, the boy rushed past his Uncle Cedric, up the portico stairs, and let himself into the house. The rest followed him. The parlor danced with shadows, lit by a candelabra with three flickering wicks. Aelfreda sat at a table, tatting lace by the candlelight.

"Where are Tommie and Janie?" Quentin asked, his hands on his hips. Aelfreda set aside the lace and rose. A floppy cotton cap concealed her hair.

"They've gone to bed, my love. You can see them in the morning."

Quentin marched up to her. "Janie makes kites," he said. "I need to know how to do that."

Aelfreda had their cook bring hot toddies for her guests and warmed milk for Quentin. They chatted in low voices until Quentin fell asleep on the couch.

Anne held her breath as she stroked his cheek, willing herself not to cry. She kissed his forehead.

After saying their farewells, Anne, Kitty, and Harald left for the Port of Southampton and boarded their private ship.

3

The Spanish Hand

February, 1623
London, England

Count Gondomar sat at his Jacobian desk, staring at the raindrops spattering the windowpanes. Thoughts of bright days in Spain occupied the ambassador's mind—memories of wineglasses being raised to the setting sun. Laughing and talking beneath the stars with candlelit guests. This time of year, the climate of his country estate stayed mild long after nightfall.

Years spent in England had taken their toll on Gondomar. He'd never adjusted to the cloud-covered landscape and endless rain. First, the weather depressed him. Then, it broke his health.

He pulled the glass lamp down so the hanging flame could better illuminate the parchment atop his desk. Although he had read King Philip's letter several times, he read it once again. The king's language was vague, which annoyed Gondomar. He preferred detailed instructions. A rare mixture of giddiness and apprehension swirled within him as he anticipated the arrival of King James's favorite, the

Duke of Buckingham. He had to get it right. The duke's vacuous arrogance, combined with his close familiarity with King James and the crown prince, made him an ideal cat's paw. If Gondomar could persuade the Duke of Buckingham to push for a match between Prince Charles and the Spanish princess, no one, not even King James himself, would talk the avid social climber out of it. Making the affair appear to be the inspiration of the willful duke would provide cover for Gondomar as he executed his king's orders.

The divided Hapsburg monarchy—with one branch in Spain, via an advantageous marriage, and the other in Austria—was more complicated than ever. Protestantism was so popular in Central Europe that the Germanic kingdoms were slipping from the grasp of the Holy See. Determined to regain lost ground, the Roman Church had set its sights on Great Britain, which is why the Vatican had suggested a match between the Spanish infanta and Prince Charles of England.

Gondomar, nearing the end of his career, longed for a crowning achievement. Forging a marriage contract between the House of Hapsburg and the House of Stuart would be the capstone of his career.

A knock sounded at the door and the Duke of Buckingham strode into the study. A tall capotain hat with a curled brim topped his dark mane, accentuating his good looks. The duke's gray eyes, aquiline nose, and flawless complexion impressed Gondomar, although his gold brocade doublet spoke to the man's narcissism. Even

Buckingham's daily attire led one to believe he was dashing off to a grand ball.

Rising to honor the social protocols the duke was ignoring, Gondomar greeted the king's favorite. "My Lord, forgive this humble setting, hardly suitable for a man of your splendor," he said with a light bow, his hand pressed to his chest.

"I cannot be delayed by trivial matters, so I hope this is important," Buckingham said, dropping gracefully into the facing chair. "The king expects me at court."

Gondomar smiled. Scheming didn't have to be dull. He sat, pulled a miniature portrait from his top drawer, and laid it face-up on his desk for Buckingham, displaying a clear view of the infanta. Although the portrait showed none of her legendary figure, her copper curls, luminous eyes, and cherubic mouth were enough to entice any man.

"The House of Hapsburg is open to a match between Prince Charles and the infanta, Princess Maria Anna," the ambassador said.

Buckingham's sleepy eyes widened.

"Such a match would benefit both England and Spain," Gondomar continued. "Spain is flush with wealth from the New World. Nonetheless, the amount of treasure lost to piracy from England distresses King Philip. Of course, the Spanish are forced to retaliate, in a similar fashion. If England and Spain were to forge this union, treaties could be drawn to curtail this practice. Think of the wealth that could be spared on both sides."

Buckingham leaned forward. "Who else knows about this?" he asked.

Gondomar kept his face straight as his quarry snapped at the bait.

"No one, M'Lord. I thought it best to bring the matter to you first, since you are close to both the prince and his father, the king. When an heir to the throne is produced from this union, he will need a godfather, and who would be more qualified than you?"

"Indeed," Buckingham said, excited. "You've brought this information to the right person. Now, I beseech you, tell no one about this, absolutely no one. May I have your word, as a gentleman?"

"You have my word, M'Lord," the Spanish ambassador said, holding his mouth firm to avoid smiling.

Prince Charles and Buckingham marched in lockstep toward the king's chambers.

"Tell me more about her," said the prince, glancing at the miniature portrait of the infanta.

"She's Roman Catholic, of course," said Buckingham, searching his mind for further knowledge of her and finding none, other than rumors about her appearance. "She's quite amiable, and I hear she is buxom, even though her waistline is as dainty as a fairy's." He took delight in the prince's blush. The duke scanned Charles's blond hair and wondered if a bit of henna would make him appear more intellectual. The old wives' tale that blonds were strong in body but weak in mind could work against him in a Spanish court.

Charles was quite handsome, nevertheless, nearly as much so as the duke himself.

The two guards outside the king's door clapped their fists to their chests and thumped their spears twice on the ground—a signal to the majordomo inside royal visitors were approaching.

The majordomo opened the door. In a theatrical tone, he announced, "Prince Charles and the Duke of Buckingham seek an audience with the king."

"Let them in," King James mumbled, engrossed in a document atop his desk.

The majordomo bowed as Charles and Buckingham breezed by him.

"Father." The urgency in Charles's voice caused the king to look up from the document. His chemise fell loosely about his scrawny shoulders. The long opening at his neck revealed a frail chest. "Father, I must marry the Spanish infanta."

"What?" The king turned in his chair and stared. "Out of the question! If you think you can set a Roman Catholic on the throne without causing riots in the streets, you are mad. I will hear none of it! You can marry any Protestant princess you like, but a Roman Catholic? Never."

"Your Excellency," Buckingham interrupted, bowing deeply, "there are sound reasons to consider the Spanish infanta as England's next queen, reasons that have nothing to do with religion. We should consider the politics of seafaring navigation and trade. The Spanish pirate our trade ships, we pirate theirs, and amidst such fiery battles, much treasure is lost. Treaties with Spain would bolster our treasury. Moreover, we could use the influence of the

Hapsburg royal house as a bulwark against the depredations of the Roman Church."

"Or the Roman Church could use the influence of the Hapsburgs against us," King James interjected.

"Unlikely. The Hapsburg's interests align more with the Stuart's than with the Roman Church," Buckingham insisted. "King Philip has demonstrated his maturity and shrewdness. I assure you he is more interested in increasing his treasury than depleting it by financing another fancy ceiling for the pope. Ignore the Roman Church. An alliance with the Hapsburgs would strengthen England politically."

"As if one could ignore the Roman Church," James huffed.

"But what about me, Father?" Charles pressed.

"What about you?" James asked. "Do you suppose the moon and stars revolve around you? That Galileo fellow never made such a claim."

"I should have some say in this. We are discussing my future wife and the mother of my heirs."

James rolled his eyes. "I would not entrust England's future to the romantic fancies of youth."

"Charles," Buckingham said, turning toward the prince, "I pray you give me a moment alone with His Majesty."

Charles hesitated before leaning into a short bow. He left without a further word.

The majordomo followed him out the door—something he never would do unless the king had given the signal.

The first time Charles heard rumors about his father's sexual proclivities, he wanted charges of slander brought against the perpetrators, but two of the king's ministers had advised him against such an action. They explained that charges of slander were brought only if the gossip threatened the royal family's political standing. A charge of illegitimacy leveled against a royal was politically toxic. Such accusations could ruin the chances of strategic marriages for the royal heirs. Even more dangerous, it could call into question the legitimacy of a crown prince and lead to a civil war. Idle gossip about a king sporting with bonnie lads was of no import, however. Such talk was common in all European courts.

As Charles grew older, he could no longer deny his father's interest in bonnie lads. The more he noticed, the more it embarrassed him. Consequently, his affection for his father waned. However, as time passed, he noticed other things. Whereas many of his friends endured ongoing abuse from their entitled fathers, his own father had never subjected him to such humiliation or battery. On the contrary, as Charles reached manhood, his father had come to treat him as a peer and even a trusted friend. They often hunted together. His father also taught him to play chess—a heartwarming gesture, considering such tasks were often left to tutors.

While young lords in Charles's entourage gossiped about his eventual ascension to the throne, the thought of his father's demise made him feel more like an orphan than a king-in-the-making. He kept these thoughts to himself.

Buckingham was a necessary evil. Charles needed his assistance in his pursuit of the Spanish infanta's hand. He focused on the sound of his footsteps as he walked toward the garden.

4

The King's Council

February 1623
Whitehall Palace, London, England

Anne and Harald sat in the waiting room outside the king's study, surrounded by a gallery of paintings by Peter Paul Rubens and Anthony van Dyck. They hung one above the other, all the way to the ceiling. The wingback chairs embraced the couple with satin tufting, yet Anne sat with her back straight, unable to relax.

"When are we going to tell King James?" she asked in a low voice.

"That a match between the Spanish infanta and our bonnie Prince Charles is in the works? He already knows."

"Not that," said Anne. "About that horrible man from the Vatican."

Harald shot a look at her and shook his head. "That won't help," he whispered.

"I feared as much," said Anne. "Will Gregory Mack arrive soon?"

"He should be here already. He may have been detained."

They fell silent.

Two men approached the open doorway. Anne turned to see Sir Gregory. The doorman announced his arrival.

Gregory strolled into the room. He preferred corduroy breeches and a leather doublet to velvet and lace. He was the sort who could splash cologne on his jaw, run a comb through his long curls, and present a more handsome visage at court than prissy lords who spent hours primping with their valets. Anne admired his simplicity.

"Forgive my tardiness," he said. "Every member of the court accosted me with questions about a Spanish match. I swore I knew nothing, but once they gaged my destination, they would not relent."

He kissed Anne's cheek then sat, clapping his hands to his knees. "Will the miracle that is The First but Third Duke of Buckingham ever cease?" He began counting off on his fingers, "First Gentleman of the King's Royal Garter, Master Architect of Personal Palaces, Lord Chamberlain of the Patent Office, and now Meddlesome Matchmaker in Service to the Crown."

"Indeed. Imagine our delight when we learned of the duke's plan," said Harald.

"The duke has a plan?" Gregory asked, arching one eyebrow.

"An ingenious plan," said Harald. "Disguise Prince Charles and himself as merchants to go traipsing through France and across the Spanish border with nothing but a pair of lackeys to guard them."

Gregory shook his head in disbelief. "Absolutely foolproof," he said. "If anything should happen to bonnie Prince Charles, our kingdom will simply devolve to our noble queen, Georgie Villiers."

"Watch your tongues," Anne said in a hoarse whisper. "The duke in question has a habit of appearing out of nowhere." She glanced at the open doorway that led to the outer hall.

Gregory tipped his head back and clapped his hand over his eyes. "I cannot believe how easily this pretender has taken the reigns of England's destiny. This will not end well."

The door to the king's study creaked open and the three of them rose. A guard emerged, clacked his stave on the floor, and stood aside to wave them in. Anne led the way. The guard followed them in and flipped through their calling cards, reading their names aloud.

"Lady Anne and Lord Harald Audley, Duke and Duchess of Southampton, at your service, Your Majesty. Sir Gregory Mack, Earl of Staffordshire and loyal equerry to the king's stables, at your service, Your Majesty."

Anne curtsied as Harald and Gregory bowed. The king stood behind his desk, next to his minister, Sir Thomas Lake, a quiet man with a short, gray beard.

"Ah, the charming Lady Anne," said King James, "how we miss you at court." His velvet coat squared his shoulders and minimized his paunch, but his bulging eyes and swollen jowls betrayed his state of health.

"Please, observe." King James waved them over to his desk strewn with maps and parchment letters. He pulled a letter written in elegant script to the top. "I must say, the generosity of King Philip's dowry proposal excites me. By far, it is the most appealing aspect of the match, but the potential pitfall of a royal marriage between a Protestant and

Catholic gives me pause. The last time England had a Catholic queen, things went rather badly," he said, referring to Bloody Mary's reign of terror. "No one has forgotten, and no one wants to repeat it."

Sir Thomas stroked his beard. "Not to sway your decision unduly, Your Majesty, but Queen Mary Tudor inherited the throne directly from her father, King Henry the Eighth. If Princess Maria were to marry Prince Charles, she could not, by law, be regent. If anything happened to Prince Charles, the crown would go to his firstborn son or to Charles's elder sister, Elizabeth, if there is no male heir."

"Yet," said Harald, "if Charles should die before his heir reached the age of majority, the queen consort would rule as proxy to the crown prince. Herein lies the danger of a Catholic queen who may be inclined to take the advice of the pope over that of her English ministers."

"This is what frustrates me," said King James, slapping his hand on the desk. "The faintest possibility of a civil war torments my soul!"

"Your Excellency," said Anne. She touched his elbow, but quickly withdrew, realizing her gaffe.

"You may touch me," said the king. "Must I, too, bow to protocol? Am I not the king of my own castle?"

His guests chuckled at his joke.

King James raised his hands, as if in surrender. "Ah, what is a father to do with a willful son?" he asked. "Sir George has stoked his passions. Now, they both insist on leaving for Madrid. I doubt a royal decree would stop them."

"Your Majesty," said Gregory, "allow me to accompany Prince Charles to Madrid. I shall devote myself to his personal safety. You have my word."

"I have no doubt you would give your life to save my son, Sir Gregory. The moment I heard of this harebrained scheme, I summoned you, for that reason. If Charles insists on disguising himself as a common merchant and journeying to Madrid with no one but Steenie to guide him, I must insist you join them."

There was a pause. Sir Thomas broke the silence. "Who is Steenie, Your Majesty?"

"Ah," said the king. "That is my pet name for Sir George, dear boy."

The lords pursed their lips and glanced at one another.

Gregory placed his hand on his heart. "I would be most honored to accompany Prince Charles to Madrid, Your Majesty. May I request Sir Varney and Sir Isley assist me on the journey? They are well-travelled, and dexterous with swords and muskets. We would all be much safer with them along."

"I know them well and heartily agree," said the king.

"Your Excellency," said Anne, "Sir Harald and I could journey to Madrid to assist your ambassador, Sir John Digby, in preparing for the arrival of Prince Charles and Sir George, if it pleases you. We may forestall a wedding and assist Ambassador Digby in negotiating an advantageous marriage contract."

"That is a delightful proposition, Lady Anne," said the king. At that, he dismissed them to carry out their plans.

5

The House of Seven Chimneys

March 1623
Madrid, Spain

A midnight rain fell on six mounted men as they approached the English Embassy. The clip-clop of hooves echoed off the surrounding walls. Behind them, a tall coach rumbled over the brick pavers. Cracks of lightning revealed the rippled roof tiles of the shadowy houses that lined the street. Their turrets stood black against strobe-lit storm clouds.

From inside the coach, Anne drew back the curtain to look about the darkened streets. The rain nearly drowned out the noise from the carriage wheels. Kitty leaned over and peered out. The light from the pole lamps on the carriage reflected in the spattered puddles.

Anne whispered, "I feel we're being watched."

"We are," said Harald. "I wouldn't worry. We'll meet the neighbors in the morning."

"Should we tell Ambassador Digby about Prince Charles and Buckingham when we arrive?" Anne asked. "Or should we wait till tomorrow?"

"Morning," said Harald. "I dispatched a letter. He should have received it two days ago. If we go into details now, we'll be up all night. My only thought is the warm bed that awaits us."

"I heartily agree," said Anne.

Kitty leaned forward. "If we don't better manage Buckingham, he and the prince could sneak into the Alcazar and leap out at King Philip as a jest. Let us pray his guards don't shoot them dead."

"It's frightful to think someone so stupid has so much influence over our king," said Anne.

"It's a source of endless gossip in the London taverns," said Kitty. "That and Buckingham's new estate, which puts the king's palace to shame."

The rain subsided. Anne tipped her head out the window and took in the crisp night air, inhaling in the essence of rosemary. The English-built House of the Seven Chimneys loomed ahead, the only mansion in the neighborhood with torches lit at the gate and at the front porch. The gables along the slate roofline clustered together like a small mountain range, their slender chimneys rising above them like sentinels. The house's windows glowed from within, making it seem alive.

They passed between the flickering torches at the gate and pulled up to the lamp-lit porte cochère between a canopy of tall cork oaks that lined the entryway. The embassy doors swung open and a flock of footmen hurried across the courtyard. Harald leapt out of the coach and nodded to the head servant.

"Sir, allow me to stable your horses and coach," the servant said. "Your men will have shelter near the stalls."

Harald nodded. Once Anne and Kitty disembarked, the coachman flipped the reins. The horses followed the servant toward the stables.

Anne sighed with pleasure upon entering the warm entry hall. A fire crackled in a grand, mahogany fireplace. As she and Kitty stood warming their hands, Lady Digby and her housekeeper assisted them in removing their cloaks.

"I know how demanding a journey from London to Madrid can be," Laura Digby said. Her kind round face and matronly figure made Anne nostalgic for her childhood nanny. "Our head housekeeper has prepared your rooms. Your lady's maid's room is next to your own and Lord Audley's."

"Dear Lady Digby, thank you for your kindness," said Anne. "My companion is my longtime friend, Lady Catherine, Baroness von Kirchheim. In the family, we call her Kitty. She has been like a sister to me for years."

"How do you do, Lady Digby?" Kitty curtsied elegantly.

"Oh, my," said Lady Digby. "Please forgive my gaffe."

"It is nothing," said Kitty, tossing her hand as if a gaffe were a floating dust bunny she could wave aside.

Lady Digby clasped her hands. "Please, call me Laura. It is my sincere hope you ladies enjoy your time in Madrid. The city is lovely and the weather is so fine, it is like being on holiday. Now, you must be in want of a good night's sleep. There are refreshments waiting for you in your chambers."

The housekeeper escorted Anne and Kitty to their rooms. Anne entered her bedchamber and found a fire flickering in a petite, marble fireplace. The tall windows had been set with glass panes. A crack of lightning exposed the orange trees in the courtyard. Anne drew the brocade curtains together.

Kitty rapped on the door and entered. "Do you need some help out of that damp dress?" she asked, letting herself in.

"Thank you. If you help me with my buttons, I'll help you with yours."

As they chatted, they could hear Harald's conversation with John Digby echoing in the entry hall.

"Ah me," said Anne. "I hope he has not done what he said he would not."

Within the minute, Harald entered the room, as if he had heard her thoughts.

"Comfortable, indeed," he said, pleased with the fireplace and the plush coverlet on the bed. "Lady Digby keeps a welcoming home."

"We'll know more about that when we see what's for breakfast," Anne remarked, unfastening the last of Kitty's buttons.

"I will see you in the morning," said Kitty, rushing from the room, holding the bodice of her dress to her chest.

Having already donned her nightgown, Anne slipped between the covers of the bed and yawned. "I'll want to hear all about the house Lady Digby has picked out for us."

"John Digby told me we'll be quartered in a large country estate near the embassy. He said it has a spectacular cupola."

Anne made no response.
Harald looked down to see she was fast asleep.

6

Incognito

The following week, Prince Charles and his traveling party arrived at the city gates of Madrid, disguised as jaunty merchants decked in tams and leather cloaks lined with beaver fur. They dismounted, then passed through the city gates, holding the reins of their horses and proffering letters of passage to the officials who stood guard.

Perched in the columned cupola above the terracotta roof of the Audley's villa, Anne held a bronze telescope to her eye and watched.

"Are we obliged to rush over to the embassy to greet them?" she asked Harald.

"Dear God, no," he said. "Buckingham will consume the entire afternoon with endless bragging, none of it to the point. Gregory Mack is the only person worth talking to, but we shall see him on the morrow."

"Buckingham and the prince rarely rise before mid-morning," Anne mused, lowering the telescope. "If we arrive at the embassy at dawn, we would have at least three hours to converse with Sir Gregory without the duke's presence."

"I'll dispatch a page to Sir Gregory," said Harald. "We need to discuss strategy."

"What is our strategy?"

Harald paused. "That remains to be seen."

The House of the Seven Chimneys was more than an embassy. It served also as a comfortable home for Ambassador Digby and his wife and would soon function as a hotel for the hearty young lords King James had dispatched to act as a merry entourage for his son, Prince Charles.

For those allowed to enter, the favorite room in the house was the fireside study. Both spacious and cozy, the room showcased a large fireplace with a Baroque mantel carved from black walnut. Several wingback chairs stood between the fireplace and a large table in the middle of the room. The walls were pale amethyst and lined with tall, narrow windows set with beveled diamond windowpanes. The windows on the far wall opened to a rose garden. The late-winter morning was unseasonably mild, much to the delight of the English visitors.

Kitty poured tea for Anne and herself, then set the Blue Willow teapot down on the silver platter and scooped a lump of sugar into both cups. Anne stirred her tea. The sound of silver clinking against porcelain relaxed her.

John Digby poked the fire, sending a rush of crackling sparks swirling up the flue. The amber glow of the flames lit up Sir Gregory Mack's face. He sat on a footstool beside the hearth, holding a brass horse's bit to the side, polishing it with a soft leather cloth. He wore plain and sturdy garb, but Anne knew he was no commoner. His family had been the

Stuarts' retainers for generations. While his eldest brother had inherited his father's ducal estate and title, Gregory had secured for himself the title of Earl, due to his successful management of the king's stables.

Laura Digby sat on an upholstered chair in the corner, crocheting. The window at her shoulder glowed pink with the breaking dawn.

Ambassador Digby scowled as he considered which of the Spanish quandaries to bring up first. His expression smoothed as he spoke. "The Vatican sent scholars to take charge of Prince Charles's conversion to Catholicism." He clasped his hands behind his back. "When the prince and Buckingham pay their visit to the Alcazar, King Philip will offer to house them there." Digby stopped to face Anne and Harald. "The invitation cannot be refused. Prince Charles must accept this arrangement or leave Spain on King Philip's orders. The prime minister, Count-Duke Olivares, made this clear."

Gregory spoke up. "If the prince had stayed home, we could have bargained an excellent marriage contract. There was no need for him to set foot in Madrid."

"That would have ruined Buckingham's fun," said Harald.

"Ah, the joys of being in service to a mischievous amateur," said Gregory. "We must insist Varney and Isley stay with them as their personal valets. The prince needs expert protection."

"I bargained one valet for each of them," said Digby. "Olivares conceded nothing more. I shall tell them their duty is to protect only the prince, which means Varney and Isley must stay with him at all times. If Buckingham wants to go his own way, he must find his own escort."

"My heart goes out to Varney and Isley," said Anne, as she considered the duke's strange and powerful appetites. "Keeping Buckingham pacified won't be easy."

"They take pride in serving the English crown," said Harald. "In the meantime, we have two reliable Englishmen to observe the activities within the Alcazar. I will take a report from them daily."

Two quick knocks at the door interrupted them.

"Come in," said Digby.

Varney and Isley walked in, both dressed for court in black doublets. Varney's black hair was pulled back and fastened with a ribbon at the nape of his neck. The simple style emphasized his widow's peak. Isley's brown hair pooled around his shoulders.

"Gentlemen, welcome to Madrid," said Anne.

They bowed and made their greetings.

"We have come to make a report," said Isley. "We sat near a papal legate at a tavern in the town of Alcala and overheard his conversation."

"Something riveting, I hope," said Anne.

"The pope is founding a Vatican bank," said Varney.

Digby's jaw dropped. "Dear God," he exclaimed. "How do they intend to capitalize it?"

"He didn't say," said Isley, "but he discussed financing a war on the German Protestants."

John Digby opened a polished rosewood box, lifted an ivory pipe, and flicked up its filigreed cap. "France recently reduced their contribution to the Vatican. It was the last thing they expected from Cardinal Richelieu," he said. He picked up a long splinter, touched it to a candle flame, and lit his pipe.

Anne shifted to face Digby. "Which means the pope will expect an even larger contribution from Spain," she said.

"This is awkward," Harald said. "King James agreed to this match, hoping a large dowry from Spain would resupply his own dwindling coffers. Now, it appears Spain may be hoping for financial relief from England."

A rapid clacking of footsteps from the hallway approached and Buckingham burst through the door. Prince Charles followed him in. The group stood to greet them.

"Well, well," Buckingham sneered, "when I rose to take breakfast, none of you were there. Who would suppose such well born notables would rise with the cowherds?"

"Good morning, Your Highness," said Anne, ignoring Buckingham and curtsying to the prince. "I hope you slept well."

"I did, indeed," said the prince, glancing admiringly at Anne and Kitty.

"We meant no disrespect," said Anne.

"I see my equerry is here," said Buckingham, glaring at Gregory. "It seems servants strive to be masters in sunny Madrid."

Lord and Lady Digby regarded Buckingham as if he were a misbehaving child abroad without his governess.

"You are new to the English court, Lord Buckingham," said Harald.

Buckingham glared at Harald. Harald regarded him coolly.

"Sir George," said Anne, striking a pleasant tone, "we are discussing Spanish climate, terrain, and the gear needed for short journeys. We hoped to spare you the boredom of such trivialities."

"Trivialities? What is trivial about warding off highwaymen, or choosing proper attire? You might have consulted with myself, not my equerry," Buckingham sneered.

Lady Digby smiled and said, "Prince Charles, Lord Digby collected telescopes during our diplomatic visit to Italy. You may wish to join him when he sets them up tonight. There are two peculiar starbursts in the sky. I believe the astronomers call them nebulae."

"Telescopes?" Charles was incredulous. "Where did he get them?"

"We have friends in Pisa," said Lady Digby. "Doctor Galileo makes them. They invited him to put on a demonstration."

"You have telescopes made by Galileo? I must see them! If only my mother were alive. She loved astronomy."

Buckingham huffed and put his hands on his hips. "We are due at court in less than two hours. We must prepare."

"The plan was to go in disguise," the prince replied. "It doesn't take much time to look like a merchant. I shall don my hat and be ready. In the meanwhile, I would like to share my tale of adventure. It appears the famous storyteller, Cervantes, is still alive and living incognito. I spotted him in a barbershop in Alcala, his hometown."

"You don't say!" Lady Digby exclaimed.

"I saw him with my own eyes," said the prince. "I even spoke with him."

Buckingham sighed and yawned in an open display of boredom while Prince Charles continued his tale.

7

Young King Philip

The magnificent palace of Madrid known as the Alcazar stretched wide before them. The columned white walls gleamed under the mid-morning sun. A row of colorful pennant flags fluttered above the parapets.

The English party approached, dressed in velvet tams and thick wool doublets with matching breeches. They looked like wealthy merchants on holiday. Buckingham produced a calling card with a flourish and the five of them—Buckingham, Prince Charles, Gregory, Varney, and Isley—followed the majordomo into the palace.

Inside, a retinue of liveried servants stood above their own reflections on the polished floor. The majordomo stopped and turned to the right. From an avenue of marble columns crowned with cathedral arches, the king's secretary approached. He wore white silk stockings and blue velvet bloomers. His matching doublet was topped by a stiff white Elizabethan collar wrapped around his neck like ribbon candy. His short black hair was combed forward and shellacked in place. A coterie of liveried servants walked in lockstep in his wake, their garb the same blue and white but made of fine wool.

Buckingham stepped forward to bow, spinning his hand before him as if unspooling a ball of yarn. "Please inform

King Philip that the merchants from England are at his disposal," he announced. He winked at Prince Charles as he straightened.

The servants bowed low while the king's secretary greeted the prince and his party. The prince kept his posture stiff as he nodded to the staff.

A beautiful matron with elaborate hair garnished by a black lacy veil appeared at Gregory's elbow. "Please, allow me to escort you, Señor. This way."

Two more women took Varney and Isley by the arm, leading them in the same direction. Gregory grinned, enjoying the attention, until he looked over his shoulder and noticed Prince Charles and Buckingham being led in the opposite direction.

"Pardon me, Señora, but I must remain with my pri— my companions."

"Not necessary," she said with a smile and a reassuring pat on his arm. "I assure you, your companions shall receive the kindest hospitality, but only they have an appointment with the king. Do you enjoy café?"

"I do," Gregory said, watching the servants lead the prince and the duke down an ornate hallway.

The women led Gregory, Varney, and Isley to a room with high ceilings and divided-light windows that revealed a green lawn dotted with weeping willows. The pale gray walls were painted with pastel scenes of oriental trees and exotic birds. The aroma of fresh café made Gregory's mouth water. The women motioned the men to chairs that were more beautiful than comfortable, but once coffee and pastries were served, Gregory cared not a whit.

As they strolled down the hall, Prince Charles whispered to Buckingham, "Why were we separated from Sir Gregory and the others?"

"Who cares?" said Buckingham.

The two escorts said nothing. The servants' suede shoes whispered along the palace floor, whereas Charles's and Buckingham's boots clopped with every step, announcing their arrival with little subtlety.

"This way, if you please," said the servant on the right, motioning them toward an open doorway.

Bright sunlight streaming through the floor-to-ceiling windows at the back of the spacious room dazzled Charles. He took a moment to make out the silhouette of King Philip seated at a large, heavy table. Two men stood on either side of him; a tall, portly nobleman dressed in a black velvet doublet over a white satin chemise, and a short, stocky man wearing a red, three-corner clergyman's cap and matching cape. King Philip's heavy eyelids made him appear indifferent. His long, reddish-brown hair touched the shoulders of his ermine vestment, which he wore as casually as one would wear a dressing gown.

"Greetings, gentlemen," he announced in a voice low enough Charles could barely believe he was a youth of sixteen. "Please seat yourselves." He motioned to two damask wingback chairs gleaming in the light. "I have invited my trusted counselor, Count-Duke Olivares, as well as Monsignor Massimi, the Vatican's papal nuncio," King Philip said, motioning to the men who stood on either side of him. As Charles's vision adjusted to the light, he was struck at the thick-necked Monsignor's reptilian glare.

"Before we get started," Buckingham said, raising his hand to shield his eyes, "could I bother you to have the drapes drawn? The sunlight is blinding to those of us on this side of the room." He finished his sentence with a chuckle.

The pause that followed left Charles counting his heartbeats.

"Of course," King Philip said, at length. He snapped his fingers at the servant standing at the door. The servant glided up to the window and took the curtain wand in his hands.

"Just the sheers," said the king.

The sheers dimmed the light somewhat, but the glare still made it difficult to read the expressions of the men facing them. Charles presumed this was calculated. The young king had disadvantaged them in a way that could not be construed as impolite. Charles marveled at the Spanish regent before him—four years his junior, yet astonishingly well-composed. He studied Philip's mannerisms, wondering which he should adopt for himself.

"Of course, we would never make such a request if we were mere merchants," Buckingham said with a staged laugh, looking toward Charles. "Please don't think us brash, but I believe the time has come to reveal our true identities."

"We know who you are," Philip said dryly.

Charles felt suddenly ridiculous in his plain merchant's garb, but there was nothing to do but ignore it and hope the Spanish king would as well.

"Let us get on with the business at hand," King Philip continued. "Prince Charles, we are honored you took the effort to grace us with your presence. I understand you seek my sister's hand in marriage?"

"I do, Your Highness, if I may be so bold," Charles said. "Her beauty is ethereal and I have no doubt she will one day be the finest queen in all of Europe."

"I am pleased to hear you are as enthusiastic about this match as I am. Of course, there are more important matters to consider than mere romance."

"Indeed, indeed," Buckingham chimed in. Philip raised his palm, keeping his eyes fixed on Charles.

"There are benefits for both sides," Charles said, hoping to be taken seriously. "Each of us could benefit from a treaty. Direct trade between our great nations could increase prosperity on both sides. And, with this match, the House of Hapsburg would be making a treaty with not one country, but three. The House of Stuart reigns over England, Scotland, and Ireland."

The papal nuncio took a deep breath, lifting his chin in indignation. Sir Digby had cautioned Prince Charles the Vatican would bristle at this claim. While the Protestant Scots were happy to put their Scottish king on England's throne, the Irish stubbornly clung to Roman Catholicism while the English, just as stubbornly, imposed their new religion.

"If I may," said Monsignor Massimi, "the infanta, Princess Maria Anna, belongs to the one true faith. She will never leave the flock, and you must be prepared to accept this." He caught Charles in his cold stare.

"Of course, but—" Charles was about to say his queen would be free to embrace his religion if this was her choice, but he sensed an icy resolve from the men before him and thought better of it. "But she, in turn, will understand that I am of the Protestant faith, and neither will that change."

Monsignor Massimi glanced at Olivares. The bulky prime minister shifted to face Charles. At first glance, Charles found Olivares's bulbous nose and elaborate moustache comical, but the man's glare and hefty stature intimidated the prince.

"Your Highness," Olivares began, "It is my great honor to put myself at your service as we prepare for the happy occasion of your wedding. But matters of such importance cannot be rushed. In preparation for this holiest of unions, you shall take Catechism, taught by the esteemed Monsignor Massimi, who was dispatched by the Vatican for this purpose. You and the infanta shall sit side by side as you learn the true faith. Of course, we understand you are a man who makes his own choices in this regard, but likewise, Princess Maria Anna was christened when she was just days old and has been a devout Catholic ever since. Her devotion shall never wane. Catechism is your opportunity to better understand the nature of her virtue. As you may recall, the late Queen Katherine of England was a woman of impeccable virtue, exactly what one would expect of a Roman Catholic queen," he said, referring to King Henry the Eighth's first wife. "She is legendary for her endless charity, even to this day."

"Indeed, she was, I mean is." Charles agreed. He refrained from mentioning their most recent Roman Catholic queen, his great-aunt Bloody Mary, whose reign was still infamous for its witch-hunts and heresy trials.

"Needless to say," the Monsignor continued, "she never once wavered in her loyalty to the Church. You can expect the same from your future bride. So, to better understand the vital connection between her faith and her virtue, we felt it imperative you learn the Catechism that underpins her immaculate character."

"And shall she, likewise, learn about my faith?" Charles glanced over at Buckingham, hoping for a show of support.

"Not the least bit necessary, M'Lord," Buckingham said before turning an ingratiating smile toward King Philip. "Princess Maria Anna is a woman. Women's minds are cluttered and disorganized. It's imperative you understand this sort of muddled thinking in regard to her core beliefs for the sake of harmony in the household. But it is not at all necessary for her to understand your mind." As he spoke, Buckingham shifted his gaze from Charles to Philip, as if seeking the young king's approval. "Indeed, this would give your bride the idea that she understood you enough to venture an opinion on your affairs—" At this remark, King Philip shook his head and waved his hand. Buckingham continued, "—and that is precisely what we do not want."

"Please, Lord Buckingham," King Philip broke in. "Do not speculate on my sister's state of mind. I do not find her thoughts the least bit disorganized. Of course, she will share her insights with her king, as would any wise queen.

"Dear Prince Charles," Philip shifted his gaze. "Once you are married, you will have all the time you need to discuss whatever you like with your wife. The purpose of the Catechism is to help you understand why my sister is so devout, and why any attempts at shifting her devotions would be futile. I'm sure Monsignor Massimi could explain this better than I."

The Monsignor took a deep breath as if preparing for a lecture. "This is not merely an opportunity to understand your future queen's faith," Massimi said. "You shall come to understand the one true faith. Those who stray from the path—"

"I shall not bow to the pope," Charles said. His voice was barely audible, but everyone heard it.

There was a long pause.

"No one's asking you to bow to the pope," Buckingham said through the side of his mouth. "Let me handle this." He turned toward Philip. "Of course, we both understand—"

"Silence," said King Philip, holding up his hand. He looked at Charles. "That is not a prerequisite to the marriage contract, so there is no need to discuss it. We need only to settle where and when the Catechism shall commence. Monsignor?"

"Tuesdays, Wednesdays, and Thursdays, at 10 a.m.," the Monsignor scowled, "each class one hour and three-quarters."

"Very well," said the king, placing his fingertips together. "You, dear Prince Charles, and your companion, the Duke of Buckingham, shall reside here at the palace in close proximity to Monsignor Massimi. This will afford you numerous opportunities to converse with my sister, Infanta Maria, with appropriate supervision. We have also prepared a room for Sir Varney and Sir Isley, whom I understand are your valets. All other staff, chambermaids, pages, etcetera, shall be provided."

A slight pulse of alarm rippled through Charles as he realized King Philip had not mentioned the man he most wanted to remain—Gregory Mack, whom he had known since childhood.

"I would like to keep my equerry with me," Charles said.

"I'm afraid there are no accommodations for horse-keepers in the palace," said King Philip. "My understanding is that your ambassador, Sir Digby, has already made arrangements for Señor Gregory. Meanwhile, you and I are destined to become dear friends. Please, tell us the news from your fair England. Anything amusing?"

In the conversation that followed, King Philip took an interest in what Buckingham had to say, which encouraged his volubility. Charles could barely get a word in edgewise as the duke described and pontificated upon every bit of English court gossip and all the lordly ventures he could think of. Philip and Olivares greeted each revelation with increasing awe until it became obvious Buckingham had divulged all he knew, insofar as he was repeating himself. At this juncture, King Philip concluded the meeting.

Philip waited until the guard closed the door behind the two Englishmen before sharing his impression with his counselors.

"Count Gondomar was right," Philip said. "The Duke of Buckingham is a useful tool. I should have been kinder to him at the onset. Gondomar was always the best of my father's counselors."

Olivares chuckled like a sportsman laughing off the competition. "Do not get too attached to Gondomar. He's in bad health. His flatulence is legendary. I wouldn't mention it, except to say his inability to control it could be symptomatic of a wasting disease."

"That's a bit dramatic," Philip said, with one cocked eyebrow. "I've never heard a few farts ever killed anyone. Unless the poor fellow were to die of embarrassment," he chuckled, looking over at Monsignor Massimi.

The Monsignor managed to curl the edges of his lips beneath his deadened eyes, but the smile faded quickly, as if the fraud of merriment was too much effort.

"But that's not the worst of it," Olivares continued. "Gondomar has overplayed his hand. King James's subjects are clamoring to put his head on a spike."

Philip sighed. "Sir Walter Raleigh?" he asked.

"Exactly."

Under King Philip's orders, Gondomar had pushed for Raleigh's execution. The English pirate had laid waste to a Spanish coastal village after Spain and England had agreed to a ceasefire. Raleigh knew about the ceasefire but had promised his men an "adventure". He feared that denying his cutthroats the pleasure of rape and murder might tarnish his reputation as a man of his word, and thus allowed the destruction of the Spanish coastal village as a form of amusement. King Philip had made it clear he wanted

Raleigh taken out. Olivares had cautioned him about sending such orders to Gondomar on the grounds they were attempting to improve and not worsen their relationship with England. Philip had relented, at first, but the following night, he awoke hours before dawn, consumed with rage. He took to his desk to write the order to Gondomar and sent it off with his most reliable messenger before the sun rose.

Olivares spoke, to quell the silence. "Gondomar was perhaps a bit too eager to prove his metal. Now, King James's subjects hate the Spanish for removing a rogue they regarded a hero. We can only hope their hatred for Gondomar won't affect the match."

King Philip stared at his desk.

"I would be happy to pray over it, Your Excellency," Monsignor Massimi said.

"That's not necessary," said Philip.

"Please, suffer the Lord's humble servant to do His work, Your Majesty. If we could be alone for a few moments, that is all."

King Philip shot a glance toward Olivares.

"Excuse me, Your Majesty," Olivares said with a bow before leaving the room. Massimi waited until the guard shut the door before speaking again.

"Could you send the guard out?"

"You can't pray in front of a guard?"

"If the guard is not part of our prayer, he is a distraction. Thereby, his presence is disrespectful to the Lord."

"I cannot comply with your request," said Philip, "It is the law in the House of Hapsburg the king is to be guarded at all times."

"But in respect for the Lord—"

Philip looked coldly at the Monsignor and slowly shook his head. The Monsignor huffed.

"Before we pray, there is something you need to know about Count Olivares," the Monsignor said, lowering his voice to a near whisper.

"Really," Philip said, as if the subject bored him.

"His family have been converso Jews for over 300 years."

"Converso Jews?"

"Jews who have converted to Roman Catholicism," said the Monsignor.

"But that's what God wants, is it not?"

"Of course," said Massimi. "The reputation of the House of Olivares is impeccable. Not a single member of their family has relapsed in the past three centuries, but that is suspicious in itself, for that is exactly what one would expect from a crypto-Jew."

"A crypto-Jew," King Philip said, like a man unconvinced goblins were real.

"The worst kind of Jew," the Monsignor said, his eyes glaring from beneath bushy eyebrows. "Jews who pretend to convert to Christianity, only to spy on us, gathering information for the battle they intend to wage against us at the end times."

King Philip took in a deep breath and let it out slowly. "I have known Olivares my entire life. He is not a crypto-Jew. Shall we pray?"

Gregory crossed one leg over the other, allowing his boot to swing as he raised his porcelain teacup to the señora who had escorted him to the café parlor. He drained the cup to the last drop, but before returning it to the table, he noticed a figure embossed on the bottom. He held it up to the light to get a better look and saw the impression of a twin-tailed mermaid. He recognized the image from the signboard of a popular Scottish tavern. It was an insult directed toward King James's mother, Mary, Queen of Scots, regarding a scandalous extra-marital affair, which led to the murder of her first husband and a disastrous second marriage.

The señora smirked as she drew near. The two women behind her tittered.

"Interesting image, is it not? Imagine our surprise when we discovered it was an insult to Mary, Queen of Scots. We would never have ordered these if we had known, but that is how we learned of the scandal. Of course, no one at the House of Hapsburg would ever pass on such calumny. But isn't it a pity? If the rumor were to catch on, every royal house in Europe will assume King James, and all his progeny, are illegitimate. If poor Prince Charles wishes to protect himself and his family from such scandal, the only way is to make an alliance with the Church. Only the Vatican can vouchsafe King James's legitimacy."

"So, this is how your royal house earned its reputation as the legendary 'Street of Lies'?" Isley chuckled. The women lost their smiles, having been reminded of their own royal family's reputation.

Varney stood up. "Top of the morning to you, Señoras." As the other two men rose, Varney lifted his cup to toast the young women standing along the wall before setting it lightly on the table.

"Please signal Count Olivares to come in," King Philip said to his guard, once Monsignor Massimi had left. As the guard stepped out the door, Philip rolled his head back. The Monsignor's prayers had left him tight around the neck. Years earlier, Olivares had warned him that being king would not consist entirely of gala balls and sumptuous feasts. The occupation was hard, and every king needed to brace himself for the stress it imposed.

"At your service, Your Majesty," Olivares said with a low bow upon entering the room. Philip was still unaccustomed to his prime minister's courtly deference. When he was a child, Olivares would generally greet him with a funny story that made him laugh.

"Please, seat yourself." Philip gestured toward one of the chairs across from him. Once Olivares was seated, Phillip stared at his desk, searching his mind for the right words. At length, he said, "I'm concerned about Spain's future." He looked up to gage Olivares's reaction, but the prime minister just gazed at him, saying nothing. "England is growing in strength and prominence, while Spain's power is waning. There is no denying it."

"Powers rise and fall," Olivares said. "For many years, Englishmen had a queen to show off for. Lord knows

Englishmen do love to put on a display for women. Now that they are ruled by a king once again, they are just another kingdom."

King Philip frowned. "Spain took the most lucrative territories of the New World. Our ships still come in, laden with gold, silver, and other precious cargo. But where is the money? I cannot help but notice the gross disparity between the precious cargo that comes to port, and the size of our treasury."

Olivares took a deep breath and held it before letting it out. "Spain has always been closely aligned with the Holy Roman Church. The Church relies on Spain to maintain the stability of the Holy Roman Empire, and as our reward, Spain receives the protection of the Church."

"Protection? What protection? The Church's wars are fought with Spanish soldiers and Spanish treasure. I dare say it is the Vatican that receives protection from Spain."

Olivares raised his eyebrows and hunched his shoulders in resignation. "I was referring to the protection of our mortal souls from the forces of evil."

Philip rolled his eyes, knowing such ignoble behavior would be excused by his friend and prime minister.

Olivares continued, "The political fortunes of Spain and the Roman Church are tightly interwoven. I don't think this union can be undone."

"And regarding this fifty-five-year war with The Netherlands," the young king huffed, "what is The Netherlands to Spain? What are we fighting for, if not the Vatican's pride? So what if they lose the so-called Republic of the Seven United Netherlands? Their pretentious name is so much larger than the nation itself, it must be spelled out in the North Sea on the map."

Olivares stifled a chuckle. "Truth be told, the Netherlands is the land of the most adept traders in the world. You would be astounded to know how much treasure moves through their ports."

"If and when we do win this war, where will that treasure go? Into the coffers of Spain, or the Vatican?"

Olivares had no answer.

8

The Parade of Coaches

April 1623
Madrid, Spain

A spatter of rain touched Anne's shoulders. She looked up at the clouds and was relieved to see them drifting apart. Anne and Harald proceeded to step into an open coach. Kitty followed.

Harald leaned close, lending his warmth. "What a charming collar," he said, glancing down at the scalloped lace around Anne's neck. It came together in a bow, ending in tassels of faceted sapphire beads. "Those blue crystals match your eyes."

Anne smiled. "Kitty made it. It's called neck-lace. It is the height of fashion, thankfully. I didn't bring along any gems to match these ostentatious sleeves." She fluffed the billowing blue satin that fell from her shoulders. Her sleeve's opulence framed a pearl-beaded bodice, which displayed her décolletage above the scooped neckline.

"The effect is heavenly," Harald said. Anne blushed.

"I told you he would love it," said Kitty. Her satin dress and organza sleeves matched the color of the pale morning sunshine. Yellow roses and blue forget-me-nots decked the thick braid at the nape of her neck.

Prince Charles climbed aboard, followed by Buckingham, who picked up the hem of his velvet coat and held it straight before sitting.

The coachman cracked the whip and the dappled mares lurched into motion, their silver coats rippling under the sun as they pranced around the gravel path to join in the merriment known as The Parade of Coaches.

Charles and Buckingham waved to spectators gathered along the street to see the infanta's fiancé. Anne, Harald, and Kitty faced backwards but had good views of the crowd. Coaches carrying other noblemen formed a broad circle around the Prado. Entertainers performed on a raised platform in the center. A troupe of dancing girls with white-powdered faces and large pink dots rouged onto their cheeks lifted one hand and spun, twirling their skirts, careful to balance the feathered tiaras crowning their heads. They danced to the music of a lute player, a violinist, and a small coffee-colored man who played a wooden flute. His hair gleamed in the sun like a black lacquered bowl. He danced about as unabashed as a tot, even though he wore nothing but a loincloth. Strings of brown beads hung around his neck. As he played his flute, Anne strained to hear the strange melody through the breeze.

She leaned toward Harald. "That's the Amerindian Duchess Olivares is hosting at her estate. She claims he's a talented musician and a good hunter, even though he refuses to ride a horse. He prefers to run along with the dogs. According to her, he keeps up with them!"

"That doesn't surprise me," said Harald. "He's from the Amazonian jungle. There are no horses there. Nonetheless, their natives are legendary hunters."

"King Philip!" Buckingham shouted, theatrically waving his hand.

Anne turned to see the royal black coach with the red-and-gold coat of arms emblazoned on the door. King Philip's flushed cheeks made him look hot in his ermine robe.

"Buckingham," Harald hissed through clenched teeth. "That is not how one addresses the king, especially when you are a foreign guest. Desist at once."

"I know him personally. We are dear friends," Buckingham said in clipped syllables. He stood and shouted louder, adding a growl to his tone. "King Philip!" He waved both arms at the bewildered king. Anne froze. Kitty bowed her head and put her fingers to her brow.

King Philip raised one hand to Buckingham. The other passengers in his coach stared at them, stone-faced, except for one. The infanta broke into a silent giggle as she looked directly at Prince Charles. Her high-necked white blouse billowed above a purple velvet bodice. A breeze sent the loose satin rippling over her décolletage.

Anne glanced at Prince Charles, who gaped at the infanta, as if under her spell.

Kitty leaned over and touched his arm. "Smile and wave at Princess Maria," she whispered.

He did so. The infanta glanced sideways at her prudish governess, then pointedly at Prince Charles before rolling her eyes, as if to say, *I would wave back, but, you know…*

"Ah," Charles sighed. "She shall be my bride one day. Soon, I hope."

"Sooner than you think," said Buckingham. "I am on excellent terms with King Philip, as anyone can see. But you have not met him, have you Sir Harald?" Buckingham turned his head toward the crowd and added, "Remind me to arrange an introduction."

Ambassador Digby had already explained to Anne and Harald a royal introduction was unlikely, not because Buckingham enjoyed playing cat-and-mouse games, but because King Philip's prime minister would never allow it. A charming English couple, well-versed in European politics, might lure the young king into a close friendship, which could jeopardize Lord Olivares's influence. Buckingham posed no such threat.

Anne scanned the other passengers in King Philip's coach and spotted a familiar pair of reptilian eyes. Startled, she clutched Harald's arm and whispered in his ear. *"That sinister priest who trespassed on our property, the so-called Keeper of the Kingdom, is in King Philip's carriage."*

Harald craned his neck to examine the passengers of the royal carriage before returning his gaze to his companions. "Does anyone know that priest sitting in the royal carriage?" he asked, keeping his tone casual.

"That is Monsignor Massimi, the papal nuncio," Prince Charles volunteered. "The infanta and I take Catechism from him."

Harald looked pointedly at Anne. "I see," was all he said.

Suddenly, a small plume of bright feathers flew out of nowhere and impaled itself on Prince Charles's coat. He reached for it, but Harald grabbed the prince's hand and removed the plume himself. He held it up by its feathers and they all saw it had a sharpened quill at the end, oozing with a green potion. The area where it struck the prince's coat disintegrated.

"Remove your coat, Sire!" Harald barked.

Bewildered, the prince obeyed. He stood and allowed the coat to fall. Harald caught it and rolled it up, with the dart tucked into the center.

"I've always liked that coat," the prince murmured. "It's quite comfortable."

"We will order you another," said Anne.

Buckingham spluttered, "We must stop and notify our hosts. This is outrageous!"

"No!" Anne exclaimed. "Stopping makes us easier prey. The assassin is clever to have chosen this setting."

"M'Lady is right," said Harald. "We can't break free of this formation of carriages. We must cluster about the prince and deny our enemy a clear target."

Harald removed his own coat. "Prince Charles, please, take this."

"It will make me look like a child," Charles said. "Yours is a mite bigger than my own."

"But, of course," Harald replied. "You will wear Buckingham's coat."

"What?" Buckingham snapped.

"The Spanish subjects have come out to see England's crown prince. You and I mean nothing to them," Harald said. "Your coat is a match to his size. If you please," Harald held out his hands toward Buckingham. Buckingham glared.

"Shall I help you remove it?" Harald asked. "Here, take mine." He slipped out of his coat. As the men donned their new coats, Harald picked up the prince's, leapt from the carriage, and went to the coach occupied by the Digbys and the prince's personal guards. The prince was supposed to ride with Isley, Varney, and Gregory, but Buckingham would have none of it.

"Varney and Isley, go to the prince's coach. He needs your protection," Harald said.

"At your service, M'Lord," they said, quickly leaping from the coach. They headed toward the prince.

"Gregory, I need your skills." Harald sat and unrolled the jacket. "We have received an unexpected gift. This dart appeared in the prince's jacket."

Gregory nodded. "Would you like me to test it when we return to our quarters?"

"I would." said Harald. "I don't know the potency or source of this venom, but perhaps you can clarify that."

Gregory scanned the crowd. "There are similar feathers on the dancing girls. The royal guards have small, feathered plumes bedecking their badges." He concluded, "They are the most likely source."

"Well-trained soldiers have strong lungs," said Harald, "but we don't want to ignore the ladies. Beautiful women also make excellent assassins."

"Agreed," said Gregory. "In the matter of poison, you can't rule anyone out. I am inclined to hunt down the local pharmacists and explore every rumor of old poisoners."

Harald returned to his carriage. As the coaches continued their parade around the colorful attractions, Anne smiled and chatted with passengers occupying other coaches as they passed by, probing them for gossip that could provide clues.

9

Supper

Sunbeams slanted low through the slender windows that lined the dining room's outer wall. Harald sat at the end of the long dining table. Anne sat next to him. Her proper place beckoned from the opposite end, but she was not in the mood for such formality. Kitty would be their only guest.

"What's for supper?" Anne asked. "I am famished."

"I requested something light," Harald replied. "I am not up for a four-course meal. I have more work to do this evening."

"I hope there's enough food to equal my appetite," said Anne.

Their cook, Ibrahim, entered the room, pushing a cart laden with a modest platter of roasted chicken, a loaf of bread, a bowl of tangerines and shelled walnuts, and a porcelain tureen of butternut squash soup, a New World delicacy. His brilliant white tunic and turban were a dramatic contrast to his dark complexion.

"Ah, yes, all in one course," said Harald.

The kitchen boy, ever at the cook's heels, filled their glasses from a large, ungainly pitcher that matched the gilded tureen. Anne took an exploratory sip and was pleased to discover Sangria. She never tired of the fruit-infused wine.

Harald wolfed down his plate of food, then stood, patting his belly.

"You're done already?" said Anne.

"I shall be conferring with Ambassador Digby tonight. If I don't get some sleep, I will be no more clever than a bag of feathers."

"I'll join you soon. Kitty's late, but I'm certain when she gets here, she'll have news to share."

Alone at the table, Anne motioned for a second bowl of soup and another glass of sangria.

"I'll take a glass, if you please," Kitty called, her voice breathless as she entered the room. She took the seat across from Anne. Ibrahim signaled the boy to serve her.

Once he was done, Anne nodded and said, "Gracías, Ibrahim," her polite signal she wanted to be alone with Kitty. Ibrahim bowed, the boy mimicked him, and the two disappeared out the door.

The instant the door closed Kitty dropped her smile.

"What have you learned?" Anne asked. "Anything?"

"The only clue I have is there is a handsome priest who has recently come to Madrid. He lives nearby and has a reputation of providing pleasing, albeit exotic intoxicants, some from the New World. When I asked if he ever made poisons, the young lords I spoke to assured me he would never do such a thing."

"What's his name?"

"Father Eremitz."

"Anything else?"

"Nothing."

The door burst open. Anne and Kitty jumped. Kenhelm Digby, the ambassador's nephew and apprentice, strolled up to their table and plopped himself into Harald's chair as if he owned it. Although the tall, lanky youth's cockiness could be abrasive, Kitty found his tan face and dark gold hair too charming to be unlikable.

"Good afternoon, dear ladies," he said. "May I trouble you for a crust of bread?"

Kitty rose to serve Kenhelm from the cart. With a large ornate fork, she piled food high onto a plate and set it before him.

"Bless you, kind lady," he said. "You know me well."

Kitty smiled with pursed lips. "You are legendary among the cooks for sneaking into kitchens to help yourself."

"I have no control over my appetite," said Kenhelm. "I'm a growing lad. So, what fascinating conversation did I interrupt? You broke off so suddenly."

Kitty told her tale. When she finished, he stared, deep in thought.

"One thing I know about poisoners," he said, "is they need a source of supply and a place to prepare the serums where no one can see what they do."

"Hmm," said Anne, "let me ponder this." She shifted her gaze out the window, then stood.

A moment later, she asked, "Are my eyes deceiving me, or is that roof peaking above the mimosas made of lathe and glass panes?"

Kenhelm rose and joined her at the window. "It is, indeed, a garden house made of lathe and glass. I've heard of such, but that one is the first I have seen."

"Why would spades and pickaxes be kept in a glass house?" Kitty asked. "That makes no sense at all." Curious, she got up to look.

"Pardon me, they are called greenhouses," said Kenhelm.

"And what is kept in a greenhouse?" asked Anne.

"As the name would suggest, greenery. A glass house creates an ideal environment for exotic plants. In Spain, the afternoon sun can create too much heat, which would explain the fast-growing mimosas just to the west of it. In the winter months, their branches are bare, allowing in the sunshine, but by the end of May, their thick foliage will provide relief from the afternoon heat."

"Exotic plants," said Anne, who had stopped listening at the mention of those words. "And what, pray tell, would those be?" She turned her head toward Kenhelm.

Before he could answer, Kitty exclaimed, "That must be his house! The handsome priest."

"What was his name?" Kenhelm asked.

"Father Eremitz."

Kenhelm blanched, then stared out the window in a daze. Finally, he said, "I knew Father Eremitz all too well during my stay in the Ambon Islands."

Kitty was about to ask questions, but Anne stopped her with a hand on her arm.

"You were there during the Dutch Ambush, weren't you?" Anne asked.

Kenhelm looked weary. "I may have caused it myself, thanks to my peculiar friendship with Father Eremitz. When I knew him, he kept an assortment of potions and intoxicants that could capture a person's mind and cause him to do whatever he wishes." Kenhelm shifted his gaze to Anne. "Would you and Sir Harald like me to renew my 'friendship' with Henri Eremitz?"

"Father Eremitz," Kitty corrected. "Be very careful. We're in a Roman Catholic kingdom."

"That man is nobody's father," Kenhelm snorted. "He is a devilish charmer, preying on the young and naïve."

Anne smiled. "Perhaps you could do it for a good cause?" she asked.

"For a good cause, I would be delighted," said Kenhelm. "I have been taking lessons from Akira, the Japanese sword master who resides at the Tavernier's estate. Have you heard of him?"

Kitty touched her hand to her throat but said nothing. Anne kept her eyes fixed on Kenhelm.

"He's an excellent sword master," he continued. "He's giving lessons to people who show talent. My sword skills are much improved. If I must, I can face down Eremitz." Kenhelm grinned mischievously.

"Oh, no!" Anne exclaimed. "You must not face him down. You need to come and go as a faithful old friend."

"Have no fear, Lady Anne. The sword master is also skilled in the art of wrestling, or rather, a sort of tumbling." Kenhelm furrowed his brow. "It's hard to explain. It's much different from what we do here. But I could give Eremitz a good thrashing without causing an international incident."

"I am sorry, Kenhelm," said Anne, locking him in her cool, steady gaze. "But we are here to gather information, not settle old scores. You were chosen by your uncle, Ambassador Digby, for your intelligence, and I have faith you will comport yourself in the most professional manner as you carry out this crucial mission. For your Uncle John's sake. He so wants to be proud of you."

Kenhelm deflated. "You're taking the fun out of it."

"Oh, Kenhelm, with your natural skill, you'll make fun wherever you find it, but not the 'facing down' kind, I should hope."

"It is my pleasure to serve you, Lady Anne," Kenhelm replied.

He returned to the table and mopped up the broth on his plate with a crust of bread. "I must tell my uncle of my plans to visit Father Eremitz," he said, then stuffed the soaked bread in his mouth and dashed out the door. Kitty and Anne stared after him.

"Are you sure getting Kenhelm to renew his friendship with the Jesuit priest is a good idea?" Kitty asked. "What if it becomes a brawl?"

"If Kenhelm follows his uncle's instructions, that will not transpire. John Digby has plenty of talented relatives he could apprentice," said Anne. "I am sure there is a reason he chose Kenhelm."

10

Sword Fight in the Boudoir

When Anne retired to her room, she found Harald propped up on pillows, reading by the light of the window. Overwhelmed by the afternoon heat, Anne slipped out of her muslin house dress.

"I thought you would be fast asleep," she said.

"I should be, but I found this book of Spanish court protocols on the bookshelf. It may help in our dealings with King Philip."

Anne sat at the edge of the bed with her back to Harald so he could unbutton her corset. He undid the last button and her corset fell forward. She slipped it off and pulled at her dimity shift to circulate the air between her skin and the fabric.

"Kitty learned something interesting today."

"Oh?"

"There is a handsome Jesuit nearby by the name of Father Henri Eremitz. He has a reputation for providing young lords with intoxicants. And we have a spot of good fortune in the ambassador's apprentice, Kenhelm."

"Kenhelm? You jest."

"He and Father Eremitz go all the way back to Amboyna. Kenhelm says he would be happy to renew their friendship." Anne raised her eyebrows, as if asking for a response.

Harald shook his head. "He's a cocky, over-confident whelp."

"He's our best chance of learning more about this Father Eremitz, master of intoxicants."

"Of course, you're right," he sighed. He laid back on the bed. "I need a nap."

Anne slipped her arm under his legs and put his feet on the floor.

"No resting now," she said. "We need to practice our sword fighting. Everyone is taking lessons from the Japanese sword master except us. We're falling behind."

"May I sleep before we do that?" Harald asked.

"No. Sometimes we'll have to fight when we're tired, so this will be good practice. We'll nap much better for it."

She fetched two wooden swords and gave him a light smack with one of them.

Harald leapt out of the bed like an attacking cat, gathering a sword as he did. "Oh, you think you'll take your liberties on a weary man, do you? En garde, woman!"

Dressed only in his long shirt, Harald posed like the master swordsman he was. As Anne leaned into her right knee and raised her arm to poise her wooden sword, her shift hitched up mid-thigh, caressing her body as it moved.

"Careful, Lady!" Harald warned. "You reveal a great deal of your tactics!"

"Too much or not quite enough, would you say?" she asked.

Harald lunged forward. Anne sprang out of the way.

"Here!" said Anne, dancing away from him. "Let me tie up my hem so you won't be so distracted." She cinched her shift up over her thigh and fastened it with a pearl button. It draped diagonally across her loins, staying in place—but just barely. Harald could see the delicate joints where her leg met her torso.

While Harald studied the arrangement of her shift, Anne poked his shoulder with her sword.

"See? You are unprepared for an attack." Before she could spring away, Harald gave her a good swat on her rear.

"Ouch! That's not a good thrust," Anne complained.

"Yet appropriate for an ill-mannered woman," said Harald.

"Ill-mannered? Me?" Anne flicked the rear of her shift, showing off the red mark the sword had made on her skin. "That is not the mark of a true gentleman."

Harald took in the effect of the red mark on her white buttocks. Anne poked him twice in the stomach before she whirled away, giggling.

They danced and fenced. Outmatched by Harald's height and years of training, Anne shamelessly deployed her shift to her best advantage. Harald threw away his sword and rushed her. Her weapon swirled off into a corner. He picked her up and tossed her on their bed.

"Do you know what the punishment is for the impudence you have shown me?"

Anne squirmed under him. "You want to play the disciplinarian, do you?" She pushed him over and slipped on top, grasping his wrists and pinning them to either side of his head. "We'll see who gets the harder thrashing!"

Exhausted, Harald lay flat on his back beside her, dozing. Anne rested her hand on his chest. As she felt his heart beating beneath her palm, she found herself in a happy, isolated moment. The breeze through the window, the gauze sheers billowing, her flesh tingling—these slow, easy seconds seemed encased in eternity. Anne's hand shifted to stroke him, sliding down the golden hair that covered his chest.

"Hmmm." Harald smiled as he slept.

A startling thought pierced her reverie. *Enjoy this moment because time is fleeting.* Anne froze. She gazed at the man she loved and recalled the words of the minister at the altar. 'For as long as ye both shall live. '

I will remember this moment forever, she thought.

Anne recalled the first time she had met Harald. She was eighteen. She and Kitty had journeyed east from Paris to Flanders and arrived early in May at the House of Salomon in a fine misty rain.

The girls opened the carriage windows, allowing the breeze and the occasional spray of mist to enter their tufted leather chamber. Anne tilted her head and breathed in the cool air, scented from the nearby evergreens. An orange bulbous sun slowly dipped below the blanket of clouds that spanned the sky. Broad shafts of golden light sharpened the tree shadows that stretched across the lawn. The château's walls gleamed saffron in the strange light. The turrets seemed to prop up the low clouds, which rippled with bright glints of copper. Anne felt a rush of certainty she would be happy here. She hadn't been truly happy in a long while.

A footman helped her and Kitty from the coach. Two liveried servants opened the double doors of the château to a deep foyer and bowed low, each sweeping one arm to gesture them in. Two rows of floor candelabras dripping with crystals formed a wide path to a massive fireplace crackling with a flaming black log.

The butler took their calling cards and left them to inform the lady of the house of their arrival. Duchess Giselle de Fueggar sailed into the foyer and greeted them with open arms. A voluptuous woman, she wore her corset loosely, her waist being considerably smaller than her hips and bosom. Although her coifed hair had streaks of gray, her complexion was smooth as a baby's.

Lady Giselle led them to their room, a splendid chamber with a bed large enough for both Anne and Kitty. A fire crackled in a dainty marble fireplace. Two matching Baroque wardrobes stood at opposite ends of the room.

Once Madame de Fueggar left, Anne and Kitty plopped onto a velvet settee before the small fire.

"How are we to be trained?" Kitty asked as she helped Anne out of her frock. "I never did understand the particulars."

"I'm not clear on that myself," said Anne, "but I am looking forward to learning the art of the rapier."

"Doesn't it seem too good to be true that they would teach women sword fighting?" Kitty turned her back so Anne could help loosen the laces of her bodice.

"There is danger all around and you never know when it will find you," said Anne. "Surely you and I should know that by now."

After they changed, they met the de Fueggars and their house guests in the dining room for a sumptuous meal.

The following morning, the chamberlain of the household, Brother Theodore, introduced himself to Anne and Kitty. The stout man wore the humble but well-made attire of one who wished to hide all evidence of his rank and wealth—a brown cloak of fine wool, matching breeches, and durable leather shoes with toes ending in long points. His long gray curls were topped by a burgundy velvet tam, his one bit of splendor.

Upon introducing himself, he wasted no time beginning their instruction. "The House of Salomon conducts trade in a unique commodity—knowledge itself," he said, as Anne and Kitty were rising from their curtsies. "Knowledge of every sort—science, politics, spiritualism, news from far-away lands—any information that can be applied to the betterment of our society."

He paused to let the revelation sink in. Anne's head swirled with questions, but her mouth could not form any words.

"When do we learn sword fighting?" Kitty asked.

"The first thing a woman must know about swords," said Brother Theodore, unperturbed by Kitty's swift change of subject, "is, although men will always be stronger, a well-trained woman can be swifter and more cunning. Come with me. We shall meet your sword master."

In addition to sword fighting, they learned how to conceal a blade in a hidden pocket and put the edge to an opponent's throat before they saw it coming. They learned wristlocks that could render an attacker helpless. They learned how to swiftly stop an attack—should they be caught without a dagger—by striking their assailant at weak points in his anatomy, such as the bridge of a nose, the collarbone, or a vulnerable kneecap.

However, according to Brother Theodore, knowledge of combat was far less important than mastering the art of commiseration.

"The lion's share of useful information is gathered from those who have a need to confide their deepest feelings," lectured Brother Theodore. "Be that sympathetic companion they turn to." He also told them to be a willing audience to gossips. "Though everything a gossip says should be cross-checked," he cautioned, "they can be notorious liars."

Toward these ends, Anne learned to play the harpsichord, Kitty learned the lute, and they both learned favored art songs by heart. Brother Theodore assured them their talents would make them popular at court gatherings. "Once you garner the affection and trust of courtiers, the secrets shall flow," he assured them.

That evening at dinner, Kitty blanched when Lady Giselle asked her what her title was.

"I'm afraid I don't have one," Kitty said in a voice barely above a whisper.

"Oh dear," said the duchess. "One day, your companion will marry a man of rank. Her lady-in-waiting should be a peer."

"Not necessarily," said Anne, rushing to her rescue. "Kitty shall always be by my side, come what may."

Kitty's stomach clenched as she wondered if she would be confined to her room, or even sent home to her parents. To her amazement, Lady Giselle consulted with her husband and had documents drawn days later to grant Kitty title to a small county under their jurisdiction. Although few people had heard of the small Bavarian shire of Kirchheim, the title of Baroness Catherine Von Kirchheim made Kitty a peer to any royal court. She swooned with delight at the news.

"The only thing Lady Giselle would like in return," Brother Theodore later informed her, "is regular correspondence. Tell her of your adventures as a Baroness. Report every formal function, who attended, and what was said. Be specific about the details so Lady Giselle feels like she's actually there."

One sunny afternoon, Anne and Kitty practiced a duet in the music room. A song about the light-hearted world of young love poured from their lips while their music teacher, a white-haired woman in a loose beige-and-white frock, strummed the lute with her eyes closed. Neither Anne nor Kitty had any knowledge of love. Life had moved too fast for them, but they were young and they understood the grand idea.

A young man, taller and more beautiful than Anne had ever seen, burst through the door, interrupting their lesson. Without changing her expression, she took in his magnificence. His auburn curls lightened to gold at the ends. His complexion held the tawny glow of a man who spent most of his waking hours outdoors.

He arranged himself on a large couch. It was meant to seat three people, but he covered it all gracefully. Anne, Kitty, and the lutist stopped their song. He waved a hand for them to continue.

Although she did not yet know his name, Anne sensed she could spend the rest of her life with this man. To disguise the thought, she haughtily lifted her chin and indicated to the lutist where she wanted her to begin, and they started again. At the final stanzas, Kitty performed a high obbligato and Anne crooned all the words. As she sang, she invented a story about lofty gods who crashed into music practice and took up all the chairs. Kitty giggled during her obbligato, but covered it well. The girls closed and curtsied to their visitor. The lutist fell silent, as if hoping to be overlooked.

The young man rose from the low couch and came to where the girls stood. He picked up a lute lying nearby and experimented with a few tones. He tuned it to suit himself and sat on a chair to stroke out the tune they'd been singing.

"Dear ladies, let's come at this again," he sang in a winsome tenor. "Methinks you regard the hero's sadness with too light a heart. Do you not feel the least bit of pity for him?"

"Not in the slightest," Anne sang in reply, "for he seeks to put a young lady into a compromise from which she could never recover. He deserves no pity."

"Perhaps he is the seventh-born son of a household," he said, returning to his baritone speaking voice while he continued to strum the lute. "No hope of inheritance to attract the maiden's family. He comes inviting her to share what he has."

"And that's the problem, isn't it?" Anne replied in song, plunking out the tune at the harpsichord. "He has nothing. Where shall she live? In a pumpkin shell?"

"But don't you see?" he returned to his singing voice. "Your love song is written for those of us who long for the impossible."

Anne smiled at him, certain he had come to make sport of her. Seeing this, he played the opening bars of their song.

"Forsooth," he sang. "Let us imagine that more things are possible, as the foresaid youth has indicated, and let us sing it all again."

He sang their first two verses, including Anne's addition. He nodded for them to repeat that. In a cheerful baritone, he then sang his own new lyrics about the practical girls that let the young man walk away to new adventures while they stayed in their shady castle.

Hearing the new voice in the song, Duchess de Fueggar came in to greet the young man. She introduced him to Anne and Kitty as Harald Audley, the eldest son of her dear friends, the recently departed Duke and Duchess of Southampton. Although the duchess never said it outright, her conversation made clear that their uninvited guest was among the wealthiest lords of England.

Anne and Harald spent the entire summer at the House of Salomon. Harald loaned her all of the books he had brought, two at a time. They rode to Lille, Anne on her dapple gray Thoroughbred while Harald rode a satiny black Percheron. During their excursions, they stopped at the River Tree Tavern, where the Irish cook made delightful scones, which paired splendidly with the tavern's Ceylon tea. They discussed the books Anne had read, such as Galileo's *Siderius Nuncius,* Machiavelli's *Discourses on Livy,* and Shakespeare's scandalous *A Midsummer Night's Dream.* They talked until the sun touched the horizon, at which point Harald would toss silver coins on the table and they would ride back to the House of Salomon in the twilight.

Anne divided her time between Harald, her instruction, and assisting Duchess de Fueggar in hosting a grand dinner party on the last Saturday of each month.

At the end of August, Harald approached Brother Theodore and asked him if Anne were available for marriage, should she choose.

The Chamberlain was amused. "You realize she will always be a challenge."

"I know," said Harald. "It is one of many reasons I want her."

"It is your prerogative to ask, and hers to answer. She comes from a good family. Her maternal grandmother is Danish royalty. Her father, Lord de Breuil, was a successful merchant, knighted by King Henry Navarre of France. Her father died the same day the king was killed. Her mother died shortly thereafter of sorrow, although the official cause was pneumonia."

One summer evening, as the sky surrendered its light, Harald and Anne sat on a veranda overlooking green fields. A lutist played gentle songs and several girls of the academy who lingered nearby sang the ones they knew.

Harald put his arm around Anne's shoulder. "I would like this summer to go on forever, but it won't. Next week, I shall journey to London to have an audience with King James. I don't know when I shall return."

Anne felt a hollow thud in her heart. "Why didn't you tell me sooner? I shall miss you," she said.

Harald reached into his breast pocket and retrieved an emerald ring. Though the gem was barely the size of a baby's tooth, it flashed so brightly, it seemed lit from within. He lifted her hand. "If you are willing, I would like to marry you and bring you with me to London."

Anne gasped as he slowly slipped the ring onto her finger. She stared at him, reveling in his beautiful face, his unruly auburn hair, and his deep blue eyes. "Where ever your journeys take you, I want to go," she said. "I want to see what you see, and hear what you think. But my friend Kitty must come as well. She is closer to me than a sister. So, if you will agree to have us both in your house, then yes, Harald Audley, I will marry you."

Harald took Anne into his arms. "Kitty will always be welcome in our house," he murmured into her hair. "She feels like my sister already."

"There are things you need to know about me before we go further," said Anne, pulling away from his shoulder and looking into his face. "I have a peculiar history. When I reveal my secrets, you may wish to change your mind."

She took a deep breath and let it out in a slow, steady stream. "I was married to a man—a Count," she said, staring at the floor. "We were joined in marriage by a defrocked priest, although I didn't know that at the time. The priest was a rogue. He tried to extort a fortune from my husband, claiming we owed him a portion of my dowry for bringing us together. My husband beat him and sent him on his way. That priest had a brother who took revenge. One day, while I was riding alone on our estate, he attacked me and would not turn me loose until he had done this."

Anne tucked her thumb beneath the gauzy fabric that formed the sleeve at the top of her shoulder and slipped it beneath the upper curve of her arm, revealing the scar of a purple fleur-de-lis on her creamy skin—the sign of a thief. She turned her head away in shame.

"I already know, Anne," said Harald, his voice gentle.

Anne gaped, stunned by the revelation.

"I'm one of those people who uncovers secrets with little effort," he said.

"I cannot believe you can excuse something so shameful."

"Anne, my fair lady, there are far worse secrets hidden by the most noble among us." Harald caressed her shoulder.

"As for this secret? It is not a sign of your sin, my love, but another's."

Anne was incredulous. Her true love regarded her darkest secret as casually as he would a small mole.

"You may tell me more as you wish," Harald continued, "but it changes nothing about what I feel for you. From that first sassy verse you sang to me, I knew you were the woman I wanted by my side on lonely nights in foreign lands."

They were wed the following month. Anne's uncle journeyed from Paris. He and his dear friends, the Duke and Duchess de Fueggar, put on a delightful wedding on short notice. All of the young ladies staying at the House of Salomon appeared in their bright spring dresses. The bride wore a dress of blue dimity cotton and a rosebud wreath the ladies had made for her hair. She saw Harald's hopeful face waiting for her at the altar. He wore a garland of roses around his neck, also made by the ladies. Kitty, her only bridesmaid, stood next to Anne. Duchess de Fueggar stood on her other side as her matron of honor. Anne felt her mother and father smiling down from Heaven as she married this wise and beautiful man.

A glorious feast followed the ceremony, along with much singing and dancing.

The next day, two trunks of Anne and Kitty's belongings were packed onto a large coach, alongside Harald's. They journeyed off to Calais, where they caught the next ship for

Southampton, England. They had lived there happily ever since.

Anne gazed at her sleeping husband. Distant church bells chimed the fifth hour. The light in the room deepened to a coral glow from the Spanish sunset. With all thought and speculation absent, Harald's face took on the innocence of a child.

Their trip to Spain to help arrange the marriage between their prince and the infanta was her first real mission with Harald. Before, she had always remained at home with little Quentin. She missed England as much as she missed her son, but she was glad to be next to her husband on his adventure, as he had promised her years ago.

Anne yawned. It was still too hot to snuggle, so she lay her head down next to Harald's, with just her hand on his chest, feeling his breath come and go with her palm.

11

Sir Kenhelm and Father Eremitz

The next day, Kenhelm hurried out the back door to see his old friend, Father Eremitz, but before he could escape the embassy, his uncle called him back. After a lengthy conversation with Ambassador Digby, laced with much cautionary advice, Kenhelm finally made his way to the stable to retrieve his horse.

The brightness beyond the open stable door lit up the dust motes within the shadowy interior. He stroked the white mare's black muzzle as he walked her out into the open. Once he mounted her, she pranced before settling into a quick trot. Kenhelm stood slightly in his stirrups and tied a red bandana around his head, topping it with a broad-brimmed hat, the sort the Spanish vaqueros used to protect themselves from the sun. He settled back into the saddle.

The road was deserted. Everyone in Madrid took a siesta in the afternoon. Although it was still spring, the day had grown unusually warm. As the mare clip-clopped along the path, Kenhelm pondered his conversation with his Uncle John Digby.

"Don't show off what you know," the ambassador had advised.

"I don't want him to think I'm the ninny I was at fourteen," Kenhelm protested. "I am far more clever than the last time we spoke, and I want him to know it."

"No." His uncle would not yield. "Ignore your foolish pride. You need to coax information out of him in subtle fashion. Put him in a boasting mood. Let him be the smart one. This is your opportunity to prove your superior intelligence by being the more cunning diplomat."

"What *can* I say?" Kenhelm asked.

"You've learned about the spice trade, so pass that along," his uncle said. "If Father Eremitz is a botanist he will find your conversation interesting."

"In other words, I am to present myself as the ninny I was when I last saw him."

"You are dismissed," was his Uncle's curt reply.

Kenhelm's horse calmed to a steady walk. As he rode by the broad lawns of the villas, his thoughts carried him to a distant island in the Indonesian Archipelago.

Eremitz's home on Amboyna was simple but elegant—beautiful paintings, gentle light beaming through louvered shutters, filled with the scent of plumeria—a dream world. In that world, Kenhelm had thought he was in love. The cynicism that comes with age taught him his erotic feelings for the errant priest were nothing more than loneliness and boredom manipulated by Eremitz's mysterious intoxicants.

Now, once again, I must play the feather-headed lad, he thought.

Sweat trickled down his neck. He lifted the broad hat he wore and set it more lightly on his head. He spotted

Eremitz's villa beyond a grove of olive trees and nudged his horse into a trot. As he approached, the sight of three palm trees with long, arching fronds rose up from the center of the house. This confused him until he realized the front portion of the villa was an enclosed courtyard, open to the sky.

He guided his horse beneath the shade. The olive trees cast speckled shadows along the outer walls of the courtyard. As Kenhelm dismounted, a light breeze shushed through the olive branches, cooling his neck and making the shadows shimmy along the wall. The mare snorted and pawed at the dirt with her hoof as he rapped on the heavy oak door with an iron-ring knocker.

An elderly servant let him in and called for a stable boy to whisk his mare off to the stables. Kenhelm pressed a coin into the boy's palm. "Please water and brush her," he said.

He walked into the courtyard. An old marble fountain shot arching streams of water into the rippling pool at its base. Eremitz rose from a divan and swept around the fountain to greet him. He wore a white robe tied loosely at the waist with a beige sash. His soulful brown eyes and neatly trimmed black beard gave him a messianic appearance that may have fooled others, but Kenhelm was wise to his true nature.

"My dear Kenhelm." Eremitz's pupils dilated as he closed the space between them. Kenhelm suppressed a chuckle. Having grown six inches over the past several years, he was now three inches taller than his friend. Eremitz took him by the shoulders, kissed him on each cheek, and motioned him to the divan. He poured a glass of lemon water, splashed it with sweet rum, and handed it to his guest. Kenhelm took the cup and gulped it down, finding it more satisfying than he had expected.

"The water is artesian," said Eremitz. "It's cold because it comes from deep underground."

"Thank you, Father Eremitz! The drink was a refreshing surprise. And now, having drunk it, I can only hope that rum was the only intoxicant contained there in."

"It is," said Eremitz, "though I have many delightful intoxicants, if you are so inclined. I would never serve them without your knowledge. Rather, we should enjoy such enticements together, like two connoisseurs."

Eremitz reached into an ornate cabinet and opened the door to retrieve a brass hookah with a long smoking stem. He set it atop the cabinet and flipped up the filigreed cap. Crumbling a wafer between his fingers, he filled the bowl with a sage-like powder.

Kenhelm's heart fluttered with anticipation as Eremitz lit a splinter from a tiny ceramic lamp. He had allowed him to smoke hashish just once, years ago, but decided afterward that Kenhelm was too young for something so exhilarating. Kenhelm suppressed his anger as he recalled the sorts of activities the errant priest deemed perfectly suitable for one so young.

Eremitz touched the flame to the bowl and drew in air from the mouthpiece. The sound of the bubbles passing through the water in the brass vessel blended with the soft cacophony of the fountain.

When they had smoked the hookah's contents, Eremitz placed it atop the cabinet, nearly dropping it on his first try. Kenhelm surveyed his surroundings, which took on a magical veneer in the haze of the Persian hashish.

"Would you like me to take your confession?" Eremitz asked.

Kenhelm's anger flared once again, but quickly faded. "In all honesty, my friend, I am a Protestant. You are not 'Father' to me. Thus, I shall not address you as such from here on."

"When did you become so militant?" Eremitz asked.

"It is not militancy but the wisdom that comes with age."

"You are still a youth, and surely no man grows so wise as to lose his faith," said Eremitz.

"My faith has not wavered," said Kenhelm. "Indeed, I believe now, more than ever."

"As do I. So what is the harm in calling me 'Father' as you have so many times before, on account of your faith?" Eremitz asked.

Kenhelm straightened his back, clapped his hands to his knees, and struck a patriarchal pose before reciting a Bible verse.

"The scribes and the Pharisees sit in Moses' seat... They love the best places at feasts, and the best seats in the synagogues, greetings in the marketplaces, and to be called by men, 'Father, Father'. Do not call anyone on earth your father; for One is your Father, He who is in Heaven."

Kenhelm paused to gage Eremitz's reaction. The priest looked bored.

"Do you remember who said that?" Kenhelm asked, recalling he had never once read the bible as a Catholic, whereas he was practically forced to memorize it, verse for verse, as a Protestant.

Eremitz responded with certitude. "Prophet Samuel."

"Jesus Christ. Quoted from Matthew 23."

Eremitz scanned Kenhelm's eyes, as if looking for signs of deception. Kenhelm suppressed a smile.

"You believe in private interpretation," said Eremitz, his tone dismissive.

Kenhelm changed the subject. "I see you have date palms," he said, motioning toward the three towering palm trees, each laden with sagging clusters of golden fruit. "Why, they make your villa a paradise fit for a hedonist—or, in this case, a priest."

"I suspect paradise is equal to all who qualify to be there," said Eremitz. He poured himself another tumbler of lemon and rum and refilled Kenhelm's glass.

"May I remove my boots?" Kenhelm asked.

"Be comfortable, old friend. We need no formalities between us," said Eremitz. "Sit on the edge of the fountain and put your feet in. The water we drink comes from the spigots on top. The palm trees are watered from the pool."

"Your palms won't object?" Kenhelm joked.

"Not at all. They have an easy life."

Even in the spray of the fountain, the day was warm. Kenhelm stood to remove his vest and tossed it over the back of the divan. He untucked his chemise from his breeches and flapped the hem over the fountain, wafting cool air upwards toward his bare chest. Glancing down, he admired his firm torso, toned from Judo lessons with the Japanese sword master. Once he felt cool, he went back to the divan and eased himself into the cushions.

"What happened to your blond hair?" Eremitz asked softly. "The last time I saw you, it was bright as the moon. Now it's mostly bronze with just a sheen of gold on top."

Kenhelm thought it an odd topic. He hated being reminded he was blond; many took it as a sign of a weak intellect due to entrenched superstitions about Vikings. He was on the verge of changing the subject when a servant came from the house bearing a large bag.

"Sir," said the burly man, "the courier has come. Would you like to take the delivery here, or shall I leave it in your study?"

"Put it on the side table," said Eremitz, motioning to a long narrow table resting beneath the eaves.

The servant allowed the leather bag to roll off his shoulder and onto the table, then left.

"I hear you are a respectable swordsman," said Eremitz.

"Enough to avoid embarrassing myself."

"You look very much like your king's former lover. The one before Buckingham."

"I haven't drawn any interest from our peculiar king," said Kenhelm.

Eremitz laughed. "I suspect your father chose to keep you well away from London's court, which explains your post here in Madrid." He refilled their glasses. "Do you ever think of our time together in Amboyna?"

Kenhelm paused. "Sometimes, before I go to sleep."

Tall and elegant, Eremitz rose and walked over to the veranda. Kneeling to open a chest hidden in the shadows, he retrieved two wooden swords and returned to the divan with a sword in each hand.

"Do you still believe in that new religion?"

"I ponder the things I've learned," said Kenhelm, choosing his words carefully. "The Catholics say suffering is good for the soul, and yet, our Savior healed the sick and took away their suffering. If suffering is good for a soul, and warranted by God, why would Jesus take it away?"

"He did it to prove his authority as God's one and only son. Stand up."

Kenhelm languidly removed his foot from his knee and stood, all the while staring at Eremitz. His speed and agility had improved under Akira's tutelage. But Eremitz had trained for many years with his uncle, a legendary sword master. Few people knew of this. Eremitz's strategy was to use his passive nature to catch opponents off guard.

He threw a sword to Kenhelm. Instead of catching it, Kenhelm deflected it with his hand and leapt toward Eremitz, putting him in a wristlock that sent his sword flying. Before the priest could react, Kenhelm had him on his knees, bent forward with his arm turned up behind his back. There was a fragrance about him, something from far away. It was more elegant than cinnamon, a whiff of patchouli and sandalwood. Glancing down his neckline, Kenhelm could see that the thin gauze robe was all that Eremitz was wearing.

"That is highly disrespectful behavior toward your sword master," said Eremitz.

"You are not my sword master. You are my wrestling partner." Having made his point, Kenhelm let go, allowing Eremitz to stand.

Eremitz regarded him coolly before lunging for Kenhelm's gut, thrusting his shoulder into his waistline.

Bending at the knees, Kenhelm easily went down on his rump, wrapped his arms around Eremitz's chest, and flipped him over his head. As they landed, Kenhelm swiftly snaked his torso around until he had Eremitz pinned beneath him.

"What is this witchcraft?" Eremitz bellowed.

Kenhelm recognized this as his playful side. "Not witchcraft. Judo." He lifted himself from Eremitz and stood.

"That sounds like witchcraft," Eremitz retorted. Instead of standing, he swept his arm behind Kenhelm's knees to upend him. Kenhelm managed to wrap his calves around Eremitz's neck on the way down.

"It's a type of Japanese wrestling," said Kenhelm, pinning Eremitz to the floor again. He quickly let him go and stood, this time helping Eremitz to his feet. He didn't want his comrade to get too angry. "A bit different from Greek wrestling," Kenhelm continued. "It's more like tumbling."

"I see." Eremitz had barely finished his short sentence when he took another lunge at Kenhelm. The two of them wrestled feverishly until Kenhelm, like a cat tired of playing with its prey, moved in for the kill. Forcing Eremitz over the back of the divan at the waist, he strong-armed him into the exact position Eremitz had forced on him numerous times in years gone by. Kenhelm pulled Eremitz's robe up to his waist. The priest struggled, but soon surrendered to Kenhelm's physical power.

When they were done, they both fell onto the divan, panting.

Eremitz pulled his hand over his glistening face and groaned in satisfaction. He leaned forward to pour himself a straight shot of rum. Eremitz had always enjoyed a good wrestling match that ended in the ultimate conquest.

That their age-old struggle had ended in Eremitz's conquest did not perturb the hedonistic priest in the least, much to Kenhelm's relief. Remorse descended over him, nonetheless. His uncle's instructions had been clear—play the vacuous adolescent and allow Eremitz to maintain his role as the wiser, more powerful partner. He had to get his mission back on track by allowing Eremitz his sword match.

As if reading his thoughts Eremitz stood, still panting slightly, picked up the wooden swords from the floor, and tossed one onto Kenhelm's lap. Kenhelm looked up at him sideways, wondering if he should match Akira's Japanese-style swordsmanship to Eremitz's European-style. He thought better of it. It was vital Eremitz win the next round.

They lay exhausted on the area rug as Kenhelm listened to Eremitz's rhythmic breathing. Certain the priest was asleep, Kenhelm eased himself away and stood. He looked over at the bulky leather sack the servant had deposited on the table under the eaves and wondered if an investigation of its contents was worth the risk. He crept toward it, keeping a watchful eye on Eremitz, as well as the front and back doors to the courtyard.

Loosening the drawstrings, he gingerly sifted through a collection of parchment letters, recognizing the royal English seal on several. One was addressed to both Prince Charles and "Steenie," King James's pet name for Buckingham. One was addressed to Ambassador John Digby, another to Duke and Duchess Audley. There were other letters as well, all addressed to Englishmen.

Kenhelm surmised Eremitz was screening them before sending them along to their intended recipients. This indicated a connection between Eremitz and the palace, but through whom?

On the way out, Kenhelm used the shady olive trees for cover as he slipped around the house to the back. He discovered what he was looking for—the greenhouse made of hardwood lathe and square windowpanes. Its construction was simple but elegant. He swept across the lawn. The padlock on the fragile door posed little challenge as he popped it open with a bent wire he kept handy.

Inside, the air smelled of warm loam. Tropical hemp trees and troughs of blood-red poppies reached for the pearlescent light beaming from the glass ceiling. Terracotta pots near the floor brimmed with little bushes sporting shiny green leaves and red berries. Kenhelm didn't recognize them. "Coca," according to the small wooden tags poking up from the soil.

Translucent bottles of potions crowded the center of a large worktable, their glass stoppers glinting in the filtered sunlight. Beneath the table, Kenhelm noticed a bulky mass covered by a black oilcloth. He knelt to lift the thick cloth and his heart leapt at the sight of Eremitz's most valuable possession: an Oriental teak chest, more valuable for its contents than its ornate woodwork. Kenhelm remembered it from Eremitz's posh apartment on the Indonesian Island. The priest kept his most important papers locked inside.

What is it doing in the garden house? Kenhelm wondered. *Is Eremitz hiding his papers from someone who could stroll into his home and allow himself into any room? His palace contact, perhaps? Who else would be so powerful?*

He was tempted to pick the lock but knew no one could touch Eremitz's personal papers without him knowing the instant he opened the trunk's lid.

On his way out the door, Kenhelm looked to the far-right corner and noticed it had been sectioned off for a lush collection of ferns. The lower portion of the structure was a three-foot wall made from cypress slats. The short wall was topped by white lattice, lined with a fine net, reaching to the ceiling. When Kenhelm gazed at the lacy green ferns, he saw a delicate, brightly colored glass frog clinging to one of the stalks. He moved closer to see there were more frogs, some balanced on the fern fronds. One was saffron yellow with thick black squiggles. Another had a delightful pattern of royal-blue bubbles. Still another was cherry-red with zebra-striped legs. All had the slick shine of fine Venetian glass. The bold colors and exquisite workmanship were obviously meant to delight visiting nobles. Eremitz likely surprised them with these charming gifts—a subtle way to curry favor. Nobles loved beauty combined with novelty.

Kenhelm looked for a door in the lattice. The temptation to touch one of the glass frogs, and possibly steal one, was overwhelming. As he fumbled with the lattice sections, searching for one that would open, the red frog leapt to a leaf that dipped from its weight. Kenhelm gaped in astonishment. They were alive. And possibly venomous.

The shadows grew long as Kenhelm trotted home on the spirited white mare. The breeze stroked his neck with cool fingers. He wanted to canter home, but an approaching carriage blocked the road. He stayed on the path and pulled his hat low over his face. As he passed the carriage, he lifted his head just long enough to get a glance at the passenger and regretted it instantly.

The reptile-green eyes of a stocky Catholic clergyman bore into him. Kenhelm had never seen the man. His black flat-brimmed hat and heavy black robes gave no indication of his rank, let alone his connection to Eremitz. Kenhelm tipped his hat and nudged his horse into a jaunty trot, thinking it best to look unconcerned, even daft.

12

The Vatican Agent

Eremitz woke to find himself alone, loosely covered by his cassock. He bolted up and sighed with relief at seeing the courtyard's white walls awash in the rosy tint of twilight. Father Massimi had told him he would arrive at dusk.

As he pulled his cassock on, his personal servant burst into the courtyard from the house.

"Father Massimi approaches," he said in a hoarse whisper, carefully shutting the door behind him. Capistrano had been Eremitz's manservant for over a decade. His devout loyalty, even as he feigned a higher loyalty to Monsignor Massimi, made the burly servant his favorite.

Eremitz and Capistrano removed all evidence of Kenhelm as Massimi approached, his ominous figure darkening the embedded glass of the main entry door.

Capistrano swept the door open and bowed deeply. "Buenos tardes, your Holiness," he said, waving Massimi inside.

Eremitz froze. Such an honorific was reserved only for the pope, but Massimi seemed to revel in Capistrano's gaffe, if it was a gaffe at all. Eremitz's manservant was an expert at subtle flattery.

"Who was that bonnie lad I saw trotting away from your villa?" Massimi asked.

Eremitz caught his breath before answering. "Just an old friend," he said, hoping to sound casual.

"Ambassador Digby's nephew is an old friend?" Massimi asked, transfixing Eremitz with his gooseberry eyes.

"He was a student of mine in Amboyna," Eremitz replied, studiously keeping a tremor from his voice. "We both survived the massacre."

"Really. Whose side was he on?"

"He was on the English side, of course. But it did nothing to impair our friendship. Politics can be a violent affair, but at the end of the day, it is just politics."

"Did you gather any relevant information from your friend? I hope your reunion was not simply for the sake of pleasure." Massimi glared at him.

Eremitz realized he meant it literally and looked away. He could hide nothing from this Vatican spy. Taking a sharp tone, he signaled to the papal nuncio he would not be intimidated. "Only an amateur would attempt gathering information on a first meeting after a five-year absence. Wouldn't you agree?" he asked, arching one eyebrow. "Kenhelm Digby is no fool. I must regain his trust before probing him."

Massimi grinned like a crocodile. "And what sort of information did he gather from you?" he asked.

"Absolutely nothing," said Eremitz, keeping his tone smooth.

"I wouldn't be so certain. He's the nephew of England's top diplomat. He was practically nursed into adulthood by

Marie de Medici," Massimi said, referring to the relentless queen mother of France who struggled to regain the reins of power even though her adult son had been coronated over a decade earlier. "Don't flatter yourself. Kenhelm Digby could be twice the spy you are, and if that were the case, you would never know it."

Eremitz took in a slow deep breath. "What can I do for you, Father Massimi? As always, I am your humble servant."

"Prepare to endure the slings and arrows of a holy cause. I plan to put the belladonna tincture you provided to good use."

A chill crept down Eremitz's spine.

"I have attracted several English lords to my Catechism. Most of them come to be next to their prince, but one, Sir John Washington, has become increasingly devout. I am on the verge of converting him."

Eremitz struggled to understand why Massimi was discussing poison one moment and Catholic converts the next.

"If he should grow gravely ill," Massimi continued, "he will surely call for a priest to conduct last rites."

"If Sir John resides at the English Embassy, his comrades will be furious at such a measure."

"I have complete faith in your diligence and endurance."

Eremitz was aghast. "You're sending *me?* The Englishmen will thrash me to within an inch of my life. Indeed, several of them are over six feet tall."

"The household staff will pull them off before they do too much damage," said Massimi.

"What is the purpose of this?"

"This will demonstrate to King Philip the animalistic nature of the Protestant character."

Eremitz's mind reeled, although he did not dare point out the blatant hypocrisy of plotting a murder for the sake of exposing the violent nature of the victim's companions.

"How will this benefit the marriage negotiations?" Eremitz asked, bewildered.

Massimi's pupils narrowed to hard, black points. "The wheels of Heaven are in motion. The British Isles shall return to the fold, but there is more than one path toward this end. And some paths are more certain than others."

Before Eremitz could ask another question, Massimi cut him short. "I fully expect an impressive collection of cuts and bruises, especially around the face." He withdrew a cudgel from the folds of his robe and smacked it rhythmically on the palm of his hand. "I can add a few more, if your injuries are insufficient."

13

The Last Rites Affair

May 1623
Madrid, Spain

Birds sang in the shrubs as Eremitz approached the English embassy. He scanned the sky. A dozen clouds hung like tossed pillows, lovely to behold, but not enough to bring the rain he craved. Capistrano walked alongside him and kept silent as the leather pouch slung across his shoulder bumped rhythmically against his hip. It was lumpy with the sacerdotal pieces Eremitz would use to perform the last rites for the ailing Englishman.

"Stay alert, Capistrano, don't knife anyone, and guard the holy instruments. We're going to get a drubbing, you understand?"

"I do," Capistrano replied solemnly.

Arriving at the embassy's entrance, Eremitz bowed to the guards. The two young men looked nervously at each other. Emboldened by their hesitation, Eremitz brushed past them, with Capistrano on his heels.

They entered the shadowy hallway that led to the ailing John Washington's room. Several of his friends sat in chairs that lined the wall. They looked up, surprised to see the priest, but remained seated.

Eremitz stopped at the dying man's door. "I understand our guest, John Washington, may be facing his last days," he said.

Washington's friends rose from their chairs.

"I have come to bring him the gift of redemption from the true faith," Eremitz continued.

The Englishmen stared at him like feral beasts.

In John Digby's study, Harald made himself comfortable on a large divan and watched the ambassador pour rum into sweetened lemon water. He had dismissed the servants, which allowed them to discuss Prince Charles and the match without their words reaching palace ears.

Anne removed a tumbler from the tray Lady Digby offered and took a sip. Rum, honey and cool lemon water were delicious on a summer morning.

"Truly the best way to ward off the heat," Lady Digby said as she brought the tray around to the other guests. "Poor John Washington. How sad to be on one's deathbed so far from home. I give him all the comfort I can, but it's not the same as getting it from his own mum."

Kenhelm went to the cabinet where the rum and lemon drinks stood and helped himself.

Anne turned toward him. "How is our young John Washington? Have you seen him?"

Kenhelm paused. "I have. No one expects a recovery."

"Any thoughts on what caused his illness?" she asked.

"All the fellows eat and drink together, yet John is the only one who is sick" said Kenhelm. "According to rumor, he is enamored of the papal nuncio, and even attends his weekly Catechism. I didn't learn of this until yesterday."

Harald scowled, "And that's the only difference between Washington and his comrades?"

"The only one I know of," said Kenhelm.

Harald slowly nodded as he looked at Anne.

A loud clatter from downstairs interrupted them. Irritated voices of the young men on the first floor rose in volume.

"He's not a Roman Catholic! He's a free Protestant!"

"Stand back, Priest! This is not your affair!"

John Digby turned to Harald. "Let's see about this ruckus." They rushed out the door.

As Kenhelm rose to go with them, Anne grasped his elbow.

"Kenhelm, it is best you have nothing to do with this. The priest downstairs is likely your man, Eremitz. The next time you see him, you can hear his story without him knowing you were here, but only if you stay put." Kenhelm wavered. "Lady Digby and I need you here to protect us." Anne pleaded with her eyes.

Kenhelm straightened up and swept his coat aside to free access to his sword.

Dear boy, Anne thought. *One day he will learn to be wary of women.*

Eremitz and Capistrano fought to get into the sick man's room, and the young Englishmen fought to stop them. John Digby and Harald Audley came rushing down the hall in time to see Eremitz and his assistant struggling to get through the door. Englishmen crowded around them like a swarm of hornets, pummeling their heads and shoulders.

John Digby called the young men by name. Harald grabbed them, two at a time, and heaved them toward the foyer. As tempting as it was to throw Eremitz into a wall, Harald restrained himself, sensing the priest's connections to the Vatican ran high.

"My dear priest," Harald said, in the tone of one nobleman addressing another, "Surely you know performing Catholic rites on a Protestant was certain to agitate his comrades. You were not invited here, after all."

An indignant cavalier jumped up from the floor. "He earned his beating, bringing his papal heresies into this house!"

The others shouted, "Hear! Hear!"

John Digby raised his cane and knocked the bronze head on the door to restore order. Turning to Eremitz he said, "Young Priest, you have not traveled this world long enough to know that sometimes one's religious beliefs are not as welcome as they are in one's own home. You are on English property."

Eremitz dusted himself off, noticing and displaying both the torn sleeve of his cassock and his crumpled collar, which was torn halfway off.

"Sir Digby, Madrid is far more my home than it is yours. I came as a courtesy." Eremitz fixed him in a cold stare before turning to leave.

"The embassy is English soil, Priest, not your home," Digby said. "I shall summon a carriage to the gate to take you to your residence." He signaled the butler to open the front door and waited, straight-backed, for his uninvited guest to leave. Harald, formidable in his height, stood beside the ambassador.

Eremitz stared at them before summoning his assistant to his side. They left quietly. Harald squinted as they exited into the bright day.

"For someone who had just received a thorough thrashing, there was something curiously smug about that priest, torn cassock and all. As if he had gotten what he had come for."

Digby nodded. "Agreed. We are not yet done with this caper. Prepare for a scandal."

The carriage pulled into the avenue of olives that led to Eremitz's courtyard.

"Stop here," Eremitz called to the coachman. "I forbid any soul from a godless country to enter my property."

The coachman said nothing and kept the horses waiting. Once Eremitz and his servant stepped out of the carriage, he pulled the horses into a complete turn and cracked his whip overhead. The horses darted away as if pursued, leaving Eremitz and his servant in a cloud of dust. Capistrano watched after the carriage. "I will remember that man," he said.

"Don't dwell on it," said Eremitz. "You and I have bigger game to hunt."

The cook appeared at the outer door of the courtyard and subtly gestured with his head that someone was behind him. Eremitz glanced beyond to see Massimi sitting on the divan, staring like a sleepy lizard. A ceramic bowl on an end table held crimson sangria topped with floating orange and lemon slices. The cook glided up and replenished the papal nuncio's cup with a silver ladle.

"I wasn't expecting you so early," said Eremitz. "When will the pamphlets be ready?"

"They are being distributed even now," said Massimi. "I brought one for you." He leaned forward with the slow deliberation of a sloth to hand it to him.

Eremitz scanned the cover. "Amazing," he said. "This illustration of me with a torn cassock and a black eye is quite dramatic." He paused to read, smirking now and then at the blatant lies, although Massimi's guess of what had transpired was fairly accurate.

"Beautifully crafted prose, would you agree?" Massimi asked. "I advised the illustrator to make you look like the suffering Christ. But that is just for dramatic effect. Of course, you look nothing like our Savior."

Far more so than you, you gargoyle, Eremitz thought.

"I've arranged an audience with the king," Massimi continued. "At the very least, this scandal will require a formal apology from the English. I want you there in silent suffering. Take care to make your wounds show." He chuckled. "I think the cassock sleeve needs to be torn a little more." He reached over and gave it a tug. The fabric gave way with a short shriek, exposing Eremitz's bare shoulder. "You'll need a fresh chemise and a new, starched collar, of course. But I want *you* to look damaged."

"I *am* damaged." Eremitz replied. "Those English thugs beat the holy hell out of me."

"Very well," said Massimi. "Here is what you must emphasize tomorrow. Listen closely."

Eremitz bit the side of his tongue as Massimi droned on. He could not afford to antagonize this man, but the priest resented the nuncio's patronizing tone. Eremitz knew what the Keepers of the Kingdom required. He didn't need this aspirational commoner instructing his every move.

Massimi concluded his instructions and paused expectantly, as if awaiting praise.

As Eremitz considered the Monsignor's plot, a question formed in his mind. He knew Massimi might regard his query as seditious, but he had grown so weary of the man that he no longer cared. "Why, exactly, are we working at cross purposes with the crown on this match?"

Massimi sat silent. The splashing fountain made the only sound.

"I realize he is Protestant and we are Catholic," Eremitz continued, "but King Philip believes his sister can lure Prince Charles back to the flock by the power of love, and I must say, I believe she can do it. When they're together, you can see his passion for her."

Massimi raised his chin. "Prince Charles and the infanta are children. So are you, for even considering a romantic solution. We don't have time for such frivolities. The

Keepers of the Kingdom shall restore God's realm to its rightful boundaries and do it promptly. For all the time we have wasted on this useless romance, we must now race to the most obvious solution. War. If the prince is assassinated on Spanish soil, the English will have no choice but to declare war upon Spain."

Eremitz froze.

Massimi rambled on—about the Heavenly Hosts pointing the way to a simpler solution; about romance being for the addle-minded; and about God patiently waiting to be done with the useless dalliance that was the Spanish match.

"Who… how do you intend to assassinate the prince?" Eremitz asked, once he found his voice. He had already provided Massimi with a prodigious amount of poison. At the time, he thought he didn't want to know how the sinister clergyman intended to use it. Now, he realized such a vacuous mindset could be his undoing.

"I've already hired an assassin." Massimi brought the bowl of sangria to his lips and took a long swig. "But he missed on the first try, which makes me suspicious. I've seen his work, and he's remarkably accurate. Perhaps the prince was too far away. I expect better results the next time."

As Massimi signaled the servant to ladle another splash of punch into his bowl, it dawned on Eremitz that he was tied to the crafty Monsignor's sinister plot some time ago. When Eremitz had first unloaded the poison dart frogs from the river dock, the priest found the brightly colored creatures even more exotic than he had expected. He had to stop Massimi from touching them. The papal nuncio hired four palace gardeners to build the habitat in the newly fashioned greenhouse. The poison extracted from the skin of the frogs was far more powerful than any Eremitz had ever seen. Massimi had tested a single drop on a large prisoner awaiting the gallows. It killed him in minutes.

Such elaborate preparations indicated a target of great importance, but the revelation Massimi was brazenly targeting the crown prince of England rocked Eremitz to his core.

"I shall give the assassin one more chance," said Massimi. "If he fails again, I may need to make use of your manservant, Capistrano. I will attempt to recruit a professional, but if the time comes to order Capistrano to assassinate Prince Charles, you must reinforce the command. A loyal servant must hear such an order from his own master. Once he has your word, he will follow it. My faith in his character is unshakeable."

Eremitz raised one eyebrow to disguise his mounting panic. His reputation and entire life could be destroyed by his own manservant. "Has this been decided by the College of Cardinals?" he asked.

Massimi studied Eremitz's face as if assessing a stranger as friend or foe. "You have been selected for the high honor of joining the Keepers of the Kingdom based on a number of virtues, the highest being devout loyalty, blind loyalty, if you will. Blind to all but the will of God."

Eremitz marveled at the irony of this blood-thirsty miscreant holding forth on the subject of virtue. As for blind loyalty, Eremitz's loyalty extended to family and God, but ended there. Massimi was neither.

"The will of God, as revealed to His vicar, the pope, I would presume," Eremitz pressed on.

Massimi paused to sip his sangria. "You are sworn to secrecy in regard to all matters involving the Keepers of the Kingdom. I have said too much already."

"But if I am to be of service, you cannot leave me fumbling in a fog of missing information. Indeed, we are all serving God, but who in the church are we serving? Can I assume His Holiness, Pope Urban the Eighth, knows about this, even though he has been pope for less than two months?"

Massimi's steely confidence retreated from his face, exposing him as the conniving, lowborn church bureaucrat Eremitz had always known him to be. Massimi had strategically endeared himself to a sinister branch of the Spanish Inquisition with the only virtues he had: a stomach for murder and an old bag of tricks. Rumors swirled that the Vatican would soon bestow the rank of archbishop on the papal nuncio in order to give him more credibility with King Philip. However, lacking the proper family connections, Massimi's rank could easily be reduced once he had served his purpose. The new pope was from the powerful Barberini family of Florence. Eremitz's family knew theirs well. Massimi was no one from nowhere.

"The pope is not your concern," said Massimi.

Eremitz met his eyes without a blink. "I cannot involve myself with the assassination of a crown prince unless I know, with certainty, I am serving the orders of His Holiness. My blind loyalty is pledged to him, not to you, Father Massimi. In all due respect."

Massimi sharpened his icy stare. "You expressed a concern for missing information, Father Eremitz," he said, his voice edged with venom. "Allow me to fill you in. Our last pope, may he rest in peace, was reluctant to see the wisdom proffered by the Keepers of the Kingdom. He kept pushing for the match. And now he is gone, after a mere two-and-a-half years. Apparently, God had other plans. If a pope can be so easily removed for failure to obey God, why trouble yourself to appeal to the pope?"

His theology was woefully wrong, but it didn't matter. Everything Eremitz thought he knew rearranged itself in his mind as he realized this artful power player could kill him at the snap of his fingers—and get away with it.

"Do not flatter yourself, Father Eremitz," Massimi continued. "I am aware of your family's ties to the pope, but our Lord came to us as a pauper to remind those of us blinded by vanity that we are all paupers in the eyes of God."

Eremitz was grateful for the heavy bruises around his eyes. Surely, they would help disguise his abject hatred for this Machiavellian viper who would never stop weaving him ever more tightly into his wicked schemes.

Massimi placed both hands on his thighs and rose. Eremitz stood as well, glad to soon be rid of his evil visitor.

"Send Capistrano to me tomorrow after our audience with the king," Massimi said. "I shall take his confession."

"But what of King Philip?" Eremitz asked, desperate to stop the disaster unfolding around him. "He has grown quite fond of Prince Charles, convinced they will soon be brothers. I doubt he will go along with this assassination scheme."

Massimi smoothed the creases in his cassock. "It is not his decision."

The resounding clang of the courtyard door closing behind Massimi came as a relief to Eremitz. He dropped into the divan near the fountain and stared at nothing, a symphony of water droplets punctuating his wretched thoughts.

He had hoped for powerful connections and an easy path to the office of cardinal when he agreed to serve as a Keeper of the Kingdom. Surely, if a vulgar peasant like Massimi could rise to Monsignor and possibly become the next archbishop, the path would be all the more swift for a nobleman. That was Eremitz's philosophy at the time. Now, his folly was plain to see. Massimi had maneuvered him into a cage.

Eremitz knew with solid certainty the Amerindian would fail to kill Prince Charles. The priest had seen the would-be assassin's display of marksmanship, too. The only reason Prince Charles was alive was because the Amerindian could not bring himself to kill the daft but charming golden-haired lad.

Ordering Capistrano to assassinate the prince was simple, brilliant, and double-edged. All of Europe would accuse Eremitz while Massimi hid in the shadows. In this way, Massimi would forever enslave Eremitz to the cult. He would be incapable of leaving their noose-like circle of protection without being torn to pieces by an English mob. Worse, a man like Massimi would think nothing of laying

Eremitz's capture on the table in any negotiations with the English.

Eremitz stared past the fountain. It didn't matter that he had spotted the trap. It was already sprung. A cold sense of doom washed over him.

14

Glass Frogs

Eremitz awoke to the sound of a carriage pulling up in the courtyard. He didn't remember falling asleep. When he rose from the divan, every muscle in his body cringed with pain.

"Señora!" he called. He would have hollered for Capistrano, but his manservant was worse off than he.

Esperanza rushed from the villa, past Eremitz, to open the courtyard door.

A red coach with a gold coat of arms stood beneath the olive trees. Eremitz recognized it as belonging to Doña Adelena, the Countess Segovia, who had managed to parlay her distant relationship to the royal family into a secure, pensioned position as the infanta's nursemaid and governess. Doña Adelena had become enamored of Father Eremitz. A tall angular woman with graying hair and mannish features, Adelena practiced piety with great fanfare. At mass, she sang the loudest, cried the longest, and closed her eyes the tightest during prayer, often sneaking glances at Father Eremitz as she did so.

Wondering why she was visiting at such an inopportune time, he braced himself as the footman leapt from his perch and opened the coach door. Doña Adelena appeared from the shadows carrying a wicker basket in one hand and a pamphlet in the other. The coachman helped her down.

Esperanza stood outside the open door of the courtyard with her head bowed, hands clasped at her waist.

"I must see Father Eremitz!" Adelena cried, waving Massimi's pamphlet with her free hand.

Eremitz rested his shoulder against the doorframe, too weary to stand upright.

Adelena rushed toward him, her basket clinking with its mysterious contents. "My Lord! My Lord! What have they done to you?" she wailed.

Esperanza turned to look at Eremitz and gasped in horror. "Oh, Padre!" she exclaimed.

"Quick!" Adelena said to the housekeeper. "Boil water. We shall prepare a bath."

Esperanza cast a worried glance at Eremitz. At his nod, she rushed into the villa.

A mule-drawn cart pulled up behind the carriage. Three workmen in loose chemises and broad-brimmed hats jumped off the cart and proceeded to unload its bulky contents.

"Where would you like your bath?" Adelena asked. "We can quickly fill the tub in the kitchen."

Eremitz could think of nothing to say. "Ah, fine. Yes, the kitchen."

The workman loaded their heavy cargo onto a dolly and rolled it into the kitchen, where it clattered on the paving stones. They unloaded near a large, arched brick hearth. When they pulled the tarp off the bulky mass, Eremitz was astonished to see a brightly polished copper pedestal tub.

Adelena grabbed his arm and pulled him into a chair. He hated her claw-like grip, but as she began swabbing his cuts with gauze and vinegar water, he felt grateful for her ministrations.

With a series of claps and barked orders, Adelena directed Eremitz's servants to draw the bath. Once they completed the task, she ordered them from the room. Eremitz wondered who would assist him—certainly not the prudish Adelena. He watched her draw items from her wicker basket and set a nearby table with a bottle of liquid castile soap, a folded washing cloth, and a larger drying cloth. She dribbled lavender-scented oil into the bath. When she donned a thick blindfold, Eremitz realized Adelena would, indeed, do the honors.

"You may disrobe, Father Eremitz," Adelena announced in a pious tone, holding her blindfolded head high.

Eremitz wasn't fooled. He knew she would be able to see through the gaps directly beneath her eyes, caused by her sizeable nose. But a warm bath was too inviting to resist.

The polished copper was sinfully smooth and the water just hot enough to fully relax him. "Ahhh," he exhaled long and softly. His wounds ached a bit but the tub's curve at the nape of his neck nearly put him back to sleep.

Standing behind Eremitz, Adelena ran her hands beneath his neck and gathered his hair up over the bath's curved edge. She removed the porcelain pitcher from the table as competently as any woman who could see beneath her blindfold. After splashing Eremitz's scalp and hair with warm water that she caught in a basin below, she set the pitcher back on the table and picked up a slender glass bottle with a handle and a beak.

Eremitz felt the drizzle of cool liquid soap along his hairline and then Adelena's fingers, strong but gentle, as she massaged it into his scalp. He breathed in the cool peppermint scent. He was somewhat self-conscious beneath her gaze, but the bath felt so good he didn't care. When the scalp massage aroused his manly spirits, he simply looked at her face. The strenuous piety that tortured her brow, combined with a forced frown of pleasure denied, snuffed those urges.

Once she gave his hair a final rinse, she took up a washrag and assaulted him with a harsh rubbing, adding new scrapes atop the old ones. Gone was the gentleness she had shown his scalp. He snatched the towel from her, which made her scowl anew.

"Thank you, blessed sister," he said in the soft, hypnotic tone that made him popular among parishioners. "You are a good and pious woman. I can attend to my ablutions from here. Perhaps you could retire to the sitting room to prepare the bandages. I shall meet you there, as soon as I am clothed, if you could be so kind as to dress my wounds."

While Adelena could see her feet, she could not see the servant's dining table, nor the storage barrels, nor the chair by the door. She bumped and stumbled her way out of the kitchen.

Once she was gone, Eremitz sent for Capistrano and Bazin, his clever stable boy. Before long, the man and boy rushed into the kitchen.

"Bazin, bring me that cloth," said Eremitz, rising from the tub and motioning toward the small table. "Capistrano, the bath is yours."

Bazin helped Eremitz towel off and assisted him into the clean robes Esperanza had brought. Once fully clothed, he called Esperanza into the kitchen and instructed her to assist Capistrano with his bath before joining Adelena.

In the sitting room, Eremitz relaxed on a wooden settee, reveling in the comfort of a bath and clean bandages. Although his bruises still pained him, he felt grateful for Adelena's care. Esperanza could have assisted him, but a member of the royal family arriving on his doorstep to tend his wounds was deeply flattering. Eremitz wondered if there was something of value he could part with to show his gratitude.

At a lull in their conversation, Adelena said, "Dear Father Eremitz, I hear you have a collection of exotic frogs that appear to be made of fine Venetian glass. I have always hoped to see them, but—" She stopped and batted her eyes.

Eremitz paused. A plan formed in his mind like a dust devil emerging from the sand. "Please," he said, rising to his feet. "Allow me to escort you to the greenhouse. I would love to show you my Amazonian frogs."

As she stepped into the glass house, Adelena's eyes darted about the lush foliage as if she feared an attack from a wild beast.

"Over here," said Eremitz, gesturing to the latticed cage in the corner near the door. Adelena approached cautiously. "Please come close and look through the lattice," he said.

She did as he instructed.

"They often perch on the larger leaves. Can you see the red one?"

"Oh, yes," Adelena gasped. "I see a blue one and a yellow one, too. They are *exquisite*."

"And entirely unique," said Eremitz. "I have been around the world and never seen anything like them."

"Can I hold one?"

"I'm afraid not. They are extremely poisonous to the touch."

"Oh, my. It's hard to believe something so delicate could be so dangerous."

"Would you like to own them?" he asked. It was a bold move, but Eremitz could think of no better way to rid himself of Massimi's tools of assassination.

Adelena pulled her face away from the lattice to stare at Eremitz, eyes wide with disbelief. "Surely, you cannot mean that." She placed her hand on her cheek, signaling she very much hoped he did.

"Actually, my meaning is more complicated, Sister Adelena," said Eremitz. "The moment I laid eyes on these unearthly creatures, it was my dream to install them at the Alcazar gardens as a wedding gift for our young King Philip and his lovely bride, Queen Isabella. Unfortunately, I am but a common priest. Who am I to offer any gift, grand or small, to the most revered regents in all of Europe?"

"Indeed," Adelena said in a breathy gasp.

"But you are of much higher rank, Doña Adelena, indeed a member of the royal family yourself. It would be more appropriate for you to present such a gift to our young king and queen, don't you think?"

"Why, thank you, Father Eremitz. You are most generous. I will instruct my gardeners to retrieve them right away."

Her eyes sparkled. They both knew presenting the royal couple with a rare and exotic gift was a far more valuable prize than the gemlike frogs themselves.

15

The Catch

June 1623
Madrid, Spain

Beneath a starry sky, smoke rose from a row of three chimneys that towered above the Audley household. Inside, a blaze crackled in the large brick oven as servants bustled about the kitchen in the pre-dawn hour. The silent Moroccan cook directed the staff with gestures of his head and hands. The crew moved like choreographed dancers, swift but never colliding, wielding their pots and pans like musical instruments. The penetrating scent of green herbs sizzling in olive oil perfumed the air as it wafted up to Anne and Harald's room.

Ibrahim appeared in the doorway, bearing a covered jug of café, hot and fresh.

"Is breakfast ready?" Anne asked.

"One-half hour," the Moor replied. He closed the door behind him as he left.

"Here's one thing Pope Clement the Eighth got right," said Harald, raising his mug in a toast.

"And what does café have to do with Pope Clement?" Anne asked, amused.

"It was he who declared café much too delicious to be left to the infidels."

"To Pope Clement, then," said Anne, also raising her mug. "How could we start our mornings if not for him?"

Anne and Harald joined Kitty and Gregory Mack for breakfast. They ate together at a long table. The omelet was savory, yet they hurried through their meal to be at the river before sunrise. Gregory finished and strode off to the stables to collect gear for the fishing expedition.

"I will wake our royal charge," said Harald. He kissed Anne and left. She and Kitty lingered a moment as Kitty poured fresh café from a heated urn, first into Anne's cup and then her own.

She sat down and looked both ways. "Thank God we have not seen another feathered dart," Kitty said, keeping her voice low. "But I am apprehensive about our morning fishing expedition. It leaves our prince out in the open. An assassin could try again." She doused her dark brew with a splash of cream and watched the white swirl transform into many shades of brown.

Anne slowly shook her head. "Unfortunately, we cannot keep Prince Charles cloistered indoors forever. Protocol demands he accept every royal invitation."

"Did Harald and Gregory manage to gather any clues?"

Anne shook her head. "They still have no idea who shot it."

"Gregory tested the poison on a mouse," said Kitty. "He scratched its skin with the barb. The mouse convulsed and died in an instant."

"Good God, Kitty, were you there?"

"Of course, I was there. I want to learn these things." Anne looked out the window. The stars were vanishing as the horizon brightened from black to teal. "We must hurry. I promised we would collect the infanta and her ladies before dawn," said Anne.

"If we arrived at noon, the doñas would still have to drag the princess and her ladies out of bed," Kitty quipped.

"No doubt," said Anne. "Perhaps our presence will encourage them to hasten."

Outside, the cool air sharpened their senses. The carriage allowed a clear view of the sky. Amidst the smattering of stars, two nebulae gleamed along the western horizon, like supernatural eyes in an inscrutable, cosmic face. Anne regarded them with awe. Harald had told her they were unique in the heavens. She pointed them out to Kitty.

The horses clip-clopped on the stone path. They passed through ornate gates flanked by torches that flickered like captured daemons.

Amazingly, the infanta was waiting impatiently for their arrival. She and her entire entourage were dressed for adventure and ready to depart.

The river gleamed with the reflection of the sunrise that rimmed the magenta clouds.

The white muslin gowns of the infanta and her ladies billowed as they ran over the grassy lawn, through the trees, and glided down the sandy slope that separated the lower garden of the Alcazar from the Manzanares River. A blended company of ladies and gallants followed behind. Anne and Kitty chatted with the doñas as they assisted them down the slope.

Once everyone had made it safely to the beach, Anne joined Harald for a stroll down the river's edge. As they walked, he bowed his head and spoke softly in her ear. "They're bringing enough food and equipment to launch a crusade. It's a simple fishing excursion. It's not as if we might get lost in the wilderness. The Alcazar is right there." He nodded his head at the palace towering above them beyond the grassy park.

Anne smiled. "Everything is done ceremoniously here. I rather like it."

Servants hurried ahead to the edge of the river to set up pavilions and lay floor cloths and cushions, under the supervision of Duchess Olivares, the prime minister's wife. With great difficulty, the doñas clambered down the sandy banks, teetering in the soft sand, their white skirts ballooning like galleons in a strong wind. Young cavaliers hurried to assist them.

"Isn't it sweet how the young lords assist the elderly ladies?" Anne asked.

"Not as sweet as you may suppose," said Harald. "Winning over a doña can smooth a lad's path to the señoritas."

Anne smiled and nudged him in reply. She looked toward the riverbank. Gregory Mack stood alongside Prince Charles as they examined an assortment of fishing poles. Anne scanned the small crowds gathering along the bank and was delighted that Buckingham was nowhere to be seen, even though he had bragged of the fishing expedition the day before as if the entire affair had been his idea. He was incapable of rising before dawn, she surmised.

Gregory stood with one foot perched on a rock, squinting at the pole in his hand. He threaded the fishing line through the wire loops along the shaft before tying a hook to the end. Bait buckets of wet moss crawling with earthworms stood at the ready.

Prince Charles noticed the buckets. "Aren't we using flies? What sport is this to fish with worms?"

Gregory smiled. "We don't want to exclude our hosts from the fun of catching a fish, and teaching them to fish with flies could start an international incident if a lord or lady were to catch a hook in the face."

Prince Charles slumped. "I was hoping to show the infanta that if we were ever forced to escape into the woods, I could provide for her and look noble while doing so."

"Another time." Gregory was firm.

King Philip wandered along the grass above the riverbank amidst a bevy of courtiers. The sun lit up his auburn curls as the breeze tossed his hair about his face, making him appear to be the sixteen-year-old youth he was. Charles failed to notice him, and Gregory decided to keep it that way.

The infanta appeared over a sandy berm like a gazelle, her company of ladies streaming behind her like the tail of a comet. The wind caught the fabric of her white dress and sent it rippling against her curvaceous form. Her bustier of bright yellow corduroy with blue satin laces held the promise of a beautiful day. Charles gaped at the sight of her.

Gregory leaned in close and whispered, "Close your mouth, Your Highness."

Arriving at the river's edge, Maria positioned herself before Gregory. "I want to catch a big fish, so give me a strong pole."

Gregory picked out a sturdy rod, not too long, and began to string the line along its metal eyes.

"Is this the best pole you have?" Maria demanded.

Gregory regarded her gravely. "It's the best one in this collection."

Maria inspected the rod, then gave a brisk nod of approval, which sent her red-gold curls dancing. "Oh, good, there's already a hook."

"Yes, Your Highness. Would you like me to bait that hook, or would you prefer to do that yourself?"

Maria looked dubious as she regarded the fat, wriggling worm Gregory held between two fingers. "You may bait the hook," she said.

Charles continued to stare at the infanta until she confronted him. "Are you a prince or a puppet? You may greet me if you like."

Charles froze for a moment and then recovered himself. "In your presence, My Lady, I am the very prince of puppets. All of my strings are in your hands."

Gregory turned his head, grinning.

Maria burst out laughing. "Spoken as smoothly as a Spaniard, Northern Prince. You and I may yet be friends. Have you any experience with this 'fishing'? I have none, but I am a quick study."

Charles was confident in this area. "Your Highness, I have fished since I could walk. I have, indeed, drowned myself many times in the brooks and streams of Scotland."

"What? Drowned?" Maria teased. "Yet I see you here, before me."

The prince was finding his footing now. "My Lady, I have able protectors. They can retrieve a large fish or a well-grown prince."

Gregory interrupted their banter. "The fish will stop biting as the sun rises. If you want to catch one, you will have to be quick." He slung a leather bag filled with fishing tackle over his shoulders. "Please, Your Highnesses," he said, "come with me down the bank. Walk as softly as possible."

Maria's courtiers trooped after the young royals, chatting and giggling. Gregory leaned in and whispered to the princess, "Talking sends the fish into hiding. This is not something a crowd can do."

Eager to succeed in this venture, Maria turned and hissed at her entourage. "Stay back, you'll drive the fish away." With an imperious arm, she motioned them to leave her. Several of the older women were torn between their need to keep track of the infanta and their reluctance to get themselves wet and muddy. Maria was tyrannical in her orders. "ALL of you! Stay here at the pavilions," she hissed. "I will not have you frightening my fish with your chatter." She addressed Gregory Mack in a low voice. "For this morning, Sir Fishing Pole, I will follow your every instruction."

"My first instruction is that you both be silent," said Gregory.

Maria obediently fell mute, but her blue eyes were enormous as they headed upstream along the sandy bank. Charles offered his arm to the infanta. For a moment, it seemed she would shrug him away, but then she reconsidered. She took Charles's arm. Pressing her breast gently against him, she said, "My brother would disapprove of this familiarity, but I am only a poor, weak girl, and it is difficult to walk on these shifting sands." She met Charles's eyes with a melting gaze.

Charles dared to take the flirtation further. "With you so close, beautiful princess, I, too, find it difficult to walk on these shifting sands."

Maria gave an un-princesslike snort of laughter, dropped her hold on Charles's arm, and ran ahead of him to walk beside Sir Gregory. Charles smiled, his heart fluttering. The princess's weakness for wit was not lost on him.

He watched Maria swaying gracefully ahead of him, interrogating Gregory Mack in a loud whisper that she was sure the fish would not notice. The prince ruminated on the pleasurable challenges of being married to such a woman. At seventeen, her bold spirit seemed indomitable.

Gold and blue pennants fluttered lazily above a grassy bluff. From here, the doñas had a view of the path curving along the bank before it disappeared into the willows where Sir Gregory had led the infanta and the prince.

Duchess Olivares and her cousin, Countess Segovia—or Doña Adelena, as her peers called her—observed the royal fishing expedition from their perch. The morning sun warmed their backs. Adelena, a childless widow, had been Princess Maria's nurse since the infanta's birth. Insofar Duchess Olivares had played a key role in securing Adelena's position, the grateful palace nanny had helped put the ambassador's wife in charge the princess's royal activities.

Two ladies wandered into the group of chaperones and their charges. Rana, Duchess Olivares's Amerindian flute player, followed them like a shadow. Bringing his flute to his lips, he piped a merry tune. The ladies turned in surprise and laughed before picking up their skirts and dancing. The other ladies joined in, skipping and twirling their petticoats as they followed the Amerindian flautist. Duchess Olivares hovered nearby, pretending not to notice their feet were bare.

"When you allow them to behave like peasants, how do you expect them to marry well?" Adelena huffed.

The duchess smiled. "They are young for such a short time. Dancing barefoot in the sand will not hurt their chances for a good marriage. Young courtiers will be attracted to their merry spirits and I'm sure their families' wealth will make them no less attractive."

Adelena grunted disapprovingly.

Upstream, Gregory led the prince and the infanta through the willows at the river's edge, then around a bend, where it was darker than on the sandy riverbank. Old olive trees screened the three from the view of the white-tented pavilions behind them. The hanging foliage also sheltered a deep, shadowy pool.

Charles caught up with Maria and Gregory. "I could try a cast or two from here. There's no one else about."

Gregory glanced at Maria. "Let's begin simply. There isn't time today for the infanta to learn fly-fishing and to catch a fish."

Maria looked at the hook on her line. "I've lost the bait."

"Don't worry, little lass, I have more," said Gregory. "Would you like to try baiting the hook yourself this time?"

Maria shook her head. "We don't have time to learn to bait the hook and to catch a fish. I have no doubt you can complete the task most proficiently."

Gregory smiled and found another worm in a packet of moss he'd brought along. Charles had already prepared his rod and hook. Keeping his shadow behind him, he tossed the baited hook to where the rushing water could bring it into the pool, as if the worm had fallen into the river from a branch above.

As Charles settled into the monastic meditation of the patient angler, Gregory turned his attention to the impatient Maria.

"Your Highness, allow me to assist you." Using gestures, he coached her to arc her worm over the deepest part of the shady waters and slowly let it down. In a long silence, they watched the bait descend through the clear upper level of the pool and drift into the lower darkness. Magically, a whirlpool began to form. Maria gasped as the worm on the hook swirled into the funnel. From the shadowy depths rose a long, powerful shape. Even Gregory was astonished that so large a fish could live in the Manzanares River. Graceful as an aquatic dancer, the fish engulfed the baited hook, and dove deep into the depths of the pool.

Unthinking, Gregory reached for Maria's fishing rod to set the hook.

"No! I can do it!" she exclaimed, jerking her rod away from his grasp, thereby perfectly setting the hook herself.

Gregory managed not to laugh. His respect for the young girl rose. "Agreed, Your Highness. May I tutor you as to how to land your fish?"

The line was tearing off into the rushing current. Maria struggled to hold the rod.

"Yes!" she shouted.

"We're going to get wet," Gregory warned.

The fish headed upstream to faster water, hoping to throw off whatever was hampering it. Maria struggled to keep her footing as she stepped into the river, pursuing her uncooperative catch.

"I shall do this!" she shouted over her shoulder.

Underwater, the stones were mossy. Maria's skirts were gauzy and multilayered. One slip plunged her under water. Without releasing her pole, Maria rose from the water, her white dress plastered about her décolletage and thighs, her copper hair flying loose.

Gregory rushed into the water. Charles rushed up and snatched a net from the tackle Gregory had set on the sandbar and sprinted into the water, upstream from Maria and her fish. The net had a long handle, but was not big enough to hold the catch. Charles alternated hooping the net over the fish's head and tail, to keep it unbalanced. Together, he and Maria herded it toward the shore. Gregory rushed into the water and grabbed the fish's tail. With a mighty heave, he hurled the slippery, flopping creature into the long grass beyond the sandbar. It leapt about until Gregory smacked it in the head with the hilt of his dagger.

"Well done, Princess Maria! We have our catch. Time to return and tell our comrades of our adventure."

"We are not done fishing," Maria said with imperial certitude. "We must catch more."

"You have already caught more fish in one cast than anyone else will catch for the rest of the day," said Gregory. "We shall go back downstream to retrieve a boat. This fish is a bit too big to carry back."

"Oh, no, we must take it back with us so everyone can see I am the best fisherman," Maria insisted. "Put it in the water and I'll drag it back by the pole."

Charles laughed. As Gregory looked up from the fish, he noticed the prince's leather jerkin sported another bright spray of feathers attached to a dart. Gregory rushed toward him.

"Let me help you out of your jerkin, Sir," he said, unable to hide his alarm. The prince glanced down to see the dart tip barely hanging on his bulky lapel.

"Looks like someone else made a good cast today," said Charles. He slipped out of the jacket and Gregory wrapped the dart on the inside, making a bundle of it. He slipped out of his own jerkin and held it out for the prince.

"We need to return to the party with haste, Your Royal Highness," Gregory whispered as he assisted the prince into the thick leather jerkin. Once the prince was lodged amidst a crowd of Spanish aristocrats, they could breathe more easily. The assailant was unlikely to take another shot under those circumstances. Whoever it was, his aim was sharp. He wasn't missing from lack of skill. Gregory felt oddly calm. A reluctant assassin, Gregory mused. Could that be a clue?

Duchess Olivares stood by the pavilion with the others, waiting for the trio to return. When she saw the drenched infanta, she shot a dark look at Gregory and Prince Charles.

"I see you have been teaching our infanta what will be expected of her as a princess in an English court."

"Not at all, Lady Olivares," Gregory replied. "The princess has demonstrated she is quite capable of pursuing great adventures of her own free will. We could only put ourselves at her service."

The duchess gave him a cold look and then turned to look after Maria, who was showing a gathering throng of admirers her fabulous catch. The young men were too busy admiring the river-drenched infanta to notice the fish.

The duchess clapped her hands. "You, young men, stand away from the infanta. Young ladies, surround her while I bring her fresh clothing."

Servants ran to the duchess, carrying a fresh frock and skirts for the infanta. The duchess herded the young ladies into a white tent to assist the princess into the dry clothes.

Charles and the young men were examining the fish when it lurched to life and thrashed about. The young men leapt away as the fish flipped past them, tumbling across the shore. The instant it touched water, it dashed away.

One of the young Spanish lords chased it into the river. "Oh, no!" he cried. "Someone get the fish! It's swimming away!"

Charles charged into the river and dived on the fish, hugging it to his chest as he wrestled it to the bottom of the river. His efforts were to no avail. The fish wriggled free and disappeared into the rippling current.

Hearing the commotion from outside, the infanta burst from the tent, wearing nothing but her soaking wet shift. She pushed her way through the astonished crowd. "What is this?" she demanded. "I can't leave my fish alone for a minute without you all releasing it back? If this is the kind of care you give the prince and myself, what might happen if we faced real danger?"

The infanta's voluptuous figure shone through the wet cotton. The young ladies were deliciously aghast. The astounded young men froze and stared at the dripping princess. Prince Charles stood in the river gaping at Maria. On the shoreline, Harald caught Gregory's eye. The Infanta's words had stung him. He and Gregory had been far from vigilant in watching over their prince.

Anne and Kitty loitered near the pavilion, quietly taking it all in.

"Thank God, King Philip has already gone," Kitty whispered to Anne.

"I'm quite certain the infanta has already taken his absence into account," Anne whispered back.

Duchess Olivares wrapped a thick cotton blanket around the infanta once she caught up. Grasping her firmly, she led her back to the dressing tent, taking care not to let her escape again.

Moments later, Princess Maria returned to her shore party, elegantly dressed, with perfectly coiffed hair. Duchess Olivares clapped her hands, signaling the entertainers to amuse the crowd. The cooks sent out trays of food for the young lords and ladies.

Harald came and stood where Anne and Kitty were sitting. He unrolled the prince's leather jerkin that Gregory gave him, revealing the feathered dart.

Anne and Kitty went pale as they stared at the would-be murder weapon.

"We have to find out where these darts are coming from," said Harald.

"Let's discuss this when we're alone," Anne said in a low voice. "We can't let the others catch on."

"I'll scout the area once the guests have retired," said Kitty

"I can vouch the infanta is above suspicion," said Gregory, joining the three of them. "She tries not to show it, but she is quite taken with our bonnie Prince Charles."

"Poor lass," said Harald. "Did you see her rush out of the tent in her shift, soaking wet? She will be humiliated once she comes to her senses."

Kitty snorted.

"Oh, Harald," said Anne. "You are so naïve."

16

Kitty and the Samurai

Kitty had no idea where to begin her search. She rushed up the riverbank, retracing Gregory and his party's path, but saw nothing, which didn't surprise her. Only a fool would remain in place after an assault on a crown prince.

She calmed herself and reflected on her options.

Akira, the sword master, of course. He had offered her sword-fighting lessons in exchange for fresh-baked pastries. Her next lesson was that afternoon. She had planned to cancel but suddenly realized Akira could be an excellent source of information. After lessons, he enjoyed expounding upon the latest news and gossip from his students, nearly all of them Spanish and English noblemen.

In the Audley's kitchen house, gleaming copper pots hung above a marble countertop. Kitty slipped her lemon tart off the counter. Pulling open the metal door of the oven, she slid it onto the rack amidst several loaves of bread. She closed the door against the blast of heat, careful not to wake the old scullery maid dozing in her rickety wooden chair.

At the entryway, the upper portion of a Dutch door hung open. A cool breeze from the garden carried the scent of sweet grass. Kitty pulled a slip of paper from her skirt pocket, unfolded it, and rested her forearms on the lower door. Scanning the charcoal-scrawled names of the Spanish lords who had attended the fishing party, she searched her memory for the ones who took sword lessons. Considering the few clues they had, any Spanish lord with martial skills was a suspect.

After pondering the matter for some time, a sweet scent wafted from the oven. Kitty removed her tart and placed it back on the marble counter. The dozing scullery maid had been charged with watching over the kitchen as the rest of the staff took their siestas. For the favor of using her kitchen, Kitty rewarded her with the privilege of a long nap. All it took was a gentle nudge to her shoulder and the old woman awoke with a start.

"I believe your loaves are ready," said Kitty.

"Oh, bless you, my dear. And how did your lemon tart fare?"

"It's cooling on the countertop. Thank you for your kindness."

The woman bustled about, removing the loaves from the oven. Kitty placed the warm tart in a linen-lined basket, dipped her arm through the handle, and headed out.

"Adios," she said, waving as she departed.

A white-washed brick wall separated the Audley's villa from the one next door, which was rented by Monsieur Tavernier, a successful merchant and longtime friend of Harald's family. Kitty passed through the ornate gate, onto the shaded grass. At the back of the Tavernier's garden was a cottage occupied by their Japanese guest, Akira—a courteous, albeit formidable, sword master.

Kitty plodded through the grass toward the sword master's cottage, grateful the Taverniers were not so gauche as to parade Akira around like an exotic creature as the Olivareses did with their poor Amazonian flautist, Rana. The Japanese sword master had become a familiar sight in the jousting yard, but his naïveté in regard to social rank was a problem. Although Monsieur Tavernier had explained aristocratic protocols to him, Akira still favored the young men who showed talent over those of higher rank—a quirk that made Kitty all the more fond of him.

She knocked on the cottage door and paused. The sound of gentle snoring was the only reply.

Kitty tapped out her special knock. A lemon tart and her charming company would buy her a one-hour lesson in sword fighting.

"Hai!" Akira called from within.

The door swung open. The cottage was one large room with a bed, a settee overhung with a canopy, a heavy wooden table with four chairs, and a countertop with cupboards above and below. His swords and other tools of war were displayed along the walls like exotic sculptures.

"Good day, Akira," said Kitty.

"Lady Kitty," he responded, smiling brightly.

Although he wore breeches, he was unaware of the inappropriateness of greeting a woman at the door bare-chested. Kitty forced herself not to stare, either looking into Akira's large, dark eyes or glancing about the room. From her peripheral vision, she could not resist taking in his torso, firm and lustrous as a bronze statue. He accepted her pastry with a formal bow.

Retrieving two spoons from the cupboard, he invited her to sit down at the table. He spun the pie around with his fingertip, brought it to a stop, and ducked his spoon into the flaky crust. He held up a translucent morsel and looked at Kitty expectantly. From the start, he had made it clear he never ate anything until the cook tasted it first. Kitty couldn't tell if it was theatrics or if he was following through on a safety protocol. It was probably both. She loved her own cooking, so she dug her spoon into the pie. As she brought the morsel to her mouth, he comically matched her motion, closing his lips over the spoon at the exact same moment as she.

When they had finished, Akira rose and snatched his sword from the wall. Returning to the table, he tossed an apple into the air and sliced it into four pieces to the accompaniment of dramatic war whoops. The apple slices fell into a ceramic bowl on the table. In similar fashion, he sliced two tangerines and three walnuts. After entertaining her, he wiped his sword clean and returned it to its wall mount. From the cupboard, he retrieved the two wooden swords they used for practice.

After half an hour of drills and choreographed sword play, Akira took her sword and set it aside, along with his own.

"Now, I show you how to fight with no sword," he said, heading for his bed. He pulled the blankets aside, took the mattress off the bed, and tossed it at Kitty's feet.

"Oh, no, no!" Kitty exclaimed. "Really, Akira—"

Before she could finish her sentence, he took her by the wrist, turned quickly as he pulled her arm over his shoulder, and in one great tumble, she was lying on the mattress, staring up at his face.

"Oh, my stars! What did you do?" said Kitty, somewhat winded.

There was a sharp rap on the door. Kitty leapt to her feet and rushed to the canopied settee. She glanced at Akira, lifting her finger to her lips before kneeling on the cushion and drawing the curtains closed.

Akira answered the door.

"Señor Akira." The man spoke with an Italian accent. "I have not yet had the honor of making your acquaintance. Allow me to introduce myself. I am Monsignor Massimi."

"At your service," said Akira, bowing.

After making some small talk, Massimi got to the point. "I understand you are not just formidable with a sword, you are also a master of the art of invisibility. Am I right? Especially at night?"

"Hmm," said Akira, as if unwilling to admit it.

"I trust you can keep secrets?" Massimi asked.

"Yes, yes," said Akira.

"You must never divulge this conversation to anyone, not even your friends, the Taverniers," Massimi continued. "You wouldn't want any harm to come to them, as kind as they have been to you. I have your word of honor?"

"Hai," Akira said.

"The English prince has come to Spain in the hopes of marrying our precious Infanta Maria Anna." Massimi's tone was officious, but he didn't waste words. "We cannot allow this. Prince Charles is a heretic. That means our precious infanta's life is in danger. She will never convert to his heretical religion. Thus, as he attempts to override her virtue with his sinful nature, he will surely torture her to death. We cannot allow that to happen. You must help us."

An uncomfortable silence descended.

Kitty counted her heartbeats, wondering if Massimi had detected her presence.

"I am seeking a trustworthy man," Massimi continued, "a soldier of the Holy Spirit, to remove this wicked prince from our presence. I need you, Señor Akira, to end his life by whichever means you find convenient. I can assist you in this. You will receive a generous reward and be protected from all consequences."

"No, no," said Akira, his tone regretful. "I'm not worthy to kill a prince. My father was a sword maker. He made swords for men who served kings. So sorry. I am lowborn and cannot accept such an honorable mission."

"There is no need for you to be his peer. God commands us to eliminate him for the sake of His heavenly kingdom." Massimi's tone took on a serpentine oiliness. "Indeed, we can go now to the chapel and pray together. By God's grace—"

"Oh, no," said Akira, cutting off the wily Monsignor. "I don't pray to your God. Forbidden. I worship the Shinto Goddess only. Hai!"

Kitty clamped her hand over her mouth to stifle her gasp. She could only imagine the astonished look on the Monsignor's face.

"Failing to comply with the will of God can have severe consequences," said Massimi, "especially for a heretic like yourself. Good day, Señor Akira."

Returning to the Audley's estate, Kitty chose to go to the riverside and take the sandy path home. As she walked, she glanced about for clues—unfamiliar footprints in the sand, a bright feather caught on a twig, anything. She wove around a thick clump of ferns and paused, wondering if she heard music. A thin, exotic melody drifted through the breeze. She crept around a bend.

Nestled amidst the ferns was Rana, the Olivares's Amerindian, playing his wooden flute. He looked up and smiled, his boyish grin strange in his weathered face.

Kitty sat next to him and spoke in a casual tone. "I suppose we'll be eating fried fish tonight."

"I like fish," he replied.

"I enjoy fish, but I love fowl. Speaking of such, could you tell me what kind of feathers these are?" She reached into her pocket, brought out a linen cloth, and unwrapped it to reveal two bright feathers—one red, one yellow.

"Oh, those are mine," the Amerindian blushed as if someone had found his dirty laundry. "You won't find that kind of fowl around here."

A cold chill slipped down Kitty's shoulders but she kept her voice calm. "Were the darts yours as well?"

"Yes, yes," Rana nodded.

"And this poison, too?" Kitty picked up the dart by its feathers and held the poisoned tip just beneath Rana's nose.

"Don't touch that," said Rana, leaning back with a grin.

"Are you trying to kill Prince Charles?"

"No, no," Rana grinned, shaking his head. "If I tried to kill him, he'd be dead now."

"But why? Why would you shoot poisoned darts at our prince?"

"The priest. He made me do it. He said Prince Charles is evil, and if he marries the infanta, he'll be cruel to her, even kill her. But I don't believe him."

"What priest?" Kitty asked, wondering if Massimi had an accomplice. "What is his name?"

"His name? Uh, Padre."

Kitty sighed. "Why did you not kill the prince as the priest commanded you?"

"Because I like him." Rana turned his head like a shy girl revealing a secret crush. "The prince won't hurt the infanta. I can see when a man loves, and when he hates. When the prince looks at the infanta, his eyes fill with love."

Kitty left Rana on the sandbar. As she made her way back to the Audley villa, the exotic tune from the Amazonian's flute followed her.

Anne was sitting at her desk writing a letter when Kitty burst into her office chamber.

"I've found the assassin," Kitty said, nearly breathless. "The poisoned darts are being blown by the Olivares's Amerindian."

Anne reflexively turned her entire body toward Kitty. "Little *Rana?* I can hardly believe it, he's so sweet-natured. I discounted him by instinct."

"He is sweet," Kitty said. "The only reason Prince Charles is among the quick, rather than the dead is because Rana didn't have the heart to kill him. He missed a fatal shot both times and deliberately struck the prince on the thickest part of his doublet. Rana thinks Prince Charles and Princess Maria are the most romantic couple ever. Isn't that adorable?"

"*Adorable?* Kitty, this is no time for romance. Who ordered the assassination?"

"Patience, M'Lady. Rana told me a priest had ordered him to kill our prince. When I asked which priest, he told me his name was 'Padre' as if that revealed all. But the truth is, M'Lady, I already knew. Before I found Rana at the river's edge, I was receiving instruction from the Tavernier's Japanese sword master—"

"Mm-hmm, who is very handsome, I have noticed," said Anne.

"I hadn't given up on solving the mystery. I was seeking further information, and who should drop by but that horrible priest, Monsignor Massimi."

"The papal nuncio?" Anne looked stricken.

"I hid on a canopied settee and drew the curtain before Akira opened the door, so I'm certain he didn't know I was there. He practically ordered Akira to assassinate the prince!"

"Did he say why?"

"He told Akira Prince Charles will torture Princess Maria to death if she doesn't convert to Protestantism."

"Balderdash!" said Anne. "He knows that's not true. What did Akira say?"

"He refused as nicely as he could, but when Father Massimi asked him to come to the chapel to pray about it, Akira told him he couldn't because he worships a foreign goddess." Kitty put her hand to her mouth.

"Oh, dear God," said Anne. "We must tell the Taverniers their Japanese friend may be in danger of the Spanish Inquisition."

"Monsieur Tavernier will have to convert Akira to Catholicism, or at least make it seem so. Let us see if Kenhelm can get his friend, Father Eremitz, to conduct the rites and make it official."

Anne shook her head. "That is far too much of a favor to ask of someone who is practically a stranger, and possibly an enemy. Far more practical would be to get Duchess Olivares to take care of it. Her husband far outranks the Monsignor, and for all the fine English lace and embroidery I have given her, I'm sure she wouldn't mind doing this small favor."

17

Palace Gossip

July 1623
Madrid, Spain

While Prince Charles and Princess Maria took Catechism in the inner chambers of the Alcazar, Anne sat with the doñas and the young ladies of the court in the flagstone courtyard, shaded by orange trees. A small creek ran through the rest area. The sound of rippling water and bees buzzing amidst the orange blossoms left Anne longing for another cup of café to brighten her drowsy mind. A servant replenished her cup and quickly followed it with a dash of cream.

Anne had agreed to teach the English pastime of embroidery to the ladies of the Spanish court, but the doñas could not focus on the needlework. Although the story was weeks old, all they could talk about was the humble Father Eremitz and the horrible injustice perpetrated upon him by English ruffians who dared to fancy themselves noblemen. They spoke in heavily accented English, but broke into rapid Spanish when discussing the English barbarians. The phrase "Inglés Bárbaros" came up a lot.

"He was beaten for no other reason than being a man of God," said Adelena, who was known to provide the best gossip."They are jealous of his holiness," a young marquesa chimed in.

Anne feigned naïveté as she adjusted the embroidery frame on her lap. "Here is how you make a rose petal with a satin stitch," she said, raising her needle to show the red silk thread. The women were too busy gossiping to listen.

Two men approached their table, unnoticed by the gabbing doñas who had their backs to them. Buckingham walked alongside the dark, handsome Father Eremitz, his cuts and bruises a distant memory for his smooth, tanned face. Anne dropped her embroidery and bent low to retrieve it, hoping to remain unseen by Buckingham. The two men passed, ignoring the enclave of ladies.

Anne heard the priest say, "There are many courtiers seeking influence over the king. Those at a distance have no advantage."

The two walked quickly out of earshot. Anne longed to follow them and hear more. She brought her embroidery hoop up from the ground.

"It is he! It is Father Eremitz! Did you see him pass?" Adelena exclaimed.

One of the ladies put her handkerchief to her eyes and sent up a tearful prayer to the Madonna.

An elderly doña commented, "Lady Adelena is most fond of the beautiful priest."

The other doñas gasped.

"Well," Adelena huffed, "certainly no more than any other faithful servant of God. Any priest as holy as Father Eremitz deserves our deepest affection."

"Exactly," said the old doña. "As we all know, there are many kinds of love, including holy love." She kept her smile demure as the other ladies broke into peals of laughter.

"Did you hear about the fire at the theater?" the young marquesa asked.

The doñas glanced at one another.

"There was a fire?" Anne asked. She had already heard the news from Kitty but thought if she asked the doñas they might offer new details.

"Not a big one," said the older woman, "but enough to cause a stir."

"Oh, yes," said the marquesa. "Queen Isabella's dear friend from the French court, Lord Tassis, swept her up in his arms and carried her out. Can you imagine? Now, everyone is wondering about, well, you know."

"Why would they wonder about anything?" Adelena asked, her face terse. "I happen to know Lord Tassis personally. His honor is above reproach. Moreover, he does not accompany the queen to such events to provide amusement. It is his duty to protect her. He performed his duty faithfully and well. Our lovely queen could have been burnt to a cinder, God forbid, or trampled in the panic at the exit. So, as anyone can see, there is nothing to discuss."

"He is very handsome, you know," the marquesa continued. "Far more so than the king."

At this remark, Adelena waved her arm.

Anne turned to see whom she was signaling. Duchess Olivares sat nearby with a local lord and his lady. She rose at once and approached their table. She was not a tall woman, but when her animal spirits were stirred, her solid figure beneath a stiff brocade bodice and thick taffeta skirts could be imposing.

"What have we here?" she asked when she arrived.

"Dear Lady Olivares," Adelena said, glaring at the young marquesa, "it appears some of us are confused about the incident at the theater. I am sure you could explain what transpired better than I."

"Indeed," Lady Olivares said, clasping her hands at her waist. "A fire broke out at the theater last Tuesday. Our queen's very life was in danger. Thankfully, a member of her coterie rushed to her rescue. As a result, she is now safe in the palace. The House of Hapsburg and the people of Spain are grateful to Lord Tassis, who saved her life." She paused, slowly nodding her head. "Unfortunately, there are rascals lurking about the brothels and back alleyways, initiating gossip about our fair queen. This will not do. Such malicious gossip is a grave insult to our king, and thereby an insult to all of Spain. Such slander to the crown is punishable by incarceration and flogging." The duchess turned her gaze on the marquesa. "If you hear anyone slandering our virtuous queen, with even the slightest innuendo, you will be sure to report it to me at once, won't you, Marquesa Urda?"

The marquesa stared at the duchess, her eyes widened by fear. "Of course," she answered in a hoarse whisper.

The duchess smiled and bid them good day before returning to her companions.

The uncomfortable moment passed, and the doñas returned to safer ground with gossip about the suffering priest and the English barbarians. Anne slipped her embroidery accouterments into a velvet drawstring bag, bid the doñas farewell, and hurried to the House of the Seven Chimneys.

Now that poor John Washington had passed, the English embassy functioned as a funeral home, as well as a hotel and ambassador's residence. The grand house was still teeming with Englishmen paying their last respects. Anne wondered if Ambassador Digby would be available for a meeting.

Laura Digby served dainty cookies and lemonade to her husband and their guests.

In the warm summer weather, the fireplace displayed a massive bouquet of roses and lilies framed by the ornate walnut mantel. The tall, slender windows of the study were hung with white sheers that filtered the direct sunlight and filled the room with a hazy glow.

Anne accepted a cool glass of lemonade from her hostess.

"It must be warm outside, judging from your flushed cheeks," said Lady Digby.

"Indeed, it is," said Anne. "The coach I rode in was as stuffy as a brick oven." She downed the contents of the crystal tumbler in three gulps and sighed as she placed the cup next to her cheek, grateful to absorb its chill. "I do thank you for assembling so quickly at my request," she said. "I have important news."

Gregory Mack poured himself a second glass of lemonade and added some brandy. "I'm ready to hear a good story about our wily Jesuit priest and confessor of Englishmen," he said.

"I saw Father Eremitz walking shoulder to shoulder with Buckingham in the palace gardens," said Anne.

"And the plot thickens," said Gregory. "How does the priest fare?"

"His scars have healed, but the doñas regard him a martyr all the more."

Gregory and Harald looked at each other and shook their heads.

"If the Jesuit's plan was to cast the English in a bad light, he did a good job of it," Anne continued.

"How the devil does Buckingham know this Jesuit?" asked John Digby.

"I don't know," said Anne.

"Did they see you there?" asked Harald.

"No. I dropped my embroidery and hid behind the table until they passed. I caught a brief part of their conversation. Eremitz said, 'There are many courtiers seeking influence over the king. Those at a distance have no advantage. 'At least, that is what I recall."

"Which king was he referring to?" asked Harald. "Our own King James, or King Philip?"

"I don't know," said Anne. "But if Eremitz is screening English mail, he could be well-informed on King James's state of mind."

"And his health," said John Digby. "Perhaps we should take the priest's remark about distance literally. If Buckingham feels an urge to make a swift return to London, he could become more unstable than ever."

Gregory turned toward Digby. "His departure could be beneficial. Buckingham's a diplomatic amateur, but he won't stop meddling. Once he's gone, we can resume negotiations on a better footing."

"Buckingham won't go without the prince!" Digby said, slamming his hand on the table.

The room fell silent.

"This marriage negotiation is going horribly awry," said Anne. "We must stabilize it."

"A garden party might do it," said Lady Digby. "One that begins just before sunset and goes long into the night. Let the wine and spirits flow."

"I agree," said Anne. "Officialdom stifles the human soul. A good, long party could break down petty grudges and build camaraderie. I know the perfect place to hold a fiesta. The merchant renting the villa next to ours would love to host. You know who I mean, Harald."

"The Taverniers," nodded Harald. "Quality people. Gabriel Tavernier has been hinting he would like to throw a grand soirée."

"They've traveled the world over and they're incredibly wealthy," Anne explained, "But they don't have the social standing to invite people of rank. If Harald and I were to host, we could send out the invitations and the Taverniers could provide the venue."

"Very well then," said Lady Digby. "A garden party, it is. And I would be happy to assist you with the task of sending out invitations, Lady Anne."

"You are most kind, My Lady," said Anne. "I will make a list of guests. Kitty and I can dream up amusements for our party."

"Gabriel Tavernier has a fine collection of telescopes," Harald volunteered. "They will either make a wonderful impression, or we'll all get burned alive by the Spanish Inquisition for looking too closely at God's work."

18

The Garden Party

August 1623
Madrid, Spain

The second week of August brought harvests of hay and hemp. The reapers arrived at dawn with scythes and baling ties. At noon, mules pulled the carts to the barns. By half past one, the fields and roads were deserted. Even the English visitors took a siesta in the heat of the day. In the last hour of sunlight, the farmers began burning the stubbly fields as a steady breeze blew the smoke away from the Tavernier's estate. The sun slipped behind the low mountain range, turning the thin clouds that reclined along the horizon various shades of pink.

Jean Baptiste, Gabriel Tavernier's 15-year-old son, placed a maple box on a table the servants had set up on the lawn beyond the terrace. He carefully lifted the lid, removed the polished brass telescope from its velvet case, and gingerly set it down on the linen tablecloth.

Prince Charles reached into the maple box for the poles that made up the stand and handed them to his valet, Isley, who offered them up as Charles started piecing the telescope stand together.

Varney, the prince's other valet and guard, sidled up to the fifteen-year-old astronomer. "Jean Baptiste, please assist the prince closely, but subtly," he whispered. "I don't believe he has ever assembled a telescope, but he wants to impress the infanta."

The infanta was resplendent in a blood-orange velvet bodice that matched in color her satin skirt, which billowed above layers of taffeta petticoats. Having discovered the velvet-lined case, she reached in and brought out little packets. She opened one and looked inside to discover small leather washers.

"Your Highness," Jean Baptiste said with a hint of alarm, "we cannot mix these things up or we'll never get the telescope to stand properly."

"Tell me what to do," said Maria, dropping the packets back into the case. "I catch on quickly."

Jean Baptiste picked up a small pouch of brass gears and carefully spilled them onto the tablecloth. "You could sort these according to size, if you wish. We shall need them in a moment."

Maria huffed and turned her nose up to the gears. "I shall sit here and watch you and our mechanical prince do it," she said, flouncing her flame-colored skirts before perching on a lacquered chair. Varney rushed over to plop a velvet cushion onto the seat of the chair just as the princess sat. "Then I will know what to do and what not to do," the princess added, glancing up at Varney and nodding.

Jean Baptiste stood next to Isley and handed Prince Charles the correct washers and gears, subtly indicating which ones went where. The three young men worked swiftly, fearing the infanta would insist on helping if they failed to assemble the telescope promptly.

Gabriel Tavernier had spared no expense in preparing his villa for the party. The chairs and sofas in the parlor were reupholstered in heavy gold silk. The drapes shimmered in Champagne gold. Bright bouquets of crimson roses and orange gladioluses decked every room. The overall effect was rich, but merry. A staff of liveried servants emerged to light scores of candles propped in crystal chandeliers and floor candelabras.

Anne and Harald stood formally at the base of the stairs, slightly behind Duchess Olivares, whose husband would arrive later with King Philip and Queen Isabella.

Anne glanced over at Buckingham to see if he was still spread out along a tufted brocade couch, seemingly determined to keep it all to himself.

"What is he doing here?" Harald murmured. "Does he even know what a salon is? I'm fairly certain he'll be bored out of his mind."

"He isn't here for the salon," Anne said with a mysterious half-smile.

Duchess Olivares clapped her hands. "Ladies and gentlemen," she announced, "we are most grateful to our kind hosts, Duke and Duchess Audley, as well as their dear friend, Monsieur Tavernier, who was so generous as to put his lovely home at our disposal. We have a medley of amusements for our youthful guests, but for those of us with a philosophical nature, we invite you to remain here, in the parlor, for our salon. This evening's topic: What purpose is served by scientific pursuits in regard to civilized society and the human spirit?"

Harald looked at Anne with widened eyes, as if he had seen a ghost. He leaned in to whisper. "A discussion on the purpose of science? Here? In the kingdom of the Spanish Inquisition?"

Anne whispered back, "I suggested the idea. The duchess sought counsel from her husband, and he approved it. I suspect, the prime minister is determined to put our friend, the papal nuncio, in his place."

"And now," Duchess Olivares continued, "may I introduce tonight's special guest and surprise dignitary, Sir Francis Bacon!"

She clapped to get the applause started. The guests were hesitant at first but stood and clapped loud and long as Gabriel Tavernier appeared at the top of the stairs with the elderly Sir Francis Bacon on his arm.

Anne glanced up at Harald to gage his reaction. He returned her gaze with a look of admiration laced with awe. She was pleased he understood without further explanation. After being blamed for Buckingham's petty corruption and criminality regarding bribes and extortion at the Royal Patent Office, Sir Francis Bacon had been incarcerated at the Tower of London by royal decree. He was forced to bargain for his life, and then his freedom, by signing nearly everything he owned over to Buckingham.

While Bacon had had a great number of friends before his incarceration, he had practically none when he emerged. Several admirers, Harald among them, had pitched in to secure a modest pension for him so he wouldn't descend into squalor. But even so, Bacon was so humiliated by his circumstances that he permanently removed himself from London society. In addition to keeping Buckingham transfixed, Anne had hoped Sir Francis would find a true friend in Gabriel Tavernier, a man who revered brilliant freethinkers, despite their fall from grace.

"So long as Sir Francis holds forth in the parlor," Anne whispered, "Buckingham will hang on his every word, because he knows if he leaves, a drunken Englishman might bring up the scandal."

"Like myself, for instance?" Harald asked.

Anne punched him playfully. "I am counting on you to keep the conversation with our gentleman scientist going, and keep Buckingham under your watchful eyes, so Sir Gregory and Sir Kenhelm can perform their duties in peace."

Next door, in the Audley's study, Kenhelm spilled a handful of pastel petit-fours topped with sugared violets and fondant bows onto an end table and took a gulp from his wineglass. The room was large but cozy. Pots of robust ferns stood on each side of the mahogany fireplace. Gregory took a seat. Kenhelm brought an ottoman into position with a kick and sat down.

"Is that what you are wearing to the party?" Sir Gregory asked.

Kenhelm glanced down at his attire, barely remembering what he had on. He ran one hand along the soft, worn leather of his favorite jerkin. His brown corduroy breeches were hardly new, but perfectly decent. For the first time that evening, he noticed Sir Gregory's attire: a black velvet doublet with suede trim, matching breeches, and black leather boots. At his neck was a small, neat, Elizabethan collar.

"I'm perfectly comfortable in my attire," Kenhelm said defensively.

"A mite too comfortable, I would say," said Gregory. "Did you not know King Philip plans to make an appearance? The lovely infanta is already here."

Kenhelm lifted his chin in defiance. "Being well-versed in international intrigue, I deliberately chose this attire to better fade into the crowd. Even in these drab garments, I assure you, I will attract far more attention from the señoritas than you, which is the exact opposite of what I want."

Sir Gregory had no rebuttal. Kenhelm found his stare uncomfortable, nonetheless. He took another gulp of wine, popped a petit-four into his mouth, and thoughtfully chewed as he stared back at Gregory.

"You can have all the sweets you want," said Gregory, "but that will be your last glass of spirits for the night."

Kenhelm swallowed. "I have a pretty good idea how to start the fire in the garden house."

"You are not starting a fire in the garden house," said Gregory.

"But I thought—"

"I will start the fire. I'm an experienced arsonist."

"May I assist you?" Kenhelm asked. "I am very good at following instructions."

"Varney will assist me. I need you to keep Father Eremitz distracted," said Gregory.

Kenhelm deflated into a slouch. “I can amuse him for an hour or so,” he said. “But if he asks me to leave after that, I won’t have much choice, will I?”

“An hour will be plenty of time,” said Gregory. “Get out your pocket watch.”

They both reached into their pockets and pulled out their gold watches.

“Your watch is running five minutes behind mine,” said Gregory. “Wind it up and set it for a quarter of eight. At ten p.m., meet me at the Tavernier’s dock on the river. From there, we can follow the river path to Eremitz’s property. It’s the shortest route.”

“Very well. Anything else?” asked Kenhelm, syncing his watch with Gregory’s.

“If Eremitz smells smoke, remind him the farmers are burning the fields. The breeze will blow the smoke away from the party, but it makes a plausible excuse, should the priest notice the fire right away. Aside from that, stay close.” Gregory slipped his watch into the pocket of his loose breeches. “I’ll be wandering between the salon in the parlor and the telescope party in the garden beyond the terrace.”

“That’s what I planned to do,” said Kenhelm.

“I don’t want you hovering about me,” said Gregory.

“Then I will be at the telescopes while you’re loitering in the salon.”

Gregory took in a deep breath. “A raucous dartboard party is warming up in the billiards room,” he ventured.

"Why don't you fraternize with the young lords and gather information until we meet at ten?"

"Without drinking a drop of wine or ale?" Kenhelm mocked him with raised eyebrows. "How could I possibly do that without looking conspicuous?"

Gregory shook his head. "Fine, then. Do what you please but stay out of my way."

The servants lit the torches on the grass. The flames shimmered against the dusky sky, lighting up the faces of the party revelers. A guitar player strolled onto the lawn, singing in a clear tenor voice. He was trailed by three sopranos who sang the chorus. They were clad in white dresses with scooped necklines and billowing sleeves.

Kenhelm sauntered around the performers, enjoying the ambiance. He could follow the Spanish language just enough to know it was a song about star-crossed lovers. The female singers played the roles of the lonely señorita and her two officious aunts.

As night descended, the villa's windows glowed from the blazing candlelight within. From the double-French doors that opened onto the terrace, Harald Audley's resonant voice boomed across the green. Kenhelm wandered onto the flagstones and entered the parlor.

Hundreds of candles flickered from a battalion of floor candelabras and a grand chandelier that hung from the ceiling. Sir Francis Bacon looked more haggard than the first time Kenhelm had seen him, but the lively conversation brought color to his sunken cheeks. He wore his capotain hat at a jaunty angle as he talked about astronomy.

"We now have new parameters of cosmic reality," he exclaimed. "Galileo has proven Copernicus right. The earth is not the center of the universe. Neither is the sun. Indeed, our sun is just one star among the myriad in the cosmos. It appears much larger, due to its close proximity, much like a horse standing next to you appears much larger than a horse one mile down the road. These revelations force scholars to question every assumption ever made about creation."

"Some say," Gabriel Tavernier cut in, "that scientific discoveries pose a threat to religious authority, Catholic and Protestant alike. How does one reconcile science with religion?"

Buckingham looked bored and out of place amongst the intellectuals, although his eyes rarely left Lord Bacon, who never once looked at him.

"East is east, and west is west," Lord Bacon declared. "The Bible is not a science book, and there is no heresy in stating this, for not a single biblical prophet has made such a claim. Clergymen minister to the human soul and concern themselves with the higher truth of spiritual matters. Meanwhile, scientific discovery adheres to material fact. Advances in science are forged as scientists share their discoveries with their peers, who, in turn, must repeat the experiments and achieve the same results. If scientific discovery cannot be proven by peer review, it is not science, pure and simple. In this manner, science and religion shall not conflict, but shall live peacefully, side by side."

After a lengthy pause, Lord Bacon's remarks were met with gentle applause and murmured admiration. Kenhelm looked at Buckingham and suppressed a laugh. The duke's usual habit of dominating a conversation was thwarted by an obvious lack of intellect.

Having grown bored with the heady intellectualism, Kenhelm wandered outside, onto the lawn, then loitered at the edge of the crowd waiting to look through the telescope. A ruckus behind him made him turn. The party revelers parted and two men bounded onto the lawn, both clad in black-and-gold livery and fool's caps. Akira, the young Japanese sword master, appeared hot on their heels, his fearsome helmet topped by a long, thin crescent. His red-lacquered armor flashed in the torchlight as he shrieked a series of war whoops and menaced the jesters with two wind-milling swords. The jesters stutter-stepped in terror. Akira rolled his eyes in a theatrical gesture of exasperation, sheathed his swords, and came at the two fools with a series of flamboyant punches and kicks. The two fools grunted and yelped as they leapt into backflips and flying summersaults, slyly clapping their hands to make it seem as if Akira was landing his blows. Kenhelm knew the fools were actually formidable guardsmen, hired by the Taverniers and trained by Akira.

After a vigorous romp, the show wrapped up, and the three performers leapt to standing positions. Arms outstretched, they bowed. The crowd applauded.

Kenhelm spotted Kitty. The instant their eyes met, she trotted toward him, her décolletage struggling to break free from the strict confines of her topaz-tinted silk bustier. He had never seen her look so fetching.

"Thank goodness you're here," she said. "I need you to keep an eye on Prince Charles. I must go inside."

"Why? Is that where Akira is changing from his costume?"

"Shame on you," Kitty hissed. She picked up her voluminous skirts and trotted toward the warm glow of the parlor, her gilded brown curls bouncing as she went.

Kenhelm groaned. He had no idea how long she would be, and for all of his ogling, he had forgotten to tell her he was at Sir Gregory's beck and call and had to leave near the stroke of ten. He couldn't exactly shout it. When he turned toward the guests gathering around the telescope, he noticed Sir Varney and Sir Isley hovering around the prince and infanta. It seemed to Kenhelm the two valets had everything in hand. The Amerindian was pointedly not invited to the party, so Kenhelm could see no harm in keeping his appointment with Sir Gregory.

The party guests passed spyglasses of varying sizes amongst themselves as they waited their turn at the large telescope, which spanned four feet. Jean Baptiste took the telescope and aimed it carefully, peering into the eyepiece and rotating the knob. He nodded at Princess Maria. "I've sighted the larger of the two novae," he said.

She approached the telescope and peered into it with one wide-open eye. "Oh! It's like a blooming rose inside a bubble of fire!" She turned toward Charles. "In our home, we must have one of these. I will need to watch all the stars every night."

The young lords and ladies crowded forward for a view of the novae. Prince Charles readjusted the lens as necessary. Seeing she was not going to run the telescope, Maria took charge of the crowd and made certain nobody tried to have a second look before others had their first.

Anne joined the revelers crowding around the telescope and wove her arm into Doña Adelena's—a bold move, considering the governess's disapproval of the salon's topic of discussion. Adelena did not pull away from Anne's gentle grasp. Instead, she launched into a lecture about uncivilized Englishmen bringing their dangerous ideas into a God-fearing country. While vociferous in her dislike of the English, the dowager had dyed her gray hair blonde and wore it in long ringlets clustered about her ears, just as Anne and Kitty wore theirs. Their signature hairstyle had caught on in Madrid, as it had in London.

Anne nodded and made sympathetic noises until Adelena's diatribe wound down to an "Ay, Maria! Tsk, tsk, tsk." The governess paused, her breaths short and quick. "And, after all of that, the dear priest was so kind as to give an amazing gift to King Philip and Queen Isabella—a collection of tiny, exotic frogs from the jungles of the Amazon, more beautiful to behold than gems. They are poisonous, of course."

Anne's blood ran cold. Kenhelm had told them of the frogs. They all suspected they were toxic, and a likely source of the Amerindian's powerful poison.

"Beautiful, yet poisonous frogs," said Anne. "That's a strange gift. Did Father Eremitz say why he was donating them to the royal couple?"

"He is a kind and generous man," Adelena exclaimed, as if schooling a dullard. "What more reason does he need? The frogs have been confined in a net-lined latticed gazebo, along with their ferns, their pond, and whatnot, so no need to worry about the venom. My own gardener supervised the installation in the place gardens."

"That is most kind," said Anne.

"Well, they are family," said Adelena.

"Really," Anne feigned surprise.

"I am a royal cousin to King Philip and the infanta. You didn't know?"

Adelena was actually their second-cousin. Anne pretended to be amazed.

As she looked across Adelena's shoulder, the sight of Father Eremitz's noble face, half-lit by a torch, jolted her. She shifted her gaze back to Adelena so she would not catch on and call attention to his presence. As she continued her conversation, her eyes searched for Kenhelm. She spotted him at the far side of the crowd.

"Oh, I must have a word with Sir Kenhelm," Anne said, unwrapping her arm from Adelena's. "Please excuse me. I shall return promptly."

"I doubt that," Adelena grumbled.

Just as Kenhelm wondered if he could take a peek into the telescope without attracting Sir Gregory's notice, Anne was at his elbow.

"Kenhelm, don't look now," she said.

"I wasn't going to," he replied, irritated.

"What? You know?"

"Uh, know what?" he looked puzzled.

"When I return to Doña Adelena, casually look past us, but to the right. Think carefully before you make your move. I shall leave the matter to your good judgment." She turned and rushed back to the infanta's governess.

Mystified, he slowly looked to her right. His heart leapt to see Eremitz's melancholy profile in the torchlight. Kenhelm suppressed a smile. The solitary priest, likely overcome by loneliness and boredom, had heard the boisterous party from his house and snuck in from the riverbank like a common vagabond.

Kenhelm scanned the crowd for Gregory Mack and spotted him standing by the terrace. To Kenhelm's relief, he caught Gregory's eye. Kenhelm raised his index finger to Gregory, signaling him to wait.

Weaving his way through the crowd, Kenhelm headed toward Eremitz. Approaching him from the side, he put a hand on his shoulder and murmured into his ear, "My dear friend."

Eremitz's cool expression softened as he turned his eyes on his former protégé. The animal magnetism was too powerful to ignore.

"I am at your service, as always," said Kenhelm.

"I was hoping to find you here," said Eremitz. "I was reluctant to attend at first, as I have much important business, but I am quite fond of the Taverniers. They are well-traveled, and quite interesting in conversation, wouldn't you say?"

"I could not agree more," said Kenhelm.

A shrill voice rose from the crowd. "The king is here! Bow to the king, one and all!"

It was Doña Adelena. She drew her skirts up and pointed her toe as she dipped into a deep, wobbly curtsy. The king received her gesture with a nod. The beautiful Queen Isabella seemed amused for all the wrong reasons. Framed by chocolaty curls, the queen's large brown eyes glittered with intelligence.

Kenhelm did an involuntary double take as the queen's gaze briefly met his. When she glanced away, he slid his hand to Eremitz's far shoulder and turned him away from the crowd.

As they walked into the shadows of a stand of trees, Kenhelm leaned his head in to whisper, "Unfortunately, I happen to know you were not invited. This would not be a problem, except the Tavernier's are not the official hosts of the party. The host, or I should say, hostess, will smoke you out instantly and have an unpleasant fellow order you to leave. But have no fear. I can get several Spanish lords to insist you are their honored guest, but this may require an in-kind donation."

"I have little to donate," said Eremitz, annoyed. "The wages of a priest fall far short of my expenses."

"You have much to donate. I am referring to your delightful assortment of intoxicants."

"Hmm." Eremitz hesitated. "I would be happy to share, but I don't want a reputation for being a wizard of exotic spirits. Providing restorative potions is one thing. Being a debaucher of the young is quite another."

"A debaucher of the young." Kenhelm faked a low, theatrical laugh. "As if you were capable of such villainy. But I understand your concern. Perhaps we can go to your place, sample your wares, and contemplate this matter of debauching the young. We can return to the party around midnight, after the old doñas have gone to bed and the real fun begins."

"I like that plan much better," said Eremitz.

Kenhelm looked toward the party revelers. "Before we go, I must consult with, uh, a dear friend of mine. I must let him know I will be gone for a couple of hours. I don't want him to worry."

"Should I be jealous?"

"Jealous of what?" Kenhelm asked, his expression displaying the false innocence of the guilty. "Wait here for me."

Kenhelm joined Gregory.

"I see your friend has come, uninvited," said Gregory.

"Fear not. I have already updated our plan," said Kenhelm.

"Without consulting me?" Gregory asked. "What—"

"He and I shall go to his house and spend an hour or two in revelry," Kenhelm said, cutting him off. "I told him we could return to the party at midnight, and the fearsome hostess, who otherwise would order him to leave, will be either fast asleep or too drunk to notice."

"And how did you explain my presence in all of this?" Gregory asked. "He is glancing our way."

"I insinuated you and I are lovers. Be sure to look jealous as I unconvincingly assure you my reasons for spending time alone with the priest are completely innocent."

"You told him we were lovers?" Gregory scowled.

Kenhelm wished his uncle John could witness how expertly he had drawn the ideal expression from Sir Gregory's face.

"I shall keep him occupied for one hour, at least, hopefully two. Don't push your luck." At that, Kenhelm spun around and headed back to Eremitz.

19

Fire

A tipsy young lord pushed his way to the front of the line, insisting on a second turn at the telescope. Varney pushed him back, gently but firmly.

"Order, order," said Princess Maria, clapping her hands. She continued to ensure everyone got their chance to look through the telescope.

Sir Gregory glanced at his pocket watch. He wanted to give Kenhelm enough time to distract Eremitz. Thirteen minutes seemed enough, perhaps too much. Gregory drifted to the outer edge of the revelers and ducked into the shadows to pick up the lantern and leather satchel Kitty had left at the far side of an oak tree. Just as he turned toward the river path, a slender hand slipped around his elbow and held fast. He turned to see a familiar pair of blue eyes mere inches from his face.

"Isn't Varney going to assist you?" Anne asked breathlessly. Her dark satin gown disappeared in the shadows except for swaths of bright ocean blue that gleamed in the lamplight, but her face and hair shone under the moon like a pearl set in gold.

"No. He has been assigned to watch the prince," said Gregory, "although it is the infanta who fascinates him, as anyone can see."

"Who will act as your lookout?"

"I don't need a lookout, M'Lady. I work much better alone."

"Of course, you need a lookout," said Anne. "Did you not see what just happened? Our mysterious priest appeared out of thin air."

"I cannot be hindered, Lady Audley. My time is limited."

"Then why do we tarry?" she asked, tugging on his arm. "Let us go."

"But, you cannot act as a lookout."

"Why on earth not?"

"With your bright hair and your pale complexion, you can be seen from a half mile, even in the dark!"

Anne pulled a black chiffon scarf from the folds of her skirt and flipped it onto her head, crossing the beaded ends over her shoulders, thereby shrouding her gleaming hair and pale décolletage.

"Your face is still quite bright," said Gregory.

"Oh, for heaven's sake. I will cover it thus, if need be," said Anne, placing a lacy, black-gloved hand over her face like a sprawling starfish. She peeked at Gregory between her fingers and they both laughed.

"You're incorrigible," said Gregory. "If you insist on coming along, you are not to leave my side. And bear in mind, 'tis a better thing to botch this mission entirely than to risk even a scratch upon Lord Audley's precious wife."

"Nonsense," she said. "We're wasting time. Let's be on our way."

Adelena had not taken her eyes off of Anne since she had left her side to converse with the handsome English lord. When they slipped into the shadows, Adelena rushed to follow them. She hated leaving the infanta's side, insofar as she alone was responsible for her virtue. However, she reasoned, the princess was surrounded by noble guests. What could possibly happen during her brief absence?

She had to rely on the bit of residual light from the Englishman's lantern up ahead to keep from stumbling. Tufts of grass flashed into view, framed by the inky darkness, as the shameless lovers ambled on to their secret tryst.

Adelena stumbled and fell to her knees, planting her hands in the damp sand to avoid a headlong crash. She picked herself up, dusted off her skirt, and forged ahead, her heart racing from the thrill of schadenfreude. Lady Audley put on an excellent pretense of propriety, but now the entire Spanish court would know the truth: English women were incapable of fidelity. No wonder the English had abandoned the true religion. It was the women! Goodness gracious, would she have a story to tell once she returned to her fellow doñas.

Anne held up the lantern, its front panel open just enough to cast a narrow beam on the padlock securing the garden house. Gregory stuck a metal pick into the lock and twisted until the upper loop popped up. The door creaked open, and Anne followed him in. She slipped the lantern's panel aside to shed light on the opulent foliage within the glimmering glass-paned walls.

Gregory glanced at the corner to his left. Two rough vertical lines at the right and left of the bare corner indicated a floor-to-ceiling structure had been removed.

"Isn't this where the fanciful frogs were supposed to be?" he asked.

"Oh, I just chatted with Doña Adelena," said Anne. "She told me Eremitz gave the frogs to the royal couple as a gift for the palace gardens. She also confirmed they are Amazonian and highly poisonous."

"Hmm," Gregory said thoughtfully. "Now, we need to learn whether Eremitz did so under orders from the papal nuncio or whether he made the decision on his own."

Beyond the garden house, the fires in the fields streaked across the warped windowpanes in flickering red lines. The farmers had taken care to keep them at a distance.

"Those fires are too far away to ignite this greenhouse," said Anne. "How can that be explained?"

"There are several pine trees nearby," Gregory replied. "Yesterday, I examined the roof through a spyglass. The wooden slats that divide the glass panes are handy traps for dry pine needles. Just a few sparks could set them ablaze."

"Then let's be quick about this before the wind does the task for us," said Anne. "Is this the worktable Kenhelm told us of?" She walked to the large wooden table, knelt down, and lifted the thick oilcloth hanging over the edge. "Here's the teak chest," she said.

"Allow me." Gregory slid the chest toward him and lifted it onto the table.

Anne ran her fingers along the ornately carved figures on the lid. "Pity to burn something so refined."

"There's no avoiding it," said Gregory as he picked the brass lock. "It has to be incinerated."

As Gregory retrieved two rolled bags from the large one he had brought, Anne set the lantern down and cleared a large space on the table. They tamped and stuffed a flurry of letters and documents into the bags. Once done with that task, Anne ferreted out every bag of dried herbs she could find and dumped their contents onto the wooden worktable, tossing the empty muslin bags on top of the mess. Harald tore the largest muslin bag into strips, then tied them together to make two long strands. He gave one to Anne. She imitated him as he draped one strand from the edge of the table to the ground, using a clay pot to anchor it.

Gregory removed four flasks from the satchel and soaked each of the strips in white rum. "Dear Lady Anne, your skirts are full and I fear for them. Now would be a good time to step out and look around. Please don't leave the threshold until I join you."

Anne stepped out into the cool night air, leaving the door open behind her. Gregory replaced the empty chest beneath the table, placed an alcohol-soaked rag beneath it, and doused the chest and table above with the rum. He walked a trail of rum around the perimeter of the greenhouse. Standing in the doorway, he put a stick to the lantern's flame to light it and set it on the ground. The liquid trail leapt to life with a pale blue and pink flame that raced like a snake through the glass house.

Anne watched the flames flicker through the warped glass panes. The tropical plants withered in the heat. "Sad to watch this magnificent garden burn," she said.

Gregory fished dry sticks from his satchel, lit them in the lantern, and tossed them on the roof, one by one. The small piles of pine needles quickly ignited in the myriad corners of the panes. A spray of sparks flew toward Gregory and Anne. She picked up her skirts and ran, Gregory following close behind. The windowpanes popped and the flames rose through the roof like the tongues of hellish beasts.

As they hurried along the riverbank, they spied two shadowy men ambling along the path. Thinking quickly, Anne ran toward them.

"Oh, dear! Oh, dear!" she cried out. "Our neighbor's garden house has gone up in flames!"

Gregory crowded behind her. "The sparks from the field fires must have ignited the pine needles on the roof."

"Why, Lady Audley," said the closer of the two men. In the firelight, Anne could make out his aquiline nose, pointed beard, and velvet tam.

"Señor Peter Paul Rubens?" she exclaimed.

"Yes, yes. I was conversing with my fellow artists and sundry musicians when the wine ran out. We were journeying back to the house when my dear friend, Señor Diego Velasquez, turned and said—"

Rubens turned toward Velasquez, who was swaying a bit on his heels, his face framed by a shock of black hair, his mustachio curled at the edges for the special occasion.

"What did you say, comrade?" Rubens asked.

Velasquez struck a theatrical pose with his hand in the air. "I said, 'Hark, the flames are closer and higher!'"

"And I said," Rubens hiccupped, morbid fumes of garlic and alcohol wafting from his lips, "something over there is on fire! So, we came to inspect."

Kenhelm lay on the bed, a messy pile of sheets at his feet. The white curtains at the window glowed with the shifting orange light from the fire outside. He glanced over at Eremitz, sprawled naked beside him with his hand on his groin, lightly snoring. With any luck, he would sleep right through it.

The sound of approaching footsteps caught his attention.

Kenhelm quickly rolled off the bed to the rug below, effectively concealing himself, thankful the door was on Eremitz's side. The door burst open. There was a rustling of taffeta skirts and a sharp shriek.

"Oh, Father Eremitz! Oh, do please cover yourself!" Kenhelm recognized the distinctively shrill voice of Doña Adelena. "I shall shield my eyes," she said, "but I must not depart until I report to you that the blonde Englishwoman, the so-called Lady Audley, invaded your garden house for a tryst with her lover, and while this wicked woman was in the throes of her passion, she kicked over a lantern like a cow in heat and set your garden house on fire! Have you ever heard anything so scandalous?"

"Please, get out." Eremitz's voice was surprisingly calm.

"But—"

"Get out."

Eremitz slowly walked toward the latticed inferno, spellbound. The panes burst intermittently, sending shards of glass flying. Some hit Eremitz in the face, but he failed to react, stunned at the knowledge his personal effects were being incinerated in the raging fire. Every letter of recommendation, every document that proved his aristocratic titles and lines of inheritance, gone. Massimi was right, and that was the worst part of it. Kenhelm had played him for the fool. He was obviously assigned to distract him while his English cohorts did their dirty work. But to what end?

The answer gradually dawned on him. It wasn't the poisons, or even intoxicants they were after, as one might naïvely suspect. It was the papers. Amidst the bric-a-brac of his identity and officialdom lay something of little value to Eremitz, but precious to his adversaries—secret letters and documents of English origin that Father Massimi had instructed him to keep safe. What a fool he had been to keep them among his personal effects. He had wondered at the time why Massimi didn't keep the documents with him, but now he knew. Once they located what they were looking for, it was his property the English spies ransacked and destroyed, not Massimi's.

Still numb from the knowledge his identity was being incinerated along with his papers, Eremitz was only vaguely surprised to discover the famous artists, Rubens and Velasquez, as he slowly paced around the fire. He overheard bits of their conversation as he passed by.

"I agree," said Velazquez, "red crimson, fading into vermillion would be a perfect choice of pigment for the flames, but why a burnt umber background? Why paint the night sky a morbid brown when you could build up glazes of cobalt blue, and get a true midnight sky?"

"At twenty francs an ounce? Who can afford an entire sky's worth of cobalt pigment at those prices?" Velasquez grumbled.

"It suppose it depends on how wealthy your patrons are," said Rubens.

The crackling flames drowned out their voices as Eremitz drew farther away. He could see Kenhelm lingering in the periphery but refused to look at him. He wanted to hate him for what he had done, but the emotion eluded him.

As he gazed upon the ruins of his life, an epiphany brighter than the flames blossomed in his mind. Kenhelm had not destroyed him but had handed Eremitz the keys to his ecclesiastical jail.

No one leaves The Keepers of the Kingdom. How often had Massimi reminded him? But where would The Keepers find Father Eremitz if there was no Father Eremitz to be found? While Eremitz could never conceive of destroying his own papers for lack of courage and imagination, Kenhelm had forcibly ripped him from his past. This, and nothing else, would break Massimi's iron grip.

Sparks drifted through the night air toward the party revelers gathered at the telescope. Princess Maria's blood-orange velvet bodice and satin skirts gleamed in the torchlight, the same color as the sparks.

"I smell smoke," she said.

Jean Baptiste looked up from the telescope. "The farmers are burning the fields."

"I know," said Maria, "but it smells different now. It's making me light-headed."

The party turned toward the burning fields. The thin line of flames beneath the horizon had burst into a bright conflagration that danced energetically above the field.

Prince Charles grabbed the telescope and swung it toward the flames. After a few second of peering into it, he declared, "I do believe that is a cottage engulfed by an unruly fire."

"It's the priest's garden house," cried a youth, barely fifteen.

"He's an apothecarist!" exclaimed an elderly doña. "Good glory! Imagine the mysterious intoxicants taking to the wind."

The lords and ladies took to sniffing the breeze with marked enthusiasm. Flurries of sparks flew above the nearby woods, and a few even drifted onto the grass near the telescope. While the prince stood with the telescope in hand and the infanta at his side, their entourage streamed off to see the fire.

"Isley," Prince Charles said, "Please go to the Alcazar and tell King Philip of the calamity. Make haste."

"I'm quite sure his own courtiers will inform him, Your Highness."

"We don't know that for certain," Charles insisted, "If he hears it from an Englishman first, it might raise our standing, which would be a welcome turn of events in the aftermath of the last-rites scandal."

Isley looked pointedly at Varney, before dipping into a bow. "As you wish, Your Highness." He raced off in the direction of the horse stables.

Charles frowned at Varney. "Shouldn't you inform Sir Audley of this alarming development?" he asked.

"Of course, I would under different circumstances, Your Highness, but I must not leave you alone. I am under strict orders—"

"Nonsense!" Charles exclaimed. "I am ordering you to tell him at once."

Varney stared, speechless. After an uncomfortable pause, he said, "As you wish, Your Highness. Please wait here. I shall return promptly."

"Be sure to tell him all you know," said Prince Charles. He watched as Varney trotted toward the house, then turned toward Jean Baptiste. "Shouldn't you inform your father of the fire?"

"Don't you suppose Sir Varney will?"

"I wouldn't count on that," said the prince, knitting his eyebrows in a pantomime of concern. "More likely he will take Lord Audley aside and whisper in his ear. If you wish your father to know of this crucial event, which may threaten the very roof over your heads, I suggest you do it yourself."

"As you wish, Your Highness," said the fifteen-year-old, his voice tinged with hesitation. "Can you take care of the telescope for me?"

The infanta piped up. "I will look after the telescope. You had best be on your way."

As Jean Baptiste strode off, Princess Maria was astounded to find herself alone with Prince Charles under the starry and somewhat smoky sky. The prince's ploy of sending his valets away on official business worked. In his nervousness, however, Charles fiddled with the telescope's adjustments. He peered through the lens every now and again as he tried to bring the larger of the two nebulae into focus. Maria fidgeted beside him.

Charles stepped back, triumphantly. "There's the big one. Take a look."

Maria peeked into the glass.

"Don't jiggle it, or I'll have to find it again," said Charles.

"I'm not jiggling," said Maria, "I'm just trying to see. Ooh, this one is green! It looks like a dragon's eye."

"I wonder how long they have been there. Even the astronomers speak of the nebulae as if they are recent arrivals," said Charles.

"What do you think they mean?" Maria wondered. "What are the heavens trying to tell us?"

"Johannes Kepler thinks they are actually very large objects but appear small because they are so far away."

The telescope slipped in Maria's hands as she became distracted by Charles. "Oh, dear, I can't see a thing, just a great blur of night." The prince's arms went around her as he reached for the device. He intended to readjust the alignment, but Maria slipped backward into his arms and placed her temple against his cheek.

Both forgot about the nebulae.

20

The Amboyna Incident

Anne hung in the shadows, hoping to remain unnoticed. Eremitz paced before the fire, his hair floating about his face like a daemon. Anne could only guess what he was thinking.

A member of the drunken fire brigade Gregory had hastily assembled rushed by with a sloshing bucket of water. He leapt forward, his back leg extended like a ballerino, and let the water fly. The soaring stream landed just short of the flames. The bright puddle sizzled at the edges as he stumbled back to the river for a refill. The others had barely more success with their buckets.

Anne looked about the gathering crowd for Kenhelm. Her heart raced when she failed to spot him.

"Gregory," she said, grabbing his arm. She put her lips to his ear. "I don't see Kenhelm anywhere," she whispered.

Gregory glanced about. "There he is," he said, nodding toward a quickly retreating figure. "He's heading back to the Taverniers."

Anne and Gregory rushed to catch up. Kenhelm's eyes were rimmed with tears. He snorted and swallowed when he saw them, as if trying to hide the evidence of his sorrow. Gregory put his arm around him and produced a handkerchief. Anne walked alongside them. They continued toward the Tavernier's estate.

"I had no idea this would be so difficult," said Kenhelm, with an embarrassed chuckle. "It caught me off guard."

"I'm truly sorry," said Anne. "We should have warned you."

Kenhelm shook his head. "Well, it's not as if he didn't deserve it. Even so, I feel like a scoundrel."

"He took advantage of your naïveté, years ago, at Amboyna," Gregory reminded him. "He didn't just betray you. Scores of Englishmen died on account of that betrayal."

Kenhelm shook his head and put his hand up to his eyes. "You forget, Eremitz lost his entire family when the natives attacked them."

"What happened there?" Anne asked. "I have heard of the Amboyna Massacre. Everyone mentions it, but no one talks about it."

Kenhelm dropped his head and stared at the ground.

Gregory took in a deep breath, then explained, "The Dutch Republic has been at war with the Roman Catholic Church for decades. Years ago, the Dutch captured the Isle of Ambon from Portuguese traders. It's a small, lush island in the Indonesian Archipelago, but it has a sizable harbor next to a broad beach, which makes it ideal for a port. The harbor allows the Dutch Republic to keep their ships safe from pirates and local tribes. The port allows them to collect all the goods they trade in the Orient, such as silks, spices, and tea, and ship them back to Europe in fleets that can easily ward off pirates.

"King James sent a contingent of English merchants and sailors to the Indonesian Archipelago to explore the possibility of trade with the Dutch. But the Dutch did not like their presence, assuming they had arrived to poach their territory.

"In response to the Dutch take-over, the Vatican sent a contingent of Italian, Spanish, and Portuguese traders to the island. They came with a group of Jesuits. Eremitz and his family were among them.

"Numerous times, the Catholics tried and failed to take the island back from the Dutch. Meanwhile, a worthless English rogue by the name of Michelbourne managed to wheedle King James into allowing him to charter a ship under the English flag. Upon arriving in the Orient, he pirated the first ship he saw, and continued pirating until he attacked a Dutch ship. The Dutch dealt with him by hiring Japanese mercenaries to attack his ship. The mercenaries didn't kill him, unfortunately, but they killed everyone else on board. Michelbourne barely escaped with his life and returned to England a ruined man.

"This incident gave the Italians an idea. In lieu of forcing the Dutch to return Amboyna to the Portuguese via military intervention, they would weaken their enemy by fracturing their bond with their strongest ally. They did so by utilizing the same Japanese mercenaries in a ploy to start a local war between the British and the Dutch traders in the vicinity.

"Their plot was simply to instruct the Japanese mercenaries to sneak onto the island and spy on the Dutch. The Italians who gave the orders to the Japanese told them they were Englishmen, knowing the Japanese could not tell the difference between Anglos and Latin-Europeans. Neither did the Japanese know that they would all be sacrificed as the plot played out.

"Once the mercenaries were in place, the Jesuits tipped off the Dutch that spies were operating on their island. When the Dutch captured and tortured the Japanese dupes, they confessed they were hired by the English.

"In the aftermath of Michelbourne's piracy, the Dutch easily believed Britain was plotting against them. They rounded up all the English merchants on the island and extracted false confessions by torture. They executed twenty of them. Four broken men were sent back to England to tell the tale."

Anne shook her head. "That was why Englishmen were clamoring for war with the Dutch Republic. I remember that. Thank heaven King James wasn't fooled. But what does this have to do with Kenhelm and Eremitz?"

"Eremitz knew," said Kenhelm in a flat voice. "For all I know, the entire plot could have been his making. He begged me to board a ship departing for England but refused to say why. I wouldn't go because my uncle had not yet called me home. How could I disgrace myself for no good reason? Eremitz drugged me and I awoke aboard the HMS Merryweather. He had put me under the charge of Father Mazin, a French priest and a good man, who looked after me and asked for nothing in return, except good humor. We reached Plymouth in ten weeks, and I didn't hear about the massacre for another fortnight."

"What happened to Eremitz's family?" Anne asked.

"Many of them were ambushed and murdered by local natives, just before the Portuguese traders tricked the

Japanese into being their dupes," said Gregory. "The Latin survivors of the first massacre didn't know if it was the English or the Dutch who set the natives on their throats, but they were certain it was one or the other."

"It could have been either of them," said Kenhelm. "They both wanted to drive the Portuguese trading company out of the territory."

Anne looked at Gregory, hoping he would give her a signal that Kenhelm would soon recover from his cynicism. Gregory looked at his boots. The three of them trudged back to the party in silence.

21

The Little Quarrel

Leading Princess Maria by the hand, Prince Charles held out the lantern as they forged through a grove of towering cork oaks. The tree trunks lit up in a deep gold, making the black spaces between them all the darker. The oaks gave way to a broad meadow of dewy grass and wildflowers, glimmering silver beneath a bright full moon. Charles's heart soared. He had led the infanta away without notice.

"We can get a better view of the night sky out here," Charles said, setting the lantern down at the meadow's edge. He doffed his cloak, twirling it toward the ground to spread it on a mass of clover, the royal-blue satin lining facing up. He took Princess Maria's hand and they both descended onto the spread, gazing at each other, breathless with anticipation. Charles reached into his breast pocket. Retrieving a small parcel from it, he said, "I brought you a gift."

"What is it? What have you brought me?"

"Be not hasty, dear Princess Maria. It is not dignified," Charles teased.

She grinned and wiggled her fingers greedily. He laid the parcel in her eager hands. Maria unwrapped the gold-shot blue silk to reveal a small walnut box, intricately carved in a design of exotic flowers with ivory insets. The lantern lit up her copper curls. She opened the hinged lid to reveal a tiny crossbow crafted of ebony and silver, set with a spray of tiny diamonds. Her face glowed like a cherub as she took the tiny mechanism into her hands. She looked at Charles in puzzlement. "What is it? A weapon or an ornament?"

"It's both. A Flemish merchant representing a guild of arbalests gave it to my mother as a gift. He told her it was specially made for her, to exemplify her loveliness and the sharpness of her mind. He said it symbolized the triumph of intellect over brute force."

Maria's busy fingers explored the little mechanism. "Is it a brooch? Did she wear it on her gown?" She placed it near the top of her velvet bodice, drawing his attention to her décolletage.

"No, once her coiffure was complete, she wore it in her hair." Charles was careful to keep his eyes fixed on hers. "She once wore it for a portrait."

Maria smiled, the orange flame of the lamp reflecting in her eyes. "Can I actually set and fire it?" She began fiddling with its mechanical parts.

"Careful! It's not a toy," Charles cautioned. "Think of it as a miniature weapon. Let me show you how it works."

"I could figure that out myself," Maria muttered. She fell silent and watched as Charles demonstrated how the tiny tip of the dart unscrewed, revealing a miniscule compartment. "In here, a person could put just a tad of strong poison, reseal the cap, and—" He positioned the quarrel as it had been before, cocked the mechanism that readied the crossbow for firing, and continued. "If you feel intellect is not winning out over brute force, you can shoot the person who offends you, and let the poison do its work."

Maria gasped, then laughed heartily. "One can only wonder how many obstinate dullards met an untimely death from this tiny dart. Is it armed to kill right now?"

"I'm afraid I have unleashed an Amazonian upon an unsuspecting Spanish court."

"But just a little Amazonian," she giggled.

"Even more dangerous. I'm afraid you'll have to supply your own poison, if you decide to use it that way."

Maria took the ornament from Charles. "Such a pretty thing." Handling it with surprising skill, she uncocked the quarrel, then cocked it again. "Absolutely exquisite. How I wish I could have met your mother."

"You remind me of her, especially that time you dove into the river to recapture your fish and excoriated my fellow courtiers for letting your catch escape." He was thoughtful for a moment. "Of course, I never saw Mother nearly naked, thank God."

Maria froze. When she could move again, she forcefully struck the prince's arm with her closed fist, expressing herself energetically in two languages.

Falsely contrite, Charles grabbed Maria's hands and held them gently but firmly against his chest. "No, no. You were lovely. No woman could be your equal in wet gauze."

Surprisingly strong for a girl, Maria struggled, her every intent to punish Charles. Unbalanced and laughing helplessly, Charles fell back as she piled on top of him. Maria was hissing in fury, but she wrenched free of his grip as Charles laughed. Before she could strike him again, she began to laugh, too. Lying at ease on the heavy satin, they fell silent and listened to the distant burbling of the river.

He pulled her close. A tiny voice inside him shouted he was going too far. She was the Spanish infanta. Prince Charles pushed the voice from his head as he tenderly placed his lips upon hers. Maria sweetly and completely kissed him in return.

22

Intoxicants

The sandy path guided Anne and her small entourage back to the Tavernier's estate. Anne looked up to see Harald. She rushed forward to kiss him.

"Thank God," he said. "I thought you were going to return as soon as—" He paused ever so slightly and added, "You were finished."

Anne sighed. "Things did not go exactly as planned, but the deed is done."

"Is something wrong?" Harald asked.

Gregory herded Kenhelm onto the lawn. Anne held Harald back. "I think it was too much for Kenhelm. We forget how young he is."

"No, you forget, my dear."

Anne sighed. "His talent met my expectations. But betraying an old friend was hard on his conscience, even though I am all the more fond of him for it. So many people at court have no conscience to speak of. It's refreshing Kenhelm has enough heart to mourn the loss of a friend, even a bad one."

"What about the priest? Could you gage his reaction?"

"Eremitz knows Kenhelm set him up, I'm sure. But he cannot reveal that to the papal nuncio without putting himself at risk."

"Losing his papers will tie him more closely to Massimi," said Harald. "He'll have nowhere else to go."

"I wouldn't be so sure about that," said Anne. "Eremitz is quite charming, not to mention handsome. And talented. If he curried favor with the right nobles, he could extricate himself from Massimi."

"You may be right. He seems to be currying favor with Buckingham," said Harald.

"Exactly. And with the infanta's governess. And with the royal couple. He is already putting his lines in the water."

They found Kitty and Akira lying on a large linen cloth spread out on the grass. Akira had changed into breeches topped by a short cotton kimono. Kitty wore a beige bustier over a white muslin dress billowing with petticoats.

"I feel dizzy," said Anne, clinging to Harald's arm. "Lord knows what we've been breathing. Let me lie next to Kitty."

"Please do, M'Lady," Kitty said, rising up on her elbow. "The smoke is clearing and the stars are spectacular."

Harald braced Anne and sank with her to the linen cloth. Her head swirled into a state unlike any she had known. She breathed in the scent of cool grass and damp earth as she grasped Harald's hand, entwining her fingers into his. Her heart swelled with gratitude. How fortunate she was to be married to her lover and best friend.

"Mind if we join you?" Anne looked up to see Gregory Mack and Kenhelm.

"Of course," said Harald. "Fiesta's down here."

Gregory snatched a linen cloth from a cleared table, flipped it on the grass, and reclined on the other side of Harald.

"I love it when parties get to this stage," said Kenhelm, plopping down next to Gregory.

"What parties have you been attending?" Gregory asked.

"Probably none you'd be interested in," said Kenhelm.

"Are there señoritas in attendance?"

"Of course."

"Bring me to the next one and let me be the judge," said Gregory.

Harald tilted his head toward Anne. "Can you see the two nebulae?" he whispered.

"The stars won't stop moving," she said. "Point them out to me."

With their fingers still entwined, Harald raised her hand, placed his index finger against hers, and pointed slightly above their heads. "There's the green one up there. That's the one Kepler discovered."

Although the nebula was the size of the full moon at midnight, it was so translucent Anne had to look directly at it to see it. "Oh, yes. It looks like a cat's eye."

He pulled their fingers down slightly and to the right. "And there's Cassiopeia A, the pink one."

"Oh, Kitty, do you see the pink one?" Anne asked, after spotting it.

"Yes," Kitty exclaimed. "It's my favorite. It looks like a blooming rose. If you look at them both, they look like the eyes of God."

Akira spoke up. "When omens appear in the sky, it means the world will change. Forever."

"It is changing," Kitty said dreamily. "What if Prince Charles married Princess Maria, and they went to the New World, then became king and queen of the New World Order? They could gather all the Indian tribes together and make peace treaties. It would be egalitarian."

Kenhelm responded in a mocking, sing-song falsetto. "Doubtful."

"You have no vision," Kitty huffed.

"Prince Charles can never leave England," Kenhelm retorted. "It is his destiny to be England's king. And once he is king, everyone throughout Europe will see he is more than capable of being an emperor."

"Emperor!" Gregory rose up slightly to get a better look at Kenhelm.

"Why shouldn't he be the emperor?" Kenhelm asked. "Why does it always have to be a German? Why can't it be an Englishman, for a change?"

"We should fight the Germans for it," said Gregory, lying back down, his hands behind his head. "I shall put my money on the Brits."

"I know we could beat the Germans," said Kenhelm. "Britain has the most powerful navy in the world."

Everyone laughed.

"It's true!" Kenhelm protested.

"I'm with you, Kenhelm," said Gregory. "We could take our finest naval vessel to the top of Mount Watzmann and wait for the midwinter snow to pile up. Come Valentine's Day, we'll jump up and down on the deck, start an avalanche, then ride that hussy straight into Bavaria, and boom! The Germans will drop their beer steins and genuflect as if Judgment Day were nigh."

"You're not funny," Kenhelm said, but his remark was barely heard above the laughter. He put his hands behind his head and listened to the others as their banter continued.

"Oh no! The eyes of God are upon us!" said a squeaky voice. Kenhelm lifted his head and looked beyond his feet to see a puppet attached to a long stick bobbing above the grass, his porcelain face lit bright by the torches in the lawn. Kenhelm could barely make out the black-clad figure holding the puppet and decided to ignore him to better enjoy the show.

The belled ears of the puppet's jester cap bounced about his apple-cheeks. "The eyes of God are upon us! We must escape! We must hide!" His arms flopped wildly at his side as he bobbed about.

A hawk-nosed hag puppet clutching a rolling pin came into view and hollered in a shrill voice, "I'll teach you to come home late stinking of ale without so much as a copper in your pocket!"

"Oh no! The eyes of Judy are upon us!" the first puppet yelled. "Run, run for your life!" He made an about face and bobbed in the other direction with Judy hot on his heels.

"I'm going to get you, you drunken sot!" Judy yelled, "Hold still!"

The party on the grass laughed. God seemed so absorbed in his enigmatic goggle-eyed thoughts, He likely didn't get the joke, which made the puppets all the more hilarious.

Anne's giggles settled down. The warmth of Harald to her left and the softness of Kitty's shoulder to her right comforted her as the two nebulae, both comical and frightening in their strangeness, absorbed her attention like a pair of all-seeing eyes in the vast face of the starry sky. Anne sensed they were being observed by an intelligence that far surpassed anything the human mind could conceive. The stars rang like tiny bells. A chorus of angels sang, but their voices were eerie, rising and falling, as if warning of impending danger. Anne sensed a deep low hum from the darkness behind the stars. She closed her eyes, hoping to see Heaven.

Instead, she saw an eerie, unrecognizable landscape creeping with fog. Ghostly owls with moonlit eyes passed her in flight hooting, "Who are you? Who are you?" A flock of magpies followed, whispering, "Come hither. Come hither." A flock of tiny wrens piped, "Over here. Over here." As she flew to catch up with them, she stared into the distance, seeing nothing but a glittering mist. Her minded drifted and darkness overcame her.

Kenhelm was fighting drowsiness when someone plopped down beside him. He turned, startled to see Eremitz. His old friend looked at him with eyes devoid of anger.

"I'm sorry about your garden house," said Kenhelm. He wondered if Eremitz had come to cut his throat.

The priest remained silent. At length, he said, "You are fortunate, Kenhelm. You have someone to be loyal to. I have no one. Your comrades have burned every trace of my identity. I am dismayed to learn how little I mean to you. But I realize now, I am not who I want to be. I'm trapped. You have forced me to seek my freedom."

"Eremitz, please do not think my affections are false." Kenhelm lowered his voice to a whisper. *"But you are involved in a plot to assassinate the crown prince of England. You have left me no choice. Did you think so little of my intelligence and integrity?"*

Eremitz stared at the sky. A tear slipped down his temple. "I didn't know of the plot until recently. If I had told you, we would surely both be dead." Eremitz turned his face toward Kenhelm. "Now that I know, I shall waste no time making my escape. I shall not have the blood of England's future king on my hands. Certainly not your future king. Please, heed my words. You and your comrades must take Prince Charles in hand and leave this place. The powers that be shall never allow this match. These star-crossed lovers were not meant to be man and wife."

Kenhelm closed his eyes and let the tears fall. He wanted to believe in romantic love. Prince Charles and Princess Maria had proven it did, indeed, exist. But Eremitz had revealed a harder truth. Much like a shooting star, true love was beautiful, but fleeting. The forces of wickedness would always tear it apart.

The breeze blowing up from the river cooled Anne. She lifted her face from Harald's shoulder. "Why are you carrying me?" she asked.

"It was either that or leave you sleeping on the grass with the snails climbing over you."

"I fell asleep? We were having such great conversations."

"Too many strange spirits in the air, my dear. You're not the only one who fell asleep, if that's any consolation."

"I didn't fall asleep," Gregory said, walking alongside of them.

"Because you wouldn't stop talking," Harald shot back. Anne found their careless banter amusing. They often carried on like brothers.

"Are you going to carry me like a child all the way home?" she asked, breaking into their conversation. "I would look less foolish riding on your back." She noticed a weedy burr on Harald's jacket and picked it off, then held fast to his neck as he marched on.

"If you're worried about what Spanish high society may have to say, there's no need for concern," said Gregory. "They've fallen asleep in their cups."

Harald and Gregory strode through the garden gate and onto the terrace at the entryway of their villa. The house was deserted, the servants likely sprawled somewhere on the Tavernier's estate. Gregory stepped ahead and opened the door.

Upon reaching their bedroom, Harald put Anne on her feet with his arm still around her. She tottered. Gregory took her arm to support her. She patted his hand. Harald guided Anne onto the bed, where she absent-mindedly turned her back to him so he could loosen her bodice, which he did, slowly and tenderly. Gregory opened the window. A breeze lifted the white eyelet curtains, revealing the nebulae hovering above the Western horizon.

Anne could feel Gregory nearby like the warmth of the sun. His involvement with their lives was so constant, his presence seemed perfectly natural, as if it were Kitty standing by.

Gregory knelt down, untied her satin shoes, and slipped them off her feet. Anne was relieved to be home and sitting on her bed. She sighed and thought, It's warm in here. A gust of air blowing through the open window brought in the scent from the smoldering garden house. All three of them sneezed.

"I tremble to think what is in that smoke from the priest's garden, but it makes everything more luminous," said Harald.

"Indeed, the room is luminous, but from the glow of your fair lady more so than the smoke. You have a pretty room. Your lovely bride finishes the bed."

Harald chuckled. "She does make it look more welcoming, doesn't she? Her hair glinting like gold, her skin smooth as satin."

Anne didn't mind them commenting on her as if she couldn't hear. It made her feel ethereal, removed from the corporeal world, like a floating body of light. She could still hear the lonely Spanish guitar from the only musician who had not succumbed to the wine and smoke. The music in her head played along, harps and flutes rising in sprays of bright pink, falling in droplets of crystal blue. The guitar beat out deeper colors—dark purple waves edged in gold. Anne stood up on the bed, easily, and gracefully like a ballerina. She danced to the music as she slipped out of her gown, kicking her skirts and petticoats off the bed until she was completely naked. Her entire body moved with sensual grace.

Harald's and Gregory's eyes captivated her like the two glowing nebulae peaking at her through the shifting curtains—the eyes of God. Her serpentine arms and legs were her sacrament. The dark, glittering intensity in her gods 'eyes grew. They approached her as she danced, putting their smooth hands upon her until she knew the pure joy of her gods fully beholding her.

23

The Flute

Kitty emerged from Akira's cottage in time to spot Harald carrying Anne back to their house, Gregory at their side. Everyone had left the party or fallen asleep. Kitty's head still buzzed from the smoke. She strolled through the grass, the dew dampening her shoes. A realization shot through her. She had not seen Prince Charles and Princess Maria since the fire. A sense of foreboding descended upon her.

She rushed toward the Tavernier's garden.

The cathedral clock struck five, its leisurely bong echoing across the river. Dawn was less than an hour away. Kitty had to locate them before the sun rose.

She went to the place she had seen them last to find it deserted. Spotting a group of doñas snoozing on the terrace, Kitty rushed toward them. She found Adelena slouched in a wicker chair, snoring. The infanta was nowhere to be seen.

Kitty plucked a torch from the lawn and headed toward the river path. The gentle burbling of the current grew louder as she approached. A faint melody emerged from the breeze whistling through the willows at the river's edge—the sound of a flute. Kitty crept into the willows that grew near the bank and discovered the Amerindian sitting on the sand, his feet barely touching the water's edge.

"Rana, why are you here?"

Rana took his flute from his lips. "My master called me to play music at the party. The priest's servant found me." His voice was weak and barely audible. "He took me here and has beaten me to death."

Kitty lowered her torch to get a better look at him. The flickering light revealed large, black bruises all over Rana's torso.

"My God!" Kitty said. "Why on earth would he do such a thing?"

"He said I did not take seriously my orders to kill the prince. That all of my arrows stuck in his clothes and the lord was angry about it."

"Who was angry about it? Which lord?"

"He didn't say. He beat me like it was his duty. He took no pleasure. Your people are strange. They call me a savage. My people only kill to defend or hunt. Your people kill for odd reasons I do not understand. It is bad luck to kill a ruler."

Kitty knelt beside him. "We must get you to a physician. If you can't move, I can bring one here."

"No. The job is well done. I should be dead by now, but I'm waiting for my people to come."

Rana looked into Kitty's face. "You are kind. Please take my flute." He slipped it into a narrow leather pouch hanging from a strap, unslung it from his neck and shoulder, and handed it to her. "Keep this for me. When I need it again, I will ask you for it."

A sharp chill shuddered down Kitty's spine. She had no idea how this dying little man would ask her for his flute again, but she was sure, somehow, he would. She placed the strap around her own neck and tucked the flute down the bodice of her dress.

Rana nodded in satisfaction. "That is the best place for it. Keep it near and you'll be safe through your adventures. When you die, your people will come for you."

He strained to lean forward and look down the river. "Here are my friends now," he said, his voice warming with joy.

Kitty glanced down the river. In the pre-dawn glow, a triangular path appeared in the water rippling toward her, but she could see nothing but the mist.

Rana sat up. "Ah, my own father is here. And village elders I haven't seen since I was a boy."

Kitty heard the prow of a boat slide up onto the bank. She even saw a triangular imprint carve into the sand, but there was no boat.

Rana stood with open arms and smiled. His body collapsed in the sand, as if his spirit had chuffed it off like a husk. The prow of the invisible boat pulled back and slipped down the river, leaving a trail in its wake. The sound of men singing a triumphant song in a strange language trailed off into the fog.

Kitty gazed at Rana's bruised body lying crumpled at her feet. Her eyes welled with tears. "Such a kind and gentle soul you were." She knelt and arranged him with some dignity, placing his head near the trunk of a willow tree in want of a tombstone. "So our Lord Jesus will recognize you as a good man," she murmured, crossing his arms on his chest.

The river and the willow grove seemed suddenly empty. Kitty shivered with the realization she had yet to find the prince. She sprinted toward the cork oak grove.

24

A Peccadillo

Kenhelm found the infanta's governess on the terrace, snoring in a wicker chair. He had hoped to find the prince and the infanta in her company. He positioned his torch to scrutinize every snoozing face on the terrace. None belonged to Princess Maria or Prince Charles.

He broke into a sweat. Varney had told him he had emerged from the Tavernier's parlor hours ago and did not see the prince or the infanta on the lawn. He assumed they had left with Adelena to see the fire. Having searched relentlessly for all of them, Varney had no choice but to seek them at the palace. He had asked Kenhelm to continue his search at the Tavernier's estate.

The horrible truth descended. The royal pair were completely unaccounted for. Kenhelm ran to the Audley's estate, the only other place they could be.

The house was quiet when he entered. A few candle stubs flickered in their glass lamps. A quick search yielded no one in the study or the kitchen. Kenhelm hurried back to the bedrooms. He opened the door to Harald and Anne's room with trepidation. Small votive candles burned on the dresser. Harald, Anne, and Gregory Mack all lay naked on the huge bed.

Kenhelm's mind reeled. He would forever hold the image among his fondest memories. He reached over and shook Gregory's shoulder. The well-trained captain woke instantly and glanced around, confused as to where he was. Kenhelm picked up Gregory's pants off the floor and wiggled them at him. Gregory silently rolled out of bed, snatched them away, and put them on. Kenhelm scooped up the rest of Gregory's clothes and headed out the door. Gregory grabbed his boots and followed. He sat in the parlor and pulled them on, glancing darkly at Kenhelm to signal his unusual circumstances were not up for discussion. Kenhelm did his best to act as a valet, mindful to keep his face blank.

Once outside in the crisp air, he told Gregory about his concern for the prince and the infanta.

"The last time I saw them, they were with the telescopes by the oak grove," said Gregory. "Have you checked with Buckingham?"

"Buckingham is prostrate on a sofa in the Tavernier's parlor," Kenhelm replied. "He kept his eyes on Lord Bacon all night until he passed out."

"Where's Lord Bacon?"

"He retired to his room upstairs at the Taverniers' over an hour ago."

Gregory took in a deep breath. "Where would you go if you were a prince and wanted to get an ethereally lovely princess alone to yourself?"

Kenhelm slowly raised his index finger. "To the meadow beyond the oak grove," he said. "That is where I would take her."

They both rushed to the oak grove and nearly ran over Kitty on the way. They quickly learned her mission was the same as their own. With torches in hand, the three of them tromped through damp weeds and weaved their way amidst the gnarled oak trunks, their torch flames lighting up the canopy of leaves that arched overhead.

When they emerged from the grove at the meadow's edge, the eastern sky was glowing with dawn. Gregory's hand shot to Kenhelm's arm. Directly before them they could see the entwined, iridescent figures of Prince Charles and the infanta, both of them naked under the stars. The brightening sky gently stage-lit the lovers. The infanta's copper curls were unmistakable.

More beautiful memories, Kenhelm thought.

Kitty doffed her cloak and rushed to Infanta Maria. The men attended to Prince Charles. Gregory and Kenhelm had the prince half-dressed before he completely awakened while Kitty gently shook the infanta awake and deftly dressed her under the shield of her cloak. Once Kitty was done, she lifted the princess to her feet.

"I must get the infanta back to the terrace with the sleeping doñas immediately," she whispered to Kenhelm and Gregory. "It doesn't matter so much where the prince has been."

The two men nodded.

"Thank God for the touch of a competent lady's maid," Gregory said as he and Kenhelm followed with the prince in tow.

Anne awoke to the eyelet drapes billowing in the late summer breeze. She lay in bed, listening to the muffled clinks of the maids bustling in the kitchen and the clucking of the chickens wandering in the yard. Harald was fast asleep, his hand lying across her thigh.

"Time to wake up," said Anne, running her hand over his chest. Harald stretched, shivered, and brought his hand back to her thigh. Anne laughed and slipped away.

"I have rejoiced so much in the pleasures of man and woman, I could join a convent and never miss it again," she said.

"I take that as a challenge." Harald rolled out of bed and came after her.

"You'll ruin me. Perhaps this afternoon?"

"Excellent," he said. "Judging from the shadows in the garden, we could have lunch for breakfast, and then be back here."

"Not at all," said Anne. "We are expected at the Tavernier's and I must have a bath."

"I need a bath, too," said Harald. "It might go faster if we bathe together."

"I'm pretty sure it would go a lot slower," said Anne, wrapping her robe around herself. She paused. "Perhaps it was the smoke from the burning potions last night, but I had the strangest dream. It seemed so real, yet unreal."

"Best it all remain a dream, my dear," Harald said.

"Was it real?" Anne asked. A sense of horror came over her. *What have I done?*

"It wasn't real, exactly," Harald said, his words hesitant. "Perhaps I should say it was real, inexactly. Have you ever heard of a peccadillo?"

"I've heard the word. I assumed it referred to some silly, trivial occurrence."

"Indeed, it does. It often refers to minor sins committed well past midnight after mysterious intoxicants have been consumed. Come morning, we laugh off such trivialities and say, 'Ah, 'twas a peccadillo.'"

25

In Broad Daylight

September 1623
Madrid, Spain

Buckingham leapt out of the carriage as it rolled to a stop. He pressed a silver coin into the footman's hand and rushed across the carriage path into the crowd of locals and tourists who loitered before the Alcazar. The vast plaza of the palace grounds was a popular gathering place for bored nobles who wanted to be seen hobnobbing with other members of their class.

The first week of September was still warm, which made Buckingham wonder if wearing black made him conspicuous. His dark attire contrasted with the other men who wore colorful doublets and ribboned pantaloons. They sashayed about even more than the women. Some wore Elizabethan collars, which Buckingham found ridiculously out of style, but he was too distracted to sneer.

He eavesdropped on their gossip, knowing the topic full well—Count-Duke Olivares was holding a soirée, commencing at seven that evening. It was a casual affair merely involving drinks, canapés, and pleasant music. It also allowed guests to invite other guests. On the plaza, uninvited lower nobility in their finest clothes eagerly vied with one another for the affections of those holding invitations. Some indulged in gossip, yet studiously avoided the scandal of Queen Isabella and her bodyguard. That sort of gossip invited unpleasant consequences.

Buckingham suppressed a grin. Before the stroke of twelve, they would have far more interesting things to gossip about. He snatched his watch out of his pocket and checked the time. Ten minutes of noon. Glancing to his left, his heart quickened. A large, two-toned black coach approached. He crossed its path on his way to the porte cochère. Several noblemen loitered near the palace entrance. Buckingham quietly joined their company. All of them were too high of rank to be asked to leave. He struck a pose between the carriage stop and the palace entrance.

A man across the way looked directly at him. Buckingham had seen the man once at a local brothel. He wore shabby boots, but his cloak was brand new—typical attire for a failed aristocrat. The stranger raised his hand in an attempt to catch the duke's eye. Buckingham studiously ignored him, hoping the man would get the hint. The stranger lifted his chin and haughtily turned his head away, flipping one side of his elegant cloak over his shoulder to reveal a large dagger.

Buckingham scowled and returned his gaze to the approaching coach. As it pulled up beneath the porte cochère, the man from the brothel crossed the path in front of the carriage, heading toward the crowd of distinguished nobles. No one else noticed the approaching stranger. The crowd fixed their gaze on the coach's door.

Weaving his way through the gathering throng, the stranger kept his eyes on Buckingham until he had maneuvered himself directly in front of him. Buckingham's pulse pounded in his ears. The stench of rancid urine and sweat nearly gagged him. He fell back a bit, so he could see the emerging passenger.

The footman swung the door of the carriage open with great fanfare. A man in a gray doublet and breeches stepped out, his brown hair waving in the breeze.

A young lady gasped, "It's Lord Tassis, the queen's guard." The ladies tittered as the men looked the lord up and down.

"Is he the one who carried the queen out of the burning theater?" whispered another lady.

"The very one," said the first.

Lord Tassis lifted his arm to place his hat on his head. One of the ladies waved a scarf at him.

It hovered in mid-air as the stranger lunged and stabbed the lord in the ribs. He pulled out the dagger, shining red, and brought it down on Lord Tassis's neck, slitting his throat so deeply, his neck gaped all the way to the white nub of his spine.

The crowd screamed in horror. The palace guards fell upon the murderer, twisting the knife out of his hand.

"I am on a mission for the king!" screamed the man from the brothel. He looked directly at Buckingham. "Lord Snare, tell them! Tell them I'm under the king's orders!"

Buckingham swiftly stepped aside and looked at the man behind him. The crowd's eyes followed his.

As the stranger from the brothel struggled with the palace guard, Buckingham pulled a stiletto from the sheath hidden within his short cloak. The world around him took on a crystalline edge that slowed the thrashing bodies. The cacophony of the crowd grew softer, yet brighter. In two floating steps, Buckingham reached the assassin and slipped the rapier between his ribs, knowing he had reached his target when the handle pulsed with his victim's heartbeat. He left the rapier impaled in the murderer and melded back into the crowd.

Two types of people hired assassins: the ones who were too squeamish to do the deed themselves, and the ones who could perform the task with ease but could not get blood on their hands.

Buckingham was well-versed in the practice. Visit the local brothels. Ask around. Give a fake name. He could tell which assassins were experienced. They quickly negotiated a reasonable price and asked for extras, like a new cloak.

26

The Soirée

Later that evening, the sky faded to a purplish dusk, revealing the first stars of the night. Buckingham trotted up the stone steps to the Olivares's estate. The orange glow of candelabras beamed from the windows and open doorway. The house buzzed from the crowd within.

"The First Duke of Buckingham," he said to the servant at the doorway of the ballroom. The servant announced his name as Buckingham swept past him and headed toward the wine and liquor table.

"Cognac," he said to the liveried servant. The servant picked up a bottle of the amber liquid and poured a generous portion in a crystal glass. Buckingham took the glass, snatched the bottle from the startled servant, and headed toward a shadowy corner. He spotted Prince Charles but turned away from him as he poured another shot of cognac. He wondered if the prince knew his father had taken ill and was close to death. The king's decrepit condition had attracted a bevy of young dandies hoping to take Buckingham's place, according to his surprisingly well-informed friend, Father Eremitz. Buckingham was now in danger of losing his status as the king's favorite.

Buckingham had also made so many enemies at court, he was certain to be locked up in the Tower of London if his enemies managed to groom a new lover for the king and thereby seize the reins of power.

The duke had been a fool to allow the marriage negotiations to draw on for so long. He had to return to London at once but leaving the love-struck prince behind was out of the question. He had no choice but to either bring the marriage negotiations to a swift conclusion or abandon them altogether.

Assassinating Queen Isabella's guard in broad daylight would signal to the House of Hapsburg he was not a man to be trifled with. It would also obligate King Philip to return the favor. No one in Madrid had the spine to restore the king's honor, so that put Buckingham in a stronger bargaining position.

He drained his shot and poured another. Once he had drunk his fill of the cognac, Buckingham set the bottle down and sauntered over to the host.

"My dear Count-Duke Olivares," he said. His own voice made his ears ring. He wondered if he was speaking too loudly. "Please, let us converse frankly." He wrapped his arm around Olivares's shoulders, but before he could get a firm grip, Olivares flipped his hand off.

"What can I do for you, Lord Buckingham?"

"You can tell King Philip we are growing bored with the fiestas, the mystifying smoke, the endless intrigues—" Buckingham paused for dramatic effect, then added, "And the numerous attempts on the life of our prince." He turned to appeal to the crowd of nobles who were pretending not to listen. "We all know there have been at least two attempts to murder England's crown prince here in Madrid, do we not?"

In the periphery, Buckingham spied the prince turning his head. Glass of wine in hand, the prince's face descended into a scowl. Buckingham lowered his voice and bent his head toward Olivares.

"Let King Philip know the party is over. If he keeps wasting our time, he will lose. Dear, oh, dear, what would happen to poor Spain, if our two great nations were to wind up on opposite sides of this endless war plaguing Europe? You do realize England has the superior navy."

Olivares huffed. "King James is desperate for the infanta's dowry. Thanks to a certain royal favorite with an endless appetite for luxury, England's treasure has dwindled to almost nothing. We both know this."

"Spain needs England's military power," Buckingham said, through clenched teeth. "Your own has withered."

"Your empty threats will not bring us any closer to finalizing these marriage negotiations."

"Do you want this royal marriage or do you not?" Buckingham's voice rose in volume, but he saw no need to curtail it. "What the bloody hell have we been doing here for the past six months?"

"It is not my decision."

"I am sick of your lies, you pig-faced peasant! Your king is a child. You are the one who tells this royal baby what to do and say. Do you take me for a fool?"

"Let us discuss this in my study," Olivares said in a low voice.

"To hell with your study!" Buckingham spun on his heels. Gesturing to the nobles around him with a grand sweep of his arm, he addressed the crowd. "Do you suppose this self-serving coward does what is best for your king? A coward who stands aside as a low-ranking member from your queen's coterie puts horns on your ruler. He thinks nothing of a rival sweeping the Queen of Spain into his arms—something we all know only a lover would do!"

Olivares raised his own voice, as if announcing his remarks to the gathered throng. "It was Lord Tassis's duty to protect our queen from harm, under any and all circumstances. He fulfilled his duty admirably, may God rest his soul."

"Who could believe that?" Buckingham laughed. "If he were a proper guard, he would come from the king's court, not the queen's. That rogue put horns on your king. You did nothing! If it wasn't for me, he would still be wearing them!"

The lords and ladies gasped. Lady Olivares rushed up to defend her husband.

"Really, Lord Buckingham, I would strongly urge you to remember you are an English duke who is representing your king in the Spanish court. One could only hope not all English lords behave so boorishly abroad."

"Who are you to reprimand me, you smelly sow?" Buckingham barked. "I know your type. In your courting days, you tried to fornicate with any lord who would have you. But the moment they got under your skirts, they ran, screaming, 'The stench! The stench! 'You had to settle for the only one who was as disgusting as you."

A heavy hand came down on Buckingham's shoulder. He spun to see who dared to assault him. Prince Charles's face loomed so close he could feel his breath. Buckingham barely saw the fist flying toward his face. A sharp pain made his knees buckle and everything went black.

He opened his eyes to a massive, glittering crystal chandelier hovering directly above him. A high-pitched buzzing in his ears accompanied a horrible headache. The duke was confused. It didn't feel like a hangover—this one throbbed more, and the pain was concentrated at the upper left side of his face. Buckingham blinked several times as his tunnel vision gradually broadened to reveal a circle of wide-eyed Spanish and English aristocrats staring down at him.

"Get up," said a voice he recognized as Prince Charles's.

Buckingham twisted himself onto his hands and knees. He tried to remember how to stand. Balancing on his knuckles, he managed to clumsily place one foot on the floor and put his weight on it, hoping the move would refresh his memory.

"Stand and compose yourself," said Prince Charles.

The rumpled duke applied enough pressure to his planted foot to elevate his knuckles off the marble floor. He wobbled to a semi-standing position.

"Approach Lady Olivares and kneel," said Prince Charles.

Silence rang from the walls. Buckingham's cheeks heated with humiliation as reality bore down. For the petty sin of insulting Duchess Olivares, his own prince had turned on him—Buckingham, his most loyal servant. Of course, Buckingham would forgive him, in time, but he would never forget.

"Offer her your sincere apologies," Prince Charles said, his voice echoing into the silence around them.

Buckingham hesitated, staring at Lady Olivares's jeweled, satin-heeled slippers.

"Do it now," Prince Charles continued. "Or risk humiliating the English Crown and all of the Commonwealth."

Looking up at the duchess with hate in his heart, Buckingham clutched one knee and eased the other down to the floor, teetering as he went.

"Oh, no, this is truly unnecessary," said Duchess Olivares.

"My dear Lady," said Count-Duke Olivares, "please stay out of this. The gentlemen have it all in hand."

Buckingham rambled something he hoped sounded like an apology, even though he studiously avoided admitting to any wrongdoing. His non-apology eventually petered out. In the expanding silence, his annoyance at the prince grew, yet he kept his face a mask of contrition.

Olivares looked directly at his wife and nodded. She accepted Buckingham's apology with a curtsy.

"Return to your apartment and begin packing for your departure," Prince Charles commanded. Buckingham turned and swiftly departed.

"Lady Olivares," Prince Charles said, looking into her eyes and taking her gently by the arm, "I couldn't help but notice the hybrid roses on your balcony. I am most fascinated by botany and would love to get a closer look at them, in all their paintbox glory."

"Please, join me on the balcony, Your Highness," said Lady Olivares, gesturing gracefully with a trembling hand. She led him outside. They stopped by the nearest potted rose. It was milk-white and edged in pink. "Here is a hybrid I cultivated with the help of my gardener. I call it 'Early Morning.'"

"If ever a man could fall in love with a rose," said Prince Charles. The duchess smiled. The prince continued, "For to be a rose is to be a man, I mean a lady, who has it in her mind, uh, her heart—" His poetry came to a stuttering, mid-sentence halt. The duchess patted his hand and led him toward the next potted rose. The blossoms were scarlet with bright yellow centers.

"Here is a new one called 'Vulcan's Flame.' It was imported from Constantinople last year."

"It's marvelous," said Prince Charles.

In lieu of hailing a carriage to take him to the Alcazar, Buckingham loitered at the front garden of Count-Duke Olivares's château, mingling with the guests who had come outside to smoke their pipes. He pulled his own pipe from the interior of his jacket, filled it with tobacco, and asked a nearby servant for a light.

He turned to look back at the château. A second-story balcony rose above a deserted terrace on the side of the grand house. He could just make out Prince Charles leading Lady Olivares back into the house. Buckingham watched to see who would come out to the balcony next, assuming their conversation would revolve around him, regardless of who it was.

He turned his pipe over to release the ashes, then casually walked toward the side of the house, staying in the shadows to conceal himself. He stopped directly beneath the balcony, holding his pipe like a stage prop. If a servant should happen to spot him, he had a handy excuse. Before long, he heard footsteps above him.

"My God, have you ever seen such an ugly display?"

"I'll be frank. Buckingham deliberately sabotaged these negotiations."

Buckingham recognized the voices of Ambassador Digby and Lord Harald.

"I agree," said Digby. "He used his drunkenness to disguise his intentions, and possibly as a cover for his prior actions. He practically admitted to murdering Lord Tassis. Although, upon reflection, that could easily be his usual braggadocio"

"Someone slipped a stiletto into the assassin's ribs to silence him," said Harald. "I know Buckingham very well. Beneath his foppish exterior, he is a ruthless cutthroat, much like the man who raised him. Remember old man Raynor?" Harald asked.

"I do remember the first time little Georgie Villiers invited his stepfather to court at the king's indulgence," said Digby. "Sir William Raynor of Orton, was it? The old fool got so roaring drunk, he nearly vomited on the king as he was being introduced, and then got into a nasty row with him."

Buckingham cringed at the memory but remained silent in the shadows.

"At any rate, Buckingham has been away from London for too long," said Harald. "I'm hearing rumors King James is taking an interest in other young men. If I've heard these rumors, Buckingham has likely heard them, too. He wants to be forcibly sent back to London. He's manipulating us, and even Prince Charles."

"How this makes my head throb," said Digby. "Whatever his motive, I fear the marriage negotiations are damaged beyond repair. The Vatican does not want this marriage. I cannot prove it, but I feel it in my bones. Spain is the Vatican's last powerful ally in Western Europe. If young King Philip is wooed by the Protestants into switching sides, the Vatican is sunk. They cannot afford the risk."

"Well, I am sorry to hear that," said Harald, "because our bonnie prince is completely smitten with the infanta. You'll never tear him away."

"We must make a clean break," said Digby. "We will tell King Philip our prince must return to London to see his father, who has taken ill, with a promise we will be back to resume negotiations in the spring. It is completely plausible. Once we are back in London and the prince's passions have cooled, we shall arrange a meeting between Prince Charles and Princess Henrietta of France. It's a much better match. She is almost as lovely as Princess Maria, and I have it on good authority that France's Prime Minister Cardinal Richelieu is a Protestant reformer disguised as a Catholic official. Apparently, this doesn't matter to young King Louis, who doesn't give two figs for religion anyway. Their father, Good King Henry, was raised an avid Protestant. The dowry isn't as much as the infanta's, but the marriage contract is far less complicated and the politics far more tame. It is the perfect way to save face on our side. And King Philip will simply have to find another match for his sister."

"The elegant coward's way out. I like it," said Harald. "We turn the page, it's over, and on to a new day."

"Speaking of Buckingham," said Digby, "what do you suggest we do about him?"

"Tie him naked to a tree and flog him?"

"Be serious," said Digby.

There was a pause. Buckingham folded his arms tightly about him as the evening chill set in. He stilled his breathing to better hear the conversation above.

"You need to dispatch a letter to the king and let him know that Buckingham has ruined this match," said Harald. "Quote Buckingham's remarks to Duke and Duchess Olivares, word for word. King James has a right to know how his favorite has represented him in the Spanish court. With any luck, King James will have a new lover by the time we return. Whichever duke or count is sponsoring the new lover will make a motion to send Buckingham to the Tower as a preemptive move."

Digby chuckled. "Buckingham has given them ample reason to bring criminal charges. Perhaps we can add the assassination of Lord Tassis to the list."

"Hear, hear," said Harald.

Buckingham ambled into the Alcazar foyer, exhausted. Drifting by the café parlor to see if anyone there interested him, he locked eyes with Father Eremitz, who regarded him with alarm.

"M'Lord, what happened?" asked Eremitz. "Did someone assault you?"

"It is of no consequence," said Buckingham, eager to change the subject. "What brings you here, might I ask?"

"I had business to conduct with the papal nuncio, but I lingered in the hopes of crossing paths with you before I left."

"Let us order a pot of café to be sent to my room," said Buckingham. "I would enjoy some company before I turn in for the night."

Buckingham fell into a velvet armchair and motioned Eremitz to sit down in the matching one. A liveried servant poured coffee into each of their cups before placing the pot on the serving table and leaving. The crackling fire in the marble fireplace filled the room with the aroma of sweet oak.

"Did you hear about Lord Tassis?" Buckingham leered at Eremitz with his one good eye.

"I was hoping we could discuss that," said Eremitz, cradling his cup. "The papal nuncio has congratulated me on a job well done. I didn't dare tell him it wasn't my work. He had ordered me to assassinate Lord Tassis by putting my manservant on task, but I stalled, hoping he would change his mind."

"Yes," said Buckingham. "I can tell you are a man of tender spirits who loathed such a morbid task, so I did it for you."

Eremitz's mouth gaped.

"I had my own reasons for assassinating him," Buckingham continued, as if discussing old friends. "But I am curious why the papal nuncio wanted him eliminated."

Eremitz meditatively sipped his coffee. "The Tassis family has risen rapidly in the past generation," he said. "They operate a private, highly reliable postal service, which makes them popular in both the French and Spanish courts. But Monsignor Massimi believes they are subversives attempting to curtail the power of the Spanish Inquisition. The Tassis family is too influential to be brought down with an inquisition, so the highest-ranking member of the family was targeted as a warning to the rest of them. Massimi arranged the fire in the theater in order to compel Tassis to pick up the queen and carry her out. That way, his murder could be passed off as a favor to the king."

"Ah," said Buckingham. "And now that favor is owed to me, but I fear there is no honor in the House of Hapsburg. My valiant effort has come to naught."

"I am indebted to you," said Eremitz. "I shall forever be your loyal servant. Massimi, as you know, is a grave threat to your prince. I would suggest—"

Buckingham cut him off. "I have it all in hand. The wheels are in motion, and we shall leave for England at the time of my choosing."

"Sooner would be better than later," Eremitz hinted.

"Indeed." Buckingham chuckled and took another sip of coffee.

"I, uh, need to leave Madrid for a short time," Eremitz said. His dark, pleading eyes sent a thrill through Buckingham. "The only thing that holds me back is my paltry finances. One needs money to travel."

"Of course, one does," Buckingham said, plopping his coffee cup on the table. "Can you tell me why? I am absolutely intrigued."

"All I can tell you is, it is a matter of life and death. And once the matter is accomplished, I would be delighted to tell you all about it, sparing no details, over two snifters of warm brandy."

"How much do you need?"

"I couldn't possibly accept an extravagant gift from you. Not after what you have already done."

"Extravagant? Why, travel expenses are among the bare necessities of life! Of course, I will provide such to a dear friend." Buckingham rose, walked over to his bedside cabinet, and opened the top drawer. He removed a lacquered casket and motioned Eremitz to join him.

The casket's interior glittered with a jumble of jewelry. Buckingham retrieved a thick gold ring, set with a large ruby. The gem glinted under the lamplight.

"This ring is small enough to hide, and valuable enough to pay for a lengthy journey. It comes from King James's personal jewelry box, if anyone should ask."

"What a lovely provenance," said Eremitz. "If I produced a parchment and pen, then wrote that down, would you mind signing it? It could double its value."

"But, of course," said Buckingham. "In fact, I keep such tools of correspondence at my bedside." He rose and went to his bedside drawer to retrieve a pen, parchment, and a corked inkwell. "Please, sit down on my bed. You can compose the provenance letter here, on the cabinet top."

Eremitz sat, uncorked the inkwell, and dipped the pen. As it hovered above the parchment, he turned toward Buckingham.

"An even better provenance, one that would provide a bit of élan in royal gossip circles, would be to say this ruby ring, this gem of passion, is a gift from the infanta's sister, the ethereal, newly-crowned Queen Ana Maria of France. Have you been keeping up with her fortunes?"

"Indeed I have," said Buckingham, his eyes widening with intrigue. "While we tarry here in Madrid, did she not just marry that royal dullard, King Louis the Thirteenth?"

"They have been married less than two months now. I hear it is not going well," said Eremitz. "But with a mother-in-law like Marie de Medici, what would one expect?"

"Not going well?" Buckingham made no attempt to hide his grin.

"To say the ring was a gift from her improves both of your images," Eremitz continued. "Yours, because it is far more romantic to receive a ring from a young queen than an old one, and hers, because to say the ring is from her, when it is actually from a king who has ruled far longer than she, why, that bestows a much higher rank upon her, wouldn't you say?" Eremitz knew his argument was ridiculous, but it stoked Buckingham's vanity, and that always made sense to the arrogant duke.

At Buckingham's urging, Eremitz wrote down the fictionalized provenance and handed Buckingham the pen for his signature. Buckingham nestled in beside him and took the pen.

"Come to think of it," Buckingham said as he scratched out his name, "There is a favor I would like to ask of you."

27

Flight of the Dark Priest

September 1623
Madrid, Spain

The chill in the early morning breeze reminded Eremitz summer was drawing to a close. He paused to listen to the gentle patter of the fountain. The courtyard walls, pink in the dawn, turned gold with the rising sun. Distant cooking fires scented the air as he stood in quiet meditation.

The past week had been sublime. Coffee and cordials with Buckingham, followed by a tryst in his palace chambers, and many secrets shared. Buckingham had told him exactly when the English would depart Madrid, and even divulged the route. The risks he took astonished Eremitz.

He strolled over to his date palms and checked the moisture level at their base. He would miss his villa, but he had to go. Buckingham's gift had lifted the yoke of Massimi's oppression.

Rather than nursing a grudge toward Kenhelm Digby, Eremitz admired him for outwitting both the papal nuncio and himself. Massimi had no idea Kenhelm's cohorts had burned down the greenhouse to hide the fact they had purloined a treasure trove of secrets from the priest's private papers. Eremitz's mind boggled at the amount of information the English had gleaned in that simple task. Since he had never told Massimi he kept the documents there, Massimi had not yet caught on they had been stolen. But the English gaining the upper hand in one swift move was Massimi's problem, not his.

A clamor at the gate gave Eremitz a start. Beyond the colored glass insets of the courtyard door, he could make out the hulking figure of Capistrano, who was opening the heavy padlock with an iron key.

Capistrano swung the double-doors open. "Monsignor Massimi approaches," he hissed.

"Jesus, what now?" Eremitz muttered under his breath. His pulse quickened as Massimi rushed over the threshold.

"I heard a rumor Prince Charles may soon return to England," he said.

"His Excellency, Monsignor Massimi, papal nuncio to King Philip the Fourth!" Capistrano dutifully said over him.

"Really?" Eremitz replied, feigning ignorance.

"We must assassinate him before it is too late."

"Why assassinate him?" Eremitz asked. "Wouldn't it be easier to simply arrange a more suitable match for the infanta?"

"We have discussed this," said Massimi. "Our only chance of regaining Britain is through war."

Does the pope know of your plan? Eremitz didn't dare ask the question out loud.

Massimi opened his cloak to reveal a jeweled sword. He withdrew it from its sheath and presented it to Eremitz. The priest took the sword and examined the hilt. A large sapphire surrounded by a bevy of small colorful gems formed an elegant diamond pattern. The blade was forged from the finest steel, judging from its mirror-like surface.

Eremitz ran his fingertips along the blade, delighting in its sharp edge.

"I purloined this sword from the Duke of Buckingham," Massimi said. "He had it custom-made by the best swordsmith in Madrid. The Buckingham coat of arms is engraved on the bottom of the shaft, as you can see. He has reported it stolen, but that will not save him from suspicion once this very sword is used to assassinate his prince."

Eremitz grasped the hilt, the large sapphire resting comfortably in the palm of his hand. He turned away from the papal nuncio and gave the sword a few swipes. In that moment, he knew it would be his.

"I thought the plan was to have the English assume Prince Charles was assassinated on the orders of the Spanish crown," said Eremitz, still staring at the glorious sword that had briefly been Buckingham's.

"You have much to learn about political intrigue," Massimi said. "Assassinating Prince Charles with Buckingham's sword achieves a number of goals. King Philip's reputation will be spared here in Spain and throughout the Holy Roman Empire, as his defenders point to the original owner of the sword. The English crown will officially deny it, but Buckingham's reputation for impulsive and violent behavior will convince influential parties in England that the king's loathsome favorite is, indeed, behind the assassination. The king is on his deathbed, and such a scandal will surely finish him off. England will be left without a regent, and every English nobleman will fancy himself a kingmaker. This will tear England apart from the inside, making them a weak opponent, ripe for conquest."

Eremitz kept his expression to a barely perceptible smile as he gently turned the sword in the morning light, marveling at the sky's reflection along the bright, smooth blade. Massimi's plan was perfect, except for one tiny flaw.

"The assassination of Lord Tassis was brilliant," Massimi said. "No one has identified the assailant. You should have told me you intended to convince your hired cutthroat the order came from King Philip, but the move was inspired nonetheless. Even the investigators were fooled. They didn't dare track down the party who hired the assassin. Was it Capistrano who killed him with a single stab before slipping away?"

"He is exceptional, is he not?" Eremitz replied.

"Indeed, he is," Massimi said, "which is why I trust Capistrano, and no other, to assassinate Prince Charles. This mission is far more important than the assassination of Tassis. We cannot risk hiring a nameless amateur. I need someone I can absolutely trust."

Eremitz waited until he could no longer hear the rumble of Massimi's coach and smiled. One thing Massimi had unwittingly taught him: if you want unswerving loyalty from your servants, give them a reason to love you. Massimi had failed utterly in this, which was why the Duke of

Buckingham had all of Eremitz's loyalty and the cold-blooded Monsignor none. It never crossed Massimi's mind to exchange kindness for loyalty, and that was his fatal flaw. In the end, Massimi would die a friendless man.

As Eremitz turned to go inside for breakfast, a coach pulled up to the portico. The footman leapt to the ground, swung open the coach door, and Adelena popped out.

"Oh, dear God." Eremitz turned to rush into his house before Adelena saw him, but it was too late.

"Father Eremitz! Father Eremitz!" she cried out. She rushed toward him in a jerky trot, her yellowish-gray sausage curls bouncing gaily along her creased jowls. Her bodice would have been fetching had it been topped by a sheer cotton blouse, as was the fashion, but Adelena was such a prude, she had opted for a thick wool shawl instead.

"Father Eremitz, I must speak with you in absolute privacy!"

"Would you like me to take your confession?" Eremitz asked, even though it was the last thing he wanted to do.

"Not exactly," said Adelena, standing so close to him he could smell her fetid breath. "But this important matter does involve a confession." She moved in so close her skirts crowded his thighs. He took a step back. "I have been to see Monsignor Gugliani," she continued. "He took my confession. So, of course, I had to tell him what happened the night of the fire." She stared at Eremitz, her eyes bulging with seriousness.

Eremitz paused and searched his mind for what she could be getting at. Was she lodging a complaint about his intoxicants? He had seen Adelena fast asleep on the Tavernier's porch while the infanta and Prince Charles went missing for several hours, according to the rumors. Surely, she wouldn't have the nerve to even mention such a gaffe.

"And what exactly happened the night of the fire?" he asked, wondering if she were such a fool as to blame him for her faux pas.

"Well, I prayed and prayed that night," she said, taking another step forward. Eremitz took another step back. "It so disturbed me, I lay awake in my bed till the wee hours of the morning, unable to sleep."

You liar, Eremitz thought. *You were passed out on the Tavernier's porch. I saw you.*

"At last, to relieve my distress, I journeyed to Alcorcon to make a confession to Monsignor Gugliani." She gripped Eremitz's forearm, filling him with an urge to escape. "I told him everything," she said, with bug-eyed intensity. "Now, he wants to see *you.*" She tightened her grip, as if on the verge of hauling Eremitz to Alcorcon that instant.

"What on earth for?" Eremitz asked, resisting the temptation to shake her claw from his forearm.

"Why, to take your confession, of course."

"What am I confessing to?" he asked, bewildered.

"Don't play the fool. You know full well what you need to confess. Especially you, a *priest!"* She threw his arm back at him.

Eremitz stared at her, hoping for a better clue. "About the intoxicants?" he asked.

"Fie on the intoxicants! You must confess what I saw that night as you lay in your bed. Your... thing. That thing down there." She glanced in the direction of his crotch. "I saw it. It was standing straight up, like some exotic mushroom."

Eremitz stood, stunned, for several heartbeats before finding his voice. "You stupid sow! I will not confess to your prurient priest. I was sleeping in the privacy of my room, trying to cool off from the stifling summer heat. But you rudely ignored the admonitions of my servants and barged in. Now, you suggest you possess some supernatural power to see in the dark? You just admitted you imagine these things as you lay awake at night, you horny old crone!"

"I saw everything because of the raging fire caused by two fornicating adulterers in your garden house!" Adelena shot back. "But what do you care, when all the while you were pleasuring yourself? How dare you accuse me of a sinful mindset!"

"Out with you! Pestilence!" Eremitz hollered and gestured pointedly at her waiting carriage. "Go home and pleasure yourself! Perhaps that will calm your rabid spirits!"

"Oh, you horrible man!" Adelena shrieked, running from the courtyard. "You are no man of God!" She lumbered into the coach, sobbing, and slammed the carriage door shut before the footman could assist her.

Eremitz turned. His entire household staff stood in a semicircle, gaping at him.

"Is breakfast ready?" he asked.

Eremitz sat, staring at his food, his heart pounding so strongly he could actually hear its beat in his inner ear. He took inventory of his meager options. While the proceeds from Buckingham's ring could easily finance a lengthy journey, he had nowhere to go. He held the bitter memories of his family's massacre in Amboyna at bay as he searched his thoughts for anyone at all whom he could rely on. There was one remaining uncle who had suffered a severe turn of fortune at the demise of their family, but who had found a respectable position serving in the newly formed French royal guard. Eremitz wasn't clear on what he did, but he led a comfortable life and would likely retire with a pension. Eremitz knew that if he reached out, his uncle would greet him warmly, at the very least.

"Señora," Eremitz called to his housekeeper, who was standing by. She rushed to his side.

"Please summon Capistrano."

When Capistrano emerged in the dining room, Eremitz motioned him to sit down. "I shall journey to Alcorcon," Eremitz said. He put a forkful of food in his mouth, chewed, and swallowed. "I must shadow Dowager Adelena's friend, Monsignor Gugliani, and make sure he does not start rumors about me."

"Please, Lord, let me go with you. I can alleviate the burden of this priest in short order."

"No, Capistrano, it is not that simple. Monsignor Gugliani is of noble birth. Not as noble as Lady Adelena perhaps, but likely more so than I. This matter must be handled with utmost gentility. All I need is Bazin."

The fourteen-year-old stable boy was agile, quick-witted, and highly resourceful, having taught himself to train horses among other things. Eremitz would have preferred Capistrano's martial skills, but Massimi had sealed

Capistrano's fate. "I need you to stay here and watch over the household. Bear in mind that as Monsignor Massimi is my master, so I am your master, do you understand?"

"My highest loyalty has always been to you, M'Lord," said Capistrano, his expression marked by a twinge of concern.

Eremitz put his fork down, folded his fingers, and looked directly at his favorite servant. "Father Massimi may ask a favor of you in my absence. Do everything he asks, except for one thing."

Eremitz's household staff stood, shoulder to shoulder, in the courtyard, staring at him with worried eyes. They had never seen him in his black doublet, breeches, and black suede boots.

"I must journey to Alcorcon on personal business," he announced, slipping on his riding gloves. "Settling my affairs may take some time, so I shall rent a room there. In my absence, Capistrano will supervise all matters outside of the household. Esperanza shall manage the interior. I trust them to keep all affairs in hand. Do not expect my quick return."

With his new sword at his side, he mounted his black Arabian horse and took off at a full gallop. Bazin and his pony could barely keep up. In one week's time, they would be in Paris. The very thought sent Eremitz's spirit soaring.

28

The Tryst

September 1623
Madrid, Spain

By late September, the heat of summer had faded. Cool mornings segued into golden afternoons that dimmed all too quickly into breezy evenings.

While the people of Madrid took their afternoon siestas, the Englishmen met in the drawing room of the House of the Seven Chimneys. John Digby, Harald Audley, and Gregory Mack gathered near the fireplace. The heat mingled with the cool breeze that wafted in from the tall windows on the far side of the commodious room.

The windows opened onto a courtyard that had geometric areas laid out in grass and gravel in majestic Moorish style. The rains had revived the roses, which bloomed exuberantly in a second flowering. The central fountain splashed. Breezes blew random sprays of water through the windows.

In the middle of the study, Anne, Kitty, and Prince Charles sat at a card table. The prince tipped back in his chair, the soles of his boots straddling the carved lion's paws of the chair's legs. Anne played a weak game of backgammon, hoping the prince would beat her. He needed something to boost his spirits.

During a lull in the conversation, Anne broached the dreaded topic. "I'm sorry to hear your father has taken ill," she said. Prince Charles fingered a backgammon chip, contemplating his next move. "Autumn is here," she continued. "If we are to journey back to England, we must leave while the weather is fair."

Prince Charles lifted his head, his face lit with hope. "Are we close to finalizing the marriage contract?"

Anne looked at Kitty. Kitty stared back, her eyes large and silent.

Anne returned her gaze to the prince. "I'm afraid we must resume negotiations when we return in the—"

"I need to see Princess Maria!" Charles snapped.

Harald, John, and Gregory looked up from their side conversation.

The prince stood. "We are so completely surrounded by incompetents, we need to devise our own plan. How can the two of us rule a nation if we cannot even rule our own lives?"

"I'm sorry," said Anne.

"Please, excuse me. I need to get some air." He walked to the open windows and stared out.

Kitty put away the backgammon board, opened the box of Snakes and Ladders, and set up the game. Anne left the table to join Harald.

As she chatted with the men, Anne kept Prince Charles in her periphery. He could easily step over the two-foot threshold of the window.

Harald spoke. "Perhaps we should make an arrangement with Monsieur Tavernier and his marshal. Akira could train the prince's guards, full-time, out in the open, on his estate."

"Why out in the open?" Anne asked.

"To intimidate possible enemies," said Gregory. "They need to respect British power as we escort Prince Charles from Madrid to the Port of Santander."

As their deliberations continued, Anne became more absorbed in the conversation. At length, she glanced across the room to see the curtain sheers drifting in the breeze. The prince was gone.

Her heart lurched. She scanned the men's faces. They hadn't noticed. Anne knew where Charles was going. She reminded herself that both attempts on his life occurred at public events. She looked at Kitty, who sat quietly, playing both sides of a game of Snakes and Ladders. Anne could tell by the glint in her eyes that she had watched him go. She breathed more easily knowing Kitty would never allow Prince Charles out of her sight unless she sensed he was safe.

Prince Charles's boyhood years of stalking deer in Scotland served him now. He used foresting skills to climb trees whose branches overhung the stone walls. He passed like a shadow through walled gardens, sprinting along the lawns—a steeplechase without a horse. Scaling one final wall, he dropped down, exhilarated to find himself in

Princess Maria's private garden. He whistled the birdcall that would bring her to him, then stood in the umbra of the rose arbor and waited for her.

It seemed like a long while before he saw her floating toward him in a cloud of white gauze.

"What are you thinking?" Maria hissed, then smiled. "I had to send all of my ladies to change their clothes. I couldn't think of anything else to get them to leave. Tonight at dinner, they will all be wearing blue and gold, or they will be eating bread and cheese in their rooms."

Charles laughed. "That seems a bit harsh."

"Dear Prince Charles, we have so little time alone, I take advantage of my royal privileges as I must."

Charles took Maria's hand and they sat on a little bench under the sheltering roses. From there, they had a clear view in all directions, but they could not be seen under the spreading rose canes. As the fountain splashed, gusts blew the water onto the graveled paths. Charles stayed watchful as he talked to Maria.

"Doña Adelena usually keeps you well-chaperoned. Where is she this afternoon?"

Maria sighed, her gauzy dress slipping off one pearlescent shoulder. "Adelena has become so odd lately. I think she and her favorite Jesuit fell out. Since their tiff, Adelena seems to have lost interest in hounding my every move. She just sits in a chair, staring out the window and shaking her head."

The warmth of the afternoon faded as the late September sun sank toward the low hills in the west, turning the horizon gold. A breeze made Maria shiver.

"Take my jacket. We can't leave yet. We have much to talk about." Charles removed his leather jacket and wrapped it around Maria's shoulders. She snuggled into the caramel satin lining, inhaling his scent.

"Can I keep this? It smells of you."

"My dearest love, keep me. I will even scent your sheets!"

Maria gasped, then doubled over, laughing. "Would they even allow us to be king and queen if they knew you speak to me this way?"

Drawing her close, Charles embraced her. "We shall pass a royal decree that all who linger in our company must fill their ears with wax. It won't hurt them, their heads are already stuffed with it."

Stifling her laughter, Maria hissed like a teakettle. "You must stop! Someone is going to hear us carrying on like this!"

Charles felt brilliant and witty, even though he could think of nothing clever to say. His arms were full of the girl. The cotton gauze was crisp under his hands, but beneath lay only softness and warmth. She smelled of violets and some essence that was only Maria. The infanta leaned against him and opened his shirt, pressing her lips against his bare chest.

"Just like this," he said. "We could be just like this for all of our lives." He shivered. "Maria, our time is short. We can't wait for the statesmen and priests to decide our future. We must take our fate into our own hands."

Maria nodded wearily. "I know, they are still fussing and talking. The papal nuncio has been shouting at the priests of the Holy Office, and they have been muttering threats back. This could go on until next spring."

Seeing her white face, Charles remembered how young she was. "Maria, take a leap. Turn your back on everything you've been taught and come with me."

"You are a daemon lover," she whispered.

"In Spain perhaps. At home, I'm an angel of light."

She couldn't laugh. "Charles, we can't do it that way. Without the agreements, I will have no authority or power in your country. I would be alone, without protection, without rights. None of my people or household would be with me." She brushed some fallen rose petals from his shoulder. A few fell inside the blousing of his shirt. Maria made a business of finding them, her soft fingertips gently stroking his chest. Charles embraced her and held her sweetly against him.

After a few minutes, she rearranged herself to put a little distance between them.

"I don't know, Charles. This raid to capture the bride might be a fine tradition in Scotland, but in the larger world, it could cause a holy war." She leaned even further away from him, but he recaptured her.

"Come live with me and be my love!"

Laughing outright, Maria leapt up from their embrace on the marble bench. Swirling white gauze and copper tresses, she struck a theatrical pose, then recited the first few lines of *"The Nymph's Reply to the Shepherd."*

"If all the world and love were young, and truth in every shepherd's tongue, these pretty pleasures might me move, to live with thee and be thy love."

Her Spanish-accented English made Sir Walter Raleigh's poem all the more delicious. Charles laughed but he could feel time rushing away. He had to have a commitment from her. He needed to bring his sweet bride home.

Maria dabbled her fingers in the water of the fountain's basin. "The water is cold. Winter will soon be upon us and they'll let the fountains go dry. I will miss the sound of falling water." Thoughtfully, she took his hand and re-seated herself. "This is a great deal to consider," she said.

"I know that my love, and there is so little time to think about it. Let your heart choose."

They were silent for a space. Charles waved a hand at the golden sun skimming the horizon. "The sun is setting. I love this time of day."

"Both of us have to dress for dinner," Maria said. "We can meet tomorrow. I doubt Adelena will be over her melancholy by then."

"Even more dangerous. Come to me." He took her by the waist so quickly she couldn't dart away. Charles held the laughing girl close.

The breeze blew stronger through the rose canes, making the spray from the fountain somewhat icy. The young lovers leaned together and watched the sunset. There was no one to see the glow around them.

As the sky dimmed, two planets sparked to life. His arms loosened and she sprang from his grasp. He reached for her, but she laughed and flitted away from him, over the lawn and up the pathway to her apartments. His leather jacket trailed from her outstretched hand, flying above her like a victory pennant.

29

The Queen and the Infanta

October 1623
Alcazar Palace, Madrid

Queen Isabella awoke at the first glow of dawn. She sat up on her pillows and gazed out the window into her garden as her French nurse snored quietly on her cot nearby.

The misty fields were green once more. Isabella hadn't slept well since the death of her dear friend, Lord Tassis. King Philip had told her he had nothing to do with his murder, but his dismissive tone led to a quarrel. He forbade her from discussing the matter and stormed out of her chambers. They hadn't spoken since, which all the more convinced her he was involved.

While others regarded her husband as wise beyond his years, Isabella found him stiff and officious. He refused to show a glimmer of gaiety for fear others might find him immature. But while he put on a pretense of piety, he never turned down the palace whores who crowded around him at every ball and official occasion. They had no shame. Isabella had stopped caring. King Philip had fallen far short of her expectations, unlike Lord Tassis. While he had devoted himself to making her life in Madrid enjoyable, he never so much as flirted with her.

Tears rolled down her cheeks. She had taken utmost care to maintain her virtue, in private and public. Now, her only friend in the palace was dead at the hands of a filthy cutthroat, and she was shown no pity. Nearly everyone took her for an adulteress. If she had known she would suffer the reputation, she would have indulged in the sin.

The rising sun glittered through the yellow foliage of a gingko biloba tree. As the mist cleared, she spied two women waiting on a garden bench. Focusing her gaze, she was rocked at the sight of her sister-in-law, Infanta Maria. The tall, thin woman sitting beside her was Adelena.

The queen wrapped her robe around her and slipped out the door. She walked to where the two women waited. Maria rushed to greet her.

"My dear sister, I am so happy you are awake this early," Maria exclaimed, clasping her hands. "We'd planned to wait until we could see your maids about."

"And what, pray tell, brings you to my garden at dawn?"

"I have heard that the English are returning home." Maria's hands trembled as her face contorted with despair. "I had hoped to hear of a wedding date and that my own ships would be sailing along with them."

Isabella clasped Maria's hands. "This happens often in wedding negotiations. Remember, the prince and the busy Buckingham arrived on their own schedule. They can't expect everything to go their way. They'll be back next spring, you can be sure."

Adelena stood behind the infanta, her rosary beads clicking through her fingers as she muttered a prayer for the girl.

"Next spring will be a good deal too late," said the infanta, tears streaming from her eyes. "During the night of the great fire, things happened that cannot be undone. I must go with the prince as his welcome bride, already married to him."

Isabella clasped Maria's hands more tightly. "I am twenty-one years old," she said. "You are seventeen. The fate of nations lies in our hands for however long that lasts. I've had unpleasant surprises in my life. An unpleasant event for other people in power won't be the least bit remarkable, especially if they never know about it."

Isabella looked kindly at Maria as the poor girl grimaced with fears and regrets. Her tears fell like a fountain, but she made little noise, other than high-pitched sobs. Having no idea how to ease Maria's pain, Isabella changed the subject.

"Do you know of anyone in the country with suitable lodgings whom you can trust with your secret?"

Maria collapsed to the ground, weeping. "No one. I have no idea what to do, not a single thought in my head. Please help me."

Isabella reached out her hand to Maria. "Get up and walk with me."

Adelena helped the infanta up and provided a handkerchief. She remained behind the two ladies as they walked, arm in arm. The governess instinctively knew to keep quiet while the young women conversed.

"We can both retire for a time to a convent in the countryside," Isabella said. "A season of prayer and reflection would be welcome after all we've been through this year."

Maria stopped and turned toward her, clutching Isabella's arm with her free hand. "Please, tell Lord Gregory Mack and no one else. He is the only member of the prince's coterie I trust. He behaves like Charles's true father, and Charles is always his best when he's with him."

Isabella reflected on this.

"That's a good choice," she said, at length. "He is one of the few Englishmen I actually admire. I know a few things about Lord Gregory, if you would like to learn about him."

"Please, do tell. I need a distraction."

"Lord Tassis kept me well-informed, one of many services he generously provided. When I asked about Lord Gregory, he investigated, and returned with a full report. I was astonished to learn Gregory and his family are second cousins and close allies of King James's family, the Stuarts. Gregory has known Prince Charles since birth. When Charles was six, Gregory Mack was sixteen. At that point, he taught the prince how to ride and hunt. When he came of age, Gregory taught Charles how to conduct himself at court. Sir Gregory was always by the prince's side when he traveled."

"So, he did raise my bonnie prince." Maria smiled. "I remember ordering him about a good deal. Now, I realize he was a good sport about it."

"There is no story that will surprise this man," said Isabella. "He will serve both you and Prince Charles admirably."

Maria stopped, clutching Isabella's arm. Fear reclaimed her eyes. "Do you think Lord Gregory will help me if I need to go somewhere for a year or so?"

Isabella draped her arms around the infanta's shoulders and held her for some time before pulling back. She looked the princess in the eye and said, "I am the Queen of Spain. I have good family connections in France. You are the Infanta of Spain. You have excellent connections as well. Lord Gregory, for one. He will be honored to give you all the help you need, I am certain."

Maria drew in several sharp breaths before entwining her arm into Isabella's again and continuing their walk, Adelena remaining silent, trailing a few steps behind. The garden was astonishing in the early golden light. Drops of dew sparkled like diamonds on blades of grass. The three ladies drew long, elegant shadows on the lawn.

"This will be a busy day for us both," said Isabella. "I shall tell my husband all of this has been a shock to your tender spirit, that you should leave for the northern chapel to renew yourself, and that I shall be your chaperone. We shall keep some things a mystery until we know exactly the shape of things to come."

"But doesn't Charles have a right to know?"

"No," said Isabella. "This is women's business. Besides, as regents of Spain, we are better able to deal with emerging events than the nouveau riche Stuarts. I will speak to my king as soon as he is awake."

"You're not going to tell him!" Maria exclaimed.

"Of course not," Isabella said. "Only about your need to rest at a nearby convent."

Maria sighed with relief. "Could you join me on my journey? I cannot bear to go alone. I need someone I can trust."

"I would be happy to accompany you," said Queen Isabella, "and stay for as long as you like."

She took Maria's hands into her own and smiled. The thought of escaping her husband filled her heart with relief. She would tell him she would be away for a fortnight or two. He could learn from a letter she would stay longer.

30

Leaving Madrid

October 1623
Spain

The royal caravan ambled through the Spanish countryside, headed for Burgos and the Santa Dorotea Convent. Fifty mounted soldiers led, sporting uniforms of sky blue trimmed with gold braid. Another fifty soldiers rode behind the royal party, with mounted troops flanking them. Sporadic rainstorms had revived the grass in the field. Trees ablaze in autumn foliage dotted the verdant landscape.

Isabella adjusted her capotain hat to keep the sun from her eyes. She rode a white Andalusian mare while Maria and Adelena huddled in a coach behind her. King Philip had sent along a dowager of proper peerage to chaperone Isabella. The woman sat in the coach with Princess Maria and Adelena, as Isabella had instructed her. The woman had family in Burgos, and Isabella resolved to encourage the friendly dowager to spend time in the city with her family so Isabella could be free from prying eyes.

Sir Gregory emerged from the front guard, trotting toward her on a brown Thoroughbred. "I've spoken to

Captain Rodriguez," he said. "Apparently, you are the only personage in the travelling party who can issue commands that outrank his."

"Indeed, I am," Isabella said, grateful he had come to converse with her just as boredom was setting in.

"I would like to suggest a change in our destination."

"Really?" she exclaimed, intrigued. "What do you suggest, Sir Gregory?"

He pulled his horse in close to ward off eavesdroppers. Isabella enjoyed the way the breeze lifted his chestnut hair from his shoulders. "I am concerned about the infanta's condition," he said. "A convent anywhere in Spain could invite rumors. I know of a lovely convent in Flanders, just over the border of France. Noblewomen, both young and old, seek refuge at Our Lady of Temple Mars. It has a lovely courtyard brimming with fruit trees and flower gardens. Most importantly, the abbess and the sisters are admired for their discretion, especially in such circumstances as we have found ourselves."

A light thrill rushed through Isabella. She relished the thought of choosing a more distant destination, especially one that put her on the far side of Paris. She trusted Sir Gregory's judgment.

"That would be ideal," she said. "Flanders is under the Hapsburg flag. If you are asking me to give the order to switch our destination from Santa Dorotea to Our Lady of Temple Mars, consider it done. I am so weary of rumormongers I am longing to leave Spain. Do we need to change course?"

"No need. We shall pass the town of Burgos on our way to the Port of Bilbao, where we can set sail for Dunkirk."

When they reached Burgos, Isabella insisted the chaperone stay with her family until their return.

"Have I offended you?" the dowager asked, her forehead creased with worry.

"Not at all," said Isabella. "You have fulfilled my every request. I will hold you in my affection forever more." She smiled convincingly at the woman.

The chaperone was still hesitant, but Isabella assured the woman she would be reunited with the traveling party when they returned, and no one would be the wiser.

Maria sat in an open carriage between Adelena and Sir Gregory. As he extolled the virtues of Our Lady of Temple Mars, Maria removed her hat, allowing the breeze to blow through her thick hair. She was beyond caring what such an action would do to her creamy complexion. She breathed in the air, scented with juniper and wood smoke.

"Will Prince Charles come to visit?" she asked. She could not finish the question without a waver in her voice.

There was no need for Gregory to answer. She could tell by his look of compassion there would be no visits from her bonnie prince. She closed her eyes, but it did not stop the tears from falling. Throwing protocol to the wind, Gregory put both arms around her and rocked her. She buried her face in his shoulder as he spoke gently.

"We must concentrate on your well-being. You are at a challenging passage in your life."

Her shoulders shook with sobs.

"We cannot know what fortunes lie ahead, but you will, most assuredly, be a powerful and noble queen one day.

Your subjects will love you and praise you for the wisdom and kindness of your rule."

At length, Maria stopped crying, but she did not lift her head from Gregory's shoulder for quite some time. The soldiers politely ignored them.

Two weeks later, they reached the Port of Bilbao. Maria dreaded the sea voyage, but Isabella assured her the winds were blowing steady in their favor and they would make it to Flanders within days.

31

The Last Kiss

October 23rd dawned cold and rainy. John Digby and his wife presided over a candlelit breakfast. The scent of fried ham and fresh bread permeated the room. The fireplace warmed Anne's face as she ate.

She caught Harald's eye. Her stomach clenched in apprehension at the grim look on his face. The journey ahead could be pleasant or grueling, depending on Spain's fickle weather. She couldn't wait to be in England, wrapped in his arms in a soft bed in a familiar room.

Once the coaches were packed and provisioned, the traveling party began to board, but when Prince Charles realized Isley and Varney would ride outside the coach on horseback, he refused to get inside. He insisted on riding his own horse out of Madrid and would not be overruled on the grounds of security.

"I am alive and well, as anyone can plainly see," he said, exasperated. "Your obsession with my personal safety is verging on paranoia."

"It wasn't paranoia that landed two poison darts in your doublet, Your Highness," Harald said.

"I beg your pardon," the prince said, indignant.

"Baroness Catherine!" Harald called out, turning his head toward Kitty. "Please be a dear and get in the coach." He held out his hand to her. Boarding a lady's maid before a royal was a violation of protocol, but it worked. The prince yielded to the fetching Kitty and followed her.

When Anne saw the prince content in the coach, she decided to ride with her husband. She knew Harald wanted her at his side, even though he would be the last to say it.

"Lady Digby," Anne asked, "is there a place I can change quickly?"

Laura Digby smiled. Anne suspected she was glad to have just a few more moments with her. She rarely had an opportunity to discuss national affairs with a lady of rank, particularly one who actually understood what she was talking about.

"Please, come with me, M'Lady," she said, taking Anne's arm, and leading her to a small drawing room.

Anne retrieved a pair of boys 'riding breeches from her satchel before sitting down to pull off her riding boots.

"Shall I beckon Kitty to help you with those?" Laura asked.

"Not necessary," said Anne, pulling off the first boot. She set to work on the remaining one. "Kitty and I always travel in riding boots. Even ladies must be prepared to march around in the brush."

"No doubt, riding boots and boys 'breeches will protect you from the morning chill. Shall I fetch some blankets for your journey?"

"That is kind of you, Laura, but there are blankets in the coach. Besides, I intend to ride out of Madrid by my husband's side."

"Really," said Laura, "and not in that nice warm coach with the prince?"

Anne started to tell Lady Digby how much she enjoyed riding beside her husband as the day grew warm and bright, but she choked up before she could get the words out.

"What is it, dear?" Laura asked, patting her shoulder.

"I don't know," Anne said. "I just can't be away from my husband today. I have to ride with him."

Laura nodded and readjusted the back of Anne's skirt to cover the breeches. "I couldn't help but notice the clasp at your waist and the pleat beneath. Is that so you can easily slip your skirt off, if need be?"

"Yes," said Anne. "Kitty and I stand ready to participate in any sudden violence that might occur as we head to Santander."

"Oh, my, how... irregular."

"It hasn't happened yet," said Anne. "Most likely, it never will."

"I suppose it is better to be prepared and never need it," said Laura. "I pray you never do."

"As do I," said Anne with a nervous laugh. She gave her hostess a quick hug and strode rapidly back to where the coach was being loaded. Twenty English soldiers lined up ahead. A second group of twenty soldiers lined up to protect them from the rear.

Harald brought his horse to the window of Prince Charles's carriage. "We had hoped to see the infanta as we left, but we now have word from King Philip that she and Queen Isabella departed early this morning for a convent in the mountains. As a courtesy to the House of Hapsburg, Sir Gregory is riding with them."

"Gregory Mack is with them and he said nothing to me?" Prince Charles was aghast. "How dare he! How—" He choked up.

Kitty frowned in sympathy and instinctively put her hand on his shoulder before catching herself and taking it away.

The prince composed himself. "Thank you, Lord Audley. I know the infanta will be safe. I had hoped to say farewell before we left."

"I know," said Harald.

The wind blew cold from the mountains. The Digbys made their farewells and hurried back to their warm fires.

Buckingham waved his hat in the air to signal the group as they began their march north toward the Spanish coast.

The air was so clear, it revealed a panoramic view of the tree dotted hills in crystalline detail. Chilly sprinkles of rain sprayed Anne's face, even as the sun warmed her shoulders. Over the scent of horses and saddles, she could smell the sandalwood soap she and Harald had bathed with the night before. Prince Charles would marry the lovely Maria, or he would marry some other princess. She no longer cared. She was with the man she loved. She smiled at her husband.

"You and I have had a lovely time in Spain, this year, no matter how it came out," she said to him.

"It was a delight, wasn't it?" he exclaimed, his smile flashing from beneath the shadow of his broad-brimmed hat. "Though, it is truly unfortunate to have to go back to poor, sick King James and tell him about the mess."

"Mess" was their code word for Buckingham's sabotage of the marriage negotiations, though Buckingham rode too far ahead to hear.

It was afternoon when they arrived at San Agustin, a town of many crossroads. Wagons bearing artisan goods from Madrid and grain from the countryside crowded the road that led into the bustling town.

Anne was pleased to see the bright cantinas at the outskirts. The aroma of broiling cutlets and herbed vegetables suffused the air.

Soon, they were seated in their own set of tents. Varney and Isley rushed off to the broilers to bring back food.

They finished their meals with tiny ginger cookies and a tureen of rum mixed with fresh orange juice. As they sipped their drinks, two large butterflies joined them, as if they'd been invited. One was bright yellow. The other was black with crimson slashes and white spots on its wings. They fluttered about the tureen before landing and dipping their proboscises in for a drink. Anne reached out to touch the yellow one, but it flew up and landed on Harald's tumbler.

"Well," said Harald. "I have never known two butterflies of different genera to travel together, but this fellow is the brimstone butterfly. It looks like a falling yellow leaf. Welcome to my drink, little fellow."

Once the butterfly drank its fill, it stepped off the rim of the glass and onto Harald's hand, then gazed at him.

"If I belonged to one of the Eastern religions, I might wonder if this fellow and I have been in previous battles together," said Harald. "He greets me like an old friend." The yellow butterfly flew up, circled him three times, and fluttered away.

Anne looked down at her own glass. The black butterfly had landed on it. A bright red strip ran diagonally across the top of each forewing, like an admiral's stripes—or a gaping wound.

"Oh, this one I know," said Anne. "It's the red admiral."

"Ah, I learned something new today," said Harald. "Any sense you may have fought old battles with your red admiral?"

Anne smiled. "More likely, we spent rainy afternoons in a library."

The butterfly finished its drink and flew onto her shoulder. It sat there a moment, gently flexing its wings before fluttering up into the air and chasing its comrade out of the tent.

Anne looked at Harald. His perfect face seemed captured in a precious locket of time. So vital, so strong a man. A tender smile graced his lips.

"What do you see, my dear lady? You look concerned."

"Nothing I can put into words," she said, blinking back tears. "Just that I love you so much and I am deeply happy for every day we spend together."

"Oh, we'll be together a good deal more, my darling."

Anne quieted her heart by promising herself she would fully enjoy every instant she spent with her husband.

They picked up the drinks the butterflies had sipped from, toasted each other, and finished them off.

"I would love to break our glasses over this magical moment," said Harald, "but the vendor would be furious, I am sure."

Anne laughed.

Holding hands, they walked to their horses. Buckingham had his horse impatiently trotting in circles.

"Well, look at that. Buckingham is ready to go before anyone else," said Harald, under his breath. "There's a first time for everything, I suppose."

"Tally ho!" Buckingham called out. "We need to be at our next destination before dark. No time for laggards," he added, looking harshly at Anne and Harald.

"And he can't resist being a cad about it," Anne mumbled.

Harald leaned toward Anne and kissed her. Before he pulled away, she wrapped her arms around his neck and kissed him long and deeply, ignoring the soldiers around them.

Varney helped Prince Charles and Kitty back into the coach. There was a bit of a delay as Prince Charles insisted Kitty go before him, once again in violation of protocol.

Anne took her dapple gray mare by the bridle. As she guided her onto the path, a rustling in the bushes beyond the road caught her attention. Two young men in hunting garb sprang from the foliage, each with a large knife in his hand. The soldiers ahead of her and behind her were distracted as they prepared to mount their horses.

Anne's world slowed. Everything in motion seemed to float in mid-air. She shed her skirt without a thought, and grabbed the foot-long knife from the scabbard at her hip.

"Ambush!" she screamed.

The soldiers turned their heads.

Kitty burst from the coach. With a flick of her fingers, her skirt dropped, revealing a pair of snug-fitting breeches.

Anne lunged toward the assailant on the right, knowing Kitty would get the other. Holding her knife tightly, Anne turned the blade horizontally as she dashed past the assailant and sliced his throat.

She turned just in time to see Kitty drop to one knee with an animalistic scream and stab the second assailant where his leg met his groin, pulling her knife through his femoral artery and muscle tissue, effectively crippling him. The man Anne had mortally wounded lay in the dirt nearby, gurgling blood.

She turned toward Harald to see him shoving Prince Charles into the coach as the reluctant royal fought to see what was going on. A few of the soldiers had turned their horses toward them.

Anne rushed toward Harald to assist him, but Buckingham was suddenly in the way.

A third man rocketed from the bushes. He held a musket in each hand and was past Anne before she noticed him. As his profile sailed by, she recognized Father Eremitz's manservant.

Her mind flashed to the vivid memory of Eremitz and Buckingham walking at the Alcazar, shoulder to shoulder, heads together, murmuring to each other.

She watched helplessly as Capistrano headed straight for Harald. Still, Buckingham would not yield. She ducked under Buckingham's long-legged horse. He maneuvered the beast into a circle and caged her in, but she scrambled free and rushed toward Harald.

He had the carriage door closed and latched when Capistrano came upon him.

Anne pointed herself toward them and ran at full speed, but no matter how powerfully she willed herself forward, she was trapped in a gelatinous nightmare of slowing time.

Harald spun around and deftly deflected the musket in the assailant's right hand, just as Capistrano placed the muzzle of the second musket above Harald's heart and pulled the trigger.

Anne grabbed the back of Capistrano's hair, her foot-long knife at his throat, and sliced him to his spine. His neck gushed blood. He looked at her with the eyes of a dead man. Anne could see no ill will, just resignation.

She tossed him aside and fell to her knees. Harald lay on the ground, looking dazedly at the sky.

"Where is the prince?" he whispered.

Gallant to the end, her soulmate and love of her life. Anne screamed to the heavens, knowing it was no use. There was no one there to hear.

The danger passed, leaving behind nothing but confusion and despair. The next moments were a blur—Kitty at her side… soldiers crowding around… Kitty pulling her toward the carriage... Isley and Varney wrapping Harald in a dark wool blanket and loading him on an old wooden cart… rushing to the cart for her husband and finding only the woolen bundle… placing her hands over layers of wool, searching for a beating heart.

"We must get back in the carriage," Kitty said softly. "I promise you, that is what Harald wants. Please, please, Lady Anne." She wept. "Think of what your Lord Harald would want."

Eyes bleary with tears, Anne silently asked the sky what Harald would want.

The soft wind assured her Harald had left the body beneath her hands and had moved on. She saw herself through his eyes looking down from above—a grief-stricken widow weeping over her lost husband. She sensed his desperation to restore her happiness, but Anne could see no happiness in her future. All joy had died with her love.

32

Skull and Crossbones

Day turned to night, and became day again. Anne found herself in the courtyard of a thatched-roof cottage, immobile in a wicker chair, looking upon a burbling stream that ran along the back of the property. A stone wall to her right was decorated with terracotta pots brimming with cascading caper flowers of lavender and white. A nearby chiminea emitted enough heat to keep the breeze from chilling her.

Varney and Isley sat at a nearby table, conversing. They had made it clear they were at her service. Anne knew they were eager to help, but she could think of nothing she needed, aside from her husband.

The landlady kept wine and cool well water in Anne's two glasses. A cutting board filled with bread and butter lay alongside a bowl of fruit. Anne sipped at the wine. She couldn't eat but didn't notice. Harald was dead. She felt void of hunger and expectation as her sense of reality grew increasingly tenuous. The chair, stream, and trees were real, but she felt as insubstantial as a ghost.

The landlady said something kind to her in Spanish. Anne had become well acquainted with the language, yet she didn't know if it was a question or a statement, and then she forgot what the lady said.

The landlady smiled and held out a dainty, rose-emblazoned teacup on a matching saucer.

"Bless you," said Anne, taking the cup and sipping the warm lemon-honey brew. It soothed her aching throat.

Kitty emerged from the back door of the house, dressed in a quilted beige bustier over white billowing sleeves and skirts. A leather satchel hung over her shoulder, barely concealing the scabbard of a long knife that hung beneath. Kitty swept a short, hooded cape over her shoulders as if she were on a mission.

"Where is Buckingham?" Anne asked. She wasn't concerned about his welfare. To her, the ruthless duke was little more than a dangerous animal she hoped to keep at bay.

"He has continued his journey to London with Prince Charles. We are staying here for a while. We need the rest."

"My throat is sore," said Anne.

Kitty put her arms around Anne's shoulders and spoke softly in her ear.

"I know," she said. "You screamed for a long time yesterday."

Anne was puzzled. "I did?"

"I have learned there is an Eritrean mortician on the far side of town," said Kitty, straightening herself. "Our hostess was kind enough to give me instructions on how to find her. Varney and Isley will stay with you. I'll take the cart with me. Lord Harald's remains will be prepared for the rest of the journey, according to custom."

Anne nodded but forgot where Kitty was going the moment she was out of sight. She resumed gazing at the stream. Doves cooed in the olive trees around her. The creek burbled along its journey.

By the time Kitty returned, the glow of twilight would be slipping across the sky.

Kitty had wrapped Harald's body in two linen sheets, but even in the cool weather, she knew she had to get him to the mortician as soon as possible. She walked beside the donkey as he pulled the cart. The journey wasn't long and she needed a good stroll.

The donkey seemed to know its way to the crossroads. They walked half a mile on the winding streets. At the far edge of town, the houses were more widely spaced, and most had workshops behind them. Kitty spotted the white stucco house roofed in apricot-colored tiles. Violet flowers lined the outer walls, climbing up vertical strings like ivy. Kitty recognized the perfumed scent of sweet pea blossoms.

She reached for the pull cord on the ornate iron gate and tugged on it. It set off a series of tubular bells hanging above. The soft harmony sounded like exotic temple music.

A tall African woman emerged from the house. Her long cotton gown was a bright geometric print, predominately brick red. The scarves that formed her towering turban were of varying shades of violet.

"Buenas días, Señora," Kitty said with a curtsy as the Eritrean woman opened the gate and waved her in. "I have with me the body of my dear master, Lord Harald Audley.

His lady's wish is to perform the funeral rites for English knights."

"Anglo knights?" the Eritrean woman asked in a rich North African accent. "Sí, sí," she nodded as she expertly ran her long hands over Harald's wrapped corpse. "We have a large cauldron in the back."

"A cauldron?" Kitty wondered if there had been a horrible misunderstanding. At the end of the ritual, Anne would be presented with the immaculate skull and thigh bones of her beloved, but did this foreign woman understand how such a task was achieved?

The Eritrean woman regarded her with peaceful eyes as it dawned on Kitty the process would, indeed, involve a large cauldron. How else would the mortician separate the flesh from the bones in a timely fashion? Kitty had no desire to further contemplate the matter.

"But, of course," she added, her voice barely audible.

Once they sorted out the services and fees, the Eritrean woman gave a sharp whistle. A boy with curly black hair and a grin rushed up to take the donkey by the harness. As he guided the gentle beast and cart to the work yard behind the house, the donkey trotted along willingly, eager to be with a cheerful soul. Kitty sighed and turned toward the Eritrean woman.

"I am Batsheeba. Welcome to my villa." The woman led Kitty toward the sprawling, one-story house. "You can sit in my parlor, if you like. It has many shadows for grieving souls. Or you can enjoy the sunshine on my porch. I can put a fire in the chiminea, to keep your feet warm."

"The porch sounds lovely," said Kitty.

She sat on a wicker chair with a curved fanback that nearly hugged her. Batsheeba bustled about, giving orders in a strange language to the maids inside the house and to the servants in the yard.

Once refreshments were served, the mortician came to rest at the table across from Kitty.

"You are in good hands," she said, patting Kitty's forearm. "I know the ritual you need. When the Anglo knights came to the Holy Land, your knights learned the ritual from those who guarded the vaults of the Temple of Solomon. My people are those people. They don't guard the temple vaults anymore. They had to come home."

"Oh, how sweet the thought," Kitty sighed, "coming home." She stared at the flames in the chiminea as tears welled in her eyes.

"I know why you weep," said Batsheeba. "When you lose someone who takes a piece of your heart, you can never come home again. I lost my father when I was young. I learned much from those who comforted me. And I learned much from those who did not. It is my calling now to care for the dead. To care for the dead is to care for the living. You are in a hard time now. But you have what you need to face it, come what may. After the grief, new doors will open, and you will be ready to pass those thresholds."

Kitty smiled through her tears. "Thank you for your kind words," she said.

Batsheeba left to check on the progress of the work. Kitty dozed in her chair while the sun's rays sparkled through the canopy of grapes and warmed her shoulders. She awoke at the touch of a cool hand on her arm.

Batsheeba's eyes were calm in her smooth, bronze face.

"Come," she said.

Kitty followed her into the house, all the way to the back. They entered a room where the outer wall above the three-foot paneling was comprised of glass panes, much like Father Eremitz's garden house. Beyond the warped panes was a broad field where green grass waved in the breeze.

Two tall Eritrean women waited in the sunny room. Their bright cotton turbans and long slender dresses were made from exotic prints, similar to Batsheeba's. On a table before them was a polished wood case, bright copper-red with wavy streaks of bronze, exactly like Harald's mane of hair.

"I noticed your master had lovely hair," Batsheeba said, stroking the box. "I hope this acacia wood will be a remembrance."

"I'm sure his wife will love it," said Kitty. "May I view his remains?"

Batsheeba nodded to her staff and the woman on the right opened the case. A gleaming white skull rested upon an indented bed of burgundy satin. Beneath the skull were two crossed thigh bones—bones that had carried the man to all the amazing places he had seen.

"What will become of the rest of him?" Kitty asked.

"We shall bury his remains in the field," Batsheeba said. "The spring rains shall deck his grave with spires of larkspur and fronds of wild roses."

Kitty placed her palm on the skull's broad forehead. "The breadth of his forehead is evidence of the brilliant man he was," she said. "In life, we basked in his wit and wisdom. All contained in this mortal vessel. All gone." Tears sprang to her eyes and ran down her cheeks.

Batsheeba placed a hand on her shoulder. "You don't know how far he has gone, nor where he is. You may, at times, run into this brilliant mind. Your mistress, too."

"You are not Catholic, are you?" Kitty remarked.

"No, I am Eritrean. We belong to the Old Religion. The Ark of God is made from acacia wood, as you know."

"Really?" Kitty knew nothing of such things.

"Oh, yes," said Batsheeba. "My people are the guardians of the Ark. The Queen of Sheba took more than a son from King Solomon. She took the Ark of God, too, as a favor to King Solomon. If it stayed with him, his enemies would have destroyed it long ago. My people kept it safe, from then till now."

The Eritrean woman had divulged an ancient secret, not that Kitty knew what to do with it. She wished she could tell Harald.

Batsheeba's workers carefully lifted Harald's acacia case, took it outside, and gently placed it on the cart. As Kitty passed beyond the gate, they bowed to her, and Batsheeba recited a blessing in a foreign tongue.

Anne hadn't moved from her chair since Kitty had left, neither had she sensed any passage of time. Varney and

Isley were still nearby, sipping ale and nibbling on the bread and cheese the Señora had left for them. Keeping their voices low, they conversed about the best type of horseshoe and choosing an ideal route for their journey homeward. Anne wasn't interested in the topics, but their familiar voices comforted her. The wall took on a golden hue as the day drew to a close. The streams of flowers pouring from the terracotta pots cast long shadows along the stone surface.

The back door of the cottage creaked open, and Anne heard the familiar rustle of Kitty's skirts as she came around and placed the acacia box on the table. Anne ran her fingers along the smooth surface. The afternoon sun had left it warm to the touch. The bronze-streaked copper wood grain reminded her of something familiar. Her fingers discovered the gold-plated hook in front. She opened the box with great care and tenderly took the skull into her hands. After staring at it for a good long while, she kissed its forehead and placed it back in its nest of burgundy satin. "What will happen to the rest of him?" she asked.

"The Eritrean woman will bury his remains in the grassy fields that lay at the outskirts of town," said Kitty. "He'll be surrounded by wildflowers, come springtime."

Anne carefully lowered the lid of the case and caressed the smooth wood, as if Kitty's response pleased her. "What kind of wildflowers?" she asked.

"She mentioned larkspur and wild roses."

"Wild roses," Anne murmured. "Harald was my wild rose."

After a night of weeping over her husband's remains by candlelight, Anne knew it was time to continue her journey.

33

Our Lady of Temple Mars

November 1623
Port of Dunkirk, Flanders

Princess Maria and her party sailed into the Port of Dunkirk on a bright, cold, ear-stinging morning. The ship laid anchor in choppy waves. With Sir Gregory's assistance, Adelena boarded a rowboat that bumped against the ship's hull. Gregory balanced in the wobbly boat as he grasped Maria at the waist and hoisted her aboard in one deft move. Kenhelm and Queen Isabella joined them. Once they were seated, the ship's crew lowered the boat into the dark, chaotic waves.

The oarsmen shoved against the ship's hull with their oars to create space between the vessels, then heaved the oars into the rocking waves and rowed in powerful, steady strokes. Sir Gregory wrapped his arm about Maria's shoulders to stabilize her as the rowboat's prow dipped and rose.

A sharp wind sprayed drops of water into Maria's face. She barely noticed as she marveled at the glittering waves.

The sun's rays splayed through a cluster of clouds, lighting up sections of the bright green sea below with broad shafts of sunlight. She had never seen anything so beautiful.

The oarsmen guided the boat straight onto the shoreline, where the prow sliced through the sand with a hiss before coming to a neat stop.

Gaily painted row houses crowded the far side of a broad thoroughfare that ran atop the seawall. The scent of rotting seaweed assaulted their nostrils as they ascended the stone stairs. They piled into a coach wherein Maria sat shoulder to shoulder with Adelena, taking comfort in her familiar scent of rosemary and lavender. The coachman cracked his whip and the wheels creaked into motion. They rolled onto the road that led up a sloping hill into town. Adelena rolled her wool shawl and placed it behind the princess's neck. Maria fell asleep and did not wake until the coach came to a full stop.

They stayed at an inn overlooking the bay in a room decked with white eyelet curtains and coverlets. A fire crackled in a hearth between two louvered shutters, which opened to a view of the sea.

Since their sea voyage had been fraught with rough waters, Queen Isabella ordered the traveling party to take a short respite from their journey. Over the next three days, Maria, Isabella, and Adelena drifted from their cozy beds to the sofa and armchairs near the fireplace, where they read and chatted. They sent for tea and pastries in the afternoons. Isabella commandeered the small desk. She offered to provide Maria with a pen and parchment for writing letters of her own, but Maria declined. She had nothing to say.

They journeyed south toward Lille. The days crackled with cold that bit at their fingertips and toes while their horses snorted steam as they marched through flurries of snow.

Massive windmills dotted the broad fields, their great sails creaking as they rotated in the breeze. Maria squinted to examine their details. She had heard of them. Señor Cervantes's tale of a ridiculous old aristocrat going to battle with windmills and losing badly had been the gossip du jour throughout her childhood. Aristocrats and clergy alike found the story insulting, although they had a hard time pinpointing exactly how the windmills mocked them. They settled on the accusation the story was an outrageous lie and therefore, a type of heresy.

Our Lady of Temple Mars dominated the broad, flat-topped hill that lay ahead. Stone towers with slate-shingled, pyramid-shaped roofs rose above the evergreens. The expansive walls of the convent were lined with windows.

As their carriage approached, the massive arched doors of the bell tower slowly swung open, pushed by two nuns. A coterie of black-clad women in white wimples topped by black head cloths streamed through the doors and formed a reception line. A tall woman in a black gown swept around the line of nuns. Her headdress appeared to be white gauze wrapped around a pair of goat horns. As odd as it was, it gave her a look of authority.

Abbess Louise stepped near the carriage doors and greeted the occupants.

Sir Gregory jumped out and spoke with her, his voice low. After a short conversation, he extended his hand to Maria and helped her step down from the coach. The fragrance of cedar smoke wafted through the chilled air.

The abbess led them through the convent gates into the hollowed tower. Stone walls reached high over their heads. The beveled diamond panes of the high cathedral windows displayed a fractured blue sky. At the top, a massive bell hung from a wooden beam.

They traversed the pathway beneath the vaulted tower, and the abbess waved them through a pair of ornamental gates on the other side. A vast courtyard awaited them, surrounded by the walls of the convent's chambers and offices. Bare trees stood in neat rows, their black branches reaching no higher than the sills of the second-story windows. Gregory smiled as he pointed them out.

"Come springtime, you will be surrounded by cherry, apple, and peach blossoms. All through the summer, you will eat your fill of fresh fruit."

The abbess chuckled. "You can eat your fill of stewed fruit and clotted cream at tea time, if you please," she said. "We dry the fruit we don't eat in the summer and enjoy it at breakfast during the winter months."

A flock of chickens pecked at the dry grass.

Maria turned her head and could barely believe her eyes. Along a far wall was a row of massive flowers. Spanning over two feet in diameter, they sported velvety, green petals shot through with burgundy-tinted veins. At each center was a perfectly round, deep red orb. She had never seen anything so exotic. She grasped Isabella's arm and pointed.

"Dear heaven!" she exclaimed. "Have you ever seen such grand flowers?"

Isabella laughed. "Those are *cabbages*."

"You jest!" Maria retorted. She looked more closely. Upon realizing the violet orbs at the center of the incredible flowers were, indeed, red cabbages, she blushed. They both laughed merrily as she wove her arm through Isabella's.

Maria breathed in the scented air. Just as she allowed a spark of happiness into her heart, her tears sprang anew. She closed her eyes tightly, willing them away. They disobeyed and rolled down her cheeks, but the bitterness was gone. Isabella clasped her hand and said nothing. Adelena handed Maria a handkerchief. Relief mingled with sadness.

Maria put off unpleasant worries as to who would be foisted upon her at the altar, or what would become of the baby stirring within her belly. Instead, she looked forward to seeing her new apartment, and an early dinner.

34

Home Again

December 1623
Southampton, England

Anne wandered through her cozy home, catching glimpses of Harald everywhere—reading letters at his desk, stoking the fire, gazing at stars from the balcony. When she turned to look, she saw nothing but shadows. The empty spaces reminded her Harald was dead and she was alone.

I can't stay here, she thought. The emptiness suffocated her.

Aelfreda, her sister-in-law, arrived shortly after breakfast one morning, and invited Anne and Kitty to stay in the château with her family.

"Your son wants you," Aelfreda said with a sad smile. It was a white lie. In Anne's ten-month absence, the five-year-old had cleaved to his new family.

At the château, Quentin engaged in his new custom—paying his respects to his mother for two minutes before dashing off to play with his cousins. Although Anne could no longer feel happiness, she still enjoyed the sight and sound of happy children. Their innocence lifted her spirits.

Aelfreda respected her solitude there, but when Anne stared mindlessly out the window for too long, Aelfreda would engage her with some busy task. They sorted the linens, gathered bouquets from the garden, or tatted lace. On Christmas Eve, they gathered in the kitchen with the children to make gingerbread cookies. Anne supervised Quentin as he iced cookies cut into shapes of woodland animals. Amidst the giggling, flour-dusted children and the warm scent of baking cookies, Anne's happiness returned for a fleeting moment.

One snowy afternoon, Anne sat in the parlor listening to the fire crackle within the shelter of its Baroque mantel while she tatted lace. The long velvet curtains, pulled to each side of the window, created a frosty triangle of light. Beyond the window, snow fell softly and quietly as cotton. Anne felt the chill of winter to her left, and the warmth of the fire to her right. She paused, resting her needles and lace in her lap. There was great pain in her unfathomable loss, but there was warmth, too. She resolved then and there to move past her grief and return to the land of the living.

The sound of the front door opening and clanging shut made her look up. Her brother-in-law trotted up three curved steps and sailed into the parlor.

"Have you heard the news from Venice?" he asked. He knelt at the fire to toss on another log.

"No," said Anne, sitting up straight. "Please, tell me. I am eager for news."

Cedric rose and took a poker from the stand. A few jabs at the charred log on the bottom sent a rush of sparks up the flue. He went to the table containing the spirits and poured out two walnut cordials. He handed one to Anne before sitting down in a nearby armchair.

"This comes straight from the Horse and Brimstone," he said, referring to his favorite tavern. "The Venetians are buying Italian translations of King James's Bible, as if it were plated in gold. The Vatican is furious." Cedric grinned. "The printers cannot keep up with the demand. Everyone of fashion is reading it, in open defiance of the pope. Isn't that rich?"

Anne smiled. She found Cedric's likeness to her husband more comforting than disturbing. He wasn't as tall, and his hair was more brown than auburn, but his face, with his prominent nose, intelligent eyes, and strong jaw, was all too familiar.

Cedric settled in to sip at his drink. "Even in Italy, the King James Version of the Bible is more popular than the official Latin Vulgate. Everyone wants to read the scriptures in their own language. I proudly give credit to our visionary king." He raised his crystal glass toward her.

"Hear, hear," said Anne, clinking her small glass to his. She paused. "This makes me wonder if Buckingham is feeding the tavern's gossip mill to obfuscate his deliberate sabotage of the marriage negotiations." She looked directly into Cedric's eyes. "He had Harald murdered because Ambassador John Digby instructed him to make a full report to King James."

Cedric's face grew cool. Anne sensed he had something to tell but hesitated on account of her condition. He looked away but looked toward her again.

"Everyone knows Buckingham's a fraud and they hate him all the more—" he stopped.

Anne looked at him warily. "Why do they hate him all the more?" She studied his face. "Is it because King James is on his death bed and Buckingham is casting his spell over our crown prince, more powerful than the one he has cast over his father?"

"We hoped to keep that from you."

"Did you think Kitty would keep me in the dark? I wonder how long it will be before I am sent to the Tower," Anne sighed and looked out the window.

Cedric took a deep breath. "You are most dear to us, Duchess Audley."

"I am no duchess," Anne sighed, "not without Harald."

Cedric paused. At length, he said, "We have another family title you would be most welcome to take on, if you prefer. It belonged to a great aunt on our mother's side. She was a lonely woman with a sad life. Her own peers floated a rumor she had murdered her second husband. Harald and I found that monstrously unlikely. He was a beastly man who beat her, so her peers assumed he was too cruel and arrogant to take his own life."

"How did he die?" Anne asked, turning her face toward him.

"Our aunt found him hanging," he paused. "He'd been beaten severely. Our family assumed he'd fought at a tavern, taken a thrashing, and while in a drunken stupor, decided to end his life. At any rate, you can't blame Her Majesty Aunt Jane for his ignoble end."

"Her Majesty Aunt Jane?"

"That's what Harald and I called her."

Anne smiled and imagined Her Majesty Aunt Jane beating her beastly husband to death. She wondered if Jane's first husband had been like Harald, and her second like George Villiers. "What was she like?" she asked.

"She was thin and delicate, but tall. Her eyes crinkled when she smiled. She kept her tresses tucked beneath a floppy muslin cap. One day, Harald and I popped over while her maid was combing her long hair. It shone as bright as polished silver and reminded me of Lady Godiva. We begged her to wear it hanging down her back, just for the day. She found us amusing and had her maid pin her tresses into a great spiral at the back of her head, like a silver nautilus. When she served tea, it came with amazing canapés and petit-fours, the sort of treats you find at a grand ball. She made us feel like royalty." He fell silent, lost in his memories.

Anne cleared her throat. "What was her title?" she asked.

"Ah," Cedric chuckled. "I quite forgot. Lady de Winter. It is a wonderfully respectable name, I assure you."

"It is perfect." Anne looked out the window at the bare, snow-covered trees. "My summers are gone, and so, I become Lady de Winter."

35

The Ring

December 1623
London, England

Prince Charles gazed through crystal windowpanes at the brilliant field of snow. At the far edge, a row of bare-branched elm trees glittered with frost against the deep blue sky. The day was bright but icy cold. Sunlight flashed through the beveled crystals with prisms so beautiful, he couldn't stop staring at them. His frock coat failed to ward off the chill emanating from the window, so he pressed his shoulders into the velveteen upholstery of the armchair and hugged himself, caressing the plush velvet of his sleeves.

What makes sunny winter days colder than overcast ones?

His mind drifted from that thought to his tribulations. Upon his arrival in London, his father's ministers made a great fuss over him, even as they pointedly ignored the perils of his journey. They shrugged away his fears when he recounted the numerous attempts made on his life. In their view, the crown prince was clearly safe and sound. Thus, Spain's numerous assassination attempts were dismissed as a moot point. The ministers were consumed with the subject of primogeniture, which involved far more than a crown prince being coronated upon his father's demise.

The ministers ordered him to attend their morning meetings, as if he had no choice in the matter. And apparently, he didn't, for if he tarried so much as one minute, his valets grew anxious and hurried as if their very lives depended on his punctuality.

Every day since his return, he was awakened at an hour unnatural for even a common man and forced to endure one long meeting after another. When summed up, matters of trade and politics could be intriguing, but when the ministers made endlessly long sermons around every single topic, needling each matter to death with redundant points and counterpoints, the process devolved into mindless boredom. He encouraged them to sum things up, but each time he did so, they added more verbiage, assuring him every syllable that slipped through their lips was as precious as those uttered by the Savior Christ our Lord. Charles suspected the lot of them just loved to hear themselves talk.

This was what was in store for him as ruler of Great Britain. Who knew being king could be so boring? He felt like a bird beating its wings against its cage.

Buckingham was not invited to the Royal Council meetings, but came anyway, and when the ministers attempted to order him out of the room, he claimed Charles had invited him. Charles had not, but he didn't want to create an ugly scene, so he pretended he had. The minsters glowered at Buckingham but did nothing more. Buckingham rarely said anything in the meetings. Rather, the duke would slip into Charles's study when the meetings were long over, preferring to take his counsel with the crown prince alone.

Charles's thoughts turned to Sir John Digby. The ambassador had caused an uproar by leveling accusations against Buckingham at court. Charles wished the hoards would simmer down and go about their business. Yes, Buckingham had a volatile temper; this was news to no one. Charles couldn't see the point of tattling to the Royal Council about it. The sooner they put the Madrid events behind them, the better. Everyone's tempers were shortened in that beastly heat. Of course, Buckingham made the chaos worse by suggesting Digby was trying to take over the government and might even incite English subjects to take up arms against the royal family. Buckingham could be counted upon to provide the most extreme point of view on any given matter.

Be that as it may, nobody but Sir John Digby cared about the disaster that was the Spanish Match, and his stubborn insistence that the Royal Council investigate the matter was becoming annoying. At that moment, Charles cared only about his father, who would never again rise from his sick bed. That was the news from the king's physician, and that was the only thing that mattered now.

A knock at the door disturbed his thoughts.

"Come in," he said.

Buckingham entered, dressed in black, trying to avoid attracting attention these days.

"I hear tell the wedding negotiations between the English and French Crown are going smoothly," Buckingham announced. "I was surprised to hear Cardinal

Richelieu is writing the marriage contract. I thought it would be the queen mother, Marie de Medici. It was she who made the first overture for a match between you and Princess Henrietta. We can't say that in public, of course."

"Women are bustling hens when it comes to planning their daughters 'nuptials," said Charles. "I'm not surprised the queen mother initiated the proceedings. But why wouldn't the prime minister be negotiating the contract? It is the king's prerogative to leave contract details to his best counselor, isn't it?"

"Indeed, it is," Buckingham said. "What I meant was, Marie de Medici is an obstinate little thing when it comes to having her way, and you'd best watch out for her. She will be your mother-in-law soon. Not to suggest the adorable Henrietta wouldn't make the perfect little queen for you. She is only fifteen—not yet old enough to be dangerous. And no matter how clever she gets with age, you will always be nine years her senior, and all the more clever. But be advised, whereas her mother has the face of a satin pillow, she has also the heart of a viper."

"So I've heard," said Charles. "I have no intention of setting foot in France. I've decided, once the wedding contract is drawn, I will send a proxy to Paris for the wedding ceremony. Then Henrietta can sail to London accompanied by a French fleet, and we can be married here."

Buckingham raised his eyebrows. "An excellent plan, Your Highness. I'll bring it up at the next Royal Council meeting."

"No need, Buckingham," Charles said. "It is not such a hefty idea that I cannot wield it myself."

Buckingham huffed and changed the subject. "That's a lovely ring you're sporting. Is it new?"

Charles raised his left hand to get a better look at the delicate gold ring set with a dainty half-karat emerald. It caught the light from the window and sparkled bright green.

"Lady Anne Audley gave me this shortly after her husband died. We were back in the carriage. She, Kitty, and I were rushing along our way. She appeared to be in shock, just staring ahead at nothing, but then she caught me in her watery gaze, slipped this lovely gem off of her ring finger, and said, 'Your Majesty, this ring was my husband's. Harald wants you to have this ancient talisman. It will bring you wisdom and make you a more effective ruler.'

"I accepted her gift and slipped it easily onto my little finger, where it has been ever since," Prince Charles continued. "When Lady Anne fell asleep on Lady Kitty's shoulder, Kitty related the rest of the story.

"Lord Harald bought the ring in Cairo from an elderly antique dealer who told him the emerald had been fashioned from a small shard that had chipped off the legendary emerald tablet of Hermes Trismegistus as it was being installed in the Alexandria Library. According to the finest secret societies, Hermes Trismegistus was a famous prophet of the ancient world—human in form, but divine in thought and wisdom. It was he who taught the ancient architects the numbers, angles, and formulae that would allow their grand monuments to stand. He engraved his secrets onto a massive emerald boulder, one side of which had been sheared off and polished to provide the surface for the magical text. The dealer claimed that via the power of Mercury, herald of the gods, the ring bestowed wisdom on anyone who wore it.

"Lord Harald didn't believe the man's fairytale, according to Kitty. But the emerald was genuine and of exceptional quality, so he bought it and wore it just past the first knuckle on his ring finger. The moment he placed it there, the business he was conducting in Cairo became swifter and smoother. When an inconvenience blocked his progress, he would instantly imagine a solution, such as strategizing a quick shortcut when a coach was delayed, or realizing a lonely, retired official with a treasure trove of information would enjoy a visit, along with a box of sweets and a forbidden bottle of brandy. The ideas usually came to him as he was gazing at this pretty emerald ring, flashing in the light. He gave the ring to Anne as a token of his affection, shortly after they met. She received it as her ring during their wedding ceremony."

Prince Charles folded his fingers together as he wrapped up his narrative. "An utterly charming story, is it not? I have found the ring to have a similar effect on me. Even though I know the Spanish were attempting to assassinate me, and we absolutely owe them retribution for it, I refuse to allow those assassins to navigate my will. I used to fear my dear father was a bit lily-livered, concerning his aversion to war. Now, I see the wisdom of it. Whereas it is easy to start a war, war takes on a life of its own, and no mortal man, regardless of bravery, can bridle that unholy beast. Like a raging forest fire, a war tends to burn out in its own time, and often with no clear winners. I couldn't see that before, but now, I see plainly that my father was right. A regent is well-advised to steer clear of war, wouldn't you think?"

"Not if you want to be truly great!" Buckingham protested. "The world's greatest empires were built by conquerors—Alexander the Great, King David, Julius and Augustus Caesar."

"In ancient days, yes," Charles replied. "But now, the French Catholics and Protestants have recently knocked themselves senseless in a nasty civil war, and for what? The war settled nothing and nearly obliterated the French treasury. If not for their wine and cheese exports, King Louis and his lovely queen would dress in rags, no doubt. Think of the dowry Princess Henrietta would bring, if not for war. Why, the poor thing is nearly a pauper. Thank goodness her holdings are productive lands else she would have nothing at all. That is what war brings." He raised his left hand and admired the ring. "I do believe this gem of Hermes has made me a wiser man."

"I do believe you are being tricked by a very crafty woman," Buckingham replied.

"What on earth are you talking about?" Charles asked.

"Clearly, Lady Audley is attempting to put you under her spell with that bewitched ring," Buckingham sneered.

"She gave it to me as a gift from the man who had just saved my life."

"But she certainly didn't save *his* life, did she?" Buckingham arched one eyebrow. "You saw her murder two men with your own eyes, I might add. Unnatural behavior for any woman, but beyond the pale for an entitled one. Her victims might have told us who was behind the assassination plot, but she prevented that, didn't she?"

"She was trying to save her husband's life as he was saving my life."

"No! You are mistaken, my dear prince. It was her plot to murder her husband. He was the one the assassins were after, not you. This was obvious from my vantage point. I was mounted on my Thoroughbred while you were looking out the tiny window of a coach, in all due respect, Your Highness."

Charles shook his head, incredulous. "She loved her husband, and why wouldn't she? Aside from being among the most powerful lords in England, he was the most handsome. And he treated her with great respect. What could be her motive in killing her own husband?"

"Why, your affection, of course!" Buckingham exclaimed. "She gave you that ring so you would think fondly of her, as you obviously do. If you spend time with her, she will surely seduce you into marriage, because Lady Anne wants to sit on England's throne. I would suggest you seize her and incarcerate her at the Tower before she kills again! Why, the woman will stop at nothing until get what she wants. She may send assassins to kill you as well!"

"My dear George, I do appreciate your concern, but I am certain it is unfounded. I don't believe a man as wise as Lord Audley would marry such a woman as you describe."

"Love is blind, my dear prince. Even the wisest can be blinded by it."

Charles shook his head. "I will have none of it," he said.

"Ah me," Buckingham shifted in his chair and changed the subject again. "Well, then, the Globe Theater will be featuring playwright Thomas Middleton's most recent production, 'Women Beware Women,' this spring. I hear it is a cautionary tale about deceptive trollops and the chaos they bring. Sounds delightful, doesn't it? I suggest we reserve the entire theater on opening night for our favorites. What say you?"

Charles seized the change in subject and launched into a discussion of the artistry of Thomas Middleton as compared to the antiquated Shakespeare of their grandparents ' generation. As they chatted, Buckingham fetched a bottle of liquor to serve himself and Prince Charles, pouring the amber liquid from a Bohemian crystal decanter into two snifters. He expertly wove the fingers of one hand through the two stems of the snifters and used the other to carry the decanter, which he placed on a small round table between the armchairs. He handed a snifter to Charles.

The prince took a sip of the vanilla-scented liquid and breathed out the bitter aftertaste while Buckingham threw a log on the fire and stoked it. Charles tilted his snifter toward the fireplace to catch the glow of the flames through the swirling cognac.

Their conversation glided from playwrights to courtiers who might be invited to opening night—and who might come uninvited. As the conversation rambled on, Buckingham refilled Charles's drink every time it dwindled to a puddle. The duke rambled on about the latest fashions, a topic that bored Prince Charles. The duke's voice slowed to a monotone. He sounded as if even he were bored by the subject, but he kept talking. His droning voice was the last thing Prince Charles heard before falling asleep.

Buckingham rose from his chair and approached Charles with catlike footfalls. He reached for the prince's hand but touched only the emerald ring with his thumb and forefinger. With his ear cocked to Charles's rhythmic breathing, Buckingham slowly and gently slipped the ring from his finger.

36

The Capo of Rome

January 1624
Rome, Italy

Massimi walked out of the townhouse and locked the heavy, domed door behind him. In the street, fog billowed a somber gray as morning dawned. A fine rain softened the mist and slickened the ancient stone pavement. Although the surrounding townhouses loomed like shadows in the fog, he could still see his boots well enough to avoid the deep cracks between the broad paving stones.

He didn't mount his horse even though he had a six-mile journey ahead. His mission utterly botched, failing to show deep contrition by riding in on a fine horse would be a fatal error.

The damp chill penetrated his cloak as the mist thickened. Thanks to the best roads in the world, Massimi could follow the street to the city gate, and from there, blindly follow the ancient Roman highway deep into the countryside.

His footsteps echoed around him as uncomfortable thoughts from the pit of his conscience rose to torment him. He had failed dozens of opportunities to assassinate Prince Charles, and the prince had returned home, safe. He would never convert to Catholicism. Sparking a war with England had been the only hope of bringing Great Britain back into the fold of the Holy See. A slither of nausea quaked in Massimi's belly, and he broke into a sweat.

Ghostly apparitions of the ruined Roman aqueduct materialized beyond the drifting mist, the crumbled rows of stone arches rising high above his head. He was now beyond the Roman city limits, heading into the countryside.

As he continued, the fog grew so thick he could see nothing through it. When he stopped to listen to the perfect silence, a quiet panic came over him. He resumed walking, welcoming the sound of his own footsteps. His mind turned to Rome's geopolitical landscape.

The tide of Protestant heresy had begun to overwhelm the Inquisition, and being all too familiar with the parties involved, Massimi knew why. An invisible power structure of European communities consisted of a local capo—who was sometimes a common monk with close ties to his community—his consigliere, his team of captains, and thousands of soldiers drawn from surrounding farms and villages.

While the Vatican put on an excellent show of controlling the Inquisition, in reality, local capos ordered the interrogations, the tortures, and even the executions, which were carried out by the captains and soldiers. Their favorite targets were wealthy Jews and Muslims. Convinced that their wealth should be transferred to devout Catholics like themselves, Inquisitions throughout Europe had evolved into bands of thugs shaking down easy prey. Since Jews and Muslims had no power base in Europe, they made handy victims, but that was a problem. While Inquisition capos dallied with inconsequential heretics to line their collective pockets, the Protestants were gathering their forces throughout the Holy Roman Empire, particularly in the Germanic kingdoms, and the German emperor had allowed it.

Now, cardinals packed themselves before the Vatican Council, postulating with pedantic certitude that the German emperor should have been called upon to turn back the Protestant tide a decade prior. Massimi had made that very claim before those very cardinals, a dozen years ago! How he despised their blindness and pretentions of wisdom as they paraded their petty ignorance.

At least Padre had shown faith in Massimi's foresight. Massimi had informed him first, and the Roman capo had put Massimi's dissertation on the calendar of the College of Cardinals, though this act of wisdom had been in vain.

Padre. Who is Padre? Massimi wondered. He still didn't know, though he had once overheard Padre's housekeeper call him Jacopo. Had she slipped and called him by his real name, or accidentally called him by the name of another? She was an old woman, so there was no way of knowing. Massimi knew Padre was a Dominican friar, but that was the full extent of his knowledge of the man. That, plus the fact Padre ran the Roman workforce, including the Vatican housekeeping, guard, and gardening staff, which meant Padre could kill any pope or cardinal at any time.

Perceiving the unique opportunity his position provided, Padre had created the Keepers of the Kingdom, a brotherhood of exemplary seminary students whom the capo groomed to become papal nuncios, secretaries, and messengers throughout Europe. All of them were sworn to secrecy in regard to their true master—Padre, and Padre alone.

The organization had no name when Massimi arrived. He eventually suggested the name to Padre, postulating that allowing the brotherhood a modicum of publicity would attract talent. The capo agreed.

Massimi joined the brotherhood to become part of a network of papal nuncios who gathered information from the most powerful kings in Europe in order to put together the larger picture. That picture clearly showed that the only way the Catholic Church could maintain its hegemony over Europe was through all-out war.

At the crossroad to his destination, the fog thinned enough that he could make out the signpost. He turned and continued his journey on a small dirt road. After a quarter-hour, the fog lifted, and the golden landscape lit up as if the world were waking from a dream.

Up ahead, a two-story cottage with terracotta roof tiles nestled within a half-circle of tall cypress trees. Massimi took a deep breath and let it out slowly. He quickened his pace, eager to get the matter over with. He had given up all attempts at crafting an explanation. Better to gage Padre's mood once he arrived and take it from there.

Massimi rang the bell at the gate. A minute passed before the door of the house creaked open. A clergyman emerged wearing a black velvet cape over a white muslin robe trimmed with lace and pearl buttons. A fringe of black shiny hair encircled the shaven dome of his head. Around his shoulders hung a heavy gold chain terminating in a gold crucifix the length of a small dagger. He waved with an exquisitely manicured hand.

"Good morning, Monsignor Massimi," he called out as he approached.

Massimi didn't like his tone. Though respectful on its surface, there was a faint hint of mockery to it.

"Good morning to you, Friar," Massimi replied, a stinging insult considering the clergyman before him was clearly an aristocrat—most likely an abbot, judging from his pectoral cross. But Padre was a friar, and no one in Rome rose above Padre's rank. The man winced.

"I am here to pay my respects to Padre," Massimi continued. "Forgive me for asking, for I have been away quite some time, but who might you be?"

"Brother Marcos, Padre's new consigliere, at your service, Monsignor," he said with a nod. "Padre's former consigliere passed away last summer. May God rest his soul."

Massimi tamped down his jealousy. He always hoped he would be promoted to consigliere. He wondered what qualified Brother Marcos, and further wondered if Padre was losing his eyesight. The Dominican capo had shunned assistants who gave off even the faintest whiff of vanity.

"Please, follow me," Brother Marcos said, gesturing toward the front door.

Massimi followed the new consigliere into the house. Although Padre's cottage had many rooms, the white stucco walls had no adornment, save for sprays of flowers painted above arched doorways. Large open windows framed bucolic views of olive groves and the rolling hills in the distance. Aside from a cook, housekeeper, and gardener, Padre had no servants. A pack of dogs policed his property at night. If he felt the need for more protection, the surrounding villagers were at his beck and call.

The consigliere led him through the house, past the study, and out into the garden's broad crescent-shaped lawn, walled off by a row of giant cypresses, all a hundred feet tall. Massimi had forgotten their formidable size. From a distance, they appeared quaint.

At the base of the middle cypress, Padre worked at a wrought iron table, sitting in an armchair, clad in an olive-brown cassock. The base of his hawkish nose and his cleft square jaw were visible beneath the hood.

Massimi presumed the smaller chair at the table opposite Padre was intended for him. This gesture of kindness gave him hope for absolution.

He bowed deeply. "Your humble servant, Monsignor Massimi, at your service, Padre."

Padre sat still for several moments before speaking. "Is that how they talk at court nowadays? You used to come to me and say, 'What can I do for you today, Padre? 'But now that you've lived in a palace, you need to be fancy, huh?"

Massimi froze. He had hoped to honor Padre with courtly manners, but now wondered if the old man assumed he was putting on airs. He bowed his head. "You deserve at least as much respect as any king, considering all you do for God's kingdom," Massimi said. "But I realize I have erred by ignoring your direct connection to our Savior, which fills you with divine humility. You do not need courtly theatrics meant to flatter far lesser mortals. Please, forgive me, Padre."

A long silence followed. Massimi broke into a sweat. He had asked forgiveness for a trifling faux pas, when a deadly transgression dangled above him, held back by a thread.

"Sit down," Padre said. He didn't sound angry.

Massimi sat.

"How is young King Philip? Is he devout?" Padre asked.

Massimi breathed a sigh of relief. Of course, Padre wanted to know who the Roman Church could rely on in a holy war—the information he always wanted. The meeting might be nothing more.

"The king of Spain will remain devout so long as he has the right advisors. I do not trust his prime minister, Duke Olivares, as he is a converso Jew. But if we constantly remind him of his status—subtle hints, as he has a temper—he will be obliged to show his loyalty to Catholicism in order to survive politically. If we can coerce him to make Catholic hegemony his priority, he will convince King Philip to follow suit."

Padre nodded. "And what about England?" He asked in slow, measured syllables. "Why is the prince still alive?"

A flash of heat rushed over Massimi and dripped down his back as cold sweat. He opened his mouth to speak but his tongue went dry.

The sun breached the tips of the towering cypresses and stabbed his eyes with harsh rays.

"I failed you, Padre." Massimi's voice broke. "I throw myself at your feet and beg for mercy." He clenched his hands together and resisted the temptation to get on his knees. "I recruited an assassin who was a perfect shot but he failed. At first, he said he couldn't get close enough, so I forgave him, but he failed twice. It is a good policy to forgive just once. I recruited him because he was a really, really good shot, you know? He showed me many times!"

Massimi realized he had slipped back into his old vernacular but didn't care. Indeed, he hoped his Roman peasant accent would resonate in Padre's heart, for it was the very same as his own.

"The second assassin I recruited had an assassin's heart. I made sure," Massimi continued. "His loyalty was absolute. But the two witches with that heretic English prince struck like vipers, laying men low at the point of their knives, their slashes falling like driving rain. They took out the entire brigade I sent. Just those two, because they were filled with the power of Satan!"

Massimi was crying now. "We are fighting a war with Satan. Are we not, Padre?"

Padre slowly nodded. Massimi felt a surge of relief. His display of sincere contrition seemed to soften the old capo's heart.

"Those witches decapitated the assassin right after he executed the heretic prince's guard. My assassin was at the prince's throat! But Satan thwarted us, because that worthless German emperor has allowed Protestants to rise in the Holy Roman Empire. And now, Satan's forces on this wicked earth have overcome even the Inquisition!"

"Exactly," Padre said in a cryptic tone. "That is why we needed the English prince to die. This is what *you* explained to me."

Massimi crumbled inside. "You have all of my apologies, Padre. You have my full contrition. Please bear in mind, I have been a devout soldier of God. I will continue to serve you with utmost humility. I am your eyes and ears in the Holy See. Anywhere you see fit, I will journey, and report back to you. I have failed as an assassin, but I can still serve God. I will give the Almighty the most devout service." Massimi placed his hand on his heart, blinking back tears.

Padre leaned back in his chair. As he did so, his monk's hood rose, revealing his scrawny cheekbones, but not his eyes.

"I have power here in Rome," Padre began, "but beyond these fields, my power wanes to nothing. Here in Rome, the Inquisition doesn't make enemies because we're easy to deal with. We need the flock to stay in line. That's all. We don't shake people down to feed our vanities. Look at me. I live a simple life. I drink two glasses of wine a day. Just two. I eat barley soup, a bit of fish, and fresh greens." He waved a veiny hand as if shooing away a fly. "I don't need fancy things. The Dominicans taught me simplicity, so I keep things simple. In Rome, we arrest the heretics and put the fear of God in them. When we let them off easy, they are so grateful they give us gifts—very generous, these heretics. This is how we do things in Rome. Yes, we need to show unyielding strength, but at some point, we need to win over the people. These amateur inquisitors outside of Rome don't understand. They turn people against the Church. Then, Satan finds his way into their hearts.

"Years ago, you came to me and said, 'Padre. We have this problem. The Inquisition isn't working, and the German emperor is allowing Protestant heretics to roam free in the Germanic kingdoms. If things go on like this, the Protestants will rise in power, they will overthrow the Holy Church and conquer Europe with their heresies.' Then, you said, 'We need to set up marriage negotiations between Spain and England and convert the English prince. If he won't convert, we will assassinate him in Madrid, and drive England into a war with Spain, and thereby, a war with the Holy Roman Empire, which, by the grace of God, we shall win.'

"And I said, 'Thank you for telling me this, I will put the best soldiers on the job.' And you said, 'I am the best soldier for this job! Anyone else will miss. Only I can get the English prince!' I had my reservations, but you were convincing. I believed in you." Padre draped one arm over the back of his chair. He laid his other elbow on the chair's arm, allowing his hand to dangle. "What will you do to bring Britain back to the fold? Tell me."

A sensation of being watched from behind made Massimi's skin crawl. He turned and noticed a large monk in a black-hooded cassock lurking behind him to the right. He snapped his head in the other direction. A second monk stood behind his left shoulder. The decision had been made.

In the periphery, he spotted Brother Marcos standing at the door into the house, a smirk on his face.

In that instant, Massimi knew he understood Padre more than Brother Marcos ever would. The consigliere never witnessed an execution. That was a house rule. Brother Marcos was a one-man leering mob anticipating the show.

Massimi turned back, surprised at how calm he felt now that he knew there was no point in begging for his life. He took in one last breath, intensely aware of the refined aroma of the cypress trees—so cleansing, yet so earthly. He had been breathing in their scent since he had arrived but hadn't noticed until now.

"Will you grant me one request?"

Padre pulled back his hood, as if to get a better look at Massimi. When he did so, he revealed what he had been hiding. Cataracts had claimed both eyes. Padre stared with whitened orbs set in the death mask of his hollowed face.

"What is it?" he asked.

"Could you ask Brother Marcos to step back into the house? My death should not provide him amusement. For all of the service I have devoted to you, please spare me that."

Padre lifted his head.

The sun had continued its onward trek through the heavens, and now, its rays fell upon Padre's eyes, making them flash pearlescent. The old man scowled, snapped his fingers, and pointed at Brother Marcos.

Massimi turned to watch the monk on the right rush at the aristocrat. Brother Marcos tore open the door and fled into the house, the executioner on his heels. The monk tackled him in the hallway, punched him senseless, and then dragged him onto the grass by his ankles, smearing green stains on his pristine gown. Brother Marcos came to and began to struggle, but the monk wrenched his arm behind his back and pinned it with his knee as he drew a long dagger from the folds of his thick robe. Pulling Brother Marcos's head up, he sliced his throat as casually as a farmer slaughtering a pig.

As Massimi stared at the dying clergyman, a cold knife slipped along his own throat. The blade was extremely sharp, so it didn't hurt as much as he had feared. The second monk kindly avoided Massimi's throat, merely slicing both arteries before pushing him onto the thick grass.

Massimi wanted to die staring at Brother Marcos's face as they both bled out. But his eyes closed against his will, and he forgot everything.

37

The House of Salomon

March 1624
Southampton, England

A loud knock on the front door interrupted Anne and Kitty's breakfast. The knock's coded rhythm indicated an important visitor. They fell silent and listened to the announcement in the foyer.

"Brother Theodore, from the House of Salomon, has come to offer condolences to Lady Anne Audley, Duchess of Southampton," the messenger announced.

Anne and Kitty rushed out of the dining room and through the front door.

"Did you know he was coming?" Kitty asked.

"No," Anne said. "He must be in England on some business matter and decided to pay a visit."

A stocky man sporting a burgundy velvet tam over his gray curls stood at the tall gate. They recognized him instantly.

"There," Kitty said.

Anne ran to embrace him.

"I am extremely sorry for your loss, my dear," he said. "I came as soon as I heard."

On their way back to the house, they shared warm memories of Harald. Kitty threw another log on the parlor fire before heading to the kitchen to prepare tea.

"Have you been to London yet?" Anne asked, once they were alone.

"I have. Your life is in danger," Brother Theodore said, getting right to the point. "Buckingham convinced King Charles you hired an assassin to murder your husband."

Anne went numb. His words were nonsense, but his face was as serious as death itself. "How could anyone believe anything so horrible?" she asked.

"Simple minds lend themselves to exotic fantasies," he replied. "Buckingham plays up the fact you valiantly dispatched your husband's attacker. He constantly refers to you as a cutthroat. His argument is that any woman who could do such a thing is unnatural, and thereby untrustworthy."

"A wife who fights to save her husband from a ruthless murderer is untrustworthy?" Anne exclaimed.

"Buckingham is spreading the rumor you killed the assassin to silence him."

"But you know that's not true." Anne's heart thumped in her chest, powered by rage and fear.

"I refuse to be fooled by a depraved miscreant like Buckingham," said Brother Theodore.

"God bless you for that," she said. "What are my options? Shall I go to court to defend myself?"

He shook his head. "That would be suicide. King Charles has issued a decree for your arrest. The royal guard would remove you to the Tower of London upon your arrival. Your only hope is to return to the House of Salomon. We can protect you."

The following morning, they set sail for Dunkirk and arrived days later. They journeyed on and upon reaching the town of Lille, they traveled three miles west and crossed the border into France, arriving at the House of Salomon at half past noon. The massive château's snow-topped turrets glittered in the sun. Anne felt as if she had come home.

Duke and Duchess Fueggar embraced them as if they were their own kin. Winter at the château was far quieter than in the summer. Gone were the scores of chatty visitors crowding the sitting rooms. Though the dinner party was small, they enjoyed discussing the latest scientific discoveries and the dramatic turns in the ongoing ideological wars. They remained at the dining table sipping hot toddies until well after dark.

The next morning, Anne rose and peered out the window at a cloudy day. She sensed Harald nearby but instead of leaving her forlorn, his presence comforted her. She still ached from her loss, but her pain eased in the quiet glow of candlelight.

Anne and Kitty took a stroll and noticed purple crocuses springing through melting clumps of snow. Anne had been cloistered in the house for so long that the reflection of the sun glancing off the snowdrifts blinded her. She tipped the brim of her hat forward and blinked until her eyes adjusted. At the sound of approaching footsteps, they turned to see Brother Theodore.

"That pleasant breeze is a zephyr," he said, trotting a bit to catch up with the women.

"Mother Nature has blessed this place," Anne replied. "How rare to feel a mild breeze so late in winter. Almost tropical."

"Nubile spring is pushing Old Man Winter aside," Kitty quipped.

They laughed.

"I have good news, Kitty," Brother Theodore said.

Kitty raised her eyebrows in expectation.

"In the French court, women of fashion have taken to mocking the drab hairstyles of royal debutantes who send out their portraits to eligible noblemen. Subsequently, artisan hairstylists are all the rage in Paris."

Anne smiled. "Oui, vanity comes with sacrifice, does it not? Thank goodness, I have never had a complaint about Kitty's hairstyling."

"Exactly," said Brother Theodore. The sun warmed their faces as they walked. "The two of you have set a trend throughout Europe. When you left the House of Salomon years ago, all the ladies adopted your style. Placing the curls over the ears and pulling the rest of the hair back in a chignon is extremely distinctive. I have summoned a Parisian hairdresser to train you, Kitty. You shall become the most sought-after hairstylist in Parisian high society."

Kitty and Anne exchanged curious looks. Since when did old Brother Theodore take an interest in women's hairstyles?

Later that evening, Anne joined Brother Theodore on the balcony. She could always find him there at dusk leaning on the balustrade, watching the stars emerge from the purplish sky. A light breeze carried the clarifying scent of evergreens from the surrounding hills. She handed him a steaming cup of mulled wine.

"How very kind of you, Lady Anne," he said, cradling the mug in both hands.

She took a sip from her own mug and relished the exotic spices blending with the tart berry flavor of Burgundy. The concoction left a delicious afterglow in her throat when she swallowed.

"Any thoughts you'd like to share?" she asked.

"Are you seeking wisdom, gossip, or humor?"

"I'm curious as to why you want to train Kitty as a Parisian hairstylist. Do you have plans for us? We come as a pair, of course. The two of us are inseparable, in case you hadn't noticed."

"I want to prepare you and Kitty for an opportunity, the kind that comes only once in a lifetime. These are not merely pensioned positions at the French court, mind you. This is your chance to change the course of history."

"One updo at a time?" Anne asked with raised eyebrows. "Aside from styling hair, what, pray tell, shall we be doing at the French court?"

"You will soon meet someone who can give specifics on that topic. In the meantime, I can tell you the history surrounding the matter. It revolves around Quentin Boyle."

Anne braced herself at the sound of her father's name. She was ten when she last saw him alive. Her father worked in Paris while she and her mother lived in a château in a nearby town for their safety. News of his death had hit hard. Anne never learned who was behind his assassination. She wondered if Brother Theodore would draw back that veil.

"Quentin was nine when he first began assisting your grandfather in crating his exquisitely crafted cabinets to ship overseas."

"Ah, yes, my grandfather, the cabinetmaker. I remember Father telling me how he and his brother would help him wrap his cabinets in wool before crating them for shipment."

"Quentin cultivated an interest in mercantilism from an early age. Perhaps he told you about joining his mother on trips to London's market square. Your grandmother was enraptured by exotic foods. She would spend not a penny on apples if pineapples imported from Jamaica were available."

Anne laughed. "She kept her own herb garden so she could afford vanilla beans from Mexico City. She became one of London's most popular hostesses by serving such fare as pineapple cake with vanilla foam frosting at her fashionable tea parties."

"Your grandmother's taste in exotic foods is what paved the way to your father's future as a merchant. When he accompanied your grandfather to the shipping dock to deliver crated cabinets, young Quentin would chat up the ships 'captains, making them aware of which cargo was likely to be the most lucrative based on his mum's tastes in merchandise, considering all the fashionable ladies in

London followed her example. Merchant captains found this information invaluable. When Quentin was twelve, one of those captains offered him a job on his ship. The captain had a good reputation, so your grandfather allowed it. That was the beginning of your father's career as a merchant."

Brother Theodore's detailed knowledge of Anne's father surprised her. "Why did you not share this with me before now?" she asked.

"There is a proper time for everything, I suppose."

A chill set in as the stars brightened against the black sky. Anne put both hands around her warm mug, prepared to endure the cold for fear the magic of the moment would vanish if they went inside.

"Please continue," she said.

"Your father traveled to Shanghai as a young man, hoping to initiate trade in legendary Cathay. He hired a reputable scholar as a tutor of Chinese history and culture, hoping it would help him connect with vendors, but he learned far more than he expected. The scholar taught him about the dynastic cycle. When an old dynasty fell into decay from an abundance of corruption and mismanagement, the peasants would revolt, which led to civil war. The victor seized the imperial throne and became the new emperor. The winner of this contest was not necessarily the wealthiest warlord, or even the best military tactician. Rather, the leader who showed the most kindness and generosity to their soldiers and the peasants would triumph in the end. Soldiers who received the best pay and treatment fought the hardest in battle. Peasants who received kindness and generosity from a general would protect his troops, and act as his informants. Those commoners believed their leader would take good care of them once he became emperor. They were never disappointed.

"The first emperor of a new dynasty customarily enacted sweeping land reforms. Farmlands were parceled out to peasants, who then owned the crops they worked hard to produce. That is why most Chinese dynasties thrive in their early days. The current Ming Dynasty likewise thrived in its early days. The new wealth generated by peasant farmers gave rise to a mercantile class of traders who traveled thousands of miles to sell Chinese silks, porcelain, tea, and other luxury goods to wealthy Persians, Arabs, and Indians. A rising merchant class thrived there, but some imperial bureaucrats grew jealous, perceiving the wealth of successful commoners as a sign of insubordination. A cabal of powerful officials convinced the emperor to curtail trade. The emperor did so, claiming everything the Chinese people needed could be bought and sold within their own borders.

"Their merchant class collapsed overnight, and poverty swept through the land like a plague. This diminished the nation's tax revenues. But rather than admit their mistake, the emperor and his favorites levied increasingly heavy taxes on craftsmen and farmers, which made their poverty worse. Farmers who could not pay their taxes were forced to sell their land cheaply to high-ranking court officials. Today, China is a nation mired in corruption and poverty. A tiny number of court officials own virtually all of the land, and most of the peasants live on the verge of starvation. This scholar predicted the current dynasty would likely fall within this century.

"That was the first time your father had encountered the theory that a thriving common class would lead to a thriving empire. Conversely, an empire's wealth decays when a small number of rulers control too much property, especially if they engage in unnecessary wars.

"Quentin eventually bought enough Chinese goods to fill an argosy trading ship and sailed back to Europe. During fair weather he would lean on the ship's deck rails, stare at the rocking waves, and recall stories his parents had told him of Queen Elizabeth's reign. Elizabeth spent her childhood under the constant threat of her sister's wrath. Queen Mary initiated heresy trials in England, and hundreds of Protestants were burned alive at the stake.

"One day, Queen Mary issued an arrest warrant for Princess Elizabeth and ordered soldiers to transport her to the Tower of London. When word got out, Englishmen followed her carriage through the countryside, and would get out ahead when they approached a town to herald her arrival. Villagers flocked to her carriage and showered her with gifts, such as baskets of fresh fruit, or stacks of clean linens for her bed and bath, so eager were they to show their generosity.

"This effusive demonstration of support for Princess Elizabeth caught the attention of the queen's ministers. Whereas Queen Mary intended to charge Elizabeth with treason and have her executed, her ministers would not cooperate, fearing the wrath of the English subjects should anything dire happen to their beloved princess. This ultimately saved her life.

"Your grandparents finished their tale by explaining that for the many kindnesses English commoners had shown her, when Elizabeth became queen, she always put their welfare first, protecting them from heavy taxation, encouraging English inventors to get patents for their inventions, vigorously enforcing those patents, and so many other policies that benefited peasants and craftsman alike.

"Quentin had delighted in these stories as a child, but it wasn't until he received instruction from the Chinese scholar that he drew a line between Queen Elizabeth's generosity with her subjects and the unprecedented prosperity, inventiveness, and even military might that England enjoyed throughout her reign.

"While your father was widely traveled and had conversed with many learned men, these were the primary experiences that formed his new ideology, which held that the quickest path to prosperity for any kingdom was to lighten taxes on the commoners and levy taxes on the wealthy to pay for roads and bridges. Such decrees open trade and allow the commoners to prosper. If the nobility cooperated and waited patiently, they would see a significant rise in their fortunes, too."

"That is most remarkable!" Anne exclaimed. "I had no idea my father was so brilliant."

"Quentin hoped to share what he had learned from the Chinese scholar with an enlightened European regent, preferably a Protestant king. Such a man would be well out of reach of the Inquisition, and too powerful to be bullied by narrow-minded Protestant evangelists.

"He saw an opportunity in France's King Henry the Fourth. When he rose to the throne, France had been ravaged by a vicious civil war between Protestants and Catholics, brought on by the Inquisition and their heresy trials. All of France had been ground into poverty.

"But your father found in King Henry a revolutionary thinker who desperately wanted to raise France to an unprecedented level of prosperity. Quentin convinced him he could accomplish this by employing his policies. Inspired by your father's ideas, King Henry lowered taxes on the poor and levied taxes on the entitled class. Quentin played the diplomat, explaining to France's nobility how they would benefit from the roads and bridges that their king was financing with the revenues. He organized grand openings and fêted the lords and ladies who chose to attend.

"Meanwhile, King Henry appealed directly to France's commoners, famously promising them 'If God grants me life, I will make it so that no plowman in my realm will lack the means to have a chicken in his pot on Sunday!'

"As prosperity took hold, French noblemen admitted their fortunes were indeed rising along with those of the peasants and commoners. Many of them acknowledged King Henry's wisdom. But some lords still resented the king for eliminating their power to tax French subjects in their counties. They felt the extra wealth the commoners enjoyed from selling their home crafts and wares at the market was rightfully theirs, and they should be allowed to tax it away. But Good King Henry would not allow it."

Brother Theodore fell silent and stared at the stars. Anne sensed what was coming. A gibbous moon slowly rose over the eastern horizon, glowing like a smoldering fire.

"King Henry's reign lasted a decade before he was assassinated," Brother Theodore said quietly. "A brief golden age in France's long history of struggle. The king and your father died on the same day. As they rode to an official event, an assassin wielding a large knife broke through the crowd and jumped into their carriage. Your father wrestled the knife away, but not before the assassin slashed the king's throat. Quentin also died from his wounds."

Anne put her mug down and hugged herself, suddenly noticing she was very cold. She shivered violently.

"I'm so sorry, my dear," Brother Theodore said. "Although it was long ago, I'm sure it must be hard to hear."

"I'm glad to know he died a good man," Anne said, wiping tears from her cheeks. "Who killed them?"

"The assassin was an insignificant monk. No one knew him."

They both fell silent. Anne stared into the night.

"My goodness," Brother Theodore exclaimed. "We have strayed far off the topic of Parisian hairstyles, haven't we?"

Anne nodded and sighed. "Indeed. I am truly curious to see how you will come back to that topic after that long, winding journey into my father's past."

"First, we must bring you inside, my dear. I apologize for keeping you hanging on my every word as the night grows cold." He put his arm around her and led her inside.

The parlor was deserted. A log in the fireplace flickered with a low flame. Three votive candles in crystal goblets lit up a nearby table, providing a sparkling glow within a cave of shadows. They sat in plush armchairs. Anne rubbed her hands and held her cold-stung fingers out to the fireplace.

"Good King Henry is gone, but he's not forgotten," said Brother Theodore. "There are forces in France who are keeping the ideological flames that your father lit alive. An opportunity awaits you and Kitty in Paris. I have no doubt the two of you could handle the positions with ease. Should the two of you accept, your combined skills will serve both of you well in Parisian high society. I can say no more."

Anne's mind scrambled. Who wanted Kitty and her to rub elbows with French courtiers, and why? Before she could ask, Brother Theodore slapped his forehead.

"Oh, fie," he said, "I forgot to tell you, Anne. Your dear Auntie Louise would be delighted to receive a visit, if you are up to it."

"Ah me," said Anne, "I should have paid her a visit weeks ago. Do you know if she is displeased?"

"Not in the slightest," said Brother Theodore. He bit his thumb in hesitation, as if unsure how to proceed. "Sir Gregory convinced Queen Isabella to bypass the abbey of Santa Dorotea in Burgos and journey on to Our Lady of Temple Mars."

Anne stared at him, stunned. "Sir Gregory is in Flanders? Mere miles away?"

"He is," Theodore said. "But before you see him, you must first pay a visit to your Aunt Louise. She is expecting you tomorrow morning, at the stroke of nine."

38

Abbess Louise

March 1624
Our Lady of Temple Mars, Flanders

The next morning found Anne strolling behind a young nun who rushed ahead in an attempt to lead rather than follow. Anne knew the way to the abbess's office, having resided at the convent in her childhood. A four-story, stone turret with a conical roof jutted up from the back of the compound. When they arrived, the nun fumbled with an iron ring of keys before wrestling one into an ornate lock. The door swung open with a low creak. Familiar stone steps lit by narrow windows ascended the perimeter of the tower's curved wall.

The nun rushed ahead and the two of them trotted up to the third-floor landing, which segued into an expansive foyer. Light from the windows reflected off the polished wood floor. The young nun pushed open the door to the abbess's outer office. The elderly nun at the desk looked up, and Anne recognized her aunt's secretary.

"Sister Meredith," Anne exclaimed, rushing to her.

"Lady Audley," she said, rising from her desk, her chubby face beaming. They clasped hands and kissed each other on each cheek.

"How I would love to chat," she said, patting Anne's hand, "but your Auntie is looking forward to seeing you." Sister Meredith knocked on the door that led to the abbess's chambers.

"Come in," a voice called from inside.

The old nun pushed through the door. "Mother Louise, your niece has arrived."

As Anne entered, her aunt came around her desk. Her oval face was dominated by glitter-gray eyes. A white wimple draped her head and pooled around her shoulders. Though her slender black dress flattered her figure, the mannish leather shoes on her long feet squelched any hint of vanity.

She cupped Anne's cheeks in both hands and transfixed her with a silver stare.

"Your angelic face is so like your mother's," she said in a soft, girlish voice, "but that icy glint in your eyes? You get that from your father." Anne instantly remembered her aunt's penchant for remarks that wavered between flattery and criticism. Abbess Louise believed souls who received compliments should also consider their shortcomings.

She returned to her desk and motioned Anne to sit across from her.

"I was saddened to hear of your tragedy, Anne. How horrible to lose your beloved in such a cruel and senseless act. I remember what a dashing pair you two made at your wedding. You were so in love. One rarely sees that at the altar. And when the two of you danced? Such grace. It was pure poetry."

Anne took comfort in her aunt's warm memories of Harald. The conversation segued to family news. During a lull, Anne broached the sensitive topic they had avoided since her arrival.

"I understand Sir Gregory persuaded Queen Isabella to bring her royal charge to Our Lady of Temple Mars."

"He did, indeed, and I am proud to say, both Queen Isabella and Princess Maria are comfortable here. I was deeply flattered Sir Gregory felt our convent would be appropriate for such illustrious guests. How did he hear of us?"

"From me, I'm sure," said Anne. "I have spoken fondly of my days at the convent. I hope to pay him a visit. Is he in Lille?"

"No. He is residing here. I have made an exception for him. Princess Maria is as fragile as a flower, the poor dear. I don't think she would survive her travails without him by her side. All of us must devote ourselves to her well-being, which is why I must forbid you from seeing Sir Gregory, so long as he is here."

Anne gasped. Aunt Louise blinked slowly and continued.

"If you were to distract Sir Gregory with your affections, I fear the poor girl's spirits may plummet. She's not used to this cold, damp climate. If pneumonia were to afflict her, she could be gone in a twinkling. I know you need Sir Gregory's comfort as well, Anne, but you are the stronger one. Princess Maria is just a girl, really."

Anne kept her voice calm. "You speak as though I wish to kindle a romance."

"Don't you?" Aunt Louise raised her eyebrows in concern.

Heat rose in Anne's cheeks. "Of course not! Sir Gregory is an old friend, especially dear to my departed husband. Nothing more." Even as the words left her mouth, she realized her aunt was right. She was desperate to see him. The epiphany ran through her with a flash of anger. Ashamed of her reaction, her throat clenched.

Aunt Louise tilted her head as her eyes filled with compassion. "Have you heard the legend of Temple Mars?" she asked.

"I didn't know there was a legend," Anne said, grateful for a change in subject.

"Yes, a lovely one. The first time I heard it, I was fifteen, and standing right out there in the courtyard," she said, pointing out the window to the garden below.

Anne's mind filled with questions. "You were here when you were fifteen? I never knew. I would love to hear how you came to be the abbess."

"I was being groomed for marriage. My family was just wealthy enough to afford two extravagant weddings. Your Aunt Matilda was the eldest. One year before I was sent to a convent, she married a duke. It was a great expense for our parents.

"By the time they were planning my betrothal, I understood the heavy cost my wedding would impose on our family's dwindling fortune. Mother was a Danish princess, so of course she felt it crucial to keep up appearances. I found the entire idea of marriage repugnant. I absolutely hated the very thought of it.

"As my father and mother firmed up my marriage contract, I was sent to Our Lady of Temple Mars. When I arrived, I met other young ladies also waiting to be wed. We sang in the choir, played musical instruments, and learned geography and history from Jesuit priests. I'd never had so many true friends. There was none of the snobbishness of court life. Something about this place brought out the best in all of us.

"One day, as I loitered with my new friends near the kitchen garden, Sister Meredith came out to gather herbs and vegetables for our supper. She asked us to assist her. As we plucked parsley and carrots, she recounted the legend.

"Back in the days of Roman rule, the local peasants agreed there was not enough love in the world. The wise women had grown up hearing tales of men who were kind and benevolent to the local maidens, but when the Romans came, they heaped humiliations upon the village women.

"When Goth King Alaric laid waste to Rome, the Goths in the Rhineland followed their example and sent their Roman captors fleeing. As the Romans prepared to leave Lille, the wise women saw an opportunity. Still wishing to restore romance to their land, they asked the Romans if Venus would come to them if they built a temple in her honor. The Romans laughed and said the esteemed goddess would never condescend to visit such a shabby village, but if they built a temple to her lover, Mars, she might seek him in a moment of passion.

"So, they built a simple temple of marble columns. At the center, they placed a sculpted altar with a relief of Mars's beautiful face—strong, but almost feminine in its grace. The local maidens brought fruits and flowers as their offering. They sang love songs and danced with each other. The village youths saw them and joined in the dance. From that day on, men throughout the countryside were kinder, gentler, and far more romantic to their wives and mistresses.

"The temple is gone, but the legend lives on. Sister Meredith claimed every abbess who had ever presided over our convent devoted herself to maintaining an ambience of love."

Abbess Louise stared out the window, lost in her story. "When Sister Meredith said this, I felt a vibration all around me, like the wings of a thousand bees were creating a vortex that nearly lifted me from the ground. In that moment, I knew I would one day be abbess of Our Lady of Temple Mars, and I would vouchsafe every kind of love, even romantic love, on our humble hilltop."

The abbess fell silent. Anne realized she did not know her aunt at all.

"How did you convince your parents to break the marriage contract?" Anne asked.

"I asked the abbess if she would take me on as her apprentice. She agreed, perhaps because I was the daughter of an influential Dutch count. But the honor was all mine. When my parents sent for me, the abbess wrote back and told them I had the ideal temperament to be her apprentice. I wrote back as well, telling them I felt called by God, and wanted nothing more than to stay at the convent.

"My parents arrived at the convent within the week. I feared they had come to remove me, but bless their souls, they just wanted to see for themselves if this was what I truly wanted. I convinced them it was. Their consent came quickly. At the time, I assumed it was the work of God, and I still do. But I later learned that, shortly after I left for the convent, my betrothed and his family had come to visit mine. In the course of the formal dinners and dances, my flirtatious sister, Lysbeth, enticed the young heir.

"When my parents heard my wishes, they realized they could guarantee a fortunate outcome for two daughters, in lieu of one. Lysbeth married the heir, and I took the veil. Your mother was the most beautiful of us four sisters, so it came as no surprise when your father, a wealthy merchant recently knighted by the King of France, asked for her hand in marriage. Despite being a wealthy merchant, he was marrying up. My father then secretly arranged for him to pay for the wedding as part of the contract, and all was well."

Anne pondered her aunt's story. "How many years passed before you became abbess?"

Her aunt smiled. "It's difficult to say. The Reverend Mother taught me how to manage the convent from Day One. The more I learned, the more responsibility she passed on to me. By the time I was twenty, I could explain a challenge at hand, suggest a course of action, and she would say 'Yes, Sister Louise, please do that.' We carried on that way until she was on her deathbed, whereupon she had me draw the appropriate papers, and send for the appropriate signatures and seals, and arrange for a priest to come to her side. Before she took her last confession, she made me abbess."

Abbess Louise returned her gaze to Anne. "I believe I was brought to this place by the very hand of God. Every day, I devote myself to creating a safe haven for love to flourish, which brings us around to our original topic. Sir Gregory and Princess Maria have a special kind of love. I have never seen anything like it. It is pristine, powerful, and free of lust. It is a love that transcends even romance. We must not interfere."

Anne kept her face still, clinging to the words "free of lust" the way one would cling to a tree in a storm. She stared at the floor. Tears welled in her eyes.

"Oh, Anne, really," Louise said.

Anne looked up. "Auntie, I have lost the love of my life. I have never felt such pain. I don't know if it will ever leave me."

Louise reached across the desk to take Anne's hand, her eyes as cool as a lake beneath cloudy skies. "It won't leave you, Anne. But you are strong, like your father. When you were a girl, I thought you would grow to be soft, like your mum. She was of a delicate constitution, practically made of silk. You are more like a polished gem—beautiful, but hard, and sharp."

Anne gasped at her aunt's assessment. Louise stood, walked around her desk and put her arms around her niece.

Anne let her tears fall as Aunt Louise patted her back.

The abbess added, "How I would love to sit with you on the sofa, tell you fairytales, and give you sweet biscuits and tea, as your mother did when you were a girl. But you do not have the luxury of being soft. I've heard the news from London. You must be strong to survive, Anne. Be strong like Harald. I am sure that is what he would want."

Anne lifted her head, extracted herself from the embrace, and took her aunt's hands into hers, not as a gesture of affection so much as an attempt to stop the words coming from her mouth. Nothing irritated Anne more than a well-intended oaf telling her what her husband would want, her beloved aunt being no exception. Knowing her aunt was right made the remark all the more irritating.

"I must talk to Sir Gregory," Anne said in an even tone. "This is not a personal matter. We both serve the English crown, even when our young King Charles is under the spell of a sycophant. Indeed, the present circumstance makes it all the more urgent I consult with Sir Gregory. To do otherwise would be a dereliction of duty."

Louise withdrew her hands from beneath Anne's and returned to her chair to study her niece with a cool gaze. No abbess had the authority to interfere with the duties of royal officials. She could not stop her niece from consulting with Sir Gregory. All she could do was decide whether she would meet him on the convent's premises, or off.

"You were not always this way," said Louise, "and it is not your fault. This is the path that God has laid before you. Being strong where others are weak is nothing to be ashamed of, Anne."

The abbess reached into her desk drawer and pulled out a square sheet of parchment, and added, "Before you leave, I would like you to take a message to Sir Gregory."

Anne was surprised at her change of heart.

Louise dabbed a quill into an inkwell and scratched at the parchment. Her efforts seemed in vain, because no ink came from the quill. As she wrote, she seemed oblivious that her penmanship was invisible. After waving the parchment dry, she folded it into three sections and sealed it with hot wax and her insignia ring. She handed the neat parcel over to Anne.

"I'm sure Sir Gregory will know how to read this, but if he seems confused, tell him to hold the paper over a candle flame, just enough to heat it. The message will become clear."

Anne rose to leave. She went to the other side of the desk to kiss her aunt goodbye.

"One more thing," Aunt Louise said, taking Anne's hand in her own. "An old friend of mine recently wrote to me. He is interested in meeting you."

"I'm not interested in meeting anyone right now," Anne said, keeping her voice cordial.

"He is not seeking romance, I assure you."

"What does he seek?"

"An intelligent, capable woman—one with the heart of a knight, and the grace of a queen. You'll see."

"Who is he?"

"You shall meet him soon."

The young nun who had escorted Anne to her aunt's office now led her down the stairs and into the courtyard. They walked between rows of fruit trees whose black, spindly branches were studded with pink and green buds.

They arrived at an ivy-covered wall and stopped where the vines opened up to reveal a diamond-paned window and a wooden door, which was rounded at the top and adorned with a bronze knocker.

"Wait here," the nun said. "Sir Gregory uses this chamber while the princess takes her siesta. He should be along shortly."

Anne waited, staring at the orchard. She was wondering if the buds would bloom that day when she spotted Sir Gregory strolling through the trees. Their eyes met and he smiled.

"My dear Lady Anne," he exclaimed. He unlocked the door of his chamber and bowed as he waved her in. Once the door was shut, he embraced her. Anne let her tears fall freely but remained silent. After several moments, he pulled back to look at her.

"I was devastated when I heard the news," he said.

"I am certain Buckingham was involved," Anne replied.

"The moment I heard the news I was convinced of his treachery. Nonetheless, your presence is a delightful surprise. What brings you here?"

"Buckingham convinced King Charles to sign an order for my arrest. An old friend from the House of Salomon rescued me. If it hadn't been for him, I would be shivering at the Tower of London this very moment, or cold in my grave."

Gregory hugged her once again. He released her with a squeeze to her arms before turning to stack split logs into the cold hearth.

"Did you know you can start a fire with a flintlock pistol?" he asked. He gathered some kindling from a rusty box and sprinkled it on the logs. He then retrieved his musket and rapidly clicked the trigger, allowing a shower of sparks to fall.

"Bravo," said Anne, clapping as the smoking twigs sprang into flame. Gregory motioned her to sit at the table.

"My mother no longer feels safe in Scotland," he said. "I shall send for my family soon."

"Really?" Anne exclaimed. "Will you bring them to France or Flanders?"

"I haven't decided yet. Best to see how the fates play out."

Anne reached into her satchel. "Oh, I nearly forgot, my aunt sent a message." She handed over the parchment note.

"From the abbess?" Gregory took it from her, opened it, and raised his eyebrows at the blank sheet.

"You must hold it over a candle flame to warm it, for the message to become clear," Anne informed him.

"Is this a jest?"

"No. It's black magic. Try it and see."

He did so and elegant cursive the color of toast appeared on the parchment.

"It says, 'Dear S. G.,'" Gregory announced. "An abbreviation for Sir Gregory, I suppose?"

"She was in a hurry," Anne said, beaming at Gregory's blatant indiscretion.

"'Please beware of my niece's wanton affections.' Why, your auntie is no fun at all."

Anne struggled to stifle her giggles.

"'She means no harm, but you must not allow her willful heart to become a distraction. As God has led you to our fold, so may you bow to His will as we prioritize the safety and health of his precious lamb, Princess Maria Anna. Your humble servant, Mother Louise.' I had no idea our dear abbess was so dramatic."

"She specializes in romance and conspiracies," said Anne, "but her intentions are good."

In the silence that followed, their hands touched. Anne could resist no longer. She leaned over to kiss him, but a sudden commotion at the door startled her. She sat back just as the door creaked open to reveal Sister Meredith pulling a long iron key out of the door's lock.

"Don't mind me," she said innocently. "I'm just here to sweep and dust."

It was not Sister Meredith's duty to sweep and dust, but she was duty bound to fulfill the abbess's orders. Anne took the hint and rose to leave.

"You will visit me again soon, will you not?" Gregory stood.

Anne sensed Sister Meredith's cautious eyes upon her. "Once you have completed your duties here, I would be delighted to pay you and your mother a visit, Sir Gregory." Anne extended her hand and he kissed it.

She kissed Sister Meredith's cheek and cast one final look toward Gregory before venturing into the sweetly scented air. She was pleased to see the sun had emerged and the blossoms on the fruit trees had opened during the short time she spent with Gregory.

39

The New Favorite

April 1624
Our Lady of Temple Mars, Flanders

Isabella walked down a lane of blooming cherry trees, alone with her thoughts. A bright mist hovered above the convent's towers. She felt lonely at times, but far less so than in Madrid, where every utterance she made invited a disdainful look from her husband. King Philip wanted her to remain forever like a well-dressed child, seen and not heard. The thought sickened her.

She lifted her face to a spray of tiny pink petals riding along the breeze. The sensation left her tingling. She longed for a man, handsome and gallant, like Sir Gregory. A ridiculous thought, insofar as it would be a horrible betrayal to Maria at a time when her spirits were fragile. Besides, Isabella had already given the Scottish lord several lingering glances, which he pointedly ignored.

Dipping her nose into a cluster of peach blossoms, she imagined picking the delectable fruit off the tree in midsummer. She banished Gregory from her mind, but the desire to have a man press himself against her lingered. She longed for a firm body—*like Kenhelm's!*

The thought rushed from her mind with such force that she glanced over her shoulder, hoping no one could sense the dangerous idea hovering about her.

Sir Kenhelm was dashing, and exquisitely masculine—but the rumors. He and the handsome priest, Father Eremitz, were close friends. According to the court gossips, they had once wrestled naked. Isabella found the rumor ridiculous. She had assumed the story sprung from some jester's wicked musings, until she caught a glimpse of the two of them at the English summer soirée. As they tilted their heads toward one another to whisper their conversation, the truth sank in. It wasn't their expressions, or even their postures, so much as the magnetism between them. She could almost see it glowing against the night sky.

A delightful idea formed as she absentmindedly circled the last tree and started down the next row in the opposite direction. Perhaps she could do what good Christians do: save her fellow Christian from a life of sin. Of course, adultery was a bit of a sin, too, but so common it couldn't possibly be unforgivable. Surely, God could forgive her minor sin if it was committed in the spirit of saving a mortal soul from a worse one.

Feeling empowered, she rushed toward the abbess's office. She was hopeful the wise and benevolent Mother Louise would be sympathetic to her need for a gentleman-in-waiting. Isabella had grown quite fond of the free-spirited abbess.

Later that afternoon, Isabella sat on her couch and watched the dust motes dance lazily in a beam of sunlight. A knock at the door jolted her.

"Could you please get that, Sister?" Isabella asked the nun who tidied her room. "I'm expecting a visitor." The young queen fought the urge to rush to the door and answer it herself.

The nun slowly opened the door to reveal Kenhelm, attired in black corduroy breeches and a black leather doublet. The sleeves of his chemise draped loosely about his well-crafted arms.

He stepped into the parlor. Sweeping his hat from his head, he dipped into an elegant bow, and stated, "At your service, Your Majesty." His golden hair pooled in fat curls about his shoulders as he straightened. "Please, forgive my tardiness. I was out hunting when I got your summons."

Isabella rose to press a silver coin into the nun's palm and wave her out the door.

"I appreciate you coming at such short notice," Isabella said, motioning him to the sofa. He sat on one side and she on the other, her entire body pointed toward him. A fire crackled in the small hearth.

"I must write a letter to my sister, Henrietta," Isabella said, before dropping her voice to a near whisper. "She married Prince Charles by proxy at Notre Dame in Paris, I suppose you have heard."

"Indeed I have," Kenhelm said, "But in all due respect, Your Majesty, I believe you meant to say your sister has married King Charles The First." There was no awkwardness. They had become well-acquainted on the journey to Flanders.

"Ah yes, forgive me. I've known him as a prince for so long, his new royal title is unfamiliar to me. Of course, Infanta Maria must not hear of any of this. The abbess assured me the convent has a strict ban on discussing worldly matters. I am obliged to write a letter to my new brother-in-law, King Charles, as well. I would prefer to write that one in English, which is why I need an experienced diplomat to assist me as my gentleman-in-waiting, particularly with my personal correspondence. These are sensitive matters that require utmost confidentiality."

Kenhelm got down on one knee, taking the posture of a cavalier prepared for knighthood, and said, "Allow me to be your humble servant, Your Majesty. I can do that, and much more. Feel free to request anything at all."

"Thank you, Sir Kenhelm. I do have other requests. Meet me at the front gate every morning at dawn. I will have certain duties for you to perform. Once my needs are met, you shall return to Lille, and report to the first officer of the Spanish Guard, Captain Rodriguez. You shall assist him in tasks worthy of the attention of a gentleman, such as drafting English correspondence, paying vendors, and so on. On Sundays and holidays, you shall be relieved of your duties to Captain Rodriguez, but not to me.

"For your first meeting with the captain," she continued, "I shall send along a signed and sealed order outlining your wages, which I hope you find satisfactory. The captain is instructed to burn the order in your presence. Please make sure he does so."

Kenhelm nodded, his grave expression a stark contrast to his youthful face. Isabella motioned him to return to his seat.

Captain Rodriguez was a discreet man. Placing Kenhelm on his payroll made a handy cover for any illicit behavior that might occur between the young queen and her new favorite. Mother Louise had advised her on this matter. Beyond that, the abbess simply told her that Kenhelm could enter the convent as early as dawn and stay as long as Isabella liked. "But he must be gone by sundown," she had warned, like a mysterious, wise woman from a fairytale.

Isabella regarded Kenhelm as she recalled the abbess's words.

"I'll have the sisters deliver afternoon tea," she said. "Do you like fresh, buttered scones and jam?"

Kenhelm's eyes shone.

Isabella smiled. No Englishman could resist tea, piping hot scones, and jam.

40

Infanta Miranda

One year later, May 1625
Our Lady of Temple Mars, Flanders

Maria sat at her vanity, combing her hair. Adelena stood nearby, bathing Maria's baby in a basin on a marble-topped sideboard.

A vase of roses and a painted seascape were the room's only decorations. Beveled windowpanes cast shards of tiny rainbows on the white walls. Little Miranda reached for them as Adelena brought her out of the basin and set her on a thick square of folded cotton. The governess plopped a gauzy towel over the infant's head and gently patted her dry. The baby giggled and squealed, as if it were all a game. Adelena played several rounds of peak-a-boo with her before casting off the towel and rubbing her with a light coating of almond oil shaken with rose water.

Maria watched them in the mirror and smiled as she piled her thick hair high on the back of her head. She selected a citrine-studded tortoiseshell comb from her collection and slipped it into her coif to fasten it in place.

"I should do that, Maria Anna," Adelena said as she dressed the freshly bathed tot. "A princess should not be her own lady's maid."

"Nonsense," said Maria. "I am not the baby in the room. Of course, I can pin up my own hair." She got up from the vanity and went to sit on the sofa.

Adelena brought Miranda to her. Delicate golden curls crowded her neck beneath her white bonnet. She held onto her mother's fingers as she stood on Maria's thighs and bounced with a gurgling grin. Maria sang a nursery song and Adelena joined in.

It was Miranda's first birthday. Abbess Louise had offered to host a garden breakfast. Miranda slid off Maria's lap and toddled toward the wall with her hand outstretched, hoping to capture a rainbow sparkle in her tiny fingers. Outside, the clock tower struck the three-quarter hour.

"If I may beg your indulgence," Adelena said, tucking her gray curls beneath her white muslin cap. "I need to leave early to assist in setting up the banquet table."

"Please do," said Maria. "I shall summon Isabella and we will join you momentarily."

Maria smiled as Adelena rushed out the door. The young nuns found the aristocratic nursemaid's assistance more annoying than helpful, but there was no keeping her away. The sisters would survive it.

Maria hoisted her baby onto her hip and went out the door. Isabella's apartments adjoined hers.

"Would you like to see Auntie?" Maria asked as they wandered down the veranda.

"Auntie, Auntie," Miranda chirped.

Isabella's door was closed, but not locked. Maria opened it and entered.

"Lady Miranda, Duchess of Lille, at your service, Your Majesty," Maria announced in a theatrical tone. She and Isabella had acquired playful rituals during their stay at the convent. Announcing Miranda's presence like a palace herald was one.

The fireplace flickered with a ripple of flames dancing atop a charred log, but the parlor was empty. Miranda began to squirm. Maria hoisted her higher on her hip and walked across the Turkish rug to Isabella's bedchamber.

Maria lifted the drapes that hung in the open doorway, sending a flood of light into the room. This set off a flurry of motion as not one, but two figures lounging naked on the bed scrambled for their clothes.

Miranda gasped, then squealed in delight at the spectacle. Maria dropped the curtain and quickly retraced her steps back into the parlor. She sat down on the sofa, holding her baby tight. Miranda fussed and struggled to break free from her mother's grasp, eager to rush back to the excitement of Auntie's boudoir.

Isabella emerged through the curtain wearing her favorite frock. The white muslin dress hung loosely off her shoulders but was cinched beneath her bosom with a coral satin ribbon. The loose skirts flowed down to her ankles and the transparent sleeves billowed over her arms. Her large dark eyes were as innocent as a Christmas angel's.

"What can I do for you, dear lady?" she asked. "I am at your service."

"Actually," Maria said, nose lifted in faux haughtiness, "we have come to invite you to our exclusive tea party in the orchard. The first course is tea served with peaches and cream, followed by fried trout filets served with whipped turnips, followed by a round of cherry cider. Then, pop-ups served straight from the oven with butter and jam, accompanied by a round of café a la créme. Thus sayeth my Doña Adelena."

"My, such a feast," Isabella said, running a brush through her hair. "May I bring a guest?"

"But of course. I assumed your ever-loyal gentleman-in-waiting would accompany you."

Kenhelm emerged from Isabella's boudoir, fully clothed and blushing. "I heard a rumor about a feast," he said.

Far from being scandalized, Maria had been relieved to learn Isabella had taken a lover. She owed her sister-in-law a debt for keeping her love child a secret, one she feared she could never repay until Isabella launched into an indiscretion of her own. Her affair brought them closer.

They exited the apartment and wandered into the orchard. A small herd of lambs nibbled at the grass. Kenhelm shooed them into the trees with his hat as Maria led her party through a maze of peach-laden branches. The linen cloth that covered a table waved in the breeze as Adelena put the finishing touches to the place settings.

As they sat, the bell tower struck nine. In the low reverberation of the after-ring, the sweet melody of the choir singing mid-morning prayers arose from the windows above them.

Minutes later, Abbess Louise emerged through the fruit trees.

"I came directly from matins," she said, taking a seat at the head of the table.

Sir Gregory arrived shortly thereafter. The instant he saw little Miranda, he broke into a lively song, stomping his heel and smacking his knee in the rhythm of a jig. Miranda laughed and climbed down from her mother's lap. She marched toward him, bouncing with each stomp of her tiny feet, clapping and squealing as she went. He picked her up and tossed her in the air.

Maria held fast to the moment, wishing it could last for eternity.

The following morning, Maria awoke to a knock on her parlor door. She lay in bed and struggled to hear the messenger as she conversed with Adelena. The door closed and Adelena came into her room.

"The abbess has summoned you and Sir Gregory. She would like to see you in her office at nine."

When they arrived, Sister Meredith invited Gregory to sit in the reception area before sweeping open the abbess's private office door and waving Maria inside.

The candelabras at either side of the room glowed bright, casting the abbess in a golden haze. Across from her desk sat an ebony Roman chair, its backrest adorned by a carved, double-headed eagle. An ermine throw blanket covered the seat. The abbess motioned her to sit.

"That chair," she began in a slow, dramatic tone, "once belonged to the Emperor Hadrian. He sat upon it in the Roman Forum when addressing the Senate." She paused. "The ermine throw is new. Both are gifts for you, from an admirer."

Maria's face fell. She sensed the direction the conversation was going and wanted to leave.

"You have graciously endured the stoic accommodations of our humble convent," the abbess continued.

"It's lovely here," Maria murmured.

"Thank you, my dear. But you were born to be a regent. Heaven has bestowed a great honor upon you, and such honors come with duties. The time has come for you to prepare for a new and wonderful life."

Maria struggled to look cheerful, but she could not even force a smile.

"A match has been made for you." The abbess looked down at her hands, but quickly brought her eyes back to Maria's and smiled. "He is a crown prince of the highest order. Your brother, King Philip, sends news that Ferdinand the Third, of the Holy Roman Empire, is seeking your hand in marriage. You are to be married at Our Lady of Amiens on Christmas Day. You and your groom shall winter there, and journey to your new home in Vienna, come spring."

Maria stared at the floor, her silent tears falling steadily. She was grateful she would not be whisked away immediately, but the news left her feeling helpless.

"I have received correspondence on your behalf," Mother Louise said, handing over two folded parchments, both sealed with wax and stamped with insignias. "One is from your brother. The other from Ferdinand the Third."

Maria accepted the two letters and excused herself to read them in private.

When she emerged into the outer office, Sir Gregory's sorrowful eyes told her he knew. She didn't have to say a word. Their days at Our Lady of Temple Mars were numbered. She took his arm. They descended the stone steps that curved around the walls of the tower.

"What's to become of my precious Miranda when I go?" she murmured.

He took her hand and squeezed it. "I would be most honored to offer my home, and my affections as Lady Miranda's godfather, if it is agreeable to you. I don't have a wife, but I have an excellent mother, and a kind sister who has a gentle husband. She would be a member of our family."

"Bless you," Maria said. "Could you take Doña Adelena, too? She loves Miranda so dearly, if I separated them, I fear it would kill her."

"Of course. She would be a gift unto my mother, who would love to hear the gossip from Madrid, even old gossip. No doubt, Adelena has innumerable tales to tell."

Maria giggled through her tears. "Indeed. Adelena always has the best gossip." Her face fell. "There's one more thing." She looked into his eyes and held back her tears as she whispered, *"Will Prince Charles ever know about our beautiful daughter?"*

Gregory's eyes were calm, but serious. "He can never know," he said. "If powerful schemers within Charles's coterie learn of her existence, poor little Miranda could become a vulnerable pawn for kingmakers, or worse, assassins who would thwart those kingmakers. The best thing you can do for our precious little princess is keep her parentage a secret."

Maria breathed deeply. In—out. But she did not weep.

Isabella sat in her parlor, waiting. Her head tipped back, heavy from drowsiness. She bobbed awake and shifted on her couch, catching her book before it slid off her lap. She had waited since dawn for Kenhelm. Rather than ruining her mood, she decided upon a nap. She slid into a reclining position and placed a silk pillow beneath her neck.

Time disappeared as she slipped into a dream. She wandered through the grassy orchard, strangely lit in dappled sunlight. Her golden-haired niece toddled toward her arms outstretched. A flock of startled birds took flight from the trees as Isabella lifted Miranda up. Approaching footsteps made Isabella turn around.

She shot upright just in time to hear a light knocking on her door. She laid her arm on the back of the sofa and posed with grand haughtiness, so Kenhelm would know she was annoyed at his tardiness but could be mollified.

"Enter," she said, coldly.

Kenhelm came through the door, nearly breathless.

"Halfway through my journey, I was called back to Lille. A letter affixed with the Hapsburg seal awaited you there, but the messenger required a series of stamps and certifications from various officials before he could release it. Please forgive my tardiness." He presented her with a leather valise.

She untied the burgundy ribbon, pulled out the folded parchment, and recoiled at the feel of it in her hand. She went numb as she took in the red Hapsburg seal atop a gold ribbon, a signal the letter was from her husband, and was to be handled with utmost secrecy.

She looked at Kenhelm. "Could you please excuse me?" she asked in a thin voice she barely recognized as her own. "Don't leave. I need to read this in private."

She went into her bedchamber, allowing the white curtain to fall behind her.

Inside the dimly lit room, she broke the seal and tilted the parchment toward a flickering lamp.

The language was stiff in its formality. The infanta had been matched to the heir of the Emperor of the Holy Roman Empire. Ferdinand III was an Austrian-born Hapsburg. She would marry him at Christmastime and depart with him the following spring. *In time, she shall be Empress,* Isabella thought. The letter also ordered Isabella to make preparations to return within the week, so she could travel while the weather was fair. *He won't even suffer me to attend her wedding.* She refolded the letter in two slaps and threw it into the valise. She would discuss the matter with the abbess, to be sure. Even as tears of anger rolled down her cheeks, she resolved she would not leave one minute before Princess Maria Anna.

"Kenhelm," she called. "Please come in."

Kenhelm swept aside the curtain and entered.

Without a word, she drew his face to hers and kissed him deeply, her mouth desperately searching his, even as she wept.

Maria ambled back to her chambers, arm in arm with Sir Gregory, absorbing the shock of the abbess's news.

They sat in her parlor and stared out the window as Adelena played with Miranda, who grew increasingly restless. Soon, Adelena would feed the fussy tot and put her down for a nap.

Maria took the top letter, slipped her fingers beneath the gold ribbon of her brother's official seal, and scanned the elegant script. It said what she expected. She carelessly tossed it aside.

She took the next letter and hesitated, feeling Gregory's eyes upon her. She looked at him.

"Would you like some privacy?" he asked.

"No," she replied. "I want you here."

She read the letter penned by her future husband, looking for clues to his nature. His overly ornate language indicated his desire to impress her, even though some passages seemed to make sport of his own pomp. She hoped this meant he wasn't too haughty and had good humor.

When she had finished, she handed the letter to Sir Gregory. He read it with a scowl.

At length, he said, "He seems to be a decent fellow. He is trying to impress you, rather than assuming you will be impressed by him. That is a good sign."

"I hope so," Maria sighed. "My feelings for Prince Charles still haunt me, but I suppose I must try to leave them behind when I go. I need to discuss this with Isabella." She rose. "Would you care to join me?"

They sat in Isabella's parlor, the two young women on the sofa, Kenhelm and Gregory in armchairs. Everyone had read Ferdinand's letter.

"Does anyone know about this fellow?" Maria asked.

"He is quite portly and nearly fifty," Isabella said, her tone matter-of-fact. "He has a notorious temper."

Maria gaped at her in horror. "I will *not* marry a hideous old ogre. I will remain here and take the veil. *I will!*"

Isabella put her index finger to her chin. "Oh, wait, forgive me. Ferdinand the Third is his son. He's an affable fellow. I don't believe he is yet twenty."

"Really, Isabella," Maria said, annoyed at her sister-in-law's lack of gravitas.

"Be merry, beautiful princess," Isabella said. "It could be worse. You could be marrying someone like *my* husband."

They both laughed. Maria had grown weary of her imperious brother, who hawked her on the marriage market like a Thoroughbred mare. In their correspondence, he blatantly ignored any request she made in regard to her future husband's temperament. If her husband turned out to be anything better than a bellicose tyrant, it would be by the grace of Heaven alone.

Isabella looked longingly at Kenhelm. He stared back at her, sullen.

She put her hand on Maria's arm and announced, "I've received a letter as well." Tears sprang to her eyes.

"Will you stay for the wedding?" Maria asked.

"Philip wants me to return to Madrid on the morrow. But I cannot leave you, my dear infanta."

They embraced and wept.

"Don't go!" said Maria. "Not until I do."

"I shall seek the abbess's intervention."

"She will help. She will."

In her return correspondence to King Philip of Spain, Abbess Louise requested Queen Isabella stay in Flanders since the wedding could not commence without a royal witness from Madrid.

King Philip instructed his clerk to pen a letter, explaining he had already arranged to send a proxy for the wedding.

The abbess responded, explaining the proxy would be welcome, but the witness absolutely had to be a royal relative. The only one available was Queen Isabella; this circumstance was beyond her control.

Upon receiving her letter, King Philip stomped his foot and threw the parchment on the polished floor. Scribbling sloppily in his own hand, he penned another letter, explaining once again, in detail, he would send a proxy, which would be perfectly legal since the Spanish king's word was law throughout the Hapsburg Empire.

In response, Abbess Louise once again apologized, in pretty language and elegant cursive, that alas, she had not the authority to remedy the situation, considering her humble status.

The proxy arrived in Amiens, but the artful abbess remained stubbornly obtuse until the matter became a moot point.

41

The Groom

October 1625
Flanders

By the time Prince Ferdinand's courtiers arrived in Lille, Maria had made peace with the inevitability of a forced marriage. At least her fiancé was a few years younger than she. Ladies in her circumstances were often matched with old ogres, partly as a warning to other wayward maids, and partly because they were a type of damaged goods to be matched to another type of damaged goods. Perhaps her brother and his ministers had not been callous in regard to her good spirits after all.

Days after their arrival, Abbess Louise invited Ferdinand's royal party to a luncheon, which she explained was a Spanish and English custom of gathering in the afternoon to enjoy casual conversation along with wine and appetizers. News of the event threw Adelena into a fit. She raced to the convent's head office, with Maria at her heels, and demanded to know why Abbess Louise had done something so improper as to make the Infanta of Spain appear eager to meet her future husband.

"Not eager," Abbess Louise responded with a languid blink. "Bold, as a future empress should be. Prince Ferdinand will be impressed, and whatever flattery he suffers will only counteract the awkwardness he will surely feel in the presence of our ethereal princess."

Maria nearly looked behind her to see whom the abbess was referring to before remembering she was, indeed, not just a princess, but destined to be the next Empress of the Holy Roman Empire. In the other-worldliness of the convent, she sometimes forgot.

Maria brought her guitar to the courtyard of the country estate Mother Louise had secured for the luncheon. The flames that flickered within the terra cotta chimineas matched the colors of the surrounding beech trees, radiant in autumn hues of scarlet and gold. A lady from Prince Ferdinand's court dampened her spirits with news that the prince was unable to attend but sent along his kindest regards.

Maria could only wonder at the news. *Does he have a touch of fever? Exhaustion from his long journey? A reluctance to be married?* She forced the last thought from her mind, even as the conviction it was the most likely reason grew within her like black ink spilled into water.

Refusing to show her anxiety, she brought her guitar to her lap and sang along to the haunting melody of an old ballad. The courtiers paused in their conversations and turned to listen. As she sang, a young man in fine attire emerged from the crowd, his dark brown hair loose and resting on his shoulders. A downy moustache crowded his perfect lips, and his golden-brown complexion contrasted nicely with his gray-blue eyes.

"My beloved Infanta Maria Anna," he said, "allow me to introduce myself. Prince Ferdinand the Third, of the Holy Roman Empire, at your service." With a charming combination of elegance and clumsiness, he swept off his hat and bowed deeply.

Months later, he would confess he had heard so many reports of her beauty and charm, he had grown convinced his courtiers were lying to him. It had been his plan to sneak into the luncheon to spy upon her, and sneak back out if he wasn't pleased with what he saw. She would laugh and kiss the tip of his nose, before kissing him deeply on the mouth.

That afternoon, she played her guitar and sang Spanish folk songs to him. She also knew a few love songs, but prudently chose to save those for another day—to warm the cockles of her marriage and make the fire burn ever brighter. She always followed Abbess Louise's kind advice. As she sang, she gazed into the eyes of her future husband. Clearly, a love song wasn't necessary. He rose and sat next to her.

"Lady Maria, I must learn every one of your lovely ballads so I may sing with you. Although my voice will be mere croaking alongside to your angelic notes, please, indulge me, I beg you."

Maria kept her smile modest. The Spanish guitar had cast its spell. It was the only musical instrument she had insisted on playing, ignoring Adelena's admonition it was completely inappropriate for a lady of her station to wield such a clumsy device. It appeared the young prince didn't mind.

The next day, as they walked side by side on a country stroll with their chaperones trailing them, a hare leapt out of the bushes and raced past them.

"Dear me!" Ferdinand said. "That hare rushes as if he's late for church and the parishioners are gabbing about him!"

The hare's anxious face so perfectly matched his description, Maria burst into laughter. Ferdinand's eyes flashed with delight at her outburst. Taking her hand in his, he patted it, as if their budding romance had reached a new plateau. He was not as glamorous as Prince Charles, but he was amusing, and she found his desire to make her smile endearing.

As the weeks rolled by, she grew more comfortable with him.

One afternoon, as they walked through the garden, Prince Ferdinand took her hand and spoke to her in a low voice.

"I know of your secret here at the convent."

Maria froze in mid-step and looked at him. He glanced at her before casting his eyes down again, as though he were the one embarrassed by the news.

"I say this because I don't want you to worry. I don't care. You are unsurpassed in your wisdom and beauty." He looked into her eyes and took her other hand into his. "I want you, and only you, to be my bride and empress."

Tears welled in Maria's eyes. "Thank you. That is the kindest thing you could possibly say."

"Well, since I likely made you a bit melancholy, I suppose now is as good a time as ever to tell you some bad news."

She looked at him, dreading his next words.

"About your friend Lord Buckingham."

Maria's voice was firm. "He is no friend of mine," she said.

Ferdinand proceeded as though he hadn't heard. "Apparently, in an effort to dispel rumors he's fond of young lads, the duke has taken to groping the ladies-in-waiting. One day, he groped a particular lady. Her husband, a man of considerable size, pursued Buckingham, urgent to converse with him. Buckingham evaded him by weaving his way through the crowd. The pursuit became so obvious the courtiers could not contain their mirth. When the children of England overheard the gossip the following day, they devised a charming poem to honor Lord Buckingham. Would you like to hear it?"

Maria smiled in anticipation. "But, of course," she said.

"Very well." He clutched his hands at his midsection with his elbows out, striking the pose of a poet at a formal recitation. "Georgie Porgie, pudding and pie, kissed the girls and made them cry. When the boys came out to play, Georgie Porgie ran away."

Princess Maria guffawed in a most unladylike fashion.

42

The Wedding

Christmas Day, December 1625
Amiens, France

Princess Maria arrived at Our Lady of Amiens on Christmas Day's bright, frosty afternoon. The bone-white cathedral towered over the coach, its spired parapets scraping the clear blue sky.

Sir Gregory leapt from the carriage and offered his arm. Maria clung to him as she navigated the frosted flagstones in her pearl-encrusted slippers. She had chosen a gown of white samite. The gold threads of her billowing silk skirts reflected the blinding sunlight. Although her shoulders were bare, the heavy satin lining of her dress kept her warm.

Maria could hardly believe her time at Our Lady of Temple Mars had come to a close. Even while the convent had come to feel like her only real home, the past two years had flown.

A military officer opened the high door that led to the sanctuary. They passed beneath the ribbed portico and entered a massive hall with buttressed arches that stretched high above their heads. They walked down the aisle of the sanctuary, engulfed in a haze of color emanating from the gigantic rose window that loomed ahead. The clock tower struck three just as they reached the back of the sanctuary. In the lengthy pause of the after-ring, a quartet of violins struck up a breezy tune. Flutes and cellos came in, lending a sense of force to the music.

Maria spotted Ferdinand standing at the altar, flanked by his royal witnesses. He glanced her way, then raised his eyebrows. She bowed her head to hide her smile.

Queen Isabella led an assigned entourage of gowned ladies down the aisle to gather on one side of the bishop. When the percussion sounded, Sir Gregory offered his arm to Maria. She entwined her arm with his, and he led her toward the altar.

Her heart thumped in her chest. She felt so light, she wondered if her feet might leave the floor. Her life was on the verge of changing completely. As she stood before her groom, she took a deep breath and remembered to let it out only when he whispered, "Breathe." The priest babbled on, but she heard nothing. She trembled when Ferdinand took her hand and slipped a ring with a large pink ruby flanked by narrow, emerald-cut diamonds on her finger.

Their sealing kiss was not their first, but it was the most tender and sweet.

That evening found them dining in the Hotel Royale ballroom beneath candlelit chandeliers while snowflakes swirled beyond the windowpanes.

After they had a bit of the wedding feast, Ferdinand took his bride to the ballroom floor, where they lined up with their guests to dance the allemande, the galliard, and an elegant minuet before they left for their private chambers.

Once Maria's ladies-in-waiting had helped her into her delicate dimity nightgown and velvet robe, they escorted her to the bedchamber.

Prince Ferdinand stood by the bed in a long dressing robe, holding his arms out to her as if asking her to dance. She nervously pulled her velvet collar closer to her neck, went to him, and gave him a tender kiss. He embraced her, then turned to pick up a velvet satchel resting on the bed. He untied the front flap and brought out a colorful collection of feathers.

"My stepmother gave me these as a nuptial gift with instructions to take them out on my wedding night and use my imagination," he said. "I have absolutely no idea what she was getting at."

Maria gave a shriek and collapsed on the bed in a paroxysm of giggles.

"Let me see those feathers," she said, once she composed herself. "I have a feeling your stepmother and I could easily be friends."

While Ferdinand was somewhat clumsy at first, he was eager to please, and soon became comfortable. Maria found him to be an enthusiastic and passionate lover. In time, they would be known as the most romantic couple in Europe.

Downstairs in the ballroom, the party crescendoed. The orchestra played while fashionable guests leapt and swirled through the steps of the sarabande, a scandalous dance banned in prudish Spain.

Abbess Louise wore a horned headdress covered with a shimmering white cloth shot through with silver thread.

Over the contours of her elegant black dress swayed a long gold chain terminating in a golden crucifix with a peacefully dozing Messiah. Although she did not join in the dance, she clapped her hands and tapped her foot along with the rhythm, her mannish shoes peeking from beneath her long gown.

Queen Isabella danced with Sir Gregory. To everyone's surprise, he knew the sarabande and taught it to her on the dance floor. Giddy from all the spinning, she could feel her hem swirl above her silkened calves. A chorus of gasps assured her the wedding guests had noticed. She glanced at the abbess for signs of disapproval. Mother Louise smiled and waved, before returning to clapping her hands to the beat.

After several more rounds of leaping and swirling, Isabella found herself facing Sir Kenhelm, who skillfully twirled her away from an astonished Sir Gregory, for Kenhelm, too, had studied the sarabande.

He brought his lips close to her ear. "How often does one get a chance to dance with a beautiful queen?" Kenhelm murmured to Isabella, artfully avoiding other swirling couples.

Sir Gregory hunted up Adelena, plucked the tiny Lady Miranda from her lap, and returned to the dance floor with her on his shoulders. Holding her hands and keeping his shoulders level with the ground, he danced a comical jig while little Miranda giggled in delight. Gregory kept dancing until a warm, wet blotch formed on the back of his neck, at which point he swiftly returned the tot to her nursemaid.

The party went on, long into the night, until the violet glow of dawn shone through the windowpanes.

"Sir Kenhelm," Isabella's voice was urgent. "Please escort me to my chambers. The clock strikes seven."

"It can't be that late."

"And yet it is," she replied. "Let us be subtle and retire unnoticed."

They left the ballroom with a bevy of lady's maids crowding around them, as per her instructions. Isabella took Kenhelm's arm and they all ascended a broad spiral staircase to the hotel suites on the second floor.

When they arrived at her chambers, she thanked her entourage and bid them a good morning while Kenhelm unlocked the door and swung it open for her. The ladies were well-paid for their utmost discretion.

Kenhelm helped Isabella out of her elaborate gown and corset. Once the job was done, he quickly cast off his own clothes, then embraced her, reveling in the silky softness of her warm skin.

She kissed him deeply. They fell onto the bed, entwining their legs as they landed. They writhed in ecstasy until they were exhausted. Once they rested, they made love again, but slowly and with a heightened sense of imagination. Having satisfied themselves a second time, they fell into a deep sleep.

They slept all day and crept out at sunset to enjoy the French city's fashionable evening revelries.

The following morning, an ominous knock woke Isabella. Its aggressive rhythm and volume indicated a high-ranking official with urgent business. A baritone voice called through the door.

"King Philip the Fourth's agent, the honorable Count of Seville, requires a signature for a certificate of guardianship from Her Majesty, Queen Isabella."

Isabella's head throbbed. She stared at Kenhelm. They knew their time was short but hadn't expected the end to come so suddenly.

Kenhelm snatched up his clothes and all other evidence of his presence, then slipped through a secret passage—one of many delightful features of the Hotel de Royale.

Isabella gathered her thoughts. Clearly, her king had deciphered she was reluctant to return home, and how right he was. But she wasn't the sort of fool who would sign away her personal sovereignty. Certainly not to a courtier far beneath her station. Sitting up in bed, she tamped down her anger and spoke like an actor projecting from the stage.

"I am not prepared to open my door to an official of the court on such sudden notice." Her voice dripped with indignation. "Please return in two hours and I will be happy to receive your company."

"I shall return in one hour. At that time, I shall insist on a signature." The sound of footsteps echoed down the hall.

She slipped out of bed, pulled on her dressing robe, and followed Kenhelm through the secret passage.

"Please call my ladies and send them to me, swiftly," she whispered. "He shall return in one hour."

Back in her room, she waited. The ladies arrived within minutes. They dressed Isabella in a long-sleeved gown that covered her chest all the way up to her collarbone. The young women topped her bulky dress with an Elizabethan collar so completely out of fashion, it had become the hallmark of prudishness.

When the imperial official returned with the certificate of guardianship, Queen Isabella was resolute. "I will not sign your certificate, as you already have my word we shall leave at once with my full cooperation. My entourage and I shall be ready to depart at dawn. You must gather my military escorts. As soon as you summon them, we will be on our way."

"I am under the orders of the king to obtain your signature."

"You are under my orders to gather my entourage and equip them for the journey. If they are unprepared, the king will know of your incompetence."

The count spun on his heel and stormed out of her room. Isabella rushed to slam the door behind him. She sat and pulled the stiff collar from her neck.

"Do you know any sad love songs?" she asked.

One of the ladies reached for a lute and sang a beautiful melody. Isabella asked her to continue while she went behind the curtain to her bedchamber to write a letter.

> *Dearest Kenhelm,*
> *Had I the choice to marry anyone I wished, it would be you.*
> *Please think of me often. I shall warm my heart with the memories we share.*
> *May we be together in spirit, now and forevermore.*
> *Eternally,*
> *Your Beloved*

She took a sharp knife from her desk drawer, sliced off a lock of her hair, and folded it into the parchment before sealing it.

43

The Cardinal

February 1626
Paris, France

The walls of the Parisian shops lit up butter yellow in the early morning. Eremitz headed for the headquarters of the king's guard, an old Tudor-style hotel with a slate roof. An icy breeze stung his cheeks and lifted his broad-brimmed hat off of his head. He caught it and pressed it more firmly to his scalp.

Sounds of clicking swords and witty repartee crescendoed from a large courtyard as he approached. The officers of the king's guard practiced their fencing, as they did every morning. No one could approach the hotel's main entrance without engaging in swordplay. Eremitz had no time for their antics, determined to demonstrate his discipline with precise punctuality.

He ducked into the narrow passage at the side of the hotel and sought the hidden door. After twisting an iron key in the Gothic lock, he gently pushed, and the door creaked open.

The interior offered little respite from the cold, although the deserted corridor was brightly lit from a large east window at the end of the hallway. A clock tower chimed in the distance as he rushed toward the staircase, taking the steps two at a time up to the second floor. He stopped at the door of his uncle's office and knocked at the clock's final stroke of seven.

"Come in," Captain Treville said, his voice muffled beyond the door.

Eremitz entered and folded into an elegant bow. "Aramis de Genoa, at your service, Captain Treville," he said, using the cover name they had agreed upon.

His uncle sat behind a plain wooden desk, looking amused. A wide glass-paned window offered a broad view of Paris's bustling street life below. A flickering fireplace kept the room warm.

"Shut the door," he said.

Eremitz did so, and Treville stood to kiss his nephew on each cheek. A gray-haired man in his fifties, Treville was still handsome.

Eremitz removed his coat and hung it on a rack with a vanity mirror set in an oak frame inlaid with ebony. The polished woodwork was the only display of luxury in the room.

"And how is the Duchess Chevreuse? Any news?" Captain Treville referred to the wealthy noblewoman who had sponsored Aramis de Genoa as a candidate for the prestigious Musketeers of the Guard, as the king's guard was known.

"I have received two letters from her since my return."

"Two? And you've been back in Paris for less than a fortnight! I take it she is still smitten with you." He chuckled. "I was once in your place. Women like the duchess are amusing, but you must find good reason to leave while the romance is fresh. If you allow it to sour you could ruin the goodwill crucial for an excellent recommendation."

Eremitz was relieved his uncle understood the exact nature of his relationship with the duchess. This alleviated any need for explanation.

When he arrived in Paris a year earlier, his uncle had explained his influence with the king could secure a position on the king's guard for Eremitz only if he had the papers to prove his experience and accomplishments. A man with no papers could not hope to qualify.

Eremitz swallowed his pride and became a fencing instructor. Months later, he was instructing his students in a field on the outskirts of Paris when his uncle called upon him to report good news. An influential palace official of his acquaintance knew a duchess who was in want of a personal guard. She had specified a young man, fair of face and lithe of body. Treville made certain Eremitz understood the implications. "While the duchess is spirited and in need of constant flattery, she is also a beautiful young woman, so take your blessings where you can. Although she may provoke you at times, you must be always the ardent lover, for Duchess Chevreuse is Queen Ana's senior lady-in-waiting. She's close to King Louis as well. He will grant her favors, if it's easily done. If all goes well, a letter of recommendation from Duchess Chevreuse will win you an appointment to the Musketeers of the Guard."

Realizing he'd become lost in thought, Eremitz lifted his head to see his uncle gazing at him.

"You are still on good terms with the duchess, are you not?" his uncle asked.

"As near as I can tell," said Eremitz. "Her letters gush with romantic sentiments, but I'm afraid I have not yet received a letter of recommendation. How does a gentleman go about asking for one?"

Treville chuckled and leaned back in his chair. "That matter is well in hand. The recommendation letter has been received by the king's office. I feared we might be fully staffed by the time the duchess's letter arrived. But the cardinal still has one opening for a man with outstanding talent."

"Did you recommend me as a man of outstanding talent?" Eremitz asked.

"I did," replied Treville. "Please don't disappoint."

"When it comes to swordplay, I have never disappointed anyone, save for the man on the losing side."

Treville looked at him sideways. "This job encompasses far more than swordplay," he said. "Your tryst with Duchess Chevreuse is a perfect example. Whether you wanted it or not was beside the point. It was simply a thing that had to be done as a prerequisite for the job. There will be no more trysts of that sort for you, however. You must not invite Duchess Chevreuse's jealousy. A tavern girl can be easily waved aside, but a rival among the duchess's peers could be dangerous to your career."

"I have no desire to be any noblewoman's pet saddled with the constant task of amusing her. But I do appreciate knowing the rules of romance. Such a gem of wisdom could make me more popular among my fellow men."

"Indeed," his uncle said. "Many a fair-faced gentleman has found a bright future along this avenue."

"Speaking of bright futures, what sort of talents does this particular position require?" Eremitz asked.

"Nothing I can put in specific terms. I can say this: you shall be on duty at all hours, night and day, even when you appear to be off duty. There will be no room for merriment, unless you're under orders. While you may have a glass of wine or two with dinner, you must never get drunk. Specifically, you must constantly be on the lookout for the king's enemies, mindful that most come clad in brocade and drip with charm. And you must keep a constant vigil over your own person, you will never be safe."

"I haven't been safe for quite some time," Eremitz said. "And indeed, I have no inclination toward my personal safety, but only toward that of the king I serve. I would gladly die a noble death for him. Aside from that, my hopeful expectation is decent food and lodgings."

Treville chuckled. "You'll have that. But be frugal with your wages, especially while fraternizing with your fellow musketeers. If they know you are in possession of a single coin, they'll insist you buy them a round. I suggest you feign piety and tell your brethren you give all of your discretionary income to the church. Otherwise, they will spend your wages out from under you and then explain what you owe the tavern. Or worse, the gambling house."

"Thank you for your insights."

Treville stood. "If we leave for the cardinal's apartments now, we'll arrive in plenty of time to enjoy a light repast at a quaint café whose owner is a friend of mine." As Eremitz stood, his uncle moved to clap a hand over his shoulder.

"No need to worry. I'm certain you will soon be an officer of the king's guard. The cardinal will explain your duties."

Eremitz took his uncle's face in his hands and kissed him tenderly on each cheek. "Thank you, Uncle Armand. I will never forget all you have done."

"You always strived to be your best, Henri. I could not have done this save for the fact you truly are exceptional."

They walked a brisk half-mile to Richelieu's neighborhood. When they entered the warm café, the owner swept up to Treville and silently waved him over to the back of the restaurant, where they found a table for two.

After a light breakfast of coffee, fresh bread, and fried fish, the two sauntered to the cardinal's ornate five-story townhouse, which occupied a small city block. Treville stopped at a black lacquered door and pulled a gold watch from his pocket. He flipped open the ornate cover and tilted the mother-of-pearl face toward Eremitz to show him the time—five of eight. The watch's high-pitched ticking sent a fine vibration pulsing through Eremitz's veins.

Treville nodded toward the doorknocker, a heavy ring set in a brass lion's mouth. Eremitz smiled, put one fist on his hip as he struck a pose, and rapped sharply on the door.

It opened to reveal a liveried servant dressed in black and white.

"Monsieur Aramis de Genoa?" the servant asked.

"At your service," Eremitz said with a nod.

"The cardinal awaits you." the servant waived Eremitz into the foyer. Once he stepped in, the servant shut the door.

The black marble floor was dotted with large ceramic pots of rosemary, evergreen boughs, and fragrant flowers, which helped ward off foul odors from the street. Eremitz followed as the servant trotted three flights up a spiral staircase.

The door of the cardinal's study stood half-open. Eremitz turned toward the servant, but the servant was gone.

He gently pushed open the door to see Cardinal Richelieu looking straight into his eyes. The slender, silver-haired minister sat at a Baroque desk, wearing a crimson cap and matching cape over a white robe.

Eremitz closed the door behind him and bowed. "Aramis de Genoa at your service, Your Eminence. May I humbly submit myself to your inspection?"

"Please, have a seat," the cardinal said, motioning to a chair on the opposite side of the desk.

Eremitz sat, basking in the ecstasy and terror of being so near his goal.

"You are escaping the Keepers of the Kingdom, I take it?" Richelieu asked, his tone matter of fact.

"I am," said Eremitz, feeling stripped bare beneath the cardinal's hawkish gaze.

"We have forged a new identity for you. Here are your papers." The cardinal handed over a leather satchel.

Eremitz took it and pulled out a thin sheath of papers topped by a letter of recommendation. At the bottom of the fine parchment was the signature of Duchess Chevreuse in her characteristic florid script. With a fanfare of verbosity, the letter introduced Monsieur Aramis de Genoa—an expert swordsman, perfect gentleman, and respectable scholar. The duchess claimed he had served her admirably for a conveniently unspecified "number of years." French perfume wafted from the parchment.

Eremitz drew the letter aside to reveal Aramis de Genoa's records from a seminary in Genoa, Italy, one that Eremitz had briefly studied at in his youth. He felt a twinge of loss, having attended a far more prestigious seminary in Florence, which now had to be denied. He perused the document, noting it would account for his youth from age seven to twenty-one. The next page was an attestation of Aramis's birth record, signed and sealed by a Genoan priest, which filled in the rest of his new identity.

The last page was a synopsis of his new life up to the present, including a flirtatious and somewhat scandalous story about how he became an expert swordsman, obviously crafted to please the tastes of French gossips. Eremitz assumed the unspoken instruction was to give that exact account of his history and no more when discussing his background with fellow musketeers.

"You are more than kind," Eremitz said as he slipped the papers back into the satchel. "I am and shall ever be your humble servant."

The cardinal extended his hand. "You may leave the papers here for safekeeping," he said.

Eremitz handed them back. Although the arrangement ensured the cardinal's complete control over his life, the papers would be far safer here than in the cheap hotel room Eremitz rented.

"Do you have questions?" the cardinal asked.

"I do, if I may be so bold. Why is my new name so similar to my old one? Does that not put me at risk of discovery?"

"Quite the opposite. If an old acquaintance were to recognize you, it is far easier to make a case of mistaken identity if the names, and even the histories, are similar. For instance, you won't be able to hide the numerous mannerisms that indicate you are a priest. Aramis de Genoa was raised in a seminary, which perfectly explains those subtle affectations. Here in Paris, if a foreigner claims you are a priest named Eremitz, a swarm of local busybodies will surround him and insist that you were never a priest, but that you were raised in a seminary and hope to enter the priesthood one day. The more the Parisians explain this, the more they will believe it. Even if your prior acquaintance is unconvinced, he will quickly see the futility of making the Parisians believe you are anyone other than Monsieur Aramis, proud officer of the Musketeers of the Guard."

Eremitz realized he could learn a great deal from the cardinal.

"In your service to the king of France," the cardinal continued, "you shall function at a considerably higher level than your fellow musketeers, but they cannot know this. You shall be informed of further duties as I see fit. In the meantime, circumstances compel me to introduce you to the political landscape that forms the backdrop of your service to the king."

The cardinal folded his hands on the desk. "There is a power struggle between King Louis and his mother, Marie de Medici. She served as France's regent during the time of Louis's minority, but she refused to allow her son to advance to the throne when he came of age, so he was obliged to take his throne by force. His mother still refuses to accept his rule, and since her immediate family is among the most wealthy and powerful in Europe, she has limitless resources to entice some of France's most powerful noblemen to her side. She seeks to regain her power by deposing her firstborn and replacing him with his younger brother, Prince Gaston, Duke of Orleans. The queen mother finds in her younger son a man malleable to her will."

The cardinal's strange tale was made all the more surreal by the fact he was making Eremitz, a foreigner at his mercy, privy to the darkest secrets of the royal family.

"In addition to keeping King Louis safe on journeys both long and short," the cardinal continued, "this position calls upon you to constantly be on the lookout for insidious enemies. I understand you were once a poisoner."

The cardinal's last remark hit Eremitz like a punch to the gut. It was hardly something he wished to discuss while offering his services to a king.

"Those days are behind me now. Forever." Eremitz said, desperately hoping this declaration would not end the interview.

"I fear you will need to put a portion of those days before you again. You shall not be required to concoct or deliver poison, I give you my word as a gentleman and a man of God. Rather, I wish you to tutor this office on eliminating opportunities for would-be poisoners, and to teach early diagnosis of poisoning symptoms."

"Of course," Eremitz said with a sigh of relief. "I shall gladly render my expertise for the sake of the king's health and safety."

"You will also keep your ears open as people chat in the taverns, or gossip in the jousting yard, constantly aware that the greatest threat to King Louis is poisoners, as our poor king has been poisoned several times. His mother has the strongest motive, the means, and influential connections. There is also the king's brother, but he is far too daft to pull it off. My guess is it's the queen mother's physician. I have the three under constant surveillance.

"That is not the only threat posed by the queen mother. She is in league with the Roman Church, as they stand at the precipice of war against the Protestants throughout the Holy Roman Empire, encompassing all of continental Europe. Yet even as we are flanked by Spain, which vies to be the pope's favorite among nations, and the Germanic kingdoms, where Europe's largest population of Protestants shall soon meet with imperial armies, we strive to keep France out of this war. Marie de Medici is eager to pledge the French army to the pope, but the office of the king shall prevent it."

It dawned on Eremitz that by "office of the king" the cardinal meant his own decision-making authority. The walls seemed to buzz with power.

The cardinal placed his fingertips together. "The greatest threat to any kingdom is war. This is another topic you must monitor. Aside from asking clarifying questions, which I recommend, never take a side in the discussion. Simply observe, and later record who said what about whom. You shall be trained on how to keep such records accurate and secret.

"That is enough for now," the cardinal said. "Please, remember what we have discussed." He reached into the leather satchel to withdraw the synopsis of Aramis's new identity. "Take this with you. I had my secretary write this essay to make it appear as if you composed it yourself and had it professionally penned. This vain indulgence is not uncommon among Parisian gentlemen. Memorize it and keep it as part of your effects."

At this, the interview was over.

Aramis found his way down the three-flight spiral staircase alone and stepped out into the bright winter day. The branches of a row of locust trees reached in great exaltation for the royal blue sky. He headed back to the café feeling taller, lighter.

Cardinal Richelieu stared out the window watching Aramis walk down the street. He trusted Treville to recommend only the best candidates. The most talented musketeers Treville had recruited were his own blood. His distant cousin, Athos, was the best swordsman in the King's Guard. Athos brought with him his nephew, Porthos, a youth the size of a buffalo whom Athos had trained to flank him as they took on ten of the king's best swordsmen at once.

This time, Treville had recommended far more than an outstanding musketeer. Between Treville and Aramis, Richelieu now had two strategically placed spies to protect the king's guard from the influence of the queen mother and her network of loyalists.

Richelieu was confident he could trust Aramis, knowing he had broken his vows as a priest, and worse, escaped the brotherhood of the Inquisition. Switching his loyalty back to the pope was out of the question. No man wished to go back to the prison cell from whence he escaped. Now that Aramis had severed himself from his religious underpinnings, Cardinal Richelieu hoped to steer him toward a new ideology—preferably one that did not involve a belief in God so much as a belief in a better society.

The cardinal preferred to work with spies who had lost their faith—ironic for a man whose belief in God was unshakable. Since he was a boy, Richelieu was convinced God had a plan for him. He told no one, his conviction was too personal. Through the years, God spoke to him—not every day, just now and then. Cardinal Richelieu had come to know His voice. As he watched Aramis disappear into the café on the street corner below, he felt God at his shoulder, grateful His servant had put into action His divine counsel.

Recruit those who believe in Me no longer. Upon the clean slate of their hearts, I shall restore their faith.

44

Her Father's Calling

May 1626
The House of Salomon
Lille, Flanders

Kitty left Anne's chambers and raced down the banister-lined hallway in search of her. The late afternoon sun lit up the tall, glass-paned windows across the foyer, filling the chateau with soft, apricot light.

Outside, a cadre of servants lit party lanterns. The guests would be arriving soon. As Abbess Louise headed the planning committee for the May Day celebration, she asked Anne and Kitty to provide a friendly ambiance while the guests wandered in.

Kitty found Anne in the study sitting at the baroque desk, her face tear stained as she labored over a sheet of watercolor paper that had been washed in pale blue and inscribed with delicate black script. A painted dove soared in the upper corner of the paper. Anne positioned her paintbrush over the lower left corner of the sheet, and from its tip poured the image of a cottontail bunny with long ears and big eyes—the kind she and Quentin had painted together at a homey desk, at a cozy parson's house, somewhere on an estate a lifetime ago.

Kitty's throat tightened as her own tears trailed down her cheeks. Looking over Anne's shoulder, she scanned the letter. It was addressed to Quentin and told of a meadow near the House of Salomon, and wild animals Anne had seen there. And what she and Kitty had had for breakfast that morning (tea and fresh bread with strawberry jam). She asked Quentin what sort of jam he had for breakfast that morning, knowing Aelfreda prided herself on her vast collection of homemade preserves.

Anne washed her brush in a mug of water and dipped it into a small ceramic paint pot. In the lower right corner of the paper, three luscious strawberries emerged from the brush, followed by a cluster of green leaves. While in Spain, Anne had written so many illustrated letters to Quentin her artwork had become impressively swift and accurate.

"'Tis beautiful," said Kitty.

"I thank you. But you did not come here to tell me that. You came to tell me the party is starting."

"It is," said Kitty. "But have no care, M'Lady, your correspondence with Quentin is far more important. Take your time, I beg you."

"The task is done," Anne said, swishing her paintbrush into the mug of water and placing it on a faded rag. As she stared at the letter beneath her, a tear slid down her cheek and fell upon it, blurring the word it landed on—*path.* Anne reared back and wiped her cheeks with a handkerchief before standing.

"Kitty, have I chosen this path, or has it chosen me? When I look around, my thoughts turn to Quentin, and all I can think is 'How did I get here? What have I done?' Everything has gone so horribly wrong."

"Fate is not always a pleasant thing," Kitty replied. "Please don't assume your circumstances are the result of any mistake you have made, M'Lady. You have done what you must to keep dear Quentin safe. I cannot allow you to blame yourself for the outcome of this misadventure, my dear friend. We are fortunate to have such excellent guardians in Uncle Cedric and Auntie Aelfreda. I know you miss Quentin terribly, but we must take comfort in knowing he is happy and safe."

Anne's eyes met Kitty's. "Will he forget me?" She gasped at her own words and her face crumbled in anguish.

Kitty held Anne's hands in hers. "No! Never. He cannot forget you." She hugged her friend and they embraced for some time. "He will cherish these letters, I promise you," Kitty said, stroking her back. "He will keep them in a special place and read from them again and again."

Anne pulled away, smiling through her tears. "As I have kept his precious letters. I know Aelfreda is writing for him, but I can tell the words are his own."

"As are the illustrations of his frogs and bugs," said Kitty.

They both laughed.

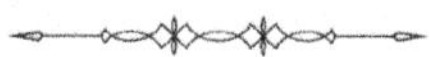

As twilight faded to dusk, a distant clock tower struck eight. Two rows of elm trees intertwined their boughs, forming a canopy over a broad avenue. Their serpentine limbs were lit from below by Chinese lanterns hanging from a network of ropes crisscrossing between the rows of trees. The paper orbs glowed in rose, saffron, and many shades of blue.

Arm in arm, Kitty and Anne passed beneath, marveling at the constellation of spheres floating above their heads. A damp chill suffused the evening. Kitty welcomed it, having grown warm under her short velvet cape.

"I missed these parties," said Kitty.

"I did too," said Anne. "The pretty lanterns and summer gowns remind me of all the gaiety we shared with Harald."

"Do the memories make you happy or sad?" Kitty asked.

"Both," said Anne. "Until recently, I felt only sorrow when reflecting on the past. But now, I can feel his presence. Indeed, it feels as if he never left me."

"Us," Kitty corrected. "He never left us. I've felt him all along and waited for a sign that you felt him too."

"Oh, Kitty, I should have known Harald would be hovering about you."

"Not me, M'Lady, he hovers about *you*, but you're too melancholy to notice."

Anne smiled. "He is here, isn't he? Kitty, how do you think he would feel if Gregory and I were to marry? Do you think he would mind?"

"I'm afraid it's more complicated than that," Kitty said. "Brother Theodore has matched us to a mission ideally suited to our expertise. And he is under the impression we have agreed to this, is he not?"

"Agreed to what, exactly? You dressing hair for queens and duchesses in Paris? To what end, Kitty?"

"To what end? We shall know everything about the Parisian court—every detail of political intrigue, who is loyal to whom, who is flush with treasure, and who is in debt. We shall hear it all from nobility of the highest rank, and when I learn what the servants have to say, we will be the most informed courtiers in all of Europe. We shall move among them as dainty flowers, far too daft to be conduits of intrigue. Moreover, you will build a circle of influence, and what better way to protect little Quentin?"

Anne humphed. "Surely, we will not be mingling with France's highest nobility for our own convenience. Who shall be the beneficiary of this knowledge?"

"Who, indeed?" Kitty asked with wide eyes. "I believe we will find out tonight. Did your Auntie Louise not tell you? She hopes to introduce you to a dear friend of hers. She wouldn't say who, but she slipped and mentioned he's at the elbow of the king, night and day. The young King Louis the Thirteenth of France, I would presume. Why else would Brother Theodore be talking about Paris? I hear he's quite handsome, now that he's lost his baby fat. The French king, I mean."

"Of all the handsome men still breathing, there is only one I hold dear. I must be honest, Kitty. A life of Parisian intrigue may not win the competition of my heart, not with Sir Gregory in the picture." She put her lips to Kitty's ear. "I yearn for him," she whispered.

When she pulled back, Kitty leaned in and whispered into her ear. "Then take him with you!"

Anne looked at her quizzically.

Kitty looked ahead and spotted Abbess Louise in her plain black gown and gauze-draped horned headdress. She stood chatting in a cozy circle of acquaintances.

"There's Auntie!" Kitty exclaimed, glad to change the subject.

The abbess looked up as they approached. After greetings all around, she bid her companions adieu and strolled between Anne and Kitty as they continued on to the buffet tables. They walked in silence as the paper lanterns shrank from large colorful orbs to an array of small white balls the size of hen's eggs. The lights trailed overhead like pale gold bubbles on a dark stream.

"Anne," Aunt Louise said at length, "there is a man here I would like you to meet." She lifted her chin and looked ahead, searching. Her regal profile reminded Kitty that the abbess was the daughter of a princess. "I've invited him to the party to meet you. He has journeyed all the way from Paris."

"May I assume he is not seeking romance?" Anne asked.

"Nothing so trivial. This man has the power to change the world, but he needs assistance from a wise and extraordinary noblewoman, like yourself. And you, Lady Kitty."

"Really?" Anne mused. "How dramatic. Now, I'm wondering if you are engaging in a bit of theater to distract me from Sir Gregory."

"There is no need for me to wonder about anything," Aunt Louise said. "You are behaving like a girl hoping for romance. But you are not a maiden, Anne. The world needs wise, intrepid souls. Many decades from now, when you are on your deathbed, will you be satisfied with the life of an ordinary woman, when you could be guiding history? I can't allow you to make such a mistake, my dear." At that, the abbess waved her hand and announced, "Here they are!"

She smiled sweetly as they approached two men at the outer edge of the crowd milling about the buffet table. The men turned from what appeared to be an engrossing conversation. Brother Theodore, dressed comfortably in an open frock coat over a chemise and twill breeches, lifted his chin in acknowledgement.

Kitty eyed his companion, a tall, tightly built man with steel-gray hair wearing a black doublet and breeches tucked into knee-high boots. At first glance, he appeared to be Brother Theodore's age, but as they neared, Kitty realized he had the smooth, tan face of a man in his early forties. *That must be Aunt Louise's mysterious friend*, she thought.

Aunt Louise spoke in perfect French. "Your Eminence, may I introduce you to my niece, Lady Anne de Winter."

Kitty's mind raced through a series of official titles, trying to remember which rank and office was addressed as "Your Eminence." She glanced at Anne, who was dipping into a curtsy, and could tell by her expression she, too, was trying to remember.

"And her dearest friend, Catherine, Baroness von Kirchheim." Aunt Louise motioned to Kitty.

"Cardinal." The word popped out of Kitty's mouth before she realized she was saying it out loud. She blushed deeply as she dipped into a slow, respectful curtsy.

"And may I introduce to you, Cardinal Richelieu, viceroy of France. He has honored us by attending our annual May Day celebration."

"You flatter me, Reverend Mother," he said. "It is my honor to attend your lovely celebration and mingle among such fine company."

They chatted amiably as they drifted toward the buffet. After acquiring plates of hors d'oeuvres, Aunt Louise led them to a round table with paper signs at each place, all scripted with their names except for one that said "Guest." Brother Theodore pulled out chairs for Aunt Louise and Kitty.

The cardinal pulled out a chair for Anne, then sat next to her.

"I knew your father well," Cardinal Richelieu said.

At that, he had her full attention.

"He was my mentor. He taught me how to play the game of global politique. I've learned important lessons on my own, but your father's guidance was a most important factor in my success." The cardinal fell silent.

Anne stared, her sky-blue eyes attesting their willingness to absorb information. "Who are you?" she asked. "I mean, who were you, before you were cardinal?"

"I was born Armand du Plessis in the year of our Lord 1585. When I was five years old, my father died in the war between the Catholics and Protestants in France. Since it was a civil war, French subjects suffered twice the casualties. I became an orphan, as did many of my generation.

"My father had fought valiantly for the king, who rewarded him with the bishopric of Luçon. Upon my father's death, my mother went to the city of Luçon and bargained with their council. She had used her connections to secure a scholarship for me at the prestigious College of Navarre in Paris. The Luçon City Council agreed to grant her a pension so she could reside in Paris and supervise my education. In return, she swore to them that once I achieved the office of bishop, I would rebuild their town, which had been ravaged by war."

"And did you keep the promise?" Anne asked with a sweet smile and a level gaze.

The cardinal could tell she was probing him. "Of course. The city of Luçon is on the verge of reopening their glorious cathedral, and many other fine buildings have been restored."

Her lids lowered, indicating doubt. "It gives me comfort to know you are a man of your word," she said.

He knew she would corroborate his story, find it true, and come closer to trusting him.

"How did you meet my father?" Anne asked. "Please forgive me, but my curiosity will leave me no peace."

"Although I was only nine years old, I passed the entrance exam for the college, thanks to my dear mother, who schooled me well. Mother rented an apartment in Paris, and with my six-year-old little sister in tow, paid a visit to every socialite in Paris with whom she had maintained a correspondence."

Anne relaxed into her chair and stared past him, bored. The cardinal suppressed a smile. "These were not merely social visits. Rather, Mother sought an introduction to an intriguing Englishman who functioned as King Henry's prime minister."

Anne's eyes snapped to his.

"I am, of course, speaking of your father," the cardinal continued. "My mother arranged to meet with him. She took me along, to show off my skills as a secretary."

"You were a secretary at the age of *nine*?" Anne asked.

"My mother was a remarkable tutor. She presented me to your father as an ideal assistant, and he accepted. He arranged to have me work at his office for four hours a day, excluding Sundays. The principal of the college allowed it, because it was an excellent opportunity to further my education. While the College of Navarre is second to none, I must admit I learned far more from your father than I did from my professors."

"What did he teach you?" Anne asked.

"The most important lesson was the power of information. It is not the mightiest army that wins. Rather, it is the most informed player at the table. Information drives all of my victories, though I do not seek victory for myself, but for all of France. I have sworn to God I shall accomplish this feat in my lifetime."

Anne's eyes widened. "And what will France win from your victory?" she asked

The cardinal studied her face. "Religious freedom. The right to worship as one chooses."

"No more holy wars?" she asked.

"This shall be the last."

Anne paused as she continued to stare into his eyes. "Where do I fit in this schema?"

He kept his face impassive. He needed to reel her in with care. "The war between the Catholic Church and the Protestant Reformation is raging over the Holy Roman Empire like wildfire breaking out everywhere. Every nation in Europe has a force within driving it to the battlefield. In France, that force is the queen mother, Marie de Medici. The Medici family consistently throws in their lot with the Holy Roman Empire. It is the substratum of their strategy and how they remain in power.

"When Good King Henry the Fourth died, his royal heir, Prince Louis, had just turned nine, far too young to be king. His mother, Queen Marie de Medici, ruled in his stead, and no lord or commoner would have complained, had she not plunged France back into the hell of religious warmongering, which likewise plunged France's fortunes. War is expensive and produces nothing, aside from the bounty extracted from its starving victims. At last, a group of noblemen formed a cabal against the queen. The crown prince attained the legal age of coronation, and this became their chance to depose the angel-faced tyrant who was Marie de Medici."

"Not every queen can rise to the standard of Queen Elizabeth," Anne murmured.

The cardinal smiled. "Today, there is a new standard. In the aftermath of Queen Elizabeth and Good King Henry, and the prosperity they engendered for their subjects, lords and commoners alike expect more from their regents, which is why Queen Marie failed with those age-old tactics.

"As it came to pass," the cardinal continued, "Prince Louis's favorite, a handsome and clever man, staged a coup d'état, and eliminated Queen Marie's favorite, an odious foreigner who knew which lords to intimidate and how. All of France rejoiced upon news of his demise. And they rejoiced in their newly coronated king, a sensible youth of fifteen, who brought an end to the holy wars, the ulterior objective of every lord who supported the royal lad. This one act made King Louis extremely popular. Unfortunately, his now legendary sarcasm and bad temper quickly turned many friends into adversaries. This is why young kings need to be supervised by ministers until they acquire the art of tact, which can take decades.

"Following the coup d'état, King Louis incarcerated his mother and assumed her reign was over. But the Medicis, well-practiced in the art of persuasion, doled out formidable fortunes to create a battalion of powerful noblemen gathered behind Queen Marie.

"The exiled queen raised an army, arranged her escape, and declared war on her son. I approached our young king with a solution. In the end, the queen mother agreed to cease her war, and King Louis allowed her to live in a Parisian palace, but she would remain under house arrest, taking fresh air only in her palace gardens. The queen is allowed visitors, who must register with the office of the king and exit the palace after a specified length of time."

"Is she allowed to speak with her guests in private?" Anne raised an eyebrow.

"A question that brings us to the topic of how you, Lady Anne, fit into this schema. I would place you and Lady Kitty in the queen mother's coterie. Kitty would become the royal hairdresser. Her position creates a pathway to the royal servants, a fertile field of gossip.

"Duchess Chevreuse, the young Queen Ana's first lady in waiting, and a favorite of the queen mother's, shall introduce you, having no idea we are connected. I have no doubt that you and Kitty will work your way into the queen mother's trust within weeks."

Anne stared into space. "Brother Theodore recently told me things about my father I'd never heard before, but he would not tell me what I most wanted to know." Anne leaned forward, her eyes locked on his. "Who killed him?"

The cardinal remained inscrutable. "One can only speculate," he said. "But I can tell you what transpired that day, if you like."

"Please do," she replied.

"On May fourteenth in the year of our Lord 1610, your father left in the morning to join King Henry in his carriage. I remained behind to manage the office.

"The queen consort was to be coronated and given a new title: Queen Regina Maria."

He paused. "Do you understand?"

Anne's heart grew cold. "The queen consort cannot rule in the event of the king's death. But if she is queen regina, she becomes sole regent over the kingdom, should her husband die before her eldest son reaches the legal age of coronation."

"Exactly so," the cardinal said, his voice barely audible. "It took her years to talk King Henry into it. His ministers advised against it, but she wore him down."

"And my father died next to King Henry in a carriage that had been stopped by traffic on the way to her coronation," Anne said.

"The king and your father were assassinated moments after the ceremony was complete. Your father killed the assassin, but he bled to death in the carriage. There was no hope for either one."

A pounding anger pulsed through Anne. She gazed into the dark theater of her mind, seeing only a silhouette in the shape of Marie de Medici. She had never seen so much as a drawing of the woman. In time, she would be looking into her eyes, entertaining her with court gossip as Kitty dressed her hair. She would gently pin this woman down in her own boudoir.

She hesitated. She had a dark secret the cardinal would figure out in time. If she told him now, he might reject her.

Seconds ticked by.

At last, she spoke. "There is something I must confess. It may cause you to change your mind."

"I doubt that," said the cardinal.

"After losing my husband, I came to reassess all I believe." She blinked slowly. "Everything. I believe in the perfect symmetry of mathematics. I believe in the certitude of science. But I no longer believe in God." She held her breath.

A faint smile graced the cardinal's lips.

"You're perfect," he said.

End Note

While a significant amount of research formed the basis of this story, some of the dates are slightly off to allow the authors enough artistic license to prioritize plot and character development. For example, while Lord Tassis was assassinated in Madrid in the manner described in Chapter 25, this incident took place in May of 1623, not September. The wedding in Chapter 42 took place at a later date and different location than described, however the scene wherein the future bride and groom meet is historical.

The Initiation of Lady de Winter is the first of a series. If you enjoyed this novel, please feel free to leave a review on BarnesAndNoble.com or GoodReads.com.

Acknowledgments

Writing and publishing a book is a long journey full of surprises—some good, some bad. Our mentor, author and publisher Megan Edwards (Imbrifex Books), made an excellent trail guide as she navigated us through the fog of inexperience, pointing out crucial publishing milestones and goals.

Deep thanks to our editors, H. G. Mac and Lorraine Reguly, whose work was invaluable to the quality of the final manuscript. Our book club—Margie, Virgie, Lynn, Kim, Holly, Joan, Kayla, Anne, and Connie—also provided crucial feedback as alpha readers. Thank you, one and all.

Thank you to our cover illustrator, Abdul Momin Ariu, for expertly translating our design idea into an image that elegantly captured the mood and tone of the story.

Most importantly, I (Crystal) would like to thank my wonderful husband, Ken Allen, who never wavered in his support. His faith in my talent was all the inspiration I needed.

And I (Carole) would like to thank my wonderful husband, Bill McKinnis, whose praise of my work was especially endearing, since Bill is a man of discriminating taste who does not offer compliments without a great deal of consideration.

Many, many thanks to all of you.

About the Authors

Crystal McKinnis Allen's career includes several years as a journalist before becoming a communications consultant in far-flung metropolises, including Boston, Manhattan, and Silicon Valley. Her work has appeared in the Boston Business Journal, European Pharmaceutical Executive, and MetroActive, a popular Silicon Valley weekly. She now lives in Las Vegas with her husband, Ken, and their two rescue cats—an affectionate Ragdoll named Pia Zadorable, and an adventurous bullseye tabby named Amen-Ra. She is currently mastering the art of desert landscaping. The Initiation of Lady de Winter is her first co-written novel.

Carole McKinnis is a self-taught historian with a library of more than a thousand books on the European Renaissance and Reformation. Her research includes an extensive examination of the lives of King James, his son, Charles, Infanta Maria Anna of Spain, and other fascinating historical characters of the Reformation era. A professionally trained opera singer, Carol performed in theatrical productions of The Mikado, Kiss Me Kate, Lil 'Abner, and other popular musicals. While raising four children, she was also an art dealer for a gallery featuring local talent. Today, she lives in Las Vegas with her husband, Bill, and their sweet, silver-gray American bulldog, Brittany. The Initiation of Lady de Winter is her first co-written novel.

Hierarchy of the Royal Peerage of Europe

Emperor/Empress

Emperors occupy the highest monarchic honor and rank, and rule over an empire (a group of states or countries). In Europe, the first emperor was Charlemagne (Charles the Great), who was crowned by Pope Leo III on Christmas day in the year 800. The Vatican granted this power to Charlemagne with the understanding he would devote his military might to the protection of the papacy and the Holy Roman Empire.

From Charlemagne onward, Europe's emperor was always German. (Emperor Napoleon Bonaparte presided only over France.) Europe's emperors were elected by a college of electors made up of Germanic kings and other high-ranking nobles.

The wife of the emperor was given the title of empress and often ruled in her husband's place when he was called away to the battlefield or on other state business. The last emperor of the Holy Roman Empire, Francis II, abdicated his position in 1806.

King/Queen

A king or queen rules over a nation, country, or kingdom. Kings and queens who have the authority to rule their country are called regents. A regent's spouse is usually considered a prince consort (male), or a queen consort (female). The term "king consort" was rarely used because the high-ranking title might cause commoners or foreign kingdoms to assume the regent's husband was the ruler.

Royal consorts do not take over the throne upon the regent's death. If the spouse of a regent is coronated as a "king regent" or "queen regent," that king or queen has the authority to take over as ruler in the event of their spouse's death, usually until the crown prince, or princess, is old enough to rule. A regent is addressed as "Your Majesty." A queen consort or prince consort is addressed as "Your Royal Highness."

Crown Prince/Crown Princess
The crown prince is the oldest living son of a regent and inherits the throne upon his royal parent's death. If there are no surviving sons in the royal family, the oldest daughter rises to the throne and rules as regent.

Prince/Princess
These are the younger siblings of the crown prince or princess. All princes and princesses are addressed as "Your Royal Highness."

Lords and Ladies
All nobility beneath the rank of prince or princess are addressed as "Lord" or "Lady." However, a duke or duchess who is also a prince or princess would be addressed by the higher-ranking title "Your Royal Highness."

Sirs and Dames
A nobleman or commoner who is benighted by his regent can be addressed as "Sir." The female equivalent of knighthood is damehood, and the female equivalent of "Sir" is "Dame."

Duke/Duchess
A duke presides over a dukedom or duchy. In England and France, regents often give their royal children ducal titles

and the duchies that go with them. In France and several other European countries, a crown prince is called "Archduke."

Marquess (Marquis)/Marquesa

A Marquess rules over a marche, which means frontier in Latin. While a duke is often an entitled member or close relative of the royal family, a Marquess is like a general who protects the kingdom's border, which is why a Marquess's land holdings are always on the border lands. This is also why Marquesses out-rank all other noblemen with the exception of dukes and royal family members.

Earl/Count/Countess

Earls and counts rule over counties. A duke wields more power than a count or earl, because his higher rank allows him more leverage with the regent. A count is obligated to fall in line with the king's orders, whereas dukes can argue their case if they feel a royal order disadvantages them. The title of earl is often granted to a king's companions, so an earl can sometimes outrank a count on this basis.

Viscount/Viscountess

This title literally means vice-count. The relationship between a count and viscount is similar to the relationship between a president and vice-president of a corporation. A count could appoint a viscount as a helpful administrator. This role was traditionally filled by a talented, educated man, not necessarily an entitled one.

Baron/Baroness

While the title of "Baron" is an entry-level position in Europe's system of royal peerage, barons were often wealthier than their higher-ranking peers for an interesting reason. A very wealthy commoner, like a merchant, could buy his way into the peerage system, usually by arranging an advantageous marriage. If the wealthy commoner had a daughter, she would come to her marriage with a generous dowry. If the wealthy commoner's child was a son, he could marry an entitled lady in exchange for a much-needed cash infusion into her family's treasury. Part of the marriage contract would include the title of "Baron," which royal peers with the right influence could arrange. Baronies were also bestowed on commoners who had made themselves extremely useful to a king during a war.

Hierarchy of the Roman Catholic Clergy

Pope

The pope is also known as the Bishop of Rome. Before the Peace of Westphalia treaties signed in October 1648, the pope derived his power from an ancient pact forged in the year 800 between Pope Leo III and Charlemagne, the first emperor of the Holy Roman Empire, which was considered the continuation of the earlier Roman Empire. Under Pope Leo III, the Vatican acknowledged the emperor's authority, and in exchange, the emperor agreed to devote his military might to enforcing the authority of the papacy throughout Europe.

The Bishop of Rome is differentiated from lesser bishops with titles such as: the Vicar of Jesus Christ, Successor of the Prince of the Apostles (Apostle Peter), and Supreme Pontiff of the Universal Church.

Cardinal

A pope can appoint bishops to the College of Cardinals when there are open seats. The cardinals reside at the Vatican in Rome. They advise the pope, and also elect a new pope when the sitting pope dies.

Bishop/Archbishop

Bishops and archbishops preside over a diocese in much the same way a governor presides over a state. An archbishop presides over a large diocese, which could be a large city or large geographic area.

Abbot/Abbess

An abbot is the male head of a monastery. While monks are usually commoners, abbots and abbesses are usually drawn from the entitled class.

An abbess is the head of a female-only monastery or convent. An abbess can also be referred to as a prioress, or by the title "Mother Superior."

Monsignor
A pope can confer the honorary title of "Monsignor" upon a priest in the service of the Holy See. This title allows the priest special privileges that help him better serve the pope.

Priest
A priest serves a parish, which is a collection of neighborhoods (i.e., a district within a diocese). A parish priest celebrates daily Mass, takes confessions, offers marriage counseling, visits shut-ins and the sick, and provides spiritual guidance to his parishioners.

Deacon
Deacons are laymen who fulfill the duties and responsibilities of priests, even though they are not ordained. Whereas a married man can become a deacon, if a deacon is single, he cannot maintain his position as deacon if he marries. Catholic seminary students often take the title of "Deacon" in their last year of seminary school. This allows them to train as priests in the year proceeding their ordination.

Monks and Nuns
Monks and nuns live in communal compounds known as monasteries. Most female monasteries are referred to as convents. Monks and nuns take vows of chastity, obedience, and poverty. They are not allowed to earn or keep money with the understanding that their room, board, clothing, and other necessities will be provided by the convent or monastery.

Friars

A friar's status equals that of a monk, but whereas monks live a cloistered life cut off from the public, friars serve the laity and are supported by donations and other forms of charity. Monks and friars belong to different orders. While there is no female equivalent to a friar, nuns can either be cloistered or serve the public depending on their order.

Cast of Characters

This is the legend for understanding the characters found in this book.

In the cast of characters that follows:

- fictitious characters are in **bold**
- semi-fictitious characters (characters mentioned briefly in history but with few details) are <u>underlined</u>
- characters in plain text are real people recorded in historical documents and books

In the descriptions:

- fictitious material appears in *italics*
- factual material appears in plain text

Abbess Louise

- *Abbess of Our Lady of Temple Mars*
- *Lady Anne's aunt*
- *supports all forms of true love*

Adelena, Countess of Segovia

- *Infanta Maria Anna's prudish governess*
- *cousin to Duchess Olivares*
- *has a secret crush on Father Eremitz*

Aelfreda (aka Aelfie) Audley

- *wife of Cedric Audley*
- *sister-in-law to Anne and Harald Audley*

<u>Akira</u>

- Japanese sword master

- guest of world traveler and trader Gabriel Tavernier

Ann Stanley, Countess of Castlehaven

- royal cousin of Prince Charles
- likely would have inherited the English throne after Queen Elizabeth's death had she not been a devout Roman Catholic

Anne Audley, Duchess of Southampton

- *English diplomat in service to King James I*
- *wife of Lord Harald Audley (Duke of Southampton)*
- *mother of Quentin Audley*
- *at the close of the year, she changes her name to Lady de Winter*

Armand du Plessis

- see Cardinal Richelieu

Athos aka Comte de la Fére

- based on Armand d'Athos, musketeer for King Louis XIII
- distant cousin of Captain Treville of King Louis's guard
- character in Alexander Dumas's "The Three Musketeers"

Batsheeba

- *Eritrean mortician residing in Spain*
- *familiar with Templar knight funereal rituals*

Bazin

- *Father Eremitz's 14-year-old stable boy and horse trainer*

Brother Theodore

- *Chamberlain of the House of Salomon*

Buckingham, aka Duke of Buckingham, aka George (or Georgie) Villiers, aka Steenie

- favorite of King James
- best friend to Prince Charles
- schemer, charmer, and social climber

Capistrano

- *Father Henri Eremitz's loyal servant*

Captain Rodriguez

- *accompanied Princess Maria and Queen Isabella to convent in Flanders*
- *functioned as Kenhelm's supervisor when Queen Isabella hired Kenhelm as her secretary*

Captain Armand Treville, aka Jean-Armand du Peyrer, Comte de Troisville

- entitled French officer and captain of King Louis XIII's personal guard known as *Musketeers of the Guard*
- historical basis for the character *Monsieur de Tréville* in Alexander Dumas's novel *The Three Musketeers*
- *uncle to Father Eremitz*

Cardinal Richelieu, aka Duke of Richelieu

- *longtime friend of Abbess Louise*
- *prior acquaintance of Lady Anne's deceased father*
- French clergyman and prime minister who served King Louis XIII from 1624 to 1642
- formerly known as Armand du Plessis

Cedric Audley

- *younger brother of Lord Harald Audley*
- *married to Aelfreda*

Count-Duke Olivares, aka Prime Minister Olivares

- served King Philip IV of Spain from 1621 to 1643

Diego Velasquez

- famous Spanish artist

Doña Adelena

- see "Adelena"

Duchess Giselle de Fueggar

- *hostess of the House of Salomon*

Duchess Marie Chevreuse

- influential French duchess
- first lady in waiting to Queen Anne (aka Ana Maria) of France

Duchess (Lady) Olivares

- wife of Count-Duke and Prime Minister Olivares

Edward Michelborne

- English sea captain and pirate
- blamed for igniting the Amboyna massacre

Esperanza

- *Father Eremitz's housekeeper*

Father Henri Eremitz

- based on Henri d'Aramitz, nephew of Captain de Troisville of King Louis XIII's personal guard
- *mysterious priest*
- *botanist*
- *keeps a greenhouse with an apothecary*
- *silent partner to Monsignor Massimi*

Ferdinand III

- crown prince of Austria, destined to become Holy Roman Emperor

Francis Bacon

- 1st Viscount of St. Alban
- gentleman scientist
- friend of Queen Elizabeth (d. 1603)
- *friend of Anne and Harald Audley*
- betrayed, framed, and socially disgraced by the Duke of Buckingham

Gabriel Tavernier

- wealthy gem merchant and world traveler
- *friend of Lady Anne and Lord Harald Audley*

Gondomar

- Spanish count and ambassador residing in London

Gregory Mack, Earl of Staffordshire

- *best friend to Lord Harald Audley*
- *escorts Prince Charles on his cross-border quest to woo Infanta Maria Anna of Spain*

Harald Audley, Duke of Southampton

- *devoted husband to Lady Anne*
- *diplomat in service to King James I*

Infanta Maria Anna

- Spanish princess
- King Philip IV's sister
- courted by Prince Charles

Isley

- *valet and royal escort to Prince Charles*
- *best friend to Sir Varney*

Jean Baptiste Tavernier

- Gabriel Tavernier's 15-year-old son
- telescope enthusiast

Johannes Kepler

- German mathematician and astronomer

John Digby

- English earl and ambassador in Madrid
- tasked with negotiating a marriage contract between Prince Charles and Infanta Maria Anna

John Washington

- young lord residing at the English embassy
- died of a mysterious illness shortly after converting to Roman Catholicism, which caused a violent outbreak when a priest came to give him his last rites

Kenhelm Digby

- nephew of Ambassador John Digby

- *former lover of Father Eremitz*

King Henry IV of France, aka Henry of Navarre,
aka Good King Henry

- contemporary with King James I of England
- legendary for shifting tax burden from the poor to the entitled class
- first leader in history to promise a chicken in every pot: "If God grants me life, I will make it so that no plowman in my realm will lack the means to have a chicken in his pot on Sunday!"
- assassinated in 1610 after one decade of rule

King James I of England

- Prince Charles's father
- commissioned King James Version of the Holy Bible

King Louis XIII

- son of King Henry IV
- became king of France in 1610 at age nine, while his mother ruled as queen regent
- seized the throne from his mother at age fifteen and exiled her
- married Infanta Ana Maria of Spain, Infanta Maria Anna's elder sister

King Philip IV of Spain

- Hapsburg king coronated at age 16
- brother to Infanta Maria Anna

Kitty aka Lady Catherine, Baroness von Kerchheim

- *official lady's maid*
- *unofficial diplomatic partner to Lady Anne and Lord Harald*

Lady de Winter

- *formerly Lady Anne Audley, Duchess of Southampton*

Laura Digby

- wife of Earl John Digby, English ambassador to Spain

Louise

- see "Abbess Louise"

Maria Anna

- see "Infanta Maria Anna"

Marie de Medici

- member of the powerful House of Medici
- acted as regent for her young son, King Louis XIII, after her husband, King Henry IV of France, was assassinated

Monsignor Massimi

- monsignor and papal nuncio to King Philip IV of Spain (a papal nuncio is an ambassador sent from the Vatican to advise powerful regents)

Olivares

- see "Count-Duke Olivares"

Padre

- *Capo of Rome*
- *Dominican Friar; leader of the Roman Inquisition and the Keepers of the Kingdom*
- *Monsignor Massimi's mentor and unofficial master*
- Author's note: Capos, which means head men in Latin, were common in European cities and other regions. A capo was often a Dominican friar with longstanding ties to the peasant and craftsmen class.

Peter Paul Rubens

- famous Flemish artist

Porthos

- based on Isaac de Porthau, musketeer for King Louis XIII
- distant cousin of Captain Treville of King Louis's guard
- character in Alexander Dumas's "The Three Musketeers"

Prince Charles

- crown prince of England and son of King James I
- travels to Spain, seeking Infanta Maria Anna's hand in marriage
- becomes King Charles I after his father's death

Princess Henrietta Maria of France

- younger sister of Queen Isabella of Spain

Princess Maria Anna

- see "Infanta Maria Anna"

Queen Ana Maria of France (aka Queen Anne of Austria)

- wife of King Louise XIII of France
- sister of Infanta (Princess) Maria

Queen Isabella of Spain

- wife of King Philip IV
- sister-in-law to Infanta Maria Anna

Quentin Audley

- *Lady Anne's and Lord Harald's four-year-old son*

Quentin Boyle aka Quentin de Breuil

- *Lady Anne's Father*
- *English merchant and world traveler*
- *prime minister to King Henry IV of France*

Rana, the Amerindian

- *Amazonian flute player*
- *cheerful house guest of the Olivares's*

Tassis

- royal escort (bodyguard) to Queen Isabella of Spain
- his family owned and operated a lucrative secured mail delivery service

Theodore

- *see "Brother Theodore"*

Thomas Lake

- King James's most trusted minister

Varney
- *valet and royal escort (bodyguard) to Prince Charles*
- *best friend to Sir Isley*

William Raynor of Orton
- Sir George Villiers's (Duke of Buckingham's) stepfather

Made in the USA
Monee, IL
18 July 2023

39127942R00246